THE (half) TRUTH

ALSO BY LEDDY HARPER

THE (half) TRUTH

LEDDY HARPER

Montlake
Romance

Published by Montlake Romance, Seattle
www.apub.com

Amazon, the Amazon logo, and Montlake Romance are trademarks of Amazon.com, Inc., or its affiliates.

ISBN-13: 9781503905184
ISBN-10: 1503905187

Cover design by Erin Dameron Hill

Printed in the United States of America

You were with me when I got the email for this opportunity, and you have been there every day since. I couldn't have done this without you, Kristie.

PROLOGUE

Tatum

The soft glow of the overhead lights bounced off the brilliant diamond that sat high on my left ring finger. It'd been two months since Michael had put it there, and not a day went by that I didn't lose time admiring it.

Silverware clinked, conversations carried on at the tables surrounding us, and the heavenly aroma of cloves filled the air. Nothing could ruin this night for me. It was my twenty-fifth birthday, I had the love of my life next to me, and as soon as my friends and family arrived, I would be surrounded by people who meant the world to me.

"It's not too late, Tatum." Michael leaned into the table with his forearms, pulling my attention away from my ring. "We can skip dinner and celebrate at home—alone."

I rolled my eyes and smiled, playfully waving him off. He'd spent the better part of the last week trying to get me to change our plans. As the owner of a popular restaurant in town, he hated dining at a rival establishment, but I didn't care to have my birthday dinner at the place I worked five days a week.

"You'll be okay, Michael. We'll be home in two hours, maybe less, and then you'll have me all to yourself."

"Yeah right," he muttered under his breath as he turned his head toward the door. He didn't need to explain what that meant; he wasn't pleased that my family would be staying with us for a couple of days.

When I'd found out that my parents and brother planned to fly in for the weekend to celebrate my birthday, I couldn't have been happier. Michael, though, didn't feel the same. He'd always seemed to avoid my family, yet he insisted he loved them. Apparently, he just wasn't thrilled to have others stay at our house, stating that it made him feel like he had to "perform."

"Oh, come on. It's not like they'll be in our room."

He glared at me as though I'd said something ridiculous. Most couples would probably avoid being intimate while guests slept down the hall, but I didn't see that as an issue. I might not have had any experience prior to Michael, but based on some of the wild stories I'd heard from friends, I thought we were rather tame. I mean, aside from heavy breathing, we didn't make much noise. So I wasn't sure where his reluctance stemmed from.

I reached for his hand, needing the reassurance I typically found in his touch. Except, I didn't get it this time. Instead of reciprocating the gesture, he pulled his arm away and began to tug on his tie. He fidgeted with it so much that the knot appeared to have been made by a child rather than a thirty-five-year-old man.

Michael had always been able to calm my uneasiness, yet now, he was the cause of it. And the longer he sat there, clearing his throat, the worse it got. I couldn't recall a single time in the last two and a half years that I had ever worried about the future of our relationship. Well, beyond the first few months. But once I felt at home with him, we were good. So, seeing him this uncomfortable and anxious freaked me out.

"What's going on, Michael?"

He shook his head, and for a split second, I thought he was about to tell me it was nothing. But then he pushed away from the table and glanced toward the front door. "I can't do this, Tatum. I thought I could . . ." He brought his despondent gaze to me and whispered, "I'm so sorry."

Even though my heart was in my throat, I forced a smile to my lips. I refused to believe this was what it looked like. "It's okay. We can leave and go home. I'll just text—"

"No. I don't mean tonight."

I stared without blinking, ignoring the painful dryness that stabbed my eyes. I had to have heard him wrong or misunderstood what he meant. Because there was no way that my fiancé—the man I shared a home with, worked with, planned to spend the rest of my life with—would break up with me like this.

On my birthday.

At dinner.

While waiting for my family to join us.

There was just no way. So, I held my breath and waited for clarification.

"Everything just caught up to me, and I don't think I can handle it."

When he stood, I followed, hoping for one last chance to change his mind. "You're leaving? Just like that? Michael, everyone will be here any minute now. What am I supposed to tell them?"

"It doesn't matter what you tell them, Tatum. That's up to you. I just can't sit here and pretend everything's okay when it's not."

"I don't understand. What's not okay? And where did this come from?"

There was a good chance we'd garnered the attention of everyone around us, but I didn't care. I wouldn't give up until I had an answer or until he resumed his seat next to me.

"We're moving way too fast." He shook his head, dismissing the tears that lined my eyes.

"Too fast? We've been together for two years. You asked me to marry you." I kept my voice low but made sure he heard my pain.

"Let's talk about this another time. People are starting to stare. I'll leave the house tonight since your family already planned to stay there. We can figure out the rest after they leave."

"Where are you going?"

"I don't know, Tatum. I'll find a couch to sleep on for the weekend."

Too stunned to speak—or do anything, really—I stood there and watched him leave. At some point, I sat back down, though I wasn't sure how long that had taken or how graceful it had been. I only broke free from the trance when I heard, "There's the birthday girl!"

Ever since my brother, Tanner, had moved to Alaska, I was lucky if I got to see him and his family once a year. My parents had become so active in their retirement community that visits had to be arranged and on the calendar months in advance. Needless to say, I didn't see my family often, so when I turned to find the three of them—Tanner, Mom, and Dad—my lack of enthusiasm might've been alarming had they actually paid attention.

They each took turns kissing my cheek before taking a seat. "Where's Michael?" my mom asked, pointing to his vacant chair.

"Oh, he's . . . in the bathroom." I sucked at lying, though I wasn't ready to admit the truth, and my mind was too muddled to come up with anything better. At some point, they'd wonder why he hadn't come out yet, but I figured I'd cross that bridge when we got there.

Before anything else could be said, Kelsey approached the table. She was my best friend, and right now, all I wanted to do was tell her what had happened and cry on her shoulder. Except I couldn't, because breaking down in the middle of a restaurant would likely come with added attention I didn't care to have.

Kelsey sat next to me, put the bright-pink gift bag on the floor between us, and regarded the empty seat to my left with a furrowed brow. "Where's Michael?"

"Bathroom." I wondered if I'd be able to make it through the rest of the night without saying anything other than a word here and there. Doubtful, but it was a challenge I'd willingly accept.

"Excuse me." Tanner placed his napkin on the table and slid his chair back. With a courteous nod, he walked away. No one bothered to ask him where he was going or even acted like it was odd that he'd just get up and leave, so I ignored it and returned to the conversation around me—I mean, pretending to listen.

Until Amanda arrived.

She and I worked together, which meant she also worked with Michael—technically, *for* him, as we all did. We were friends, though not super close. More or less, she was the kind of friend who showed up one day and never left, and her sarcasm made her spot in your life worth it.

"Here you go." Amanda handed me a small bag and shrugged. "It's an apron. I didn't know what else to get you."

After I set it on the floor with the gift from Kelsey, Tanner returned to the table. But rather than sit, he leaned down to whisper into my ear. "Nod like you're listening to what I'm telling you." It was an odd request, but I did as he instructed. "Now, act concerned and ask if he's okay."

I had no idea what he was talking about, but I did it anyway. Leaning away from him, I asked, "Is he okay?"

That's when Tanner slid around the back of my mom's chair, moving away from me. "He will be."

"What's that about? Everything all right?" Mom asked, and the slight smirk on Tanner's face told me that was the reaction he'd expected.

"Yeah. I ran into Michael in the bathroom. He's not feeling well. I told him to go home and rest; being around food isn't the best idea when your stomach is upset. Anyway, Tatum, I told him one of us will drive you back when we're done. And I'll get a hotel room for us just in case it's contagious. We can't afford to get on a plane with a stomach bug."

Conversation carried on around the table, each person discussing Michael's illness, while I just sat there without saying a word. Tanner was aware that something was up, because we both knew he hadn't seen Michael in the bathroom. This was his way of protecting me like an older brother should. I was thankful for the rescue, though I wasn't sure how I would play it off once they all found out the truth.

The rest of dinner was a blur. Luckily, Mom managed to entertain the table, which kept anyone from asking questions. I'd lost my appetite, and when my meal arrived, I couldn't do much more than pick at it. I thought I'd gotten by without suspicion . . . until Kelsey drove me home.

When she pulled into my driveway, she turned off the car and opened her door. Tugging on the sleeve of her shirt, I asked, "Where are you going?"

"If you think I'm going to let him get away with ditching you tonight, you're crazy."

"He was sick." We both knew that was a lie.

And the way she pinned me with a glare told me she had no intention of letting me get away with it. "You're my best friend, Tater. You might be able to lie to Amanda or your mom or even the waitress, who couldn't get a simple order right. But not me. I saw it in your eyes the moment I walked in. I don't have a clue what happened . . . but it was *something*."

"It's fine, Kelsey. Really."

"No, it's not. It's your birthday. And I'm not blind; it's obvious the asshole was there at some point, because his place setting was used. Which means he left. I don't care what his reason is for walking out on your birthday dinner; no excuse is good enough. If there had been an emergency at Fathom, you would've said something."

It took immense strength not to cry or break down in front of her. I gripped her hand and forced a smile. "It's okay, Kels. I appreciate your concern, but it's not needed."

Reluctantly, she sat back in the seat. However, just because she'd conceded this point didn't mean she believed the lie I'd tried to give. "Call me if you need anything. A friend, a couch to sleep on, a shovel and rug, or even an alibi."

I nodded and stepped out of the car. As soon as the door closed, the knot in my throat grew bigger. As she reversed out of the driveway, my stomach flipped and twisted. And the second I stepped inside, my world came crashing down.

He was gone. Just like he'd said he would be.

I tried to call and let him know that my parents weren't here, that he could come home and talk about everything. But he declined every attempt, only sending one text to tell me that he would see me the next day. Oh, and to tell me that he loved me.

Because *that* somehow made everything better.

But I refused to give up hope. Instead, I slept in our bed—alone—and prayed this was fixable. After breakfast with my parents, where I avoided all conversation about Michael, I went straight to work. I knew Michael had gone in before the lunch shift, so he'd be there, unable to avoid this any longer.

Except, he did avoid it. He claimed to be too busy to talk. The most I got out of him was that he wasn't ready for something so serious, and until last night, he'd thought he would be able to work through it. Apparently, he couldn't, yet that didn't mean he didn't love me. And by the time my shift ended, he had already left.

Thank God for Kelsey.

As soon as she opened the door to her apartment, I said, "I hate the words *I love you*. I never want to hear them again. From anyone. They don't mean anything to me." But the one thing that gave away just how upset I was, was the hug I took from her—likely catching her by surprise considering I wasn't a hugger . . . *at all.*

Grabbing my duffel bag from the floor next to my feet, she ushered me inside. She didn't bother to ask what was wrong, just poured the wine and waited until I filled her in. By the end of the night, we'd agreed that I would move into the spare room. The one thing we didn't agree on was my job at Michael's restaurant.

I decided to remain at Fathom 216 because I'd worked my way up the line to sauté chef. My dream was to be sous chef, and as it stood, I was next in line for that position in our kitchen. If I left, I'd have to start all over under a new executive chef. I'd made it too far to let that dream slip away.

Okay, so there might've been another reason behind my decision to stay. A very small facet. One I had vehemently denied to Kelsey—I wanted Michael back. I mean, you don't spend two and a half years with a person and just forget all the good times you had together.

Although, that was exactly what it seemed Michael had done.

Less than six months later, a new pastry chef showed up in the kitchen. A cute little blonde with a bubbly personality. She was sweet and friendly . . . and Michael Shae's new girlfriend.

1

Jason

They say there's *one* in every family.

Well, *they* lied, because I had an entire family full of them.

The best part? I was a thirty-one-year-old man living with my recently widowed mother until I found a job and a place of my own . . . and I was the normal one. Granted, I had just moved to town a few days ago, a couple of months earlier than intended, so at least I could say my situation was temporary.

But the others? I was afraid they didn't stand a chance.

On a positive note, they were great people with big hearts and even bigger personalities. And with pure intentions, even when inconvenient. Such as the barbecue Aunt Diane and Uncle Fred had decided to throw "in my honor" as if they were the welcome committee. When I'd tried to get out of it, they'd resorted to guilt trips, making me feel bad for ruining a family gathering meant to celebrate my return to Samson.

The one thing they'd left out was that they had these lunches *every* Sunday. They had just decided to claim there was a reason for this one, and then used that reason to make me attend.

"Oh, it's so good to see you." Aunt Diane wound her arms tightly around my neck, acting like she hadn't just seen me yesterday when she'd stopped by my mom's house for coffee. Or the day before, when I'd come over for dinner. Or the day before that, when I'd gotten into town.

I couldn't say much, though, considering it had been years since I'd last come home. After heading off to college, I'd basically left this small town behind. The only reason I had seen Mom and Bill so much over the last thirteen years was because they'd gone to Nevada to see me. I'd always kept up with my family, but only from a distance.

Aunt Diane released me from her embrace and tugged me inside by my hand. "Your cousins are so excited to see you. Marlena and her clan might be a little late, but Kelsey should be here soon."

I closed the front door behind me and glanced up, noticing my mother. She had left the house this morning while I was out, so I hadn't seen her until now. "Ma! What happened to your face?"

Knitting her brows in utter confusion, Mom pressed her fingertips to her cheek and asked, "What do you mean?"

I moved closer and squinted, as if trying to see clearer. Her skin was covered with some sort of caked-on flesh-colored cream. When I ran my finger along her cheekbone, I was left with a shimmery bronze powder on my hand.

"What is this?"

"Oh, that? It's makeup."

I blinked a few times, but Mom just laughed and tried to brush me off.

On the rare occasion I'd seen her wear any makeup, it was maybe a hint of pink on her cheeks or some soft color on her eyes. Hell, she'd never even worn lipstick. Nothing like the dark brown in the creases of her lids or the black ink that lined her lashes—it was a thin line, but that wasn't the point.

"It's just a little bit of color. I wanted to look nice today."

"A *little bit* of color? Ma, it looks like you ran face-first into an oil painting before it finished drying. Your lips are purple. And . . ." I leaned in for a closer look. "Are those fake lashes?"

"Heavens no." She made it sound like my question was preposterous. "I found that if I do one coat of thickening mascara and one coat of lengthening, it works best. And my lipstick isn't purple . . . it's mauve."

Mom patted my chest and turned to walk away. That's when I realized Aunt Diane had already left the room. I was willing to bet she was the culprit behind this shocking transformation. I'd been staying with my mother for days, and even though I hadn't been around her every second, this was the first I'd seen her like this.

"Are you limping?" Seeing the way she babied her left leg made me forget all about the paint by numbers on her face. "Oh my God! What happened?"

When I carefully held her arm in concern, she stilled. "I'm fine. Stop worrying. I just took a little fall last night at Derby practice, that's all."

Stunned, I wasn't sure where to begin. "Derby?"

"Yeah, didn't I tell you? I joined a local Roller Derby league."

"You can't do that. You're old!"

"Watch your tongue, young man. I'm one of the younger ones on the team. Plus, Grace says age is just a number—then again, she's likely pushing a hundred. She's one tough ol' biddy."

"So you did this last night? When? I was with you most of the evening, and you were in bed at ten when I came home."

"No I wasn't. I didn't get in until almost midnight."

"*What?*" My eyes ached from being opened so wide. "I thought you were asleep. I made sure to be extra quiet so I didn't wake you up."

With a dismissive wave, she continued toward the kitchen, talking over her shoulder. "It seems it was a wasted effort on your part, huh?"

"Ma . . . what's going on?" This had to be some sort of toxic combination of grief and denial. Considering she'd just lost her husband a couple of months ago, I guess this kind of behavior wasn't completely unwarranted.

She continued through the kitchen and out the sliding glass door to the back patio with me hot on her heels. Aunt Diane came out of nowhere and stopped me before I made it outside, holding me back with a gentle hand on my chest. "Jason Tyler Watson, you listen to me, and you listen good. Your mother is fine. She didn't want to tell you about the Derby team because she knew you'd raise hell, and ridiculing her for wearing makeup was uncalled for."

My aunt was a sweet woman, usually soft spoken and inviting. If she wasn't doting on her family, she was cracking us up with her flighty personality. So when her sternness reared its head—or she used full names—you stopped and listened.

"I just don't get it, Aunt Diane. I moved home to be closer to her because I figured she needed me after Bill died. I expected her to be sad and lonely, not . . . *this*."

"She does get sad, but she doesn't like to show it often. I think she saves the tears for when she's alone. But you can't be upset that she's not giving up. She's a strong woman—a lot stronger than you give her credit for. At sixty, she still has a lot of living left, and I'm beyond proud of her for recognizing that."

"Please don't tell me she's wearing makeup because she's starting to date. If so, someone needs to help the woman out."

She briefly closed her eyes and laughed. "No. Your mother has no desire to date. Bill never liked her to wear makeup because he didn't think she needed it. She's always loved it, though, and now that he's gone, she's kicking up her heels and enjoying the things she chose to forgo for him. She's living her life, Jason. Be happy for her. And don't worry—I think once the newness of the makeup wears off, she'll tone it down."

I glanced at my mom through the glass door, recognizing her innocence despite her age. She deserved to find joy in the things she'd once given up. And for the first time in my entire life, I was able to see her in a different light. I smiled, and with a soft squeeze of Aunt Diane's shoulder, I went outside. My uncle was down on the dock, tending the grill, so I decided to give him a little company.

The sun danced off the lake behind the house while Uncle Fred entertained me with tales from his recent trip. That man spent more time with a rod and reel than anyone I knew. Then again, I'd just spent the last however-many years in Vegas. Not that people didn't fish out there, but it wasn't as popular as in the South.

When I heard the patio slider open, I glanced over his shoulder to see which one of my cousins had arrived first. I said a silent prayer that it was Marlena, considering we had always been close and had done our best to keep in touch over the years. Not to mention that her husband would be with her, which would give me someone other than my uncle to hang out with.

Unfortunately, my prayers were ignored and Kelsey stepped outside. I hadn't seen her since her twenty-first birthday, four years ago. Even though she hadn't changed much since then, I couldn't help but picture the ugly duckling she'd been as a kid. She'd certainly grown into a beautiful swan. I made my way up the steps from the dock, and then practically tripped over my own feet when I saw someone follow her out.

It was *not* her sister.

Unless Marlena had gotten younger and shortened about six inches.

Her brown hair hung a few inches past her shoulders in waves that made her look like she'd just stepped off a sailboat. She squinted against the sun, so I couldn't see the color of her eyes, but I didn't miss the way they flashed wider when she spotted my mom. Then she smiled with straight white teeth lined by bright-red lips. That color had a tendency to give off a Marilyn Monroe vibe, yet on her, I got more of a girl-next-door feel.

With a single glance, she'd managed to knock me off my axis.

"Look who it is." Kelsey strolled toward me. "The prodigal son."

Slinging my arm over her shoulder to return her half hug, I said, "Nice to see you, too, Kelsey."

"I thought you were moving back at the end of summer."

I shrugged, not really wanting to get into the specifics with her. We were as close as two cousins of the opposite sex and six years apart could be, but that didn't mean I'd kept her in the loop on things. "I decided to come early. I didn't see the point in leaving Mom alone for another two months."

She giggled, as if anything I said was meant as a joke. "Knowing your mom, having you here early is cramping her style."

Without giving me a chance to question what she'd meant by that, she walked away. I thought that indicated our interaction was over, until she grabbed her friend by the arm and brought her over to me.

"Jason, this is my *best friend*, Tatum."

I ignored my cousin's very clear warning and regarded the goddess in front of me. She was even more beautiful up close. And when she lifted her gaze, I found myself trapped in the most intoxicating pair of brown eyes I'd ever seen.

Rich wasn't enough to describe them. Melted dark chocolate was perhaps the closest comparison I could make, and even that didn't do the color justice. They were intense, like two black holes, ready to suck me in and never spit me back out.

Captivating . . . that's what they were.

I realized I hadn't done anything but stare at her, so I cleared my throat and said, "Nice to meet you, Tatum."

She held out her hand, which I took. Yet rather than a normal handshake, she lightly held it while staring up at me. We seemed to be stuck in a time warp, both lost in each other's gazes without a word, as though no one else was around. That was, until Kelsey decided to remind us of her presence.

"Jason just moved here from Vegas. Don't get too close to him, though . . . he used to work in a landfill, so he probably smells like garbage." Kelsey pinched her nose and curled her upper lip in feigned disgust.

"You don't have a clue what I do, do you?"

Either Tatum didn't find my cousin funny, or she flat out didn't care, because instead of laughing, smiling, or even commenting on Kelsey's insult, she asked, "Have you found a place yet?"

"Yeah, but I have to wait a few weeks. It should be ready by the first."

Finally, she seemed to realize that we still held hands, but rather than shake my hand or squeeze it—or *anything* to suggest she'd meant the gesture as a greeting—she just let go. And then she wiped her palm on her jean-covered thigh. I wasn't sure how to feel about that. Maybe she'd taken Kelsey's landfill comment to heart.

She offered a forced smile and said, "Well, it was nice meeting you. Have fun." And then walked away.

There was no telling what my cousin had said about me prior to them showing up, but rather than question it, I eyed Kelsey inquisitively. "Is she leaving?"

"Nope." She stared at the sliding glass door and watched Tatum slip inside. "That's just Tatum Alexander. A bit of a nerd, that one is."

A barking laugh ripped through my chest. "No wonder you two are friends."

"*Best* friends. And speaking of . . ." She narrowed her gaze and stabbed me in the center of my chest with a finger. "Stay away from her. And that's not meant as a challenge, either. I mean it, Jason. Now that our age difference doesn't pose legal issues for you, if you'd like to screw my friends, there's nothing stopping you. But please, if you do *anything* with *any* of my friends, she's where I draw the line."

I held up my hands in surrender. "Calm down, tiger. I'm not going after anyone."

"Better not." She jutted her chin out, as if threatening to attack, and then headed inside with her mysterious friend.

It was good to see things hadn't changed too much around here.

Not wanting to be entertained by my uncle and his fishing stories again, I followed my cousin.

Tatum was in the kitchen, standing next to my mom behind the stove. They both smiled as they shared some sort of joke no one else was privy to. I took a seat at the breakfast bar, directly in front of Tatum, and propped my chin on my fist to watch her as she showed my mom how to sauté mushrooms. I wasn't sure what they thought was so funny about garlic, but I wasn't about to ask. It was just nice to see my mom happy.

"You like to cook?" I asked, catching Tatum's attention. It made me question how focused she was on the frying pan not to have noticed me sit down. I couldn't have been more than a foot away from her.

Her eyes met mine briefly before she went back to instructing my mom. When she answered me, she kept her attention on the mushrooms, as if speaking to them instead of me. "Yeah, I enjoy it."

My mom scoffed. "She's a chef, Jason. This is what she does for a living. You know that gravy you liked so much? Tatum taught me how to make it. Now that you're single and will be living on your own, maybe she could teach you how to cook *real* food."

While my mom bragged on her as if she were her own daughter, I never glanced away from Tatum's face. The slight blush on her ivory cheeks could've come from the heat wafting off the pan, although I'd say that was unlikely.

Ignoring Mom's comment, I said, "So I guess you know your way around a kitchen, huh?"

"Well, I'm pretty familiar with this one. I'm over here a lot with Kels, so yeah, I know my way around. You can only open the silverware drawer looking for a whisk so many times before you learn where everything is."

I bit my lip to hold back my laughter. She didn't know me, and I didn't know her, so the last thing I wanted to do was give her the impression that I was making fun of her.

"Tater," Kelsey called from around the corner. And without another word, Tatum was gone.

She seemed to have a knack for walking away and leaving me with women who had the power to scare me with a single glance.

"Who made most of the meals? You or Jen?" My mom knew exactly what she was doing. She was well aware I didn't care to discuss my ex, and by bringing her up, she was effectively shooing me from the kitchen.

"Great talk, Ma. But I gotta take a leak." I slapped the bar top and slid off the stool.

On my way back from the restroom, I heard voices from the formal living room, near the front door. Assuming Tatum and Kelsey were still in there, I quietly slipped down the hall to find out what they were talking about. "What are you two doing in here all alone? Gossiping? Anything that would interest me?"

There was a narrow space on the couch between my cousin and her friend, just enough for a small person. I wasn't small, so I practically sat on their laps until they scooted over to make room. With an arm over each girl—Kelsey to my left and Tatum on my right—I invited myself into their hushed conversation.

"No, you creeper. Get off." Kelsey tried to push me away, but I refused to budge.

We had always been like this, so she shouldn't have acted so appalled by my interruption. Granted, long gone were the days when I would put her in a headlock and give her a noogie. But that didn't mean she shouldn't have expected me to join her when we both knew she didn't want me to. There was something to be said about one's maturity level around family.

"What?" I played dumb. "I just want to spend some time with my cousin."

Even though I faced Kelsey, that didn't mean I wasn't fully aware of Tatum's presence. She hadn't moved or said a single word since I'd sat down, and I only hoped she was just shy and not uncomfortable being next to me.

"Fine. You wanna hear what we were talking about? I was just telling Tatum about my last period."

Liar.

I turned toward my cousin's friend and lowered my voice. "She forgets I grew up around a bunch of females."

"I bled. A lot. So much, in fact, I ruined my favorite pants. There was blood everywhere. It looked like a massacre. Everyone at the office thought I was dying. They called for an ambulance."

With my eyes locked on Tatum's, who now appeared beyond uncomfortable, I said, "You should tell your friend that when she wants to scare someone off, she shouldn't say things that would only embarrass herself."

Just then, Tatum's lips split into a smile so wide it made her squint, and I couldn't help but do the same. We just sat there, laughing as though we'd known each other our whole lives. Time stood still, until out of nowhere, Kelsey screamed, "Mom! That isn't even your phone. I took yours away for a reason. No one likes to have candid pictures taken all the time."

Kelsey launched herself off the couch and crossed the room to block her mom.

"Are you sure? It looks like mine." Aunt Diane held the cell farther away to examine it.

"Yes, I'm sure. This is Tatum's. I confiscated yours so you wouldn't spend all day being the self-appointed photographer."

"What? I like to go back and look at my shots."

"That would be totally fine, Mom, if you didn't post them all over Facebook. No one, and I mean *no one*, wants the whole world seeing the worst-possible pictures of themselves."

Aunt Diane waved her off. "You're too hard on yourself. I don't share anything that would make you look bad. See here?" She turned the screen to show Kelsey the image she'd taken. "It's a nice photo."

"How would you know? You're not wearing your glasses. You couldn't even tell this wasn't your phone."

"It's an easy mistake. It looks just like mine."

"It looks *nothing* like yours, Mom." She snatched the device from Aunt Diane's hand and held it up to show her the back. "See? This case is blue, and it has some stupid saying about cooks written on it—no offense, Tater. Yours is black. *Plain* black."

Without taking my eyes off the comedy show in front of me—or removing my arm from around Tatum's shoulders—I leaned closer and whispered, "How much do you think her arm will hurt from beating this into the ground?"

Rather than respond, Tatum giggled. I didn't hear it as much as I felt the slight rumble along my side. It gave me hope that she was, in fact, just an introvert.

"Not to mention," Kelsey continued as though she didn't have an audience behind her, "wouldn't you have noticed it wasn't yours when you couldn't unlock it to get into the camera app?"

"Oh, honey. I never have to do that. You just swipe to the left, and the camera pops up. This isn't my first rodeo, you know." Aunt Diane pursed her lips and crossed her arms. And again, Tatum's body against mine began to shake with silent laughter.

"What about the background? When you hit the button to swipe to the left, you didn't ask yourself, 'Why is there a stupid picture of the Swedish Chef on my phone?'—again, no offense, Tatum," she added over her shoulder.

"None taken."

Aunt Diane didn't give in. "You think I could see that? I don't have my glasses."

Kelsey tossed her head back with exaggerated frustration—well, it might've been genuine—and groaned. Her mom shrugged and then pivoted on her heel to return to the kitchen. Halfway down the hall, she yelled, "Fred! Where's my digital camera?"

Another groan rumbled past my cousin's lips. She quickly tossed the phone at Tatum and then turned to chase her mother. The last thing we heard was, "Don't you dare tell her where it's at, Dad!"

Once we were alone, neither of us could stop the fits of laughter from consuming us. "How have they not scared you away by now?" I asked, shifting on the stiff cushion to face Tatum.

The humor on her lips faded while she met my gaze. "I'd give anything to have a family like yours. Being around them makes me feel like I'm part of it."

"You don't have any family?" I immediately felt bad for her, never wanting *anyone* to go without at least one parent in their life.

Her brows arched in what I presumed to be shock, yet embarrassment glistened in her eyes. "Oh, no . . . I do. They just don't live here. Although, even if they did, they aren't the weekly-get-together kind of people, so I'd probably see them about as much as I do now."

"That sucks." Probably not the most eloquent thing I could've said, but since I didn't know her, I figured it was best not to pry.

She dropped her gaze to her lap, and I became desperate to engage her in conversation again. I wasn't ready for this moment to end. Somehow, her presence warded off the loneliness brought on by my recent heartbreak.

Before she could run away, I pointed to her phone and said, "Let's take a look at the picture my aunt got of us."

She unlocked the screen. The snapshot wasn't zoomed in, and we were slightly off center, but Aunt Diane had managed to capture Tatum and me in the midst of laughter, our eyes locked on each other's. On my other side, Kelsey had her face turned toward me, her top lip curled in annoyance and her arms crossed over her chest, her body angled away. No wonder she hid her mom's phone. If all the photos Aunt Diane took of Kelsey were like this one, she had good reason to ban her mother from using a camera.

"Here . . ." I took the phone and opened the edit options to zoom in and crop Kelsey out. "There. Much better."

Tatum stared at the image for a moment with a subtle, guarded smile, and before the screen dimmed, she locked it. Without meeting my gaze or even turning her face toward me, she excused herself. Apparently, she needed to finish the mushrooms before the burgers on the grill were done.

This time, when she walked away, I was all alone in the room.

I still couldn't tell if she was an introvert, although I no longer believed she disliked me. But I hoped I'd get the chance to be around her more and maybe break her out of her shell. I had a feeling there was much more to Tatum than I could see.

2

Tatum

Nothing made me dream of living in Antarctica more than the stifling heat of summer.

Even beneath a tent, the humidity was enough to leave me in a perpetual daydream of icebergs and subfreezing temperatures. Yes, I'd practically volunteered to spend a day outside, but that didn't mean I was excited to melt into a puddle of sweat.

Taste of the Town was the biggest in-person advertising opportunity a restaurant had in the area. All of Langston—and every surrounding suburb—came to enjoy food from many different businesses, large and small. I'd been picked as one of Fathom 216's employees to help man the tent and offer insight into our unique menu. It was a treat to get to do this, and I had looked forward to it for weeks . . . until I found out who else had been scheduled for it, too.

Shawn, one of the prep cooks, was there to assist with serving, and one of the hostesses, Amanda, played the part of cashier. I didn't mind spending a Sunday with either of them. It was the other person Michael had chosen to work the event with us—Rebecca DeWolf, his new girlfriend—who got under my skin.

There wasn't anything wrong with her, per se. From what I knew of her—which wasn't much, considering she'd only been at the restaurant for three weeks—she was a really sweet person. But the idea of spending most of the day listening to her gush about Michael didn't appeal to me. She could find almost any reason to bring up his name and make it relevant to any conversation, regardless of who she was talking to.

A woman could only hear about her ex—*from his new lover*—so many times before she did something unforgivable and wound up on the nightly news. And since prison kitchens didn't have sous chefs, that would've been a waste of student loans. So, instead of paying her any mind, I spent most of the day listening to local bands play popular cover songs from the stage in the center of the park. The music wasn't overly loud where we were, but it was enough to drown out Rebecca and her continuous stories of Michael.

After three o'clock, the flow of traffic began to slow—for food, that is; the beer vendors still had plenty of business. Shawn stood in front of the tent, talking to anyone and everyone who passed by, and Amanda entertained Rebecca while I pretended to be occupied with my phone.

I didn't typically pull up the photo of Jason unless I was alone in my room, where I had the freedom to salivate at his image without having to explain myself. But Kelsey wasn't around to catch me, so I tapped on the picture Mrs. Peterson had taken two weeks ago, zoomed in to see only his face, and lost myself in the daydreams his image produced.

The way the light hit the green of his irises reminded me of limes on a tree in the spring—just a hint of yellow to accentuate the color. And his lashes . . . oh my God, they were what women would sell a kidney to have. Dark and long, thick, totally capable of wooing anyone with a few bats. They were like magic, and I was under their spell.

Staring at the way we sat next to each other reminded me how hard his bicep had felt against the back of my neck when he'd draped his arm around my shoulders. And the warmth of his body pressed against mine . . . I crossed my legs to stop the familiar ache that came on every time I looked at the photo—which was often. *Far* too often. And if Kelsey ever found out, she'd kill me.

Every time I stared at his image, I wished I could redo that entire day. I'd been awkward at best, mostly trying to avoid being in the same room with him. There was a good chance he thought I was weird . . . or a bitch. For some reason, people mistook shyness for attitude. But in reality, I'd met him one week after learning of Michael's new relationship and being forced to work in the same kitchen with the young blonde. I would be lucky if "awkward bitch" was the *only* thing he'd thought of me.

"You do know Michael used to be engaged to Tatum, right?" That was enough to grab my attention, breaking me out of the thoughts of limes and muscles and body heat.

Turning to face the two women, I immediately noticed the skepticism on Amanda's face. Even without hearing their conversation, I knew it had to do with Michael. I could almost see the handwritten "Help Me" sign around Amanda's neck, which was enough to prove my theory.

I wasn't sure if I wanted to hug the sweet hostess for her obvious attempt to silence Rebecca, or cry over the reminder that my left ring finger now sat bare. That diamond had been so pretty.

"Yeah, he told me. But that was a while ago. Does it bother you, Tatum? You've never said anything about it."

I thought about pointing out that six months wasn't really *a while ago*, but I decided to let that go. And the idea of admitting how it felt to see him smile at her or whisper into her ear, let alone *hear* about all the things I didn't have to witness, made me want to disappear. "Oh, no. I'm so over it. So, *so* over it." And since stopping while I was ahead had never been my strong suit, I added, "In fact, I've been dating someone."

"You have?" Both Rebecca and Amanda asked the same question at the same time, but while Rebecca's voice was filled with excitement— which matched her bright eyes and ridiculous handclap—Amanda's was more cynical.

Hostesses always knew everyone's business.

"Yup. And he's amazing."

"What's his name?" Again with the doubtful tone from Amanda. She'd been part of my postbreakup support system, so I couldn't exactly blame her for questioning my sudden confession. After everything Michael had put me through, this was something I definitely would've told her . . . had it been true.

"Uh . . . Jay. His name's Jay."

"Where'd you meet him?" This time, it was Rebecca asking, as if we were girlfriends sharing juicy gossip over mimosas at a spa.

I had no idea why I'd even started this. I should've known they'd jump all over it like rabid dogs on a T-bone. Yet I couldn't back out now.

"We met at a barbecue." Short and sweet, not many details I'd have to remember. Perfect.

"When?" *Dammit, Amanda.* She was no longer on my Christmas card list—not that I'd ever sent any out, but that didn't mean I didn't have a list in case one year I felt ambitious. And if that year ever came, this heifer wouldn't get one.

"Two weeks ago."

"What's he look like?" Rebecca's blue eyes shimmered.

"Yeah, tell us what he looks like, Tatum." And now she could forget getting a birthday present from me. It also helped that I had no idea when her birthday was.

"He's tall. Hot. A man's man." That could've been anyone. I was still safe.

"How very nondescript of you."

"Well, you know how it is, Amanda." I glared at her, hoping she'd get the hint and go with it. "It's still new, and I wouldn't want anyone to get jealous of how perfect he is."

"No need to worry about me. I'm very secure in my relationship with Michael."

I wanted to ask Rebecca how secure she could possibly be with a man who, six months ago, had broken up with his fiancée on her birthday because he said he wasn't sure if he was ready for something so serious. But I held back the wicked comments that longed to slip off my tongue.

The next words out of my mouth were Michael's fault. Had he not forced me to spend the day with his new girlfriend, listening to every detail of their relationship, I never would've been in this position.

"He has dark hair that's trimmed short on the sides and a little longer on top, just enough to look messy if he runs his fingers through it. His eyes are this amazing shade of green—sometimes they're light, like blades of grass at the beginning of spring, and other times they're darker, similar to the color of a Christmas tree. And he's gotta be over six feet tall. When I stand next to him, I'm eye level with his chest." I glanced at my phone in my hand, noticing that the photo still filled the screen, and realized I had described Jason to a T.

"Go on," Rebecca prodded. "Is he fit like Michael?"

By this point, I was in it to win it.

"He makes Michael look like a wimp. And I'm not just saying that because Michael's my ex, either. I could wash my clothes on his abs." Well, that was taking it a little too far. I had to rein it in some if I wanted her to actually believe me. "He works out all the time, so he's totally in shape. Not an inch of fat on him."

"He sounds dreamy," Rebecca said with a sigh.

"Yeah, he does. Almost too good to be true . . . like you made him up. You probably don't have any pictures of him, do you?" As only a friend would, Amanda loved watching me dig my own grave.

"As a matter of fact, I do." I thought about sticking my tongue out at Amanda in an immature "shows what you know" kind of way, but then I realized what I'd just done. In my need to prove her wrong—even though she wasn't—I'd inadvertently dug my hole even deeper.

"Well, let's see it."

I had no choice but to show them the photo on my phone. I had to admit, though, the surprise on Amanda's face when she saw it gave me a sense of victory—like winning Monopoly only because I cheated. Rebecca's approval was simply the icing on the cake.

A cake that came crashing to the ground about thirty minutes later.

Rebecca stared at something over my shoulder and asked, "Hey, Tatum, isn't that Jay?"

"Huh? Jay who?"

"Uh . . . your boyfriend," Amanda reminded me with a quirked brow.

I craned my neck so fast it gave me a cramp. There was no way it was him. Okay, so that was wishful thinking on my part. Not only was there a *chance* he was here, but he was, in fact, *here*. At Taste of the Town. Standing a few tents away next to another guy.

My life was over.

Having Amanda believe I had lied about a boyfriend was one thing—having *multiple* people catch me in said lie was another. Add in the probability of Jason being one of those people, and . . . *shoot me now*.

My mouth gaped, denial forming on my tongue, when Rebecca said, "Yeah, that *is* him! I'm super good at remembering faces. I only have to see someone once, and I'd recognize them anywhere. Not to mention, that's the same shirt he was wearing in the picture you showed us." Damn him. Someone needed to buy him more T-shirts. "You were right, Tatum . . . he's dreamy. Did he know you'd be here?"

"I can't remember if I mentioned it to him or not."

"You should go say hi." Amanda just couldn't help herself.

"I'd rather not." I needed an excuse, and fast. "I'm working, and he's with his friend."

Unfortunately, my reasoning wasn't good enough for the excited cheerleader. "We can totally hold down the fort long enough for you to go talk to him."

"Really, guys . . . it's fine. We've only just started seeing each other, and he's out with his friends. I don't wanna look clingy and scare him off." I was proud of myself for coming up with that one on the spot. Totally believable.

Until Amanda opened her big, fat mouth again.

"You're right. You should wait for him to come to you. He's right over there; I'm sure he'll be here in no time. I can't wait to see the look on his face when he comes over and realizes you're here."

Well, that was the last thing I wanted to happen. At least if I got to him first, they wouldn't have to witness it. "You make a good point. I should go say hi. I'll be right back."

With each step I took, I dug my grave one more inch. My gaze bounced around to every person nearby, wondering who would witness the single most humiliating moment of my life. I was convinced that everyone knew what I was about to do. I could practically smell the popcorn—actually, I could, but that was probably because there were a few vendors nearby serving it.

Somehow, I made it from the tent to Jason without him noticing me. I was maybe three feet away when I realized I had no plan in place. There wasn't a doubt in my mind that the girls were watching intently, and if I just stood in front of him without any affection, the jig would be up.

Fun fact: Three feet doesn't give one enough time to formulate a plan.

Knowing I couldn't just wave or shake his hand, I practically threw myself at him. Wrapping my arms around his waist, I suction cupped my front to his with the side of my face pressed firmly against his hard chest.

"Whoa . . ." It was clear I'd caught him off guard, but at least he had a sense of humor, proven in the laughter coloring his surprise. His hands came to rest on my back as he shifted on his feet to regain his balance.

Luckily, I was able to use his unsteady footing to my advantage.

Without letting go, I pivoted him in a semicircle, putting his back to the tent so the girls couldn't see his face. Once I got him turned around, though, I had not the faintest idea what to do next. I assumed there was no possibility of getting out of this without him recognizing me. And while I clung to him like a spider monkey, I'd completely missed the way his head had dropped forward until the most beautiful sound in the world flooded my ears.

"You okay?" Humor danced in his soft-spoken question, and the heat of his breath bathed my cheek in a comforting warmth. For the last two weeks, I'd studied the picture and recalled everything in vivid detail. But somehow, hearing him speak so close to my face—much like he had that day on Diane's couch—made me realize just how much I'd forgotten.

I remembered how small my hand had felt in his, and how he smelled like he'd just stepped out of a shower when he had the side of his hard body pressed against mine. However, I'd forgotten how hypnotic his voice was—deep and almost raspy with grit. It could melt a chastity belt with as little as "hello."

Jerry Maguire had *nothing* on Jason Watson.

Realizing I still held on to him for dear life, I let go and took a step back. Running away wasn't much of an option now, and acting like it'd been an accident wouldn't be very convincing—one, there was a chance he remembered me from Diane's house, and two, I couldn't act to save my life. So, I figured I'd lift my chin and own the moment.

"Hey. Sorry about that. I saw you standing over here and thought I'd come say hi." Yeah, I was about as smooth as sandpaper. At least I could admit my inability to fit in, and in fact, I'd even learned to embrace it. Social settings became much easier when I stopped trying to hide my awkwardness—I mean, it wasn't like I was fooling anyone. Now I just had to pray he wouldn't shun me in front of my coworkers.

"That was quite a way to say hello." His smile widened, causing the subtle creases next to his eyes to deepen and spread like rays of sunshine.

Not even the slight scruff dotting his face could hide the dimples in his cheeks.

I shrugged, trying to play it off and more than likely failing. "Yeah, what can I say . . . I'm a hugger." I was *not* a hugger. Not at all. The idea of it practically gave me hives. It wasn't that I was a germophobe or suffered from PTSD. I simply valued personal space.

"You are?" He didn't believe me . . . *shocker*. "Good to know."

Just then, the guy next to him spoke up. "You gonna introduce us, man?"

"Oh, yeah. Sorry." Jason laughed under his breath and shook his head, as if he'd forgotten about his friend. "Aaron, this is Kelsey's best friend, Tatum. Tatum, this is Aaron Baucus, a buddy of mine from high school."

"Nice to meet you," he said with his arms spread wide.

Well, I'd made it this far, no point in turning back now.

Like I had done with Jason, I launched myself into him and squeezed his waist with my cheek against his chest. He didn't smell as nice as Jason, though, and his physique wasn't as impressive, either. Needless to say, that embrace didn't last long.

"Well, it was nice running into you." I began to walk away. "I should probably get back to my friends. Have fun."

Jason watched me leave with smiling eyes and humor curving his lips. Considering he was Kelsey's cousin and I'd more than likely have to see him again, I wasn't keen on the idea of weirding him out. However, if it meant he wouldn't approach me while I was with Rebecca and Amanda, I couldn't complain.

I just had to make it a little bit longer.

3

Jason

Grey clouds rolled in, giving us all a break from the blazing sun. The live music had stopped about thirty minutes ago, and half the vendors had begun to pack up. That hadn't prevented many of us from lingering near the beer trailers, though.

"What about you?" It wasn't the question or even the voice that caught my attention, but the hand on my arm. A small, attractive woman with pink hair stood in front of me, clearly waiting on an answer. However, I had no clue what question she'd even asked. I'd been too busy watching a certain brunette under the tent across from me to pay attention to anything else.

"What we want to drink," Aaron clarified for me. "They're out of the seasonal, so what do you want instead?"

We'd walked all over the park for hours, and when Aaron had struck up a conversation with this girl—Sarah or Sally or something like that—she'd brought us to this beer station. She knew the guy working it and had said she could get us free drinks. It just happened to work out that the beer truck was located right across from the tent Tatum occupied.

Ever since she'd run into me earlier, I hadn't been able to stop think-ing about her. Not the same way I was used to thinking about a woman, though. Tatum had left me with more questions than answers. After meeting her a couple of weeks ago, I'd believed her to be the shy, quiet type, maybe the kind of girl who felt uncomfortable around people she didn't know. But that had all changed when she'd practically jumped on me today and had then done the same to Aaron.

Maybe she'd been high.

I couldn't help but laugh. There was no way that woman had been on anything. It was obviously just her personality. Either way, I found her quirkiness fascinating. I'd never met anyone like her. I only wished I knew what she was like when she felt comfortable around someone.

"I'll take whatever you're having," I told Aaron, ignoring his ques-tioning stare.

The pink-haired girl told him what kind to get and then returned her attention to me. "Did you do much gambling when you lived in Vegas? I bet you're great at poker."

"Yeah . . . I'm a real cardsharp." It would be nice if I could encoun-ter *one* person who didn't assume all of Clark County lived in a casino.

Aaron handed me a plastic cup, but rather than escort us away from the vendor, he leaned his shoulder against the side of the truck to join our conversation. After all, we were only with this chick for him. I had no interest in her.

"Oh, that sounds exciting." She'd clearly missed the sarcasm. "So were you like a card dealer or something?"

I hesitated, hoping she was kidding. When it was obvious she wasn't, I said, "Uh . . . no."

"Then what do you do for a living?"

"He's a dirt guy," Aaron answered for me.

Before she could ask what that meant, I decided to clarify—if for no other reason than to save us *both* time. "I'm a geotechnical engineer, which means I study the earth before anything is built on it."

"Oh, fancy. You must be smart."

"Not as smart as this guy." I hitched my thumb in Aaron's direction. "Did you know he's a brain doctor?" I smiled inside as her eyes widened and sparked with excitement.

Aaron's groans filled my ears. He hated it when I brought up his occupation. If it were up to him, he'd downplay it until people thought he mopped floors at a retirement home. "I'm not a brain doctor," he corrected me, his monotone conveying just how disgruntled he was. "I'm a psychologist."

"Yeah . . . who works on brains." I paused and held out both hands. "Brain. Doctor."

He rolled his eyes and huffed. "I evaluate nervous system disorders and the behavior . . ."

I tuned him out, having heard this song and dance a thousand times. Then again, he repeated it only because I had a tendency to make him sound like a brain surgeon, but that didn't matter. A brunette across the way had stolen my attention. Plus, she was much better looking than my friend.

There was no way to know how long I'd watched her clean off the tables, but at some point, a small hand came to rest on my chest, fingertips grazing my collarbone, and it caught my attention. It wouldn't have been that big of a deal, but at that exact moment, Tatum glanced up. She quickly averted her gaze and dropped her chin. Even from ten feet away, I could see the color in her cheeks brighten.

I glanced down to the hand on my chest, and then trailed my eyes up the arm to find the girl with pink hair staring at me. More than likely, she'd asked me another question I hadn't heard. And once again, I waited for someone to clear it up.

"I'd hate to be your girlfriend." Giggles filled Sally-Sarah's words. I really needed to figure out her name, not because I had any need to know it but because by now, *not* knowing had begun to irritate me. This seemed to be a recurring issue when it came to women—if I wasn't related to them and didn't work with them, there was a good chance I wouldn't remember their names.

Rather than point out how I'd *never* be her boyfriend, I asked, "Why?"

"Because you don't pay attention." She finally dropped her hand. "Anyway, I was saying you guys should come up to Boots sometime. Have you ever heard of it?"

While I answered with a concise "Nope," Aaron said, "Hell yeah. I love that place." Hearing my response, he turned his attention to me. "You'd like it. It's this club in town—kind of country, kind of modern."

"If you decide to come, let me know ahead of time. It gets busy on Friday and Saturday nights, but I might be able to secure one of the VIP booths for you if I know in advance."

"Yeah, that sounds good." I offered a smile of gratitude to the woman in front of me. Stefanie . . . maybe that was her name. "Thanks. That's really nice of you. I'm sure Aaron will hit you up for that."

While Aaron walked a few feet away to throw out his empty cup, the girl with pink hair grabbed a napkin off the beer truck. I didn't think much about it until she picked up a pen and began to write something. Handing it to me, she excitedly said, "Give me a call, and I'll get a spot reserved for you. And Aaron, of course."

I wasn't the kind of guy who'd potentially embarrass someone—especially a girl. So I took the napkin and peeked at her number, hoping she'd added her name. Nope. No such luck. When I glanced up, I happened to catch sight of Tatum again, and like before, the second I saw her, she turned away.

"Thanks. We'll definitely give you a call if we make it up there." I shoved her number deep into my front pocket, ignoring Aaron's inquisitive stare. "I'm getting ready to move into my own place, so I'm not sure when I'll get a chance to go out."

"Oh, no worries. My offer doesn't expire." Her innocent smile made her appear angelic, which must come in handy for someone who worked for tips at a nightclub.

Aaron turned his face to the sky and pulled in a deep breath. "Looks like it's about to pour. I'm thinking it might be time to call it a day."

I stole a peek at Tatum and noticed she had the tent packed up. If I waited too long, I'd miss my opportunity to talk to her before she left, and after our earlier encounter, I wanted to at least say goodbye. "Yeah, I'm ready to go, too. I'm sure I'll talk to you later."

Either I'd missed an earlier conversation, or they'd built some unspoken agreement, because Aaron grabbed her hand and led her away. Instead of wasting time by questioning it, I headed toward the tent across from me.

"Need a hand with that?" I didn't wait for Tatum's response before grabbing the handle of the wagon she had packed full of various kitchen items.

Her onyx eyes met mine, full of surprise, like she had no idea where I'd come from. As if she hadn't noticed me standing not far from her for the last ten minutes. She blinked a few times and then slung her bag over her shoulder. "It's okay. I've got it."

"Just lead the way, and I'll follow," I said, ignoring her insistence on doing it herself.

She must've either been too tired to argue or figured I wouldn't give in, because rather than try to take the wagon from me, she began to walk toward the parking lot. "So . . . I see you know Cheryl."

"Who?"

Her brows knitted as she narrowed her gaze on me. "Cheryl. The girl you were just talking to. Isn't that her number in your pocket?"

I fought with all I had in me to bite back the grin of satisfaction. She'd noticed me, except I wasn't sure if it was out of curiosity or maybe a slight tinge of jealousy. "Oh, that's her name? I'd forgotten it . . . just knew it started with an *S*."

I couldn't hide my smile any longer when she giggled. "It's Cheryl—with a *C*."

It took me a moment to understand what she was saying, and then it hit me like an overstuffed bag of a bricks. I laughed when I said, "In my defense, it sounds like an *S*. Sha-sha-Cheryl. See?"

"Yeah. It's all so clear now. Not only are you an ace at phonics, you also take numbers from women without knowing their names. You're a real go-getter, aren't ya?"

I shrugged and continued to follow her past various empty tents. "What was I supposed to do? I didn't want to be rude. After all, she'd just scored us free drinks. I'd call that gentlemanly."

"Watch out, Romeo . . . people might find out you're wearing tinfoil."

"Huh?"

"You know, instead of a knight in shining armor, you're an imposter in tinfoil."

"Yeah, that would've totally made sense, except Romeo wasn't a knight."

She pulled her lips to the side in contemplation for a moment. "I'm fairly certain you're wrong, but there's no need to argue over Shakespeare."

"So is she your friend or something?"

"Who? Shakespeare? I'm positive he's a dude. And dead. Clearly, we aren't friends."

I was about to keel over laughing. "No. The girl I just met. How do you know her?"

Tatum's cheeks were the color of cherries. "We've hung out in the same group several times. I know who she is, but that's about it."

I decided to feel her out a little more. "She was nice."

Walking a couple steps ahead, she lifted a shoulder, held it for a beat, and then dropped it. "Yeah . . . I guess you could say that."

"What? You don't agree?"

"Uh, I just did when I said yeah. Typically, that's agreeing with something, right?"

"But you made it sound like you don't. If there's something I should know, please tell me, because my buddy just left with her."

"Unless you're worried she'll spit shine his knob, I don't think you have anything to be concerned about." She grew quiet for a moment and tilted her head back to observe the grey clouds overhead. "I'm in the wrong profession. I should've been a weatherperson. It's like the one job you can totally get wrong without being fired."

I was amazed how she could go from blow jobs to the weather as if they were somehow related. "I'm sure you don't have to worry about job security. I watched you in the kitchen with my mom. You look like you know what you're doing."

Her pace slowed when we entered the area lined with cars. Completely dismissing my compliment as if she hadn't heard me, she reached for the wagon, a smile taunting her lips. "Thanks for your unsolicited help, but I can get it from here."

She seemed to have this uncanny ability to walk away from me, no matter if we were at my aunt's house or in a parking lot. At the very least, it had taught me to enjoy her company—I never knew when it'd end.

"Nope. I've made it this far . . . might as well get it all the way to your car."

"And then what? Will you insist on driving me home, too?"

I couldn't be sure, but I thought she was flirting. Which only served to leave me further confused. "Possibly, but I don't know where you live. So I think you're safe."

Her brow furrowed, taking her from fun and flirty to perplexed and restrained. "You don't know where Kelsey lives? I thought you drove her home last week after dinner."

"You live with my cousin? How did I not know this?"

"She didn't mention it?"

I tried to recall what all we'd talked about last weekend at my aunt's house. Tatum hadn't been there, but her name had been brought up; apparently, her absence from Sunday lunch had been unusual. Other than that, I didn't think anything else had been said about her. "No . . . I don't think she did."

Bewilderment pinched her face—brows drawn closer together, eyes narrowed, and lips slightly pursed. But she seemed to shake it off with a dismissive eye roll and began to walk again. "Wow, she must really not want you anywhere near me."

"What's that supposed to mean?" I quickly moved to catch up, unsure if I'd heard her correctly and unwilling to let it go.

"Nothing," she said with a flick of her wrist, waving off the entire conversation. "I don't understand you two, and I'm starting to think I don't want to."

"Wait." I grabbed her hand to keep her from walking too far ahead. "You can't just make a statement like that and then dismiss it. What do you mean she doesn't want me anywhere near you? And why do you think you don't understand us?"

The color in her cheeks darkened as she dropped her gaze to my chest, then to our hands. I so desperately wanted to know what went through her mind as she stood there, studying my hold on her. She had her bottom lip tucked between her teeth, leaving me in a vacuum of anticipation.

"Really, it's nothing." She slipped her hand out of mine and dug into the bag slung over her shoulder. When she pulled out her keys, she resumed her pace. "She might've mentioned that you're a sweet talker, and even though she loves you, she'd never forgive herself if one of her friends got tangled up in your sheets. That's what I meant by not understanding you guys. I can't tell if you two actually like each other or not."

We reached the back of her SUV, and using the remote in her hand, she popped the trunk. I stepped in front of her to lift the back gate, though I didn't drop the subject. As I began to unload the contents of the wagon into the rear, I pried a little more. "Were those her words? Or are you paraphrasing?"

"Maybe a little of both. More specifically, she said you were really good at sweet-talking your way into girls' pants."

I paused for a second, desperately trying to form the right words without unveiling my true emotions. I shouldn't care what Kelsey said about me, nor should it matter what Tatum thought of me. One was my cousin, and the other was her best friend—who was more than likely around her same age. Not to mention, I wasn't interested in getting into *anyone's* pants. If I were, I had plenty of options to choose from, so this shouldn't bother me.

Yet it did.

"Is that why you've been avoiding me?"

Her head snapped back in a dramatic show of confusion. "Avoiding you? When? Today's the first time I've seen you since the barbecue, and in case you don't remember, I definitely did *not* avoid you. I gave you quite the welcome. Not to mention, I don't think what we're doing right now constitutes avoidance. Just sayin'."

She had a point, and it served to lighten my irritation over whatever Kelsey had told her. "I just mean how you act when you're around me. Like you're uninterested in talking to me and can't wait to get away."

I finished unpacking the wagon, but I had no idea how it folded up. When I turned to her for help, I found her chewing on the inside of her cheek in thought. I wasn't sure what she was looking at, but her gaze was off to the side, almost locked on the packed dirt where tires had killed any chance for grass to grow. And again, I wished I could hear her thoughts.

Then her narrowed gaze swung to my face, and she regarded me with a frown. "I'm sorry if I've made you feel that way. Honestly, I don't care what Kelsey says about you. I'm not the kind of girl who'll jump into bed with a hot guy after a few compliments—unless I've had a lot of tequila. And I don't like tequila."

My cheeks burned from the unrelenting strain of my smile, and my raised brows made my forehead ache. Not a sound came from me, yet my entire face felt like I'd spent the last hour laughing hysterically.

"I'm sorry, but . . . *what*?" I finally asked when I could no longer remember what we were even talking about. "I'm usually great at following along, but I'm pretty sure you lost me."

"Yeah . . . it happens." She bent down, took the liner out of the wagon, and pulled a string. Instantly, the cart was nothing more than a compact rectangle with wheels sticking out of the bottom. "Anyway, thanks for your help. It wasn't needed, I didn't ask for it, but it was super nice of you."

Still, I couldn't focus. It was like she'd given me ADD in thirty seconds. I could do nothing but watch her slide the cart into the back and then reach above her head to close the hatch. It wasn't until she stood on one side of the bumper and I remained on the other that I realized she was leaving.

"I'm sure I'll see you around."

"Wait!" I shouted a little too loudly and launched myself a step away from her. It was like I'd been snapped out of the attention deficit fog long enough to remember one thing. "I don't get a hug?"

One perfect brow arched high on her smooth forehead, and her top lip curled just enough to show confusion rather than disgust. That was all I needed to confirm my earlier assumption of her—although, I still didn't have answers for any other part of our awkward encounter. It was enough to prove that her outgoing personality from a few hours ago had been for show. Now, if I could only find out why.

"You said you're a hugger," I reminded her with my arms out wide.

"Oh. Yeah, that's right. I like to give hugs." If looks came with taglines, hers would have read "Kill me now" as she wrapped her arms around my waist. However, this hug was stiff, nothing like the desperate embrace she'd given me before. It was quick, and rather than rest her cheek against my chest, she kept her face somewhat turned, meeting me more with her chin than anything else. Forced . . . that's what it was.

I stood aside while she climbed into the SUV and cranked the engine, waiting until she'd backed out before heading to my car. Thankfully, I hadn't parked too far away. Without Tatum's presence pulling my thoughts in a million directions, my mind wandered back to what Kelsey had told her. For the life of me, I couldn't fathom why she'd say any of that. Yes, I had been a bit of a player in high school, but it had been *years* since then, and I'd just gotten out of a long-term relationship.

I was on the brink of calling Kelsey and giving her a piece of my mind when my phone vibrated in my pocket. Ironically, Marlena's name flashed across the screen. I answered, hoping I could gain some insight regarding Kelsey's opinion.

"Guess who I just got off the phone with?" she asked, not even bothering to say hi.

"Well, I hope it was your sister, because I have a bone to pick with her."

"No, it was Jen." Hearing my ex's name eliminated any thought I'd had about Kelsey and immediately killed my mood.

Jen and Marlena had formed a bond through me, even though they'd only met a few times. There was no way to know how often they'd spoken to one another, but it must have been enough that they'd become close over the years. I'd encouraged it at the time. Had I known just how hard this would be—going through a breakup when there were connections that extended beyond the two of us—I never would've introduced them.

"Why were you on the phone with her?" As much as I didn't want to hear the answer to that, I wanted to know, which only made the ache in my chest spread wider.

"She sent me a text asking if I could talk. I told her I didn't think it was a good idea, but then she said you refuse to answer her calls."

That was true. Jen had tried a couple of times to get ahold of me, using the excuse that I had left things behind, but I'd never bothered to respond. I was still bitter over everything, and until I could let it go, I didn't care to waste any more of my time, energy, or words on her. "There's nothing left for me to say, so there's no point in answering the phone."

"She doesn't have anyone to talk to, and apparently, you left without any warning."

"Wait a minute." I slid behind the steering wheel and started the car. "She's trying to say I just up and left without telling her? You didn't believe that, did you?"

"Not entirely."

"Excuse me? You mean there was a part of you that thought she was telling the truth?"

"Considering you moved two months before you were supposed to, yeah."

I couldn't believe what I was hearing. My own cousin, the one person in my entire family who knew me the best, had taken my ex's word over mine. "It wasn't like I woke up one morning and decided I needed a change of scenery."

This was the problem with a close family. I'd kept my mom in the loop regarding my move, and while I'd told Marlena when the decision had been made, I hadn't filled her in on the two months of uncertainty. Mom had a bad habit of telling the world things I'd rather she kept to herself, yet for some reason, she'd decided not to share this with anyone—not even the rest of the family. And now, Marlena only had Jen's side to go on.

"After Bill died, I wanted to be closer to my family, so Jen and I discussed the idea of moving. As in . . . I went to her about it *before* any decision had been made. We *both* agreed to relocate—it wasn't just me. In fact, she seemed excited about it. The only thing she asked was that we give ourselves a few months to get our ducks in a row."

"Well, according to her, you didn't give her enough time. She said you got pissed and left without her because she couldn't get everything done in the time frame you specified. Something about her not having a job in Langston?"

Jen was a showgirl, so she made a lot of money, and in her opinion, without a degree or experience, she wouldn't find anything in Langston that paid as much. "Are you serious? That's what she told you?"

"Don't be mad at me, Jason. I'm only relaying what I've been told." She was right; she didn't deserve my anger. That should be reserved for Jen and the twist she'd added when recounting the events that had led to our breakup. But it was hard to keep a lid on it when Marlena was the one on the other end of the line.

"We decided to wait four months so she could save and pay off debt. Knowing that she'd likely have to take a cut in pay, we both agreed it made more sense for her to have her credit cards and whatnot paid off before the move. After looking at her finances—*together*, because this was a joint decision—she would've had it all taken care of *and* a decent amount in savings in four months. But apparently, that wasn't long enough—despite how much money she made and how little debt she had."

"I just feel bad, Jason."

"Why? Tell me, Marlena, what more could I have done?"

"I don't know. To be honest, I'm still not entirely sure why you left."

I huffed as I pulled onto the main road and tried to regroup. It was hard to get my point across while only giving pieces of the story. So, I took a deep breath and readied myself to connect the dots for her. "When I first went to Jen with the idea of moving, had she shown any reluctance to leave or expressed any serious concern over quitting her job, I wouldn't have left. I would've stayed in Vegas with her and tried to find more time to come down and visit. But that's not what happened. Instead, she was on board from the get-go. I gave notice at my job, informed the family of our plans, and got the ball rolling with the move."

"Okay, I get that part, but if she started to get cold feet, why decide to leave instead of work things out with her? It wasn't too late, Jason. You could've rescinded your resignation and kept your job at the firm. And it's not like you couldn't have told us that you changed your mind. We wouldn't have held it over your head."

I dug my thumb into my temple, hoping the pressure would ward off the headache I felt coming on. "You're right . . . I could've done all those things if she'd told me about her cold feet or change of heart. But she never did."

"Then how'd you find out?"

"There were little things that I passed off, like her credit card not being paid off like she'd planned. But I didn't think anything of it since she technically had three more months. Then there was something she said about a new show coming to the hotel at the end of summer. But again, it wasn't enough to make me stop and question it. Tryouts going on during rehearsals didn't mean anything—I assumed she mentioned it because they were disruptive or something. She came home with new shoes once, though that wasn't unusual."

A car cut me off, making me pause to pay attention to the road.

Once I could focus on what I was saying, I continued. "During all this, I had asked a few times about the move, making sure we were still on target for the end of summer and that her bills would be taken care of by then. Not once did she speak up, and I had given her *plenty* of opportunities to express any concern. But the one thing that made me stop and question her intentions was when I called the landlord to verify the end-of-lease agreement. I had discussed everything with him at the beginning—using our security deposit to cover one month's rent and the last month already being covered when we had originally moved in. He told me that he would have to come out and inspect the house first, but it wouldn't be a problem as long as there wasn't any damage that he'd need the deposit for. I'd left that up to Jen, since she was home during the day."

Just thinking about it made my blood boil.

"Come to find out, the inspection had never happened. He told me that Jen canceled it, saying we weren't sure when we were moving and that she'd let him know when we had a date set. Which was bullshit, because we'd already set the date. When I asked her about that, she brushed it off, making it sound like it had been a misunderstanding, and said she'd take care of it."

"And during all this, she didn't even act like anything was wrong? Like show how nervous she was?"

"No. Not at all. That's why I was so pissed when she finally admitted it."

"And how'd that come about?"

"I asked to use her phone to pay rent because mine was on the charger in the room—the inspection never happened, so we couldn't use the security deposit to cover that month. And while I was on her phone, a text came through. Normally, I wouldn't have read it, but when I saw it mention the new show and her place in it, I couldn't help myself."

"Wait a minute—you mean to tell me she tried out, even though she knew it would start after she was supposed to move with you?"

"Yup. And when I questioned her, she said she hadn't accepted the position yet."

"Then why'd she try out?"

"Apparently she just wanted to see if she'd get it."

Anytime I thought of Jen and how she had effectively stolen the future we'd planned together, my entire body ignited with the heat of seven hells. My cheeks flamed, my neck sweated, and my palms burned. Anger and betrayal churned inside until I was convinced the pain would suffocate me.

"That's when I asked to see her credit card statements and savings account balance. If she truly intended to move with me, she would've been making payments and depositing money into her account. By this point, if she hadn't done those things, there was no way she'd have it all taken care of in time."

"Please don't tell me she didn't do any of it."

"Okay . . . then I won't tell you." I turned on my blinker and waited for the light to change to green. "That's when she started asking for more time. Reluctantly, I agreed and said I could push the move off one more month, but that was it. I had already trained the guy taking my place at the firm, so really, I wasn't even needed at work anymore. All the accounts I'd been in charge of had been handed to the new person. One month without pay was about all I could offer."

"And that wasn't good enough for her?"

"Oh, it was. Until a week later, when I found a two-hundred-dollar pair of shoes in her trunk. Which, of course, she tried to say were old. Unfortunately for her, she left the receipt in the bag. That was when I gave up. It was clear she had no interest in coming with me, and by that point, I couldn't change my mind and stay. I'd already given up my job—my position had been filled, so it was too late to ask for it back."

Marlena was quiet for so long I wondered if my phone had dropped the call while I was heading over the bridge from Langston to Samson. Finally, she cleared her throat and said, "I think she realized the mistake she made and genuinely wants to fix it. She said she's willing to move, but you won't give her a chance to work it out."

"If she wasn't ready to do that three weeks ago, then she's not ready to do it now. She just says she is to look good."

"I doubt that, Jason. Why would she say it and not follow through?"

"Gee, I don't know, Marlena. Why would a father tell his son that he would get him a plane ticket to spend the summer with him and then never do it? Why would he tell his son he'd have lunch with him at school while he was in town and then never show up? I'm well aware what it looks like when someone says one thing without any intention of following through with it." I'd never shared with anyone how let down

46

I'd been that day in second grade when I'd told my entire class that I was having lunch with my dad, only to eat alone at a picnic table near the playground. No kid deserved to experience that kind of rejection—by his own father, no less.

"That doesn't mean Jen plans to screw you over, too."

"I don't give second chances, Marlena. And she knows it. I never have, and I never will. That's how I've been since the day she met me, and no amount of groveling will change it. She's always known that I'm more than willing to work something out . . . until the door closes. Once that happens, I'm done. She waited too long. Calling me after I move is like writing a check after your car gets repossessed—pointless and a waste of time."

"I get that, but it's not like she cheated on you. This is totally fixable."

I gripped the steering wheel, anger over her comment rolling through me without a viable outlet. "Why must infidelity be the only form of deception? Just because she didn't sleep with anyone else doesn't negate the fact that she betrayed me."

"I don't know, Jason. I guess I'm the fool who believes if you love someone, you fight for them."

"It's just how I am. How I feel about someone doesn't change that."

She was silent for a moment, though I could tell she had more to say. "She misses you."

And there it was. The punch in my gut; the knife in my chest.

That didn't warrant a response. So instead, I asked, "Is that all she had to say?"

A long sigh drifted through the line. "Basically. She more than likely thought I could get you to change your mind. But now that you've told me your side, I won't answer any more of her calls. And I don't think Kelsey has ever spoken to her, so you don't have anything to worry about there."

"Speaking of Kelsey . . ." The sky decided right then and there to open up, the downpour making it difficult to see the car in front of me. But that didn't stop me from seeking the answer I needed. "Any clue why she'd tell people I'm a womanizer?"

Marlena laughed; at least one of us found this funny. "Maybe because you used to be one?"

"I don't see how that has any bearing on who I am now."

"It shouldn't, but you also have to remember who we're talking about here. She had to grow up listening to my friends bitch about you. At least two of them lost their virginity to you, and the rest were just tallies in your playbook. Not to mention, you guys haven't been very close throughout the years. So it would be easy for her to assume you haven't changed. Think about it . . . when I talk about Connor, do you picture him the way he looks now or as the baby he used to be?"

She had a point. Anytime she spoke of her son, I imagined an infant crawling with only two teeth in his head, not the rambunctious four-year-old who liked to growl at people for no reason. And had I not been around Lizzie, her two-year-old, for the last couple of weeks, I wouldn't have been able to picture her at all.

"My advice is to spend more time with her." Marlena never needed an invitation to offer her opinion on something. "She's older now, so I'm sure you guys will find lots of ways to bond."

She hadn't said the words, but this was her way of passing the torch. While Marlena and I had always been close, now we were in two very different places in our lives. At this point, Kelsey and I might be on more common ground instead.

And if it kept her from tainting Tatum's opinion of me, then I'd spend every second with my youngest cousin whether I enjoyed her company or not. I'd prove her wrong if it was the last thing I did.

4

Tatum

Michael waltzed into the kitchen and went straight to Rebecca. I hated the way he leaned over her shoulder while she worked, whispering into her ear so no one could hear their conversation. It's what he used to do to me, so I knew the kinds of things he'd murmur. That being said, they were never dirty or even sweet, romantic remarks. In fact, most of the time, he'd simply made comments about whatever was in the pan in front of me. How it smelled, the color of the sauce, or that he wanted me to make it for him on the next night we had off together.

Just thinking about it left a tickle at the base of my spine, as if I could still feel his fingertips grazing my lower back while the heat of his minty breath toyed with the spot just below my ear. I could practically hear him tell me how much he loved to watch me cook—he'd likened it to art on many occasions.

However, Rebecca created desserts. I could only imagine the things he whispered to her about the frosting or filling . . . or cherries. And I didn't care to find out what kind of "art" he compared her cakes to. The thought alone sickened me.

After months of not being with him and weeks of seeing the two of them together in the kitchen, it shouldn't have bothered me—I should've been used to it by now. But I wasn't. And I began to worry I never would.

He turned away from her with a smile on his face. I used to swoon at the sight of it; now it left me drowning in a pool of mixed feelings. A man who could look at another woman with the same expression he used to give me wasn't someone I should want. I wasn't sure why I still did.

"How are things with the new boyfriend?" He might have sauntered over to me, kept his head down like he'd done over Rebecca's shoulder, and lowered his voice to what resembled a husky growl—which I took as restrained jealousy—but he didn't look at me. Nor did he stand too close. Instead, he leaned against the end of my station, where I kept my dry ingredients, and eyed the ramekins used for spices.

"I take it Rebecca told you?" I tried to keep the nerves out of my voice, though I doubted I succeeded. If anything, Michael had always been able to read me—even when no one else could.

"Yeah, she mentioned it last night."

I wasn't sure if he'd worded it that way on purpose—to let me know they had been together *last night*—or if it had been an oversight. There were many things Michael did that didn't make much sense. Such as leave me alone at my own birthday dinner. And the more I tried to understand him, the less I comprehended. I tried to look busy by reaching in front of him to grab a spatula I didn't need, and being the graceful person that I was, I knocked over a set of wooden spoons and about seven plates.

Michael saved the plates at the same time I reached for the spoons. I glanced around, hoping I hadn't drawn too much attention to myself, and then groaned as everyone in the kitchen had their eyes on me.

Once we had everything put back in place, he wrapped his fingers around my wrist to hold me still. I stared at his hand for a moment.

At first, I couldn't stop thinking about the way he used to touch me, the feel of his skin on mine, or how I used to believe he never wanted to let me go. But then I remembered that he used those same hands to touch another woman.

That was enough to snap me out of it.

I yanked my arm away and went back to work. Well, I pretended to. It was near the end of the lunch rush, which meant fewer orders to occupy my time. My area had already been cleaned in anticipation of the switch from lunch to dinner service. Needless to say, I wasn't very convincing at acting busy. That might have also had something to do with my inability to pay attention to anything when he'd sidled up next to me.

Michael moved closer, halfway standing behind me with his head looming over my left shoulder. It was all too familiar. Yet this time, I didn't melt into him like butter on toasted bread. My body reacted on its own, and I became rigid, uncomfortable. The moisture of his breath grazed my neck, and I couldn't be sure, but I thought I felt the faintest caress low on my back, as if he had to fight against touching me.

I pulled in a deep breath to steady my nerves. Unfortunately, that meant I got a whiff of his cologne—the same kind he'd always worn—and it did nothing but remind me of the nights spent lying next to him, taking in the spicy yet soothing scent of the man I loved.

"I just wanted to tell you that I'm happy for you." Within the dips of his deep rasp, I picked up on a hint of hesitation.

Without waiting for any response other than a surprised gasp, he took a step back. When I cut my eyes to peek at him, I noticed the way he fidgeted with his tie—a sign of his own nervousness.

God, I knew him too well.

And I couldn't say that was a good thing.

He glanced around the kitchen, and when his gaze landed on me again, he smiled the same way he used to when we shared a secret. I hadn't seen that smile on him in over six months. And for some ridiculous reason, it kick-started my heart. Butterflies swarmed my belly, and heat licked my cheeks. Before I knew it, my lips had curled to match his, something I hadn't expected.

"Rebecca said you really like this guy."

And with that, my unexpected excitement vanished.

I blinked a few times and waited for more. Except he didn't offer anything else. Not a clue as to how I should respond to that. I said, "Um, yeah. I do."

He ran his fingers through his thick hair, and I couldn't help but notice that he had more silver just above his ears on both sides. I'd spent more than two years toying with those short strands amid the dark and pretended they were stars in the night sky that I could make wishes on. And then his slate-colored eyes met mine. They were narrowed, bringing my attention to the crow's-feet that seemed more apparent now than a year ago, and I found myself wondering if he'd been taking care of himself in my absence.

"Listen . . ." He cleared his throat and moved closer, just enough to be heard without being *over*heard. "It couldn't have been easy for you when Rebecca started working here. I think we can both agree that I haven't made many smart decisions since the beginning of the year, and that was definitely one of them."

I was on the edge, teetering, my toes touching the line. It sounded like he was about to admit his mistakes—leaving me, dating her, bringing her here. And as wrong as it was, I couldn't have been more desperate to hear those words come out of his mouth. I'd spent nearly every day since January waiting for some sort of apology or admittance of guilt from him.

"What are you trying to say, Michael?" I prodded, too impatient for his procrastination.

He leaned his hip against the stainless steel counter and bowed his head to look me in my eyes. "I'm sorry about the way everything went down. But I'm glad to see you've found someone. Even though it kills me to say this, I hope he treats you well."

Nothing else was said as he left the kitchen and headed for his office.

It took me a moment to shake free from his surprise admission. As much as I wanted to search the area for eyes cast my way or ears turned in my direction, I couldn't. Everyone around me knew of my history with Michael—okay, maybe not *everyone*, considering it seemed Rebecca had been given a variation of the truth—and my stomach knotted at the idea of seeing pity on their faces.

There wasn't much left to do before the lunch shift ended. The doors had closed, which meant once the orders already in the kitchen had been filled, it was time to leave. While I finished wiping down the burners and prepping the station for the dinner service, I ran through Michael's words and my interpretation of his tone. I'd assumed jealousy, or at the very least, a hint of it. And for the first time since I'd lied about dating someone, I didn't regret the lie. I'd wanted nothing more than to get Michael back, to make him see what he'd lost, and if letting him think I'd moved on achieved that, then so be it.

Before I knew it, my shift had ended. Everyone from the front of the house had moved into the kitchen, signaling it was time to clear out. And even though I liked everyone I worked with, I wasn't in the mood to socialize. Once I knew it was okay to leave, I had my keys in my hand and my body angled toward the exit.

"How come you haven't told any of us that you met someone?" Everyone loved Carrie, the outspoken and incredibly loud waitress, until they found themselves on her radar.

I glanced around the room, noticing half the staff had heard her and now had their attention on me. "I don't know . . . maybe I was trying to keep *something* personal around here. I mean, you all were well versed in my last relationship—including the incredibly awkward and painful breakup." And who could forget his new girlfriend in the kitchen?

"Which is reason enough to let us all know about Mr. GQ." She propped her fist on her hip and squinted at me. "We all had your back when that went down, as well as when he started dating that hussy."

All eyes, including mine, moved to Rebecca. Thank God she wasn't listening. There was no telling if she knew Carrie well enough to understand the insult hadn't been directed at her, but rather, at Michael.

"So basically, we deserve to see you bounce back," Carrie continued, self-righteousness dripping from her voice. "You know, if you rooted for a sports team through the entire season, wouldn't you want to see them play in the championships?"

"How did you find out about him, anyway? And where did you come up with Mr. GQ? You don't know what he looks like, Carrie." The sports comment didn't even warrant a response.

"Amanda told me."

"I did not!" Amanda came out of nowhere. Seriously, there might have been a lot of people in the kitchen, but she had *not* been one of them two seconds ago. This girl had a way of just popping up like a pimple.

"Don't lie." Carrie shook her head in feigned disappointment—all she was missing was the tsk and finger wag, and she'd have been my mother. "You and Rebecca were over there talking about it."

"Yeah. As in I was talking to *Rebecca* about it. Not *you* and Rebecca."

"If you didn't want anyone to eavesdrop, maybe you should've gone somewhere more private."

"Whoa, hold up." I slid between the two, arms out as if breaking up a fight. I turned to Amanda and asked, "Why in the Hellmann's were you and Rebecca discussing *my* relationship?"

"Oh, was it confidential?" She arched one brow, and all I could think about was shaving it off. I'd love to see her attitude if I did that. "It's just that you had so much to say about him yesterday."

She was onto me. Which meant I had to do something quick to drop the subject and hope no one picked it back up. Leaving gave me a fantastic excuse to cut and run. I had the next day off, so I wouldn't even see half these people until Wednesday, and by then, there was a solid chance all talk of my "boyfriend" would have died down.

"Listen, guys . . . this has been fun. I'd love to stay and chat, but I can't." Most people would shut their mouths at this point and leave. Not me. Apparently, I wasn't in control of the words that came out of my mouth, because I added, "I have plans with Jay."

I'd almost made it to the door—and by *almost*, I mean I'd taken two steps—when Amanda piped up. "Where does he work that he's off so early on a Monday?"

I glared at her while cursing the fact that I couldn't fire her. "Oh, he's not off yet. But I have to go home and shower so that when he *is* done with work, we can spend the entire evening together."

"Awesome . . . where does he work?" Oddly enough, she seemed interested—then again, she was a good actress.

Instead of fabricating something, I went with the only thing I remembered about the real Jason and what he did for a living. "He works in a landfill."

"A *landfill*?" An echo of shock and disbelief came from both Amanda and Carrie. But since Amanda found too much joy in watching me shoot myself in the foot, she handed me a gun by asking, "Doing what?"

I sucked at being put on the spot. "Filling land."

Genius, Tatum.

At least it made them speechless long enough for me to run out.

Nothing beat coming home to your best friend after a crappy day at work.

Once upon a time, I had said that about Michael—about walking through the front door after a long shift and finding him on the couch or waiting for me in bed. Now, Kelsey filled that role for me; except I never came home to find her in my bed.

Thank God.

"Do I even want to ask what happened today?" Kelsey patted the cushion next to her, waiting until I plopped onto the couch before turning to face me. "I swear, Tater . . . if you tell me he asked Barbie to marry him, I'll kill him."

I never had to utter a word for Kelsey to know something was wrong. And ever since January, when she had opened the door to find me in tears with a duffel bag at my feet, she'd never hesitated to blame everything on Michael—rightfully so. The last three and a half weeks had been the worst, though. Once she'd found out about Rebecca, the sky could've fallen, and it would've been Michael's fault.

"No. Nothing like that." It wasn't until this very second that I realized I couldn't tell her what had happened today. Well, not *all* of it. Explaining Michael's jealousy would mean I'd have to fill her in on the boyfriend I had but didn't *really* have. And I couldn't do that without admitting *who* that person was. By that point, I'd have to rationalize having the photo of Jason and me on my phone. None of which would turn out well.

I *could* tell her about everything and just leave Jason out of it completely, saying I'd made the guy up. But that would mean I'd have to lie to my best friend, and that was a rabbit hole I didn't need to fall down. The last fib had been more than I could handle.

"Then what'd he do?" Nothing would convince her this wasn't about Michael.

So I didn't bother trying. "He just got all weird today. Out of the blue . . . for no reason."

"You're gonna have to give me more than that, Tater. Weird how?"

I reclined into the couch and stared at the ceiling, knowing if she could see my eyes, she'd pick up on the pieces I left out. "He came up behind me like he used to do when he'd whisper in my ear. And I'm not positive, but I think he went to put his hand on my lower back but caught himself."

"Did anyone see him do this? Like were you guys around other people?"

"We were in the kitchen, so it wasn't like he was trying to hide it. Hell, his girlfriend was a few feet away."

She pulled her bottom lip between her teeth and nodded slowly, her gaze cast at the wall as she contemplated something. Luckily, I didn't have to wait long to find out what it was. "What did he say to you? Or did he just come up behind you and walk away? Is it possible he had to squeeze by you or something?"

This was where things could get tricky, since I wasn't at liberty to disclose that part of the story. Not wanting to lie to her, I settled on partial truth. "I guess he realized he messed up and wanted to apologize."

"Please don't tell me he wants to get back together. Because if that's what you're about to say, I should add the disclaimer that I can't be held liable for the words that'll fly out of my mouth."

I shook my head, but at least she'd managed to pull a smile from me. "No, only an apology. He admitted that it was insensitive of him to hire Rebecca, and then something about making a lot of poor decisions since we broke up."

"That's it?" She pinned me in place with her incredulous stare. "You came in looking like someone had stolen your dog. I'm not trying to discredit what happened or anything, but . . . I guess I expected it to actually be bad."

One of the things I loved most about Kelsey was her inability to take anything seriously. She was a great listener, and when a situation called for it, she had amazing advice to give. But after a certain point, she'd have to crack a joke to lighten the mood.

Allowing the humor to roll through me, I said, "I'm so sorry I didn't fulfill your need for drama." I ran my hands down my face and groaned in exaggerated frustration. "All I've wanted was to hear him admit he was sorry and that what he did was wrong. So why was that not as satisfying as I thought it'd be?"

"Because he's getting laid and you're not." When I glared at her, all she could manage was a shrug. "What? I'm not saying it to be mean, Tatum. I've been telling you for a while now that you just need to get back out there and you'll start to feel better."

"I don't understand why I have to sleep with someone else in order to *feel better*."

"I'm not suggesting you sample the whole town. At this point, a date would suffice. Hell, pay for your own meal for all I care. All I'm saying is, you'll never get over the asshole by doing what you're doing. You still see him almost every day, and if that isn't bad enough, you work with his new girlfriend. Stop moping and start living."

"Has anyone ever told you what horrible advice you give?"

"No one. Because I don't." She winked. "Why should he get to have all the fun? He's the one who left you with a broken heart, so why does he deserve someone's companionship more than you?"

"He doesn't."

"Exactly. So when can I start passing out your number? I know lots of single realtors who'd kill for a moment of your time. Just tell me if you're looking for a date or a lay, and I'll hook you up."

This wasn't the first time Kelsey had said this to me. Ever since I'd moved in, she'd told me to forget about the loser and move on—love or lust, she wasn't picky as long as I was with a man who wasn't Michael. And for the first time since she'd suggested I let loose and have fun, I contemplated it.

Kelsey was right—Michael shouldn't get to have all the fun.

I deserved to feel good, too.

5

Jason

Kelsey greeted me with a smile and waved me inside. "Give me like five minutes to get ready. I was busy moving inventory around, trying to see if I had a recliner for you. I'm still working on it, but I think so."

She didn't even wait for my response before stalking across the apartment to her room, leaving me to close the front door. And considering she hadn't told me to sit on the couch or help myself to something to drink, I stood in the three-by-three-foot area they tried to pass off as an entryway and waited for her to return. Which was where I would've been when she came back had I not been distracted by a rustling noise coming from the kitchen.

I walked closer, peering over the breakfast bar as I approached it. Nothing. It was a small area, nowhere to really hide, and unless they had a rat in one of the cabinets, the noise hadn't come from in here. I was about to turn around when I heard it again, this time, coming from the pantry at the back of the kitchen. Upon closer look, I noticed light filtering through the slats of the accordion-style door.

Standing on the other side, I quietly held my ear close to it and focused on the sounds coming from the space. I couldn't be sure, but I thought I heard the distinct click of the lid to the washing machine. I held my breath and pulled on the handle. The door opened, and I was rewarded with the sight of Tatum's very surprised eyes.

She stood in front of the washer, looking as guilty as a puppy next to a chewed-up shoe. Her dark hair was piled messily on top of her head, stray pieces framing her clean face. The last two times I'd seen Tatum, her lips had been painted red, eyes subtly lined with kohl, and her cheeks tinted a rosy hue that could've very well been natural. Now, at almost two in the afternoon on a Tuesday, she blinked up at me with nothing lining her lids other than inky lashes. No artificial coloring on her cheeks, just the purest shade of surprise.

Unbelievably gorgeous.

And she didn't even have to try.

She wore a loose white tank with what appeared to be a grey sports bra beneath it. Jogging pants painted her legs black, hugging her figure and hinting at what hid behind the flowy fabric of her top. Maybe I'd been around Vegas showgirls for too long, but there was something intoxicating about her natural beauty.

Tatum was so uniquely different that I'd be able to spot her on a congested sidewalk in front of the Bellagio. At midnight. From across the street. I didn't know much about her, but it was enough to confidently say she was unlike any other woman I'd ever met.

And one of the biggest things that set her apart from the rest was her awkwardness.

Like right now.

The way she guarded the washer told me there was something she didn't want me to see, perhaps inside. I couldn't imagine it being anything other than clothes, though there was no reason she'd be so secretive about that. Unless . . . *lingerie*. It was quite possibly filled with her bras and panties. Any normal, respectable man would bow out and let her tend to her delicates in private. However, just the thought of seeing what she wore beneath her clothes killed any chance of acting like a gentleman.

I took the few steps separating us and held out my arms. When her shock turned to disgust mixed with confusion, I asked, "Where's my hug?"

She quickly snapped out of it and threw herself into my chest with her arms wound around my torso. It was almost convincing, if she hadn't also pushed against me in a very obvious attempt at getting me out of the pantry.

"What are you hiding in there?"

She loosened her grip and peered over her shoulder, as if she had no idea what I was talking about. Then she dropped her arms and took a step back. Her lips twisted to one side while she squinted in thought, leveling her stare with mine. "I was, uh . . . just, you know, starting a load of laundry."

"Here, let me help you." I leaned into her, reaching over her shoulder toward the control panel. "I think you forgot to press the start button."

"*No* . . . wait." Her frantic tone confirmed my suspicions. "I haven't added any soap."

I glanced to my left and found the giant green bottle sitting on a shelf. Except when I went to get it for her, she grabbed my arm to stop me.

"You don't need to do that." She waved me off. "I got it, but thank you."

"Really, I don't mind."

"Kelsey should be dressed any second now. You don't want to be stuck in here measuring detergent and pressing buttons with me. It'll just make her wait, which will make her cranky. She can be a beast when she gets like that, so seriously, I appreciate the offer, but you should probably wait for her on the couch. Or outside. Maybe in your car with the engine running."

I caged her in with my arms on either side of her body, my hands pressed against the top of the washer, and leaned down to bring my face closer to hers. "You're a horrible liar, Tatum," I practically growled in my effort to stay quiet. "You're even worse at hiding something."

"I-I have no idea what you're talking about."

"There's something in here"—I tapped on the lid—"that you don't want me to see."

"Just clothes. Dirty, smelly, sweaty clothes."

I didn't bother to fight the smirk as I held her stare, silently calling her bluff.

"And socks, too." Her voice was almost inaudible, felt more in the air that drifted from her lips to my face than heard in the words she'd spoken. "Lots of socks."

I no longer believed she hid lingerie, though I was lost at what it could be. "Then it's a good thing I walked in when I did, huh? You shouldn't mix your clothes. You could ruin them if they're not separated. But don't worry, I'll help you sort."

I started to pull away so I could lift the lid and end the charade, but she stopped me by grabbing the front of my shirt. My breathing halted, as did hers, and before either of us knew what was happening, she tugged me down until our lips met. I paused for a moment, just in case it was unintentional, and when she didn't put a stop to it, I parted my lips and participated in the kiss.

It lasted approximately three seconds—if that. Her balled hands flattened against my chest right before she shoved against me, forcing me away. She gasped softly, though I couldn't figure out if it was caused by the good kind of surprise or bad. And while I stared into her dark, wide eyes, I licked my lips, tasting her on my tongue, and made sure she couldn't question just how *good* I thought it was.

On the bright side, she was too stunned by her own action to have much foresight. When I leaned closer, she tilted her head back—more than likely assuming I was about to kiss her again—not paying any attention to my fingers on the lid. It wasn't until I had it up, the contents of the drum exposed, that she realized what had happened.

Tatum twisted in my arms until she had her back to my chest. When I pulled out the bag of cheese puff balls, she snatched it from my hand, studied it with a concerned stare, and then turned her deeply creased brow to me. "How'd those get in there?"

I couldn't stop the laughter from rushing past my lips. I grabbed on to the rim of the washer to hold myself up as I let it roll through me. Tatum didn't seem thrilled, yet she didn't break out of the cage I had her in between my arms.

"Kelsey must've thrown them in when you weren't looking."

She slowly nodded her agreement. "That's got to be it."

"Yeah . . . because this couldn't possibly be *your* bag of cheese balls." I tipped my chin down and eyed her. "I'm sure someone with your gourmet experience would *never* stuff their face with artificially flavored processed food."

"I wasn't *stuffing* my face. More like nibbling." She rolled her eyes—likely at herself—and added, "You know . . . *if* they were mine. But they aren't. You said so yourself."

I couldn't have wiped off my smile if I'd been paid to. "You really think I'm that gullible?"

"No. But you can't blame a girl for trying."

"Nah, I guess you can't." I straightened my spine and lifted my fingertips to her crimson cheek, where I stroked her heated skin so lightly I wasn't sure she could feel it.

"They're my weakness," she whispered. "It's shameful, I know. I'd feel a lot better if you went back to believing they were Kelsey's."

"Too late. I can't unsee that."

Her eyes narrowed when she asked, "Unsee what?"

I lowered my hand to the front of her shirt. Her breath hitched, yet she didn't stop me. I carefully brushed the space in the center of her chest, just below her collarbone, with my fingertips. "The crumbs."

"Oh," she breathed out, not quite a whisper. With her chin tucked, she stood motionless and watched as I wiped away the faint orange-colored dust. Interesting enough, even when the last of it was gone, she didn't stop me from clearing away invisible residue.

I kept waiting for her to snap out of it or step away. When she didn't, I forced myself to stop before I discovered other areas on her body that needed attention. I dropped my arm to my side and studied her for some sort of reaction, something to let me know if I'd made her uncomfortable. Two seconds later, I got my answer . . . just not the way I had expected.

She lifted her head, yet she didn't look at me. Her eyes landed on the center of my chest, and when she brought her hand to my shirt, she used her fingertips to trace imaginary lines in the space over my pounding heart. Soft at first, then with a little more force as she flattened her palm against my sternum. Soon, her unhurried strokes became confident touches, driven by palpable urgency. Each sweep of her warm hand across my pecs heightened my heart rate; every brush of her knuckles increased my already hasty breathing.

There was nothing on me, yet I wasn't about to point that out. If she realized what she was doing, she'd stop. And much like with her outright lie about being a hugger, I figured I could let this play out, too.

When Tatum finished wiping lint off the front of my shirt, she moved to my shoulders, now using both hands. Every muscle in my body coiled tight as I fought against the desire to thread my fingers through her hair, tilt her head back, and finish what she'd started earlier.

As soon as she reached my forearms, she stilled. Visible panic stiffened her body for a couple of seconds, and then she seemed to pull herself together. Doing what Tatum did best, she played it off in the most beautifully awkward way possible. "You, um . . . you had *stuff* on you. Don't worry—it's gone now. All clean."

"Cat hair?"

She nodded and glanced up to meet my stare. "Yup. That's what it looked like."

"Yeah, I don't know how that happened. I don't have a cat."

Her eyes widened briefly, the color in her cheeks deepening ever so slightly. "Someone must've been shaving one, and the wind picked it up. Happens to me all the time."

Well, two can play that game.

I brought my fingertip to her mouth and lightly traced the line of her lips. I was playing with fire, and if I wasn't careful, I'd end up in flames. "You had cheese dust on your face."

She furiously wiped her chin with the back of her hand, but before the shock could settle into her features, she stopped and glared at me. "That was mean. I don't have anything on my face," she said with a laugh, slapping my chest playfully.

I gently grabbed her wrist and held her to me. The heat of her palm burned my skin through the fabric of my shirt, yet I didn't dare let go. "You're right, Tatum—you don't . . . *anymore.* I got it all off when you kissed me."

She dropped her head forward, hiding her ebony stare and fiery cheeks. It seemed she had a lot to learn if she thought that would be enough to make me give up. I tilted her head back with a curled finger beneath her chin, never letting go of her wrist in my other hand. "Please tell me you're hiding frosted cupcakes in the dryer."

The corners of her lips twitched, and when she exhaled, it was like her nerves had vanished. But before she could reward me with the sound of her confident voice, we were interrupted.

"What are you guys doing in there?" Kelsey called out from behind me.

I dropped my hands and turned around, finding my cousin eying us cautiously from the opening to the kitchen.

I stepped away from Tatum—begrudgingly—and moved out of the closet. "Cheese balls, soap, pressing buttons. You know, the usual."

I winked before passing Kelsey's motionless form. "Come on, I don't have all day."

"You better, because there's a lot to do."

I stopped near the front door and turned to face her. "Then maybe Tatum should come, too. An extra set of hands never hurt anyone." I'd suggested it more or less to piss Kelsey off, yet now that the idea had entered my mind, nothing short of Tatum having to work would stop me from making it happen.

"Hell no." Kelsey couldn't have rejected me any faster if she'd tried. She craned her neck to the side to regard her friend—who stood in the pantry, out of my sight—and added, "No offense, Tater."

"What exactly am I not supposed to be offended about?" Tatum walked out of the closet and crossed her arms over her chest, narrowing her gaze on her best friend.

"I'm helping Jason decorate his new place. He just moved in today, and the moron didn't bring anything with him from Vegas. So, to keep him from sitting on milk crates in front of the TV, I'm having some of the furniture from the warehouse brought over."

"I'm not following. Why would that offend me? It's *your* stuff."

"Did you not hear the part about me *decorating* his place? And you . . ." Kelsey held out her arm and pointed at something near the kitchen table behind her. "Well, you suck at decorating, evident by the photos you hung."

I turned my attention to the pictures of Tatum and Kelsey on the wall behind the small table. Although, my observation was cut short when Tatum asked, "What's wrong with them?"

"The frames don't match, for one. Two, there's no order to any of them. And they're all crooked, which might be okay if they all leaned the same way, but they don't. It throws my OCD out of whack every time I walk by." Kelsey's humor had to be the driest I'd ever heard—I felt sorry for anyone who had to put up with it all the time.

"Then why haven't you ever fixed them?"

Kelsey shrugged. "I didn't want to offend you."

Tatum's mouth opened and closed a few times. When that stopped, she blinked in exaggerated astonishment. "And you thought *telling* me I suck and using my collage of photos as proof would be less offensive?"

"Eh." She waved her off like it was no big deal. "You brought it up. It made it easier to be honest with you."

"I didn't bring it up. You voluntarily told me why you didn't want my help. And if I may point something out for just a second . . . saying 'no offense' before insulting someone doesn't suddenly make what you say a compliment."

"Wait." My cousin held up both hands, regret flashing in her hazel eyes. "You're not actually taking me seriously . . . are you?"

Tatum glanced at me quickly, and humiliation colored her cheeks. When she turned back to my cousin, she stammered, "Well, I, um . . . and then you . . ." She pointed to the wall behind Kelsey and shrugged uncomfortably. "Frames."

I couldn't help but wonder if it had to do with me being here—if she would've reacted differently had it only been the two of them.

"Come on, you two. Let's just hug it out and then go to my place." If that didn't work, I would have no choice but to call my mom and have her Dr. Phil them until they were best friends again.

"No." Kelsey held up her hand in my direction, making it known her response was directed at me, even though she never took her eyes off her roommate. "We joke like this all the time; it's our *thing*. And you always play along. Did you really think I was being serious?"

The remorse in her tone was palpable. It was obvious she didn't want to hurt Tatum over a few frames—albeit they *were* incredibly mismatched and crooked.

Tatum swung her gaze in my direction, giving up before her dark eyes landed on me, and my earlier question was answered. This had to do with my presence more than the frames. It shouldn't have, but that realization riddled me with guilt.

"What? No." She dismissed Kelsey with a flick of the wrist and laughed, though it came out apprehensive and unnatural. "Of course not. I knew you were kidding. You're such a jokester."

I wasn't the only one in the room who thought that reaction was odd. Kelsey stared at her with creases between her brows so deep they rivaled the Grand Canyon. "Jokester?" Then she set her attention on me. "Really, Jason . . . what did you two do in the laundry room? Drink the detergent or sniff the dryer sheets?"

"Nope. We only made out and felt each other up."

That got Tatum's attention. But before she could deny anything, Kelsey grabbed her stomach and howled in laughter. "Now I *know* you're lying—and more than likely high. She would never touch you."

I offered a casual shrug and smirked. "Believe what you want, but she totally initiated it."

"Whatever. Keep dreaming." With a dismissive eye roll, she returned to her roommate. "Listen, Tater . . . I'm sorry if I offended you. I hope you know I'd never do that intentionally. I was just giving you a hard time. Those pictures are my favorite thing in this apartment—there's more character on that one wall than in the rest of the place combined."

"It's fine." Her smile was forced, and the head nodding was a bit excessive, though her words sounded genuine. "I knew you were just giving me a hard time—even if you *were* telling the truth."

I glanced at the frames again. Even though I stood too far away to see their faces, I could tell by the poses in each photo that these were two people who cared a lot about each other. It made me think of my cousin's warning about staying away from Tatum. If I'd had any interest in dating her, this would've made me question it.

It was a good thing I had no desire to date *anyone*.

"Tatum, you're great at a lot of things—well, a few things. Actually, you're fantastic at one thing and okay at the rest." There was a good chance my cousin was just as awkward as her best friend—apparently, sappy moments were too much for her to handle without a sarcastic retort.

Tatum returned Kelsey's smile, leaving no doubt that she recognized the jest. "Just as long as that one thing is cooking, I'm good."

"Well, it certainly isn't cleaning." Laughter filled Kelsey's retort.

I glanced around, wondering what she meant by that. From what I could see, their place was neat and tidy. With that said, I hadn't seen much more than the living room and kitchen, though as small as the apartment was, I doubted there would be too many places to hide a mess.

I clapped my hands together, ready to get the show on the road. "We good here? Because we have a house to fill with furniture, and the clock's ticking." I tapped on my watch while leveling a pointed stare at Kelsey.

"Yeah, yeah. Hold your britches." She grabbed her purse and keys off the table. But rather than invite her friend along, like I had prior to their discussion over lopsided frames, she called out, "Later, Tater."

I could've imagined it—wishful thinking was a real thing—but Tatum seemed disappointed that Kelsey was about to leave without her. That theory was based solely on her slumped shoulders and blank expression. She might've simply been relaxed and lost in thought, yet I chose to believe she wanted to come along and felt left out that Kelsey hadn't invited her.

If my cousin wouldn't ask, then I would. "You coming, Tatum?"

"Thanks, but clearly you don't want my help decorating."

"There are plenty of other things to do. I have *nothing* in my kitchen, and since you're the queen of that area, I would be indebted to you if you'd help with that."

"You'd know better than I would where you want your cups and plates."

I shook my head and grinned, refusing to let her get out of this. "No, Tatum. I don't have *anything* . . . including food. The few pans I have won't do me any good without something to cook in them."

"So you need me to go grocery shopping?"

The purpose was to get her to my house, not send her to a store, but if it meant she'd have to put it all away, then who was I to be picky about *how* she got there, just as long as she came? "Yeah, if you don't mind taking my credit card and grabbing me enough to fill a pantry and spice cabinet."

She closed her eyes and huffed, acting as though this was such an inconvenience, yet her coy smirk gave her away. "Fine. Kels, ride with your cousin so I can go to the store on my way, and then we can drive back together."

Moving into a new place was equal parts torture and karma.

Kelsey saved my ass by selling me some of her old staging furniture for dirt cheap, and Tatum helped by setting up the kitchen. Well, for the most part. She said she'd make a list of everything I needed—cookware and whatnot—but by the time she had my fridge filled and pantry organized, Kelsey and I had finished with the furniture. Needless to say, she'd left without making me a list. At least she'd gotten me food . . . even if I couldn't eat it because she'd chosen all the fancy shit that required a culinary background to make.

Regardless, none of that mattered, because without her or Kelsey, I would've been screwed.

Jen and I had been a couple for so long that almost everything we had owned, we'd purchased together. When I'd made the decision to leave earlier than planned, the thought of dividing every single possession into two piles had made me sick to my stomach, so I'd left most of it behind. In the end, I'd taken the queen-sized bed and matching dresser that had been in our guest room, enough kitchen utensils to get me by, a small box of linens and towels, and a TV—in addition to my own personal effects.

But now, thanks to Kelsey, no one would be able to tell that I'd basically moved in with a pillowcase slung over my shoulder. This was the perk of having a professional home stager in the family. I'd be lying if I said I hadn't questioned her career choice a time or two, but I guess she ended up having the last laugh. I'd had no idea this was a real job before Kelsey. And by the time she left Tuesday night, I could see why she was so popular—aside from probably being the only one in town who did this sort of thing.

Earlier in the week, I'd received an email from the biggest engineering firm in the area. After a few calls, a dinner meeting had been scheduled for tonight. Wiseman Engineering Group had been my top pick when I'd made the decision to move closer to my family. So, my hopes and dreams pretty much came down to this.

I found the restaurant with ease and pulled into the first available parking space I saw. The second I had my car door open, my mouth watered at the aroma filling the air. There was something about the smell of a steak that could make anyone hungry.

And just like that, the mention of food brought my mind back to Tatum.

After spending most of the day with her yesterday, I couldn't stop thinking about her. Every spare minute had been spent recalling the taste of her lips and the soft hitches in her breathing when I'd gotten close to her. I'd slept soundly to the memory of Tatum's raven eyes glimmering as I'd touched her. Today had been a different story, though. Preparing for this dinner had taken up far too much energy, effectively pushing Tatum to the side.

I was too lost in my thoughts to notice the woman standing on the curb. She smiled as I approached, but I didn't think anything of it. It wasn't until I stepped to the side to get around her that she laid her hand on my arm, finally catching my undivided attention. I studied her face for a moment, hoping recognition would hit soon, yet it didn't. Nothing about her bright, aqua-colored eyes or pale-pink lips rang any bells. If I'd gone to school with her in Samson, we must not have been very close, because I didn't know who she was. And while I admittedly sucked at remembering names, I could at least recognize faces.

"Jason Watson?" Her voice was soft and light, so there was hope I hadn't done her wrong in my youth. "I'm Elizabeth Wiseman, with Wiseman Engineering Group, but you can call me Beth. I hope you found the place okay."

I tried to mask my surprise and folded her soft hand in mine. "Yes, I did; thank you. I'm sorry, but you weren't what I expected."

Smiling, she hiked the straps of a very large purse higher onto her shoulder. "Let me guess . . . you thought you were meeting someone older?"

There was no good way to answer this, so I went with the truth. "Uh, yeah, something like that." Okay, partial truth. Yes, having dinner with someone around my age wasn't what I'd anticipated, but for some reason, I'd assumed she'd be . . . unattractive. Which she wasn't.

"Don't worry. I get it all the time."

"Is David Wiseman your husband?" I stepped closer to the door and pulled it open for her.

Beth clutched her bag to her side and strode past me, the smile never falling from her lips. "Oh, no. He's my father."

As reassuring as that was to hear—considering David's age—part of me had hoped she would say yes. It wasn't that I had an issue having dinner with an attractive woman or anything, but since I was under the impression this meeting might lead to a job offer, it would've made me feel better to know she was married.

"I use my maiden name in business—makes things easier." She winked. "Unfortunately, it confuses people when they find out I'm married."

Thank God she chose that moment to turn her attention to the hostess; otherwise, she might've seen the relief on my face.

Leaning into the podium, she said, "Hi, we have a reservation for two. Wiseman."

The hostess glanced from Beth to me, then down to her clipboard briefly before finding my eyes again. She regarded me as if she knew me and seeing me here was a shock. I frantically scoured my memory for some clue that could help me place her face, and when she returned to the clipboard, I peeked at the black tag pinned to her shirt—Amanda.

That was of no help. Even if we *did* know each other, I'd more than likely called her something different—I was better at remembering famous names than those of the women I met. Not to mention, I'd probably met dozens of Amandas in my life. And not surprisingly, I couldn't recall a single one.

"Right this way, please." The hostess grabbed two menus, marked something off on the chart taped to the podium, and then led us into the dining room. Stopping at a small two-person table toward the front, she eyed me suspiciously. "Your server is Carrie, and she'll be right with you."

Beth set her bag on the floor next to her chair and picked up her menu. Apparently, she had been here many times. When I asked for suggestions, she read me the entire list of entrées. Which would've been helpful if I'd been a starving man looking to eat ten tons of food.

I was in the midst of glancing around the room, admiring the atmosphere, when a young blonde heading in our direction caught my attention. One look at her and I could tell she wasn't a waitress—she wasn't in the same uniform as the staff who served various tables with food or drinks, and hers had white dusty patches and what looked like pancake batter. However, instead of stopping, she slowed her gait, glared at me like I was beneath her, and then circled back around before trotting away.

"That was weird," I mumbled.

Beth lifted her chin, taking her focus off the menu, and asked, "What was?"

"You didn't see that?" I gestured to the far corner of the room, where the blonde had escaped, and then shook my head. "Never mind. It was probably nothing."

I went back to the list of dinner options, ready to close my eyes and point to one, when the waitress came to greet us. "Welcome to Fathom 216. My name's Carrie, and I'll be taking care of you tonight. Have either of you been here before?"

"I haven't, but she—"

"Oh, that's wonderful." The smile plastered to this lady's face was as fake as a hundred-dollar bill with George Washington on the front. "Would you like to hear the specials, or are you the kind of guy who likes to look around? You look like someone who samples."

"You offer samples?" I was surprised for all of two seconds before Carrie shook her head. "Oh, my apologies. I thought you mentioned it."

"I'm sure you did, dear." Carrie took the napkins off the table and carefully set one over Beth's thighs. When she turned to me, she didn't even bother to unfold the napkin before dropping it into my lap. "Would you like to order? The sooner you do, the faster you're out of here. I'm sure that's the endgame, right?"

I wasn't certain, but I didn't think that was an actual question. "Um, I haven't had a chance to decide yet. I think I'll keep looking."

"I bet you will." How this woman could offend me with a smile and without saying anything particularly offensive was beyond me. "I'll give you two another minute. In the meantime, what can I get you to drink?"

There was absolutely no point in her asking what I wanted, because she didn't deliver. The water with no ice and extra lemon came with extra ice and no lemon. And after my third time requesting a small plate of the citrus slices, I gave up.

6

Tatum

"So . . . Tatum." Amanda approached my station and tapped as if knocking on the rack above that held the excess pans.

"Amanda? I'm a little busy right now." I had four burners going at the same time, as well as a piece of meat in the oven below. Ironically, this was the only place I could successfully multitask. Take me out of the kitchen and I became a bumbling idiot.

That was a lie. I was an idiot with or without a saucepan.

I just hid it better in front of a stove.

"Yeah, but you see . . . this is kind of important." Her tone certainly didn't convey urgency.

"On a scale from one to my apartment burning down, how important is it?"

She hummed and tipped her head side to side. "More like the IRS found discrepancies in your return." She tapped her nail on the rack again. "And now you owe them a hundred thousand dollars in penalties and late charges . . . due immediately."

"*A hundred thousand dollars?*" I screeched. Then I blinked a few times, and reality settled over me like a bucket of cold water in my face. "Shut it. Just tell me what you came in here to say."

"I would, except . . . you see . . . I'm not really sure this is something you want to discuss *here*." She dramatically scanned the room with her eyes, never moving her head.

Leaning closer, I whispered—more for the effect than to keep others from overhearing—"What's it about?"

"Umm, Jay?"

"Are you asking? Or telling me? Because your tone has me a little confused."

"No. It's *definitely* about Jay. And you. And your . . . *relationship*."

I went back to the sauce on the front burner before I ruined it and had to start over. "As much as I would *love* to entertain you right now, Amanda, I'm sort of in the middle of something. It's called work. You know . . . that thing people do in exchange for money?"

She pursed her lips and lifted one brow. "My bad . . . I thought those were called blow jobs."

"Hmm . . . not the same kind of job I'm talking about."

"Fine. Have it your way. But I'm sure you'll be sorry later." Her huff of resignation didn't sit well with me, nor did I feel confident when she stopped at Rebecca's station. Regardless, I had too much on my plate—no pun intended—to think twice about it.

Out of the corner of my eye, I caught them both looking my way. Which ended up pissing me off, because rather than concentrating on the sauce meant for the steak in the oven, I was busy running through a million scenarios in my head. There was a good chance I added cinnamon instead of cayenne pepper. Hopefully, whoever had ordered it wouldn't be able to tell the difference.

I rolled my eyes at *myself* for that thought.

Time flew by during peak hours. That was the best part about this place—its business. An entire seven- to eight-hour shift could seem like half that. Granted, it did get slower toward the end of the night, yet even then, not one second dragged. So when Rebecca strolled over, it felt like Amanda had literally just walked away—even if it'd been close to twenty minutes.

"What's Jay doing tonight?"

Not taking my eyes off the ticket in front of me, I said, "Not sure."

"Did he have any plans?"

"Uh . . . not that I know of. He just moved into his new place, so I'm assuming he's unpacking." I should've given Rebecca a little more attention than I did—or at least given more thought to her questions—because I might've picked up on her heightened interest in my faux beau's plans.

"You doing anything with him tomorrow?"

"More than likely." I quickly glanced at her. "Why?"

"Just curious." She started to pivot on her heel, as if to head back to her station along the wall, but suddenly stopped. "Does he have any female friends that you know of?"

Had I not been in the middle of switching burners to trade tasks with Lynn, my station assistant, I would've been able to spare her inquisition a little more thought. Instead, I went into autopilot and answered her with confidence as if I had knowledge of who Jason hung out with. "Aside from family, not really."

"And when you say family . . . you mean like his mom?"

I tossed garlic into the pan that Lynn had prepared for me. "Uh, I guess. Also his cousins."

"Female cousins?"

I eyed her, still too distracted to sort through her interrogation. "Yes, he has two."

She nodded, apparently pleased with my response, and trotted away.

I shook it off and went back to the tickets that never stopped coming in.

I'd managed to complete one order before Carrie snuck in. She peeked around the corner and tried to discreetly catch my attention. By the fourth or fifth *psst*, I could no longer pretend I didn't hear her. Half the kitchen probably heard her.

"What, Carrie?"

"Does Jay by chance have a twin?"

I slowly rotated my head to face her, my stomach knotting with nerves. "Uh, no. Why?"

"What about a doppelgänger?"

"I don't even know what that is."

She dismissed me with a wave. "How serious are you two? Like still feeling each other out? Coming up with names for your firstborn?" She gasped and added, "Or are you already knocked up?"

My mouth opened in an effort to answer her, but then I thought better of it. She clearly had a reason to ask, and until I had more information about what she knew or had heard, stepping into that trap would only leave me tripping over myself. So instead, I returned my attention to the pasta in front of me. "Either spit it out, or come back when I'm not busy."

Carrie was quiet for a moment, yet she remained by my side. Her hesitancy radiated off her in waves of nervous energy, which did nothing to slow my racing heart. Carrie was never silent. She more than likely talked in her sleep, and there was a good chance what she said would offend someone. So the fact that she had nothing to say worried me.

"Get off the line!" Victor, the executive chef, yelled at Carrie from behind me. I'd seen the vein on his temple pulsate on more than one occasion, so I could only assume it was tapping out a beat to the song of her imminent death. "If you want to be in my kitchen, then go clean some dishes."

"Why does it have to be the dishes? Is it because I'm a woman?" Carrie either had balls of steel or a death wish . . . or both.

"Considering you can't cook without burning everything, including a plastic spatula, your options are limited." It could've been a reach, but Victor's knowledge of her abilities in a kitchen felt personal—especially since we didn't have plastic spatulas here. And under his breath, yet loud enough to hear, he mumbled, "Not that you're much better at scrubbing a pan."

To my surprise, she sucked her teeth and left. I stood there, my mind spinning a million miles an hour. Thank God I had someone at the burners with me. I couldn't focus to save my life. Carrie had come in here to tell me something—much like Amanda had—and now, I no longer believed it could wait until rush was over.

"Handle the station for a moment? I have to . . . uh, use the restroom." I patted my assistant on the arm and snuck toward the swinging door that led to the dining room.

Right outside was an alcove where the servers usually gathered around the computer. And just as I suspected, Carrie was there. She leaned against the half wall and stared at something toward the front of the room. I slid beside her and tried to follow her line of sight, yet I didn't see anything too interesting.

Fake candles in small red holders occupied the centers of tables where people sat in various stages of dining. Some had menus. Others enjoyed glasses of wine or stuffed their faces with some of the best food they'd probably ever tasted—at least the dishes I'd made. There was more than likely someone out there with a steak that wasn't quite right, but that was neither here nor there. Old people, younger couples, some with children. Tables for two, four, even some with six or eight gathered around. Blondes, brunettes, men, women. Kelsey's cousin. A few with napkins tucked into their—*oh shit.*

My gaze snapped back to a table near the windows where Jason sat opposite a gorgeous blonde in front of empty plates. They appeared to be in the middle of an intimate conversation. She smiled a few times, to which he did the same, yet they never took their eyes off one another.

I had no reason to be jealous; he was a single guy with the freedom to date anyone he wanted. We'd shared one kiss—if it could even be called that, considering I'd shoved him away as soon as his lips had met mine. But that hadn't stopped me from obsessing over it every second since it'd happened. Unfortunately, he didn't seem to have been as affected by it as I was.

"I take it that's not his cousin?" Carrie asked without facing me.

"Nope." I was about to be publicly shamed.

"Ever seen her before?"

"Never." When I finally blinked, I realized what I'd done. If there had ever been a time to be deceptive, this would've been it. Yet I'd been too blindsided by the sight of Jason on a date with a woman to even think of my own name, let alone formulate a believable lie.

People really needed to stop putting me on the spot.

"Doesn't he know you work here?"

Technically, I'd never told him, though he *had* been at Taste of the Town, where he'd seen me at the Fathom 216 tent. Then again, that would've required him to remember, and since I'd literally seen the man three times—the first of which I'd spent most of the day avoiding him, while the other two had been brief—it wasn't likely he'd paid that much attention.

I shrugged, hoping something would come to me quickly. "Yeah, he knows."

Crap. That was the wrong answer. I mean, I literally had two options—yes or no. How I'd failed with fifty-fifty odds was beyond me. Even though it might've been a stretch that my boyfriend didn't know where I worked, there'd been a chance I could've used the extra time to come up with a plausible excuse she'd believe. But saying he knew, yet came here on a date anyway, just looked bad.

Really, *really* bad.

"Are you going to say something to him?" She flicked her chin, gesturing to the cozy couple.

"Probably not." I didn't care to relive senior prom all over again.

I closed my eyes in the hopes that when I opened them again, this all would turn out to have been a dream. Unfortunately, I didn't have that much luck, because when I opened my eyes, Jason still sat at the table with some smoking-hot blonde.

And I still cowered in a corner.

"Are you kidding me?" She didn't just toss discretion out the window; she chucked it like an open container of absinthe while being chased by cops. "You're seriously going to let him waltz into *your* restaurant with another woman and get away with it?"

"Carrie, *shhh*." I glanced around, hoping no one had noticed the scene unfolding in the back corner. "Of course I'm not going to let him get away with it. But don't you think this is a private matter that should be dealt with at home—not in front of a bunch of strangers?"

"No. Not at all." She narrowed her gaze, and for some odd reason, she appeared to be offended. At what, I wasn't sure. "He clearly doesn't give a rat's ass about privacy. If he did, he wouldn't parade his sidepiece at your place of employment."

"Fair enough, but I can't go over there and cause a scene. I'd get fired."

"You don't have to. Just walk up to them and ask if they enjoyed their meal. The bastard will know he's caught. Then smile and walk away; let him explain to the bimbo who you are."

"*Yeah* . . . that won't end well." Just not for the reasons she thought. "I think I'll save that conversation for another time, like later tonight. Or tomorrow." *Or never.*

"If that's what you want." Then she mumbled, "He won't be leaving me a tip tonight."

I was too caught up in the tailspin of my lies to realize Carrie had started to walk away. In the direction of Jason. Had it been any other waitress, I wouldn't have worried. However, nothing was safe with Carrie.

My heart hammered out the tune to *Jaws*. I had to do something to keep Carrie from ruining my life—slightly melodramatic but true. I raced into the kitchen in search of help, and as luck would have it, the answer to my prayers shone like a beacon of light from a shiny white saucer. I grabbed it and slipped back into the dining room.

Holding the plate of chocolate cake gave me courage—false courage, but I was in no position to be greedy. I gripped it tighter with each step toward the front of the room, my sight locked on Jason. I should've been looking out for Carrie, but panic had this magical way of making me stupid, so I didn't. I was too worried that Jason would glance up and recognize me to focus on anything else.

Absurd, I know, considering I walked toward him with a plate of dessert.

I was about ten feet away when I noticed frantic movement to my left, and when I shifted my sight from Jason to the flailing arms coming from the hostess stand, I found Amanda waving. Carrie stood next to her, watching me with her elbow propped on the podium and her chin resting on her fist. Amanda frantically mouthed something to me while attempting sign language.

Unfortunately, I couldn't read her lips *and* understand her gestures at the same time. It was one or the other. Honestly, she'd make the *worst* charades partner. I glanced to my right, relieved when I realized Jason hadn't seen me, and then I put one foot behind the other to sneak off—until someone standing in the way foiled my subtle retreat.

Fun fact: Walking backward never ends well.

I almost made it.

Until his eyes met mine.

Recognition danced on his face.

So, I did the only thing I could think of . . .

"Happy birthday to you." I turned to the couple at my right and began to sing. All by myself. Halfway through, I sang louder, hoping someone would join in.

No one did.

When I finished the song, the man and woman I'd serenaded stared at each other, then at the cake in front of them, and then at me. I should've bowed out and scurried away, leaving these fine people with a free dessert. Somehow, I never seemed to do what *should've* been done.

At some point between grabbing the cake and belting out the last verse, I realized my thought process had taken a wrong turn. I understood that I'd just made a fool of myself, but I couldn't stop while I was ahead, because my insecurity overrode rationality and made me believe I could fix this.

I quickly snagged the battery-operated candle from the center of their table and stuck it in the middle of the chocolate frosting. At the time, I thought that would appease the couple's disposition. Except their confusion didn't wane—which couldn't possibly have had anything to do with me staring at them like they were baby gazelles at a zoo.

My heart rate climbed to potentially dangerous levels, warning me to run away before I patted one of them on the head. But I couldn't move. I remained paralyzed by fear, and the extreme levels of discomfort I felt from having everyone's eyes on me only fueled my desire to make it right. I genuinely believed I could convince them that I had the situation under control . . . as long as I kept going.

In my head, blowing out the candle for them made sense. In reality, it was *battery operated*.

Tears pricked the backs of my eyes when I realized how ridiculous I looked. So, I picked up the candle, turned it over, and flipped the switch. Unsure of what to do with the chocolate-covered centerpiece, I set it back into the small red dish I'd gotten it from . . . rather than, you know, taking it to the kitchen or cleaning it off.

"Umm . . ." The man hummed while regarding his wife with a furrowed brow—her reaction just as confused, though holding slightly more humor than his. "It's not our birthday."

"Oh." Slapping my hand over my chest, I inwardly celebrated the small victory. This was my out, the excuse I needed to justify my actions—getting the tables mixed up. "My apologies. I must've misunderstood the waitress." I slid the mangled dessert closer. "Well, here; have a slice of our famous chocolate cake. On the house."

"I'm not quite sure that's safe to eat." He studied the plate without touching it and mumbled, "I think you spit on it while trying to blow out the candle."

As soon as I'd thought I was in the clear, the rug was ripped out from beneath me. My chest tightened again, the stabbing behind my eyes returned, and dangerously high blood pressure caused my face to burn.

Still, I told myself it wasn't too late to salvage my reputation.

Because by now, I'd lost the option to walk away.

I had no other choice *but* to make it right.

"Not a problem." I reached to the right, grabbed a fork from the empty table, and began to scrape off the frosting. In my mind, that would take care of the issue. "It'll be like brand new."

Thank *God* Carrie decided to put me out of my misery. She took me by the arm and led me to the kitchen, far away from the scene of the crime—as well as the countless people who had witnessed the single most embarrassing moment of my life. I'd made it two steps past the swinging door when the dust settled enough that I could understand the severity of what had just happened.

I had *sung* to a customer.

Which would've been a fantastic gesture worthy of praise if I had any sort of talent, or at the very least, was capable of carrying somewhat of a tune. Unfortunately, that was *not* the case. Then there was the issue with the candle, the spit, and mutilating the cake even more by removing the icing with a used fork.

"Please tell me no one saw that," I quietly begged.

"If they didn't, I'm sure they can catch it on social media later. I wouldn't be surprised if it goes viral." She ignored my protesting groan and escorted me into the hallway that led to the front door—my escape route. "Just promise me that if you get a call from Ellen, you'll let me go with you."

I didn't get a chance to answer before Michael stepped into the corridor from the hostess area. He took one look at me and charged us both, his heavy footsteps resounding in the small space. This was it. I was about to lose my job.

Which sucked because I would've made a fantastic sous chef.

Although . . . after tonight, I wasn't sure anyone else would agree. I couldn't seem to manage myself, let alone the operation of an entire kitchen.

"Don't leave me," I whispered over my shoulder, only to be met with silence. It was enough to know I was alone. Carrie had taken off and left me to fend for myself. There was absolutely *no* coming back from this.

"Come with me." Michael's low tone surprised me. He should've been yelling, screaming, red faced while shaking angry fists in the air. But he wasn't. Instead, I was reminded of his compassion—one of the reasons I'd fallen for him in the first place.

With a gentle hand on the small of my back, he led me down the hall to his office.

"What happened?" he asked once he had the door closed.

His cologne seemed stronger in here than it did anywhere else in the restaurant. And even though I'd always loved the smell of it, I couldn't help but compare it to the balsam-and-clove scent Jason wore. Where Michael's reminded me of tender moments and calming heartbeats, Jason's made me think of passion and breathless nights, two people unable to get enough of each other.

I had to shake off those thoughts—if one kiss led me to imagine all that, I didn't want to think about how perverse my thoughts would be if Jason ever took it further. "I would love to explain, but the problem is . . . I'm not a hundred percent sure."

He stood in front of me and nodded, unconvinced yet not at all angry. "Care to tell me why you took a plate of cake to a table when you're not a server?" Oddly enough, he accepted it when I shook my head. "How about why you sang?" Again, his head slowly bobbed up and down when mine moved side to side. "Any chance you have an answer about *anything* that happened out there?"

"I'm gonna go with . . . *no*." I wasn't intentionally being defiant. I just wasn't sure how to tell him what had gone down over the last hour or so when I wasn't entirely clear on it myself.

He sighed and dropped his chin. "Rebecca told me your boyfriend's here."

"Well, she has a big mouth."

"So it's true? He's here with someone else?" Concern drifted through his voice like a strong wind, threatening to take me away if I closed my eyes and let go. Both of which I refused to let happen.

Humiliation settled in my gut, twisting my stomach into knots until bile burned the back of my throat. It wasn't that I worried about this mishap ruining any possible chance I had with Jason—I was well aware that our kiss, no matter how amazing I thought it had been, hadn't meant anything, and his date tonight proved it. The problem was, I'd have to see him again at some point, unless I stopped going to the Petersons' house.

And to add insult to injury, everyone I worked with was now under the impression that my boyfriend had cheated on me.

My relationship reputation around here kept getting better and better. Any day now, they'd have a profile for me on one of those dating sites.

"It is what it is."

He shook his head and stepped closer to take my hand in his. "You, of *all* people, don't deserve that—having a guy embarrass you the way he did."

Ironically, he'd done the same thing not too long ago. No, he hadn't broken up with me at work, but having everyone know about our split and then watch as his new girlfriend paraded around the kitchen hadn't been much better. Reminding myself of that was enough to keep me from finding comfort in his familiar touch like I'd done so many times before. Regardless of how easy it would've been to melt into his embrace and pretend the last six months had never happened, I couldn't. He wasn't mine anymore . . . no matter how often I still wished he was.

"You're not going to take this guy back, are you?"

"I can't answer that right now. Hell, I haven't even talked to him yet. My mind's all over the place."

He nodded, clearly unhappy with my answer. Letting go of my hand, he took a step away and said, "I get it. Go finish your shift; maybe we can talk after we close up."

"No . . . I mean I have to get out of this entire place. I need to go home. I can't think straight, which could be hazardous in front of a stove."

"Tatum . . ." His posture slumped, and I could tell by his elongated exhale that he wouldn't argue with me about this. He attempted a smile and added, "Have a good night; I'll see you tomorrow."

7

Jason

Ever since our waitress had pulled Tatum away from her table-side performance, I hadn't been able to pay attention to Beth—or anything
else for that matter. I couldn't stop picturing her eyes when she'd seen
me. The panic that had widened them, the embarrassment glistening
along her lower lashes, and the fear that had seemed to prevent her
from blinking. It'd taken everything in me to nod along as Beth spoke,
hoping she hadn't asked me a question I wouldn't be able to answer.

She must've sensed my distraction, though. Because she reached
out, placed her hand on top of mine, and asked, "Do you know that
girl?" Had she not grabbed my attention first, I would've missed the
question.

"Yeah. She's my cousin's roommate." Even though that was technically the truth, my reference to Tatum as if she were nothing more than
the person who lived with a family member tasted sour on my tongue.

The fabric of my pants caused my palms to heat up as I ran my
hands up and down my thighs. I'd hoped the friction would create some
sort of distraction in my mind or, at the very least, ease the unfamiliar
worry in my gut.

I'd only been around Tatum a few times, though it had been enough to recognize that she handled situations differently than most. Rather than shut down or hide in a corner, it was as though she attempted to ease the discomfort by reacting . . . and then *over*reacting when her first attempt didn't work. Based on her solo with the cake, I assumed the objective was to smooth something over.

I only wished I knew what that *something* was.

"Well, I hope she's okay." Beth's sincerity echoed in her soft tone.

As if the scene had been orchestrated by a higher power, I glanced over my shoulder just in time to see Tatum rush past the hostess stand toward the front door. Anxiety hardened her features, her expression pinched by terror. And without thinking twice, I pushed my chair away from the table.

Meeting Beth's worried stare, I said, "I'm so sorry, but I—"

"Go. The bill's already taken care of."

I didn't make her tell me twice. I pulled myself to my feet and didn't slow until I'd made it outside. I spotted the back of Tatum's white coat about twenty feet away.

"Tatum! Tatum, wait!" I ignored the unrestrained demand in my voice, as well as the frantic decibel I'd used when calling her name. It didn't matter how it had sounded, because it worked. When her steps halted and she twisted at her waist, seeing me, the tension in my chest eased enough to take a full breath. My heart slowed, no longer slamming against my ribs and beating in my ears. Nevertheless, adrenaline continued to course through my veins, refusing to relent until I could verify she was all right.

The second we stood with less than two feet between us, Beth called my name. Tatum's eyes moved beyond me toward the front of the restaurant, and in an instant, her body became rigid.

I turned slightly and gestured to my now perhaps not-future boss to give me a second. "I'll be right back. Don't go anywhere." The last thing I wanted was to walk away from Tatum, but I knew it would be brief. I only hoped she would stay so I could talk to her, make sure she was okay after . . . whatever had happened inside.

"I'm sorry, but I wanted to catch you before you left." Beth rummaged through her oversized bag—which, as it turned out, doubled as a briefcase. "I just need to give you some paperwork to fill out. Bring this to the office before Friday, and you should be ready to start on Monday."

I took the folder she offered, torn between excitement over the job and concern for Tatum. "Thank you. I really appreciate it. And again, I'm so sorry for leaving like that. I'm not normally the dine-and-dash kind of guy."

She waved me off. "No worries. We were basically done anyway. It's not like this was a real interview—Daddy had his mind made up about you before we even got here. It was just formalities. Well, an *informal* formality."

"Either way, I appreciate it. And I'll have these back to the office by the end of the week."

"Good, then I'll see you there. Plus, you'll get to actually meet my father."

I nodded with a smile, grateful for the opportunity the Wisemans had offered. "It was nice meeting you, Beth. Thank you for dinner, and please, thank your dad for me. I'll make sure to tell him how much I appreciate this when I stop by, too."

"Take care, Jason."

I held the folder in one hand and leaned forward to return her half hug. When she stepped off the curb, I moved away, but then I stopped. "Would you like me to walk you to your car?"

"Oh, no." Soft laughter lifted her shoulders. "I'm literally right here."

Beth pointed to the row of parked vehicles directly in front of the building. The giant sign over the door was bright enough to light up the entire area.

"I think I'll be fine, but thank you. You should get back to . . . umm . . ."

When her brow creased, her sight dancing in the distance behind me, I twisted around to follow her gaze. Tatum hadn't waited. Not that I'd expected her to, but I guess a part of me had hoped she would.

"Thank you again, Beth. I'll see you again before Friday." I stepped away and headed toward my car with my mind all over the place.

Wiseman had offered me exactly what I'd wanted since I had completed my master's degree. Had they hired me years ago, I would've moved home and accepted the offer—instead, I'd moved to Nevada. So getting this opportunity now, after I'd believed it wasn't a possibility, should've left me ready to celebrate. Except I couldn't, because my thoughts were stuck on Tatum . . . and her impromptu karaoke at dinner.

I could've called Kelsey to check up on her and find out what had happened tonight, or I could've simply waited until I saw her again. But I didn't do either. Instead, I drove to Samson, to their apartment about twenty miles out of my way, to find out for myself.

Realistically, Tatum's performance tonight might not have been out of character. For all I knew, this was a weekly thing for her, but I refused to pass it off as such until I could be sure.

Kelsey opened the door, surprised to see me. "What are you doing here?"

"Looking for Tatum. Where is she?" I asked as nicely as I could, hoping she wouldn't choose this moment to pick a fight. She could think what she wanted of me, but this wasn't the time to address it or question my motives.

She propped her hand on her hip, full of attitude. "She's in her room. Why?"

I should've known that I didn't have a snowball's chance in hell at getting by my cousin without some sort of interrogation. But telling her the truth would've been pointless—even I could admit my reasons for being here sounded farfetched. Friendly concern or not, there were many other ways to check on Tatum without showing up at her apartment.

Knowing that I stood between a rock and a hard place, I chose not to respond. Instead, I carefully moved her out of the way and invited myself inside—it was obvious she had no intention of doing so. But when I took a few steps toward Tatum's room, Kelsey huffed and smacked my arm.

"How do you know where her bedroom is?" Satisfaction danced on her lips, though silent threats shone in her eyes.

"It's a small apartment, Kelsey. From the front door, I can see the entire place." I waved my arm around the open space. "I'm aware your room is past the kitchen, which leaves these two right here. One is a bathroom, and the other would be a bedroom. Doesn't take a genius to figure it out."

"Or you've been in there before and just don't want to tell me because you know I'll kick your ass." She could believe what she wanted, but getting into Tatum's pants wasn't on my agenda. And regardless, even if we *did* get busy behind a closed door, it would be none of Kelsey's business.

"Trust me, cuz . . . if I'd been in there before, *you'd know.*"

"I should've guessed you'd go after her if I told you not to." Oddly enough, her feisty tone had diminished to a low, almost hopeless murmur. It was enough to gain my undivided attention.

My cousin needed reassurance, so I had to block out the fact that Tatum remained hidden away behind a closed door and focus on the here and now. "I don't even know what you're talking about, Kelsey. I'm not going after anyone."

"Admit it, Jason. You're only interested in her because I forbid it."

"It's cute that you think you have the power to forbid anything." I smiled and moved closer to her. Determined to make her aware of my compassion without sacrificing my seriousness, I relaxed my shoulders yet straightened my spine. "I'm not *interested* in her."

"Oh . . . I was under the impression that you only knock on someone's door at"—she glanced at her watch—"almost nine o'clock at night if you need to drop something off, pick something up, or it's a booty call. You don't have anything in your hands, and I can't imagine she'd have anything to give you . . . which leaves the last option."

I lifted my gaze to the ceiling and took a deep breath, if for no other reason than to steal a moment to consider my response. "I just meant that I don't have any ulterior motive when it comes to Tatum. That's it. I wasn't aware I couldn't have *any* kind of relationship with her—as in friendly or cordial, not romantic."

"She's my best friend, Jason."

"Yes, I'm well aware. Although, I have to be honest, Kelsey, I figured you'd *want* me to be nice to her. She's close with our family, spends Sundays with my mom, and lives with you—*my cousin*. It's not like she's a stranger. Why would you want me to act like she doesn't exist?"

"Because . . ." The softer, gentler side of Kelsey didn't come out often, but when it did, it made you want to find a way to give her all the stars from the sky just to make her shine again. "If you show her what a great guy you are, she'll fall for you. Either way—whether you sleep with her or make her scribble your name in a spiral notebook—it could affect my friendship with her."

That wasn't at all what I had expected her to say. Honestly, the fear mixed with dread that dripped from her confession nearly drowned me in guilt—even though I hadn't done anything other than kiss Tatum, which hadn't been intentional *or* provocative.

This was about more than my old reputation.

She worried I'd break Tatum's heart without even trying. And at the end of the day, deliberate or not, if her best friend was hurt because of me, it would be my fault.

Kelsey felt protective of Tatum, and I wasn't convinced it was solely out of consideration for their friendship. Yes, that played a definite part in her reasoning, though I couldn't help but wonder if her tireless attempts at guarding her friend's heart had to do with something deeper.

Either way, none of this had to do with me—I was only the potential hazard.

"Kelsey . . ." I rested my hand on her upper arm and waited until her eyes met mine. "If she ends up head over heels in love with me, hauling me into a closet to make out, or throwing herself at me in a public display of staking claim . . . I can't control that."

At least it made her smile, even though two of the three weren't so much hypotheticals as they were events that had actually taken place. Well, one and a half; I sincerely doubted Tatum's generous hug had been meant to stake claim, though that didn't take away from the fact that she *had* thrown herself at me.

"Whatever, Jason." She pushed against my chest playfully, forcing me to step away. It was nice to see the fire inside come to life again. "Make fun all you want, but it was *your* reputation that followed *me* around high school, and I'm six years younger than you. You can't blame me for being overly cautious. After all, *you're* the one who came here tonight looking for her."

I could've brought her up to speed on the idea of maturing, or the possibility that people *can* change over time, but instead, I decided to explain my reason for showing up unannounced. "I was at Fathom 216 tonight and saw her. She looked upset and ran out like she'd caught her ass on fire. But before I could make sure she was all right, she was gone."

"Oh, she's fine. She felt a migraine come on, so they let her go home. I guess it was a slow night." If that wasn't enough to convince me that something bigger had happened, I wasn't sure what would.

"As comforting as that is to hear, I'd still like to talk to her myself. She saw me before she took off. I asked her to wait, but she didn't. For my own peace of mind, I'd like to make sure she's okay, if that's all right with you. I swear . . . I won't make her fall in love with me before I leave," I added with a smirk.

Kelsey waved me off, dismissing me without the typical annoyance that often accompanied the action. "It's not like you'd listen to me if I told you no. But I mean it, Jason. Jeopardize my friendship with her in *any* way, and you'll regret ever moving to town. Got it?"

Backing away, I held up my hands in surrender. "Wouldn't dream of it."

With a wink, I slid into the alcove just off the living room. The door straight ahead had been left ajar. The vanity was visible from where I stood, which left only the closed door to my right. Maybe I was too caught up in what Kelsey had said, or maybe my earlier concerns for Tatum had returned and stripped me of all common sense and manners. Whatever the reason, I wrapped my fingers around the cold knob and twisted, opening it without knocking.

Tatum's wide eyes found mine before I stepped one foot into her room. She yanked off her headphones, tossed them aside, and bolted upright on her mattress in one swift move. The black pants she'd had on earlier still covered her legs, but instead of the button-up coat that had hidden her figure, a white tank hugged her body.

In that instant, I was torn, tugged in opposite directions.

Kelsey's statement echoed in my head, and the guilt it'd left me with swarmed low in my gut. Yet at the same time, seeing the surprise that left Tatum's mouth agape reminded me of our kiss. The slightest gasp that had echoed between us right before her lips had met mine played in my ears. The heat of her palms that had radiated through my chest as she'd touched me lit an unfamiliar fire inside.

But while I recalled that brief moment in her laundry room, one thing stood out above the rest. With her lips pressed against mine, she'd relaxed. She had held on to me, uninhibited and free of fear. Free of the nerves that shackled her right now. And all I wanted was to cross the room, take her face in my hands, and liberate her.

Yet I couldn't.

Had Kelsey not expressed her motivation for keeping us apart, I doubt anything would've stopped me from doing exactly what I wanted. However, I couldn't pretend that conversation hadn't happened, no matter how badly I wished I could.

Trepidation left my voice hoarse and rough when I asked, "Are you okay?"

When she did nothing but stare at me, I walked in and closed the door. With what little I knew about her, I assumed she wouldn't talk until she felt comfortable, and the only way I could get her there was to shroud us in the safety of her personal space.

Realizing that there was, in fact, room in this apartment to hide a mess, I carefully made my way around a few piles of clothes and sat on the edge of the mattress. "Why'd you take off like that? I told you to wait, and when I turned around, you were gone."

"Do you suffer from memory loss?"

I fought the need to smile and said, "Maybe. You should fill me in on what happened and see if it rings any bells."

"Yeah, that sounds like a great plan. Let me relive my most embarrassing moment just to see if you remember. Sure thing."

"We can come back to the singing portion of the night later if it'll help."

"By later . . . do you mean never? Because sure, we can do that."

I shook my head, a rush of breathless humor filling the air between us. "Fine, we don't have to talk about it if you don't want. But can you at least tell me why you left when I asked you to wait?"

"Listen, I get that you're Kelsey's cousin and I'm her best friend, and maybe that makes you feel like you have to be protective of me as well. Which is great—don't get me wrong. Having you take on the responsibility of an older brother is nice. However, it's extremely uncomfortable to stand there and wait for a guy while he goes to say good night to his girlfriend."

I hesitated to respond, needing to organize my thoughts in order to keep from putting my foot in my mouth. The first thing that crossed my mind was her insinuation that I somehow saw her like a little sister. I could say with complete certainty that a sibling was *not* what I thought of her as. But I didn't think it would be appropriate if I explained that to her, so instead, I moved on.

"That wasn't my girlfriend." A longer explanation was more than likely needed, though I didn't offer anything else. Not because I didn't want to, but because the sight of her tongue running along her lip made me think about kissing her again, and the way her breasts lifted with each breath reminded me what it was like to touch her when I'd brushed the crumbs off her shirt.

It seemed Kelsey's concerns held some validity.

"You know what I mean." She huffed and rolled her eyes.

"I'm afraid I don't. At all."

Tatum snagged a pillow off the bed and shoved it into her lap. It wasn't clear if she was uncomfortable or just frustrated, so I didn't do or say anything. Instead, I let her work through it while she explained what she meant. "You were on a date. Official or otherwise. *Girlfriend* was meant as a more generic reference, because I don't know what people are calling it these days."

This was becoming too much fun. "You don't know what people are calling *what*?"

"Hookups. Tinder meet-ups. Talking to someone, seeing them, dating them . . . whatever it is. You took her to dinner, and since I work there, I kind of have an idea about how much you spent. I didn't wait around, because after all that, you deserved to . . . *you know*."

"Yeah, I'm sorry, but I still *don't know*." I did. But making her say it was far more entertaining than correcting her. I would've stopped it by now if I thought she couldn't handle it, and honestly, I had expected her to give up already, yet she kept going.

Her cheeks turned pink as her gaze danced around the room, stopping on everything except me. "I'm just saying that after taking her to dinner and having a nice time with her—providing it wasn't ruined by that thing we're never going to talk about—I'm sure you planned to dip your toe in the water. Or maybe your whole foot." Her top lip curled, and her nose scrunched up. "That analogy just gave me a mental image I don't care to ever revisit outside of a therapist's office."

"You thought I wanted to go swimming after eating?" By now, I was pressing my luck—it was obvious that I was just messing with her. At any minute, the fun would end, and we'd have to actually talk and give answers.

"Why would I think you'd want to go swimming?"

"You said dip my toe in the water."

She blinked a few times, and in her eyes, I recognized the moment it clicked. "What are you, five?"

"You're the one skirting around the issue. Does that make you like eleven or something?"

"Fine. I won't skirt. Or short, or pants, or shirt." She paused to roll her eyes, more than likely at herself, which only made my chest rumble harder with restrained amusement. "By *toe*, I meant your . . . *penis*." She barely got that out. "By *water*, I was referring to her vagina. And when I said *dip*, I meant *thrust* or . . . yeah, *thrust* works. We'll leave it at that."

I wasn't sure how much longer I'd be able to keep it together without falling over in a fit of hysterics. "I don't believe her husband would've appreciated that. I mean, yeah, the dinner was great, but she paid."

Tatum narrowed her gaze, nearly stifling the laughter that shook my shoulders. "I'm not sure how to take that. Why would you date a married woman? More importantly, why do it if you have no intention to sleep with her? Is she your sugar mama or something?"

"No. I actually just met her tonight."

She patted my knee, as if comforting me, and said, "You're not helping your case any."

"It wasn't a date."

"Then what was it?"

"She hired me."

A smile spread across her lips. "This just keeps getting better and better. Do I want to know what she hired you for?"

"A job. You know . . . what I went to school for."

"You had a job interview at Fathom 216? Seems pretty extravagant for someone who works in a landfill."

I shook my head and covered my face with my hand, unable to refrain from laughing. "What the hell has my cousin told you about me? I don't work *in* a landfill. I'm an engineer who specializes in the *structures* of landfills. I work in an office. At a computer."

"*Oh.*" Her mouth hung open, and surprise brightened her eyes. "Yeah, that's nothing close to what I thought you did. Like . . . *at all.*"

"Kelsey's going to pay dearly for this." I took a moment to soak in the humor tugging at her lips. "Now that we have that out of the way . . . care to share with me what happened tonight?"

"You mean the thing we both agreed we'd never discuss?"

"Yup. That."

She leaned forward, bringing her face much closer to mine, which caused my lungs to freeze up. "How exactly am I supposed to share something we said we wouldn't talk about?"

"Easy. Like this . . ." I tried to reposition myself on the bed, and somehow, I ended up with my hand on her thigh rather than her knee, where I'd aimed. Yet I kept it there and acted like it was no big deal. "What made you come out into the dining room and do that thing we won't mention?"

"Oh, that?" She leaned back and flicked her wrist to wave off my question. It wasn't clear if she needed to put space between us or if it was merely a natural reaction. "Someone needed a chocolate cake, and Rebecca wasn't at her station. The plate was just sitting there, so I took it and delivered it to the table."

"And you decided at the last minute to sing?"

"You said we weren't going to mention that part."

"Right. My apologies."

"But if you must know, when I got to the table, I started to worry it was for a birthday. Then I got wrapped up in 'should I sing, should I not sing, would they get pissed if I was supposed to and didn't' . . . until before I knew it, the first verse was out. And by then, I couldn't very well stop and walk away."

"You're absolutely right. That would've just been awkward."

"Tell me about it. No need in embarrassing myself unnecessarily."

"And you blew on the candle . . . why?"

"Someone had to." Her voice lilted at the end, indicating the silent *duh*.

"That makes perfect sense. The switch on the bottom kind of ruins it, huh?"

"You saw that?"

"Saw what?" I played dumb. It was clear I'd broken through a good bit of her wall, and I didn't care to watch her erect it right now. "I didn't see anything. Much like we're not discussing this right now."

"Gee, I don't know what I would do without you, Jay." Her eyes widened in surprise. "I mean, Jason. I have no idea why I just called you that."

"It's fine. You can call me whatever you want." *Except brother*, I wanted to add but didn't.

"Well, thanks for checking on me. But you really didn't need to come all the way over here to see if I was okay."

"I don't have your number, so my options were limited."

"Oh . . ." She leaned to the side to dig around on her cluttered nightstand.

When I realized she was looking for something to write on, I assumed it was to give me her number, so I handed her my phone instead. She typed her information into my contacts and handed it back without meeting my stare.

"Thanks. I can't tell you how relieved I am to finally have this." I shook my cell, referring to her number.

Concern deepened the lines next to her eyes when she asked, "Why?"

"Allowing you to fondle me in the laundry room without even having your number made me feel a little cheap." My heart skipped a few beats when her lips curled at the corners. "I started to wonder if you were only using me."

She cocked her head to the side and squinted. "Let's go ahead and add that to the list of things never to be spoken of again."

"Add what?"

"The kiss."

"Can't make any promises." I patted her knee and shifted on the mattress to get up. "In the future, I'll call or text."

"For what?" The confusion in her eyes made me question where her mind was if she couldn't remember what we'd just talked about or why she'd programmed her information into my phone.

"To see if you're all right. You know . . . the next time you run out of the restaurant after wishing someone a happy birthday."

A huffed laugh blew past her lips as she shook her head. "I doubt there'll be a next time. I'm pretty sure I don't have a job anymore."

"Would they seriously fire you for serenading a customer?"

"No." Her gaze lowered to her lap, where she picked at the pillowcase. "I walked off the line, which is a federal offense. I wouldn't be surprised if they have my position filled before they lock the doors tonight."

"What does *walking off the line* mean?"

"That I left my post. My station. It's just a term used in kitchens since we all basically stand side by side. Regardless, I walked out—job abandonment."

"Will they call you to let you know? Or would they wait until you show up for work tomorrow to tell you that you don't work there anymore?"

She shrugged. "No idea. Never been fired before. I guess I'll find out one way or another when I get there in the morning, huh?"

"Well, let me know what happens. You still have to teach me how to cook all this food you got me, and I don't start work until next week. Maybe we can figure something out between now and then for you to come over, considering I can't exactly make anything until I've had a lesson or two."

Her smile was uncertain, and I found myself desperate to believe it was nothing more than her awkwardness. It took me by surprise—as had a lot of other realizations tonight. When I had suggested she come to my house and cook for me, or *teach* me how, it had been in jest. I'd simply tried to tease her for picking out ingredients I had never used and couldn't even identify. But now, the idea of her not following through left me unsettled, much like the thought of her seeing me as an overprotective brother. I wasn't happy with either one, and I wasn't sure what to do about it—if anything.

Instead of sitting there and picking the issue apart in front of her, I decided to leave. It was clear she'd gone back to hibernating in her shell. When she was an active participant in our banter, I was fine. When she closed herself off and grew quiet, I became uncertain of how to proceed.

I slipped off the bed and stood next to her with my arms out. She stared at me like I had eight arms, implying once more that she didn't appreciate physical contact, regardless of what she'd said. Suddenly, it dawned on her what I was waiting for—her realization came in the form of rolling eyes and a groan I doubted she intended for me to hear.

"How could I forget?" The way she dragged herself off the mattress reminded me of my little cousin Lizzie when Marlena made her tell someone goodbye—completely unenthusiastic. It was obvious she didn't *want* to. "I'm a hugger," she droned as she practically fell into my chest with the gusto of a dead body.

"Have a good night, Tatum." Laughter filled my whispered words while I tightened my hold on her. "Relax . . . everything will be fine."

The second I loosened my arms, she stepped out of our embrace and collapsed onto the edge of the bed.

I waited until she met my stare before adding, "Promise you'll call or text tomorrow to let me know what your boss says?"

"Sure thing."

As much as I wanted to stay and hang out, there was a good chance I'd end up cleaning her room. Good God, this woman could use a lesson or two—or twenty—in the art of organization. So rather than stick around, I left.

Kelsey was on the couch when I walked out of Tatum's room. She dropped her arm with the remote in her hand, the volume on the TV coming to life. As irritating as she could be, I couldn't help but find her obvious actions funny. She wasn't slick.

"See ya, Kelsey," I tossed over my shoulder and closed the door behind me.

When I made it to my car and folded myself behind the steering wheel, I grabbed my phone. I sent Tatum a text so she'd have my number, and while I stared at the screen, at Tatum's name, I wondered if I'd been lying to myself.

It hadn't quite been a month since I'd walked away from Jen—the woman I'd spent the last five years with, planned to marry, thought I had a future with. A relationship, no matter with whom, was not in my cards for the foreseeable future.

But that didn't stop me from thinking about Tatum every chance I got.

8

Tatum

The second Jason closed the door, I threw myself face-first into a pillow.

This must've been my punishment for lying. Tell one, and the embarrassing moments would never end. It was enough to deter me from ever lying again. Well, once I made it through this one, that is. I still had to deal with everyone at the restaurant believing my new boy-friend couldn't go a few weeks without cheating on me. If that wasn't a ringing endorsement to date me, I didn't know what was.

And as if things couldn't get worse, I had maybe twenty seconds to absorb Jason's visit before my door opened again. I popped up, praying he hadn't returned for a second round, and found Kelsey's head poking inside. She had moments of peculiarity, and it seemed this was one of them—sniffing the air in my room wasn't normal.

"What are you doing?" I questioned her.

"Just making sure it doesn't smell like sex in here."

I groaned and sat up. "He was here for like two minutes. Even if it *did* smell like sex, I think that alone would ensure it wouldn't happen again."

"Good point." Kelsey invited herself in, and I wondered when my room had become the after-school hangout. She collapsed onto the bed with her arms above her head and eyes cast to the ceiling. "Has he ever hit on you? And be honest with me. I won't think less of you if he has."

"No, Kels. He's never hit on me." At least, as far as I was aware. I'd never claimed to be any good at telling the difference between flirting and normal adult conversation.

"Good." She paused for a moment and then turned her head to look at me. "You'd tell me if you had the hots for him, right?"

"Had the *hots* for him? Is that term still used these days?"

"Well, it was either that or *have a crush* on him, and I'm fairly certain that's not acceptable to use outside of a playground. Stop deflecting. Do you or do you not have a thing for Jason?"

"I barely know him." I prayed that would be enough to pacify her, because I doubted I could convincingly tell her that I hadn't given her cousin the starring role in every fantasy I'd had since the day I'd met him. *Or* that I'd led everyone I worked with to believe we were dating.

My phone vibrated from somewhere on my bed, but with the pile of blankets and random pieces of clothing that never made it to the floor, there was no telling where it was. I would've looked for it, but Kelsey stopped me when she said, "You don't have to know a person to be attracted to them."

"Oh, you just want to know if I think he's hot? Of course I do. Have you seen him?" There was a good chance that hadn't been the right answer, so I tried again. "I mean, he's okay. If you're into guys like him. Which I'm not. Does that answer your question? How's work?"

"Either you took something for your headache that's not FDA approved, or we need to get you to a hospital, because I'm fairly certain something is wrong with your brain. Actually, now that I think about it, a CAT scan might be a good idea either way."

I turned to the side and stretched out across the mattress next to her. I'm sure she assumed it was to settle in for quality time with my best friend, but in reality, I'd moved from sitting to lying down to keep her from seeing my face. If I couldn't be completely honest with her about something, I'd rather not look her in the eye while doing it.

In my defense, I didn't *choose* to be dishonest with her. I couldn't help it if I found her cousin beyond physically attractive. And it wasn't my fault she asked questions she wouldn't like the answers to.

It was my duty as her best friend to tell her what she wanted to hear. Dishonest or not.

"Just because I'm related to him doesn't mean I'm blind. It's not like I can be upset if you think he's hot." She turned her head toward me, while I kept my gaze glued to the fan above us. "I only ask because I'm trying to keep you from doing what every single one of Marlena's friends did back in high school."

"What do you mean? What'd they do?"

"I can tell you all day long what a player he is or recount every story that ended with a broken heart, but at the end of the day, there's a reason he always got away with it. Marlena's friends were well aware of his reputation, but I guess he smiled enough or said the right words, because at some point, they all ignored the red flags and gave up the goods."

"So you're worried that I'll fall for his charm, too?"

She grabbed my hand and waited until I rolled my head to the side and looked at her. "From what I've heard, it's easy to do. And you're in a really vulnerable position right now. I highly doubt Aunt Lori would appreciate it if I prevented her from ever having grandkids. Jason is her only child, and if I'm forced to castrate him for hurting you, there's a good chance I won't be her favorite niece anymore."

I wanted to roll my eyes, but instead, I returned my attention to the ceiling and nodded. "Yeah, I can see the predicament his good looks have put you in. You certainly wouldn't want to forfeit your position as favorite niece and let your sister take the throne." It was difficult, but I managed that without laughing.

Kelsey's family were amazing people. In some ways, they reminded me of my own, only more involved in each other's lives. I might have had a close relationship with my parents and brother, but we couldn't have been more spread out geographically if we'd tried, which made direct involvement difficult. At least with the Petersons—Jason's mom included—I had that sense of belonging. They made me feel like I fit in, welcomed me into their tightly knit unit, and automatically included me in everything.

With that being said, I felt a stronger connection to Lori than to Kelsey's mom. It was difficult to explain, but it seemed like she got me the most. And since we had this unspoken bond, I could accurately say that Kelsey was *not* Lori's favorite. Not Kelsey's fault or anything, but I'd heard enough stories about how close Marlena and Lori were to feel confident in that conclusion.

"Too bad I'm weak and helpless." I hoped she heard more of the sarcasm in my tone than the defeat her words had left me with. "Otherwise, I'd be capable of making my own decisions rather than stripping naked and spreading my legs at the first hint of attention from Jason."

She huffed—my pessimism and hurt feelings didn't go unnoticed. "That's not what I meant by vulnerable, Tater. I was only trying to say that when our hearts are broken, we tend to seek validation in unhealthy places. If one guy hurts us, we look to another to make it better."

"Aren't you the one who told me the other day that I need to get laid?"

"Yes. But there's a big difference between a no-strings romp with someone to get you over the heartache and confusing validation for emotion. Sex can be just sex. Where things go wrong is when feelings come into play—when you mistake the attention for something deeper. And that was always the issue with Jason. My sister's friends would fall for him, assume his desires were more than surface level, and in the end, they were the ones who suffered."

"So what you're saying is . . . sex is okay as long as I keep my feelings out of it?"

"Exactly. It doesn't have to always be like that, but until you're completely over Michael, I'd say it's best to refrain from an emotional connection of any kind. You know, like if you find yourself wanting to call the person up to talk about your day, or smile at the sound of his voice, or get that dreamy look in your eyes when you think about him . . . that's when you know it's gone beyond sex."

I bit my lip while nodding slowly in thought. Based on that, a sexual relationship with Jason wouldn't technically be wrong. I didn't have any desire to share my day with him; the sound of his voice did many things to me, but making me smile wasn't one of them; and while I'd never seen myself when he crossed my mind, I felt confident *dreamy* wouldn't be the word for the look in my eyes. The only reason he was off limits was because Kelsey had said so, and from what I gathered, her reasons stemmed from a need to protect me from getting hurt. However, if I had no emotional connection to him, and my desires were strictly physical, then there wouldn't be a problem because he wouldn't hurt me.

"You make very good points, Kels." I patted her hand that remained between us on the bed. "I'll definitely remember that if I end up taking your advice and sleep with someone."

She pushed up on one elbow and leaned toward me. "Just be careful, Tater. It's super easy to fall for a guy you're sleeping with and not realize it until it's too late, especially for someone who's inexperienced with booty calls."

"I appreciate the advice, but I'm pretty sure I'll know if I start to develop feelings for someone. Someone who's *not* your cousin." I might have been a novice when it came to casual sex, but I was fully aware of emotions, especially of the romantic variety.

My phone vibrated again, and this time, Kelsey got up. "Who keeps texting you? Don't they know you're supposed to be at work right now?"

I laughed while searching the bed for the missing device. "My guess would be Tanner. I called him on my way home from the restaurant, but he had to hang up—one of the kids got into something, and Loraine needed help. I didn't ask. Anyway, he said he'd call me back, so that's probably him."

"Fine. I'll leave you alone so you can bore your brother with tales of the kitchen. Tell him I said hi, and that my offer to join him in Alaska still stands." She winked, and before leaving the room, she added, "Hope your migraine goes away."

That made me feel like crap, reminding me that I had lied to her. However, once I located my phone, a different kind of guilt crept in. While the last message had been from my brother, the first one hadn't. Had Kelsey seen the unknown number, followed by, "Hey, it's Jason. Now you can get ahold of me whenever you want. Call or text me tomorrow," she would've flipped out.

I ignored Jason's text and responded to Tanner's, texting to him back and forth for a few hours. I finally said good night and closed my eyes, but sleep didn't come easy. My brain refused to shut off, bouncing between Jason, Michael, Kelsey, and my job until the next thing I knew, my alarm sounded, alerting me that it was morning.

Kelsey wasn't home when I walked through the door. It was much earlier than I usually got off work, so I shouldn't have expected her to be here. But damn, I could use my best friend right now. Not that I could really tell her much, other than Michael was a jackass who'd allowed Victor to put me on a four-day suspension. She already knew he was a jackass, and I'd have to keep the details of *why* I had an unpaid, unrequested four-day weekend vague. Especially since I'd told her last night that I'd gotten off early because I hadn't been feeling well.

My messy, unmade bed called to me, reminding me of how tired I was after tossing and turning all night long. It was so inviting that I stripped down to my panties and threw myself into the pile of blankets and pillows.

The cool sheets felt so amazing there was no fighting it. The second my eyes closed, I was out, not once waking until three thirty in the afternoon. Sleep continued to cling to me while I stretched and kicked off the covers, but as soon as the air hit my bare skin, the numbness in my limbs vanished, and the fog in my head disappeared. I grabbed my phone, wondering how I'd managed to block out the world for over four hours without being interrupted by calls or texts. The answer never came to me, especially after seeing a message from my brother, two from Jason, and a few missed calls from the restaurant.

I jumped up while playing the voice mails on speaker.

"I heard about you getting suspended, and I wanted to tell you that I think it's bullshit." Amanda's voice droned on from my bed while I rummaged through the pile of clean clothes in search of something to wear. "If you want to talk, you know my number. I'm off at four. Or . . . you could totally call the restaurant and fill me in."

Settling on the least-wrinkled shirt, I pulled it over my head and adjusted it so the oversized neck hole fell to one side, exposing my shoulder and bra strap. And with a pair of denim shorts in my hand, I heard the next message begin—unsurprisingly, also from Amanda.

"Okay, so I tried to act all nonchalant about you calling to tell me what happened, but I'm gonna have to be real with you right now. I'm not that patient. Everyone is starting to talk, and I'd like to set the record straight." Her voice grew distant as she mumbled, "I'll be right with you." Then she came back on the line, her voice lower and her words almost running together. "Seriously, Tatum . . . call me back."

I rolled my eyes and finished putting on my shorts. I fastened the button, pulled up the zipper, and then went in search of a hairbrush. When I didn't find one in my nightstand, I pushed open the door to the adjoining bathroom to rifle through the drawers while Amanda's third message began. "Since you haven't returned any of my calls . . ."

The toilet lid was down, which I found odd since I never lowered or raised it, as I was pretty much the only person who used this bathroom—we'd have to *have* guests for anyone else to use it. And while questioning if it had been that way when I'd come home this morning or if someone had been here while I'd napped, I missed the first part of her message. However, I stopped obsessing over the toilet as Amanda's continuing message yanked me out of my thoughts.

"I won't lie," she said in a hushed voice, more than likely cupping her hand over the mouthpiece. "I highly doubted your story about Jay. I mean, you weren't exactly convincing when you spoke about him. I knew he was real, but I didn't think you were actually *dating* him. I assumed you made it all up to get back at Michael." Then her voice became clearer when she finished it up with "Okay, call me back."

I ran into the room and started it over again from the beginning.

"Since you haven't returned any of my calls to give me the scoop, I've been unsuccessful at quieting the rumors. Which, you should know, have gotten worse ever since Jay came in with a bouquet of flowers for you with a card attached. I'll read it to you . . ." There was a bit of rustling in the background, and then she cleared her throat. "It says, 'Here's to forgetting last night and that thing we agreed not to talk about. Have a great day at work. Jay.' I won't lie, I highly doubted—"

I ended the playback and exited the phone app, remembering the notifications for two texts I'd gotten from Jason while I was asleep. I was so discombobulated that I ended up hitting four other icons before finally tapping the right one. Bypassing the message from my brother, I zeroed in on the bold letters that formed Jason's name.

My heart hiccupped, which apparently affected the amount of oxygen my brain received, because I grew light headed and had to sit down in order to open it. Perched on the edge of the mattress, I carefully took in each word—twice. Then again for a third time, hoping I'd read the last text wrong.

Jason: Hey, just checking in to see how today went. I haven't heard from you, so I'm hoping that means you didn't lose your job. Text me when you get done. Or if you did lose your job and just didn't think to call, text me when you get this.

Jason: So . . . when you didn't respond to my last message, I assumed that meant you were at the restaurant. I took some flowers over and left them with the hostess. I can't say for sure, but I don't think she likes me. Anyway, Kelsey had called and asked me to grab something from the apartment while I was out. That's when I realized you were asleep in bed, not working. Let me know when you're awake.

By the fourth time, it became rather clear that I had not, in fact, read it wrong. Which only left me with the hope that he'd *written* it wrong. Autocorrect could mess up a lot of words, so it wasn't that far-fetched to assume it'd screwed up the entire message. Because if he'd been here . . .

All I could think about was the toilet lid.

And the door from the bathroom to my bedroom being slightly ajar.

And the lack of clothes covering my very naked body as I slept.

I groaned and fell backward onto the mattress with a *hmmph*. Everything had gone wrong. I'd hoped the talk at work about Jason would die down, but unfortunately, that wouldn't happen now that he'd decided to show some grand gesture and bring me flowers. He should've done that when they had all believed we were dating. Now, I probably looked weak, like I'd forgiven him rather than kicking the cheating asshole to the curb. The only thing I had in my favor was the four-day suspension. There was still a chance they'd forget about it by the time the weekend was over.

Unlikely but possible.

And as if that wasn't bad enough, there was the very real possibility that he'd seen me naked. Granted, I'd had on panties, but let's be honest . . . nowadays, those don't cover enough. If only I knew what position I'd been in while sleeping, I'd be able to figure out how to handle it. If I'd been on my stomach, he more than likely wouldn't have seen anything other than maybe a cheek and bare back. I could've lived with that—after a few shots of vodka. However, if I'd been on my back, he would've gotten a full view of the high beams as if facing oncoming traffic. That, I doubted I'd be able to get over no matter how much vodka I chugged. In fact, tequila probably wouldn't even be strong enough to wipe my memory clean.

Which meant every time I saw him, I'd be reminded of the time he saw my boobs.

My phone rang in my hand, pausing my mental meltdown. Thank God it wasn't Jason . . . or Amanda. It was Kelsey's mom. I already knew what she was calling for, and considering I'd flaked two times already, I wouldn't be able to ignore her again. "Hello?"

"Hey, Tatum. I hope I'm not bothering you. I just thought I'd see if you were available to bring over that pasta thing you were telling me about. If you're too busy, I completely understand." This woman had mastered the art of guilt trips. I was convinced she could guilt a dying man into coming back to life if she tried.

"No, Mrs. Peterson, I'm not too busy. I can bring it over now if you're home."

"That would be wonderful. Are you on your way?"

I sat up and pulled myself from the bed. "Yes, ma'am—in about two minutes."

"The front door will be open. Let yourself in, dear."

After saying goodbye, I disconnected the call and made my way into the kitchen. I pulled the pasta machine off the top shelf in the pantry and then shuffled out the door. The last thing I wanted to do was leave the apartment—even to go to see Diane. If I could've gotten away with it, I would've buried myself under my blankets and hidden for the next four days. Just the thought of Jason seeing my bare breasts left me paranoid that *everyone* I passed had seen them, too.

The man who lived across the hall from me smiled. *He saw them.*

The woman pulling the baby carrier from the back of her car waved. *Yup, her too.*

The teenager in the Explorer next to me at the light . . . he probably had pictures of them.

And when I made it to Diane's house, I was certain the man in her living room had most definitely seen them. The way his lips curled in the most obvious grin while his summer gaze held me hostage screamed, "*I know what you look like without clothes on!*"

"Oh, good! Tatum's here with the pasta thing," Diane greeted me when I came to a sudden stop in her kitchen, frozen by the hungry stare of the one and only Jason Watson.

9

Jason

I hadn't been able to get her off my mind all day, and there she was. I couldn't believe my eyes. It had taken every ounce of self-control to keep myself from calling or showing up at her apartment . . . again. If she knew what I'd seen when I walked by to use her bathroom, she'd never come around, and I couldn't take that risk.

I also refused to analyze *why* I couldn't chance never seeing her again.

I didn't need to get lost down that bunny trail.

Her deer-in-headlights stare let on that she might've been aware of the view I'd happily locked into my memory, though. Then I realized I had a shit-eating grin plastered on my face. Nothing said "I'll be thinking of your breasts while I take a shower tonight" more than a goofy smile and lust-filled eyes. I couldn't be sure if that's what I looked like or not, though her withdrawal today seemed more than normal. Which could've been paranoia on my part.

It also could've been her knowledge of the pornographic images of her I had in my head.

Aunt Diane took the box and set it on the counter. She was oblivious to Tatum's inner freak-out. I wasn't sure how, because it had been written across her face from the moment she'd stepped into the kitchen.

"Thank you so much, honey. I can't wait to use this bad boy." She ran her hands along the edge of the box. "Are the instructions inside?"

Tatum stared at me, ignoring my aunt. So I figured I'd help her out. "Why don't you open it, Aunt Diane? I'm sure Tatum doesn't need instructions, so who knows if they're in there or not."

Tatum nodded, her eyes still locked on mine.

Aunt Diane turned to her and set her hand on her shoulder, jolting Tatum out of her daze. "You should stay for supper. Kelsey has plans tonight, so it'll just be me and Fred here." Then she swung her bright eyes my way. "Oh, you too, Jason. Join us."

My aunt returned her attention to the gadget Tatum had brought over. Apparently, since she hadn't technically asked a question, that somehow meant she didn't need to wait for our responses.

But that didn't stop me from getting Tatum's answer.

"What do you say, Tatum?" I cocked my head slightly and waited for her to speak.

"Oh, um . . ." She twisted her lips to the side and squinted for added effect. "I have plans, too."

"With Kelsey?" I prodded.

"Yup. Sure thing."

"Interesting." I narrowed my gaze and crossed my arms. "Then maybe you can tell us which high-end home builder she's meeting with."

Her throat dipped, and to my personal delight, she shifted from one foot to another while moving her arms through various positions. Crossed, then hands on her hips before shaking them slightly, then back to crossed. She even threw a head scratch in there somewhere.

Finally, she said, "The um . . . the big one. They build those, uh . . . those big houses. Real high end, those people are. Everyone knows them."

"Yeah, so I've heard. Who exactly are you guys meeting?"

"The owner. Manager. The uh . . . builder guy."

"*All* of them?" I raised my brows, fully invested in the act I put on. She shrugged and said, "More or less."

Aunt Diane had long since stopped paying attention, her focus glued to the contents of the box, but I refused to let it go. This was far too entertaining. "What exactly is the meeting about? You know, since you have more details about it than we do."

"I'd love to tell you, but I have everything written on my day planner, which I left at the apartment. So unfortunately, I'm unable to give you that information at this time. Until I check my calendar. Where I write all my plans. Including the one for tonight." She blinked a few times, apparently snapping out of the awkward trance she'd been in. "Thanks again, Mrs. Peterson. So great seeing you."

"You too, dear," Aunt Diane said without turning her inquisitive stare away from the wooden handle in her hand. "Have fun."

Tatum offered me a very uneasy, forced grin, but before she turned around, I held my arms open. For once, she understood the sentiment without needing to be reminded. But I didn't get the embrace I sought, because my oblivious aunt chimed in with, "Oh, Jason. Tatum hates hugs."

Her onyx eyes grew wide, and without warning, she turned and took off.

I wasn't about to let her get away, so I patted my aunt's shoulder and muttered, "See ya later, Aunt Diane."

"You too, dear," she repeated. My cousins were such liars—their mom could've been distracted by dust floating in sunlight.

I ran out the front door, making sure it closed behind me before trapping Tatum in the driveway. "You hate hugs, huh? Why did you tell me you loved them?"

With her keys in her hand, she stalled about three feet from her car. It still amused me to picture her small frame sitting behind the steering wheel of something so big. Yet at the same time, the SUV suited her. "Would you believe me if I told you I tripped and fell into you by accident, having no idea you were even there, and to save myself from public humiliation, I said the first thing that came to mind?"

"Not for a second."

She nodded. "Well, it was worth a shot."

When she shifted on her heel to turn away, I asked, "Really, where are you going? And don't lie, Tatum. You're not very good at it."

She rolled her eyes to the sky, paused in a show of deep thought, and then shrugged. "Fine. I was planning to go home and hide in my room. And not come out until Monday."

It didn't matter how hard I fought against the rolling humor, I lost. My shoulders bounced as I pinched my lips together to at least keep the laughter inside, and when it had slowly faded away, I took a deep breath to compose myself. "You should come teach me how to cook this food you stocked my kitchen with. Call it charity or community service. I'm hungry, and I can't eat anything because I don't know how to make any of it."

"Your aunt has a perfectly good pasta machine. I'm sure she can feed you."

I glanced over my shoulder, on the off chance my aunt was outside, and then faced Tatum again. "You do realize she doesn't have the first clue how to use that thing, right? You pretty much handed her a weapon."

She giggled, and I never wanted the song to fade away. "It's a pasta machine. Manual—not even electronic. It's pretty difficult to mess it up. But in the event she has as much difficulty as you suggest, maybe you should go in there and help her with it."

"Tatum . . . she doesn't have anything to put in it."

"I don't understand. You literally feed dough through one side, turn the handle, and out comes noodles."

"Exactly."

Her confusion was palpable in her creased brow as she blinked slowly. "*Oh*-kay. What am I missing here?"

"Well, if you were my aunt, you'd be missing the dough."

One corner of her mouth gradually curled, as if she couldn't believe what she'd heard. "She has a pasta maker without pasta?" When I nodded, she released the restraint on her laughter and let it bubble out. "What did she think she'd do with it?"

"Your guess is as good as mine. But now do you see why I'm starving? Seems like the women in my life are out to get me. Mom pretends she's not home, even though I can see in the windows and know she's there. My aunt thinks that contraption will spin air into spaghetti, and you decided to fill my fridge and pantry with shit I've never heard of."

Referring to her as one of the women in my life, in the same breath as my mom and aunt, twisted me up and left me more lost than if I'd awoken after a twenty-year coma and discovered aliens had taken over the planet. I wasn't sure how to feel about that, and even worse, I wasn't sure what to do about it. Granted, I couldn't do much with the ban my cousin had put on her, though that didn't stop the knots from tightening in my chest.

"You make it sound like I went shopping at a pet store."

"I wouldn't be surprised if you did."

She shook her head in mock disbelief. "Well, I'm sure you know where the grocery store is, and you seem to be a rather competent individual, so navigating the aisles shouldn't be too much of a task. You're a big boy." Crimson licked her cheeks just before she dropped her gaze to the ground.

"You'd really make me live off microwavable dinners?" I even stuck out my bottom lip in the hopes she was one of those people who couldn't resist a pout. My desperation knew no limits.

"I'm fairly certain the store carries other options. If not, you might want to ask a manager."

"If I knew how to cook, that would be great advice." I wasn't a moron in the kitchen, but I wasn't about to tell her that. At this point, I'd be willing to lie and say I couldn't differentiate between a pot and a bowl if it meant she'd come home with me.

"You seriously don't know how to make anything?"

I shrugged, and without thinking, I said, "My ex used to handle dinner."

Sympathy fell over her face like a veil. My initial reaction was to laugh it off, tell her I'd been joking. Bringing up Jen had been a mistake, but I couldn't take it back now. And no matter how badly I wanted to retract everything I'd just said, her intoxicating gaze refused to let me.

However, her reaction taught me some vital information. A pout she could resist, but she couldn't deny a man suffering from a broken heart. If dredging up my feelings of Jen worked in my favor, then Tatum just might be the ticket to dealing with the pain I refused to acknowledge.

"Fine. I'll show you how to make *one* meal. After that, you'll have to figure it out yourself. Search Google for recipes, or hire someone— I don't care, but after tonight, I don't owe you anything." Her words might have been harsh, yet her tone was teasing and light, much like her smile.

Tatum appeared very out of place in my kitchen. I tried to do everything I could to loosen her up, yet nothing worked. The way she moved was robotic, and I wondered if she even heard half of what I said to her.

"Here, hop up." I set a glass of wine at the end of the counter, the small side of the *L* shape without cabinets hanging above it. I patted the granite and then waited for her to give in. As happy as I was that she was here, I needed to figure something out before her nervous energy gave *me* an ulcer.

"You want me to sit on the countertop?"

I glanced between her and the spot I'd slapped a few times. "Generally, that's what *hop up* means. Unless we're playing Simon Says. But we aren't, so . . . yeah, I want you to sit up here."

"How am I supposed to help you cook?"

"You're not." I slid my palm in a circle on the space in front of her, hoping it would entice her to climb up. "You're here to *teach* me how. So, make yourself at home right here, and instruct me on what to do."

Wary, she did as I said and lifted herself onto the counter. When I slid the glass of white wine closer to her, she regarded me with an arched eyebrow. "Why are you giving me something to drink? Just because it's five o'clock doesn't mean it's mandatory."

"You seem like you could use it—to relax, I mean."

"And how are you going to feel if I become an alcoholic?"

"As long as you're not acting like I kidnapped you, I'll feel fantastic. Now, drink up."

She took the glass from my hand and studied the contents. "Well, you kind of *did* kidnap me, so I guess my reaction is authentic."

"Oh yeah? Didn't you follow me here? In your own car?"

She shrugged, still staring at the wine in her hand. "I think that falls under Stockholm syndrome or something."

"Hmm . . ." I nodded, catching the faintest grin twitch at the corners of her mouth. "Interesting. I wasn't aware I had that much control over you. Although, now I understand why Kelsey is so adamant that I stay away from you."

That caught her attention.

"She's under the impression that you won't be able to resist my charm, so she's *forbidden* me from having anything to do with you." That was meant to be playful, except it had more of an opposite reaction in my chest. Bringing up how my cousin had asked me to stay away from Tatum, while Tatum sat in my kitchen, filled me with mixed emotions I would've rather ignored than dealt with.

"Yet you guilt me into coming to your house and then force-feed me wine? You might want to research the definition of *forbid*. I think you have the wrong idea of what that means."

Her teasing response was enough to settle the guilt that would've suffocated me if it hadn't been for the lightness in her tone. That was how I would have to justify her presence—it might have been a selfish reason, but if being around her softened the turmoil inside, then Kelsey would just have to deal with it.

"What can I say?" I peered over my shoulder and winked. "I'm a rebel."

"I can see that. From my experience, most outlaws wear cargo shorts and graphic tees with Iron Man on the front. It's the ultimate disguise, really. Especially the Nikes with no socks. No one would ever look at you and guess 'rule breaker.'"

Good thing she couldn't see the smile burning my cheeks. "I *am* wearing socks, thank you. Not all criminals prefer sweaty feet."

"Do you iron your sheets, too? I bet you do. And your boxers."

Either a few sips were enough to take the edge off, or she'd reached the deliriously awkward stage of her nerves, because in the two minutes since she'd sat down, she'd relaxed tenfold. It was nice to see, and even nicer to be around when she was as open as this. If only I could get her to be this way all the time around me. Around anyone else, I didn't give a shit. But around *me*, I never wanted to see her closed off in her shell ever again.

"You probably shouldn't make fun of a total badass when he's in the middle of cutting something." I held up the knife and quirked a brow.

Her humor waned as she flicked her wrist in my direction, dismissing my empty threat. "I don't have anything to worry about. I've watched you chop that onion for like an hour already. I think I'll be all right if you ever decide to turn it on me."

"Excuse me?" I slapped my free hand over my chest in feigned surprise. "First of all, I have *not* been chopping this for that long. Secondly,

122

I'm very skilled with one of these things; I just didn't want you to know and then fear for your life. You've already told me that I'm holding you here against your will, and the only reason you haven't left yet is out of some sort of affection you have for me. The last thing I wanted to do was make you run off."

"I gave you one task, Jay." God, I loved it when she called me that. Which was odd, considering I vehemently corrected anyone else who tried to shorten my name. Yet from her lips, it was different. "*Dice* the onion. It looks like you mutilated it more than anything."

I dismissed her insult and went back to the bane of my existence— this onion. It wasn't that I didn't *know* how to cook anything, because if I wanted to, I could throw something together and it would be edible. The problem was, I'd never been taught how to prepare anything. So if something called for garlic, I used the powder. If I needed onion, I used the powder. If I needed fresh herbs . . . I used the kind that came in a plastic bottle on the spice aisle.

"This is just sad," she muttered. When I turned my head to see what she was doing, I caught her sliding off the counter. "You don't want it too small, or you'll lose the flavor. And if it's too big, you'll be crunching on it for days. Let me show you."

I started to take a step back so she could have the cutting board, but before my foot slid along the tile, she slipped beneath my arm and made herself at home, trapped between my chest and the counter. This proved it—I needed to stock up on whatever wine I'd given her. Less than half a glass, and her nerves had mellowed out.

As she maneuvered the blade, she offered tips and suggestions to make it easier. Yet I didn't hear a single one. I was too busy losing myself in the fragrance of her hair to listen to anything she said—other than the sound of her voice. With her dark silky locks piled on top of her head in a very disorganized knot, it was easier to catch the clean scent while I stood behind her, despite our height difference.

And as if that wasn't enough to distract me from my cooking lesson, there was the way her back would gently graze my chest when she moved, or how she'd lean to one side, fitting my arm in the crook of her neck when she pointed something out. That was honestly the only reason I knew when to respond. Without that, she'd know immediately that I hadn't paid a lick of attention to her instructions.

"Okay, now it's ready to go in the pan." She stepped out of my slightly imaginary embrace and pointed to the stove. "You're going to mix the ingredients for the sauce while that's heating up. Just keep an eye on it so they don't burn."

I did as she instructed and then grabbed a mixing bowl—a plastic cereal bowl, since I didn't have anything else. She got a good laugh about that, and then she finally began the list she was supposed to have written for me days ago. It consisted of basic kitchen items I would need to survive without resorting to the tried-and-true college diet.

"What kinds of things did your ex used to make?" she asked after reclaiming her spot on the countertop.

I watched as her mouth met the rim of the wineglass. The liquid left her pout moist, giving off the appearance of lip gloss, even though I already knew she didn't have any on. Other than a small amount of color on her eyelids and a very thin, inky line tracing her lashes, her face was completely bare. When her tongue peeked out and captured an errant drip, I almost lost it. Though not nearly as bad as when she glanced up and caught me gawking.

Shaking it off before she could witness my struggle, I wholeheartedly blamed my cousin for this. Had she not put the idea in my head, I wouldn't have entertained the thought of Tatum licking something else, or what it would look like to see her tongue savor every drop of—

Nope, I couldn't allow myself to go there.

"She, uh . . ." I desperately fought to control my thoughts and steer them back to her question about my ex. *Jen*—that was enough to put the lid on anything remotely sexy. Being rejected by a woman you were in love with had a way of stifling anything appealing about her. "Normal shit. Like meatloaf, chicken, alfredo from a jar. Things you'd probably turn your nose up at."

"What happened?" Her voice was so small, had I not been looking at her, I would've missed the question. "With you guys, I mean. Why'd you break up? Your mom said it was recent."

"She doesn't know when to keep her mouth shut."

"Who? Your ex or your mom?"

I smiled and closed my eyes, thankful for her unintentional humor. "My mother."

"Nah. She has good intentions."

"Yeah, well . . . wait until it's *your* personal shit she's talking about. She keeps her own business under lock and key; you can't pry it out of her with a crowbar."

Just thinking of Jen put me in a funk. Anger churned in my gut while intense pain swelled in my chest, making it difficult to breathe. My mind bounced between my physical discomfort and the agonizing memories of when I'd finally left so that my world consisted of only me, closed off by a black tarp that had trapped the ache in more than it had shielded me from it.

"My ex is a douche." Her soft voice tugged me out of the fog, and the more she spoke, the closer to safety I became. "Last year, during the Thanksgiving dinner we had at the restaurant for the employees and our families, he asked me to marry him. I never pressured him to pop the question, didn't even make a big deal about taking the next step in our relationship. As far as I know, that was his decision, and his alone."

I shifted the diced onions around in the pan with a wooden spoon while she shared her pain with me. She didn't have to, and on some perverse level, I was thankful she did. It gave me an odd sense of relief to know I wasn't alone in the broken hearts club.

"Less than two months after that, my friends had planned a dinner for my birthday. I wanted to get there early, he didn't, and in the end, I won. Except I guess I technically lost, because while we waited for everyone to show up, he told me he wasn't happy and left."

Facing her wasn't enough. I was drawn to her, and I couldn't stop until I'd made my way to the end of the kitchen and stood in front of the woman with sad eyes yet determined spirit. Fitting myself between her dangling legs, I pressed my palms against the granite on either side of her and leaned forward until we were eye level with each other.

"Why wasn't he happy?" I asked, my voice barely a whisper.

She shrugged, licked her lips, and swallowed hard. For the briefest moment, her gaze dropped, but in an instant, she returned her attention to my face. "I have no idea. It all came out of nowhere. It's not like there were any warning signs or anything."

"He never told you what caused him to change his mind so quickly?"

"Not really. I had my suspicions, but he never wanted to have a conversation about it."

I didn't know who this asshole was, yet that didn't stop me from wanting to knock his teeth in. Tatum was an amazing woman—from what I could tell, at least—and she'd wasted her time with a man who didn't deserve her. Meanwhile, guys like me weren't scared of a lifelong commitment with the right person, yet we couldn't get there because the women we chose didn't comprehend the meaning of sacrifice.

We were two damaged souls, incapable of a future because we each had a past with the wrong person.

"For what it's worth, he's a dumbass." Looking into her eyes, I could see how difficult it was for her to hold my gaze. The fight within her to glance away and avoid whatever connection there was between us in this moment was strong, and I worried I'd lose her.

After a deep breath, something in her shifted. It wasn't so much a wall that had come down as it was a page that had turned. Her eyes brightened, and the lines along her forehead lessened. "Seems to me like *you're* the one who can't resist *my* charm."

I pushed away from her and laughed to myself. But my retort was stifled by the sizzling coming from the stove. I stirred the onions some more and, per her instructions, moved the pan to a different burner.

"She didn't want to come with me," I answered, realizing I hadn't made it very clear as to what I was talking about. "When Bill died, my priorities changed. My entire family lives here, and for the last thirteen years, I've been gone. In that time, Marlena got married and had two kids, all of which I wasn't around much for. So, moving home wasn't a difficult decision to make. I guess the choice wasn't as easy for her as it was for me."

Silence met my confession for a moment, and there wasn't enough strength in me to face her while she hesitated to come up with something to say. To my surprise, her response wasn't at all what I'd anticipated. "If Bill practically raised you, why do you call him by his first name?"

I craned my neck to peer at her over my shoulder. "Because he wasn't my dad." It felt like a betrayal even uttering those words aloud, but I wasn't sure how much of my life story she'd been privy to.

"Oh. I'm sorry, I guess I just figured since your dad wasn't around, and you were so young when your mom married Bill, you would've eventually called him something else." She must've seen the confusion on my face, because she arched one eyebrow, smirked, and added, "Your mom doesn't know when to shut her mouth, remember?"

I shook my head and returned to stirring the onions. "My dad might not have been around, but when Bill first came into the picture, he was still somewhat in my life. He made it known that *he* was my father. I thought if I didn't call Bill dad, then maybe my own would come back."

"And when he didn't?"

I shrugged. "Bill knew he was the only father in my life—no matter what I called him."

"Move the pan to the back burner, and add in the mixture from the bowl."

I loved how she conveniently dropped the subject and moved on.

Once we had everything done and simmering in a pan, I leaned against the counter and waited for the timer to beep. "Where'd you get this recipe from?" I asked, sipping on my own cocktail.

She picked up her glass and studied its contents for a moment. I'd refilled it while she was in the bathroom, and I thought she was about to question why there seemed to be more than when she'd left. Thankfully, she didn't. Instead, she offered me a knowing grin and brought it to her lips.

"I made it up."

"Then how do you remember it?" I was in awe over how she'd spouted off the directions as if they'd been from a family recipe.

"No . . . I literally just made it up as we went. Well, *technically*, I kind of put it together in my head as I pulled everything out of the fridge. But I more or less invented it on the fly."

"You do that often?"

She shrugged, helping herself to more of her wine. It was nice to see her so relaxed and comfortable, not wound up and shy. It gave me an idea to turn the spare bedroom into a cellar so I'd always have a supply for her.

"If I have random things, yeah. They don't always turn out the way I'd like, but at least when it's done, I can see where I went wrong and try again some other time—as long as it was at least decent to begin with. The creation of something new is my favorite part of cooking."

"Ever thought about making a cookbook?"

She huffed and rolled her eyes. "Yeah, right. I wouldn't even know where to begin. Not to mention, you haven't tasted that yet. What if it's horrible?"

I sucked in a lungful of the aroma that filled the kitchen. "Something that smells that amazing can't possibly be bad. But I'm serious. You could totally be like that chick on TV and have your own show. Not the butter lady; the hot one."

She laughed through her fingers, and all I wanted to do was pull her hand away so I could see her smile, because as sexy as she sounded, nothing beat the sight of her lips curled, showing off a row of perfect teeth, while her eyes glistened with mirth.

"Okay, if a cookbook doesn't appeal to you, have you thought about opening your own restaurant? Why work in someone else's kitchen when you could have your own? I think that'd be amazing. I'd eat there every day."

It was obvious in the dismissive flick of her eyes that she didn't take me seriously. Either that or she didn't agree with my opinion or the value I saw in her. "Again, Jay . . . hold off on the compliments until you've tried dinner. Actually"—she held up her hand—"you might want to wait until tomorrow to make sure it doesn't poison you."

"If it's bad, does that mean I get a redo? I think it should. If dinner sucks—and-or is poisonous—then you have to come over another night and teach me something else to make."

"That wasn't the original agreement," she teased, losing the battle against her grin. "I said *one* night. There were no contingencies in place for unforeseen errors or death."

"Technically, you were supposed to show me how to cook so I'd be able to feed myself in your absence. Would you really make me eat the same garbage night after night? That's rather sadistic of you, Tatum. Maybe Kelsey is so determined to keep us away from each other to protect *me*. I bet it has nothing to do with you."

"Fine." That one word stopped the world from turning and left me feeling like the biggest winner . . . until she continued. "If this meal is that bad, then I'll come back—with a stack of take-out menus from places around here."

"That's just cruel."

"I never claimed to be innocent."

Fuck. Me.

10

Tatum

I was rather pleased with dinner, not that I doubted it or anything. Yes, I'd failed at a few experimental dishes from time to time. But that only happened when we were in dire need of groceries and all I had were random items left in a nearly bare fridge, not when I had plenty of options to choose from.

However, Jason complained about it with every spoonful he shoved into his mouth. The texture, the taste, the *after*taste. Ask him, and nothing was good about it. He also claimed to have cleared his plate and gone back for seconds only because it was so awful he didn't want leftovers he'd be forced to eat again. Or, as he added, for someone to come over and taste it and think he sucked at cooking. I got a good laugh from that one.

I hadn't planned to stay and eat with him, but since we'd made so much—and I was actually curious as to how it turned out—I took him up on his offer. That, and I'd enjoyed enough wine to leave me giddy. Besides, I couldn't very well leave him with all the dishes to clean. Anytime I ate at someone else's house, I never left without making sure the kitchen was wiped down and everything was put away. That could've explained why Diane always invited me over for dinner.

Jason argued about it until he realized I wouldn't back down. That's when he grabbed a dish towel. I washed, and he dried. We were like a well-oiled machine. Several times I had to remind myself that this was my Cinderella moment, my one night to be carefree and have fun with a hot guy—and help him clean his kitchen, just like the original cinder girl.

I finished scrubbing the last pan, and when I lifted it to rinse off the soap, the water hit it at the perfect angle, soaking the front of my shirt. I groaned; the irony of making it to the end before getting wet was not lost on me.

"Should've let me wash the dishes," he teased with a goofy grin plastered onto his face. It appeared I wasn't the only one enjoying the relaxation a beverage had to offer. "I guess this means you have to take off your shirt now, huh?"

"Or I could just go home and change."

"That wasn't an option."

I set the pan in the other side of the sink and turned off the faucet. "Oh, yeah? I don't recall being given options."

"You had two—let me clean up, or take off your top. Since you wouldn't move out of the way so I could wash while you perched yourself on the counter, that leaves you with the latter."

"Interesting. There's another option you've yet to offer, which is to lend me one of your shirts. It would be rather gentlemanly of you to do."

He tucked his bottom lip between his teeth in thought. "I guess I could spare something. But don't steal it. I know how you women are . . . nothing but thieves when it comes to men's clothing."

"I don't think you have anything to worry about. Why would I want it, anyway?"

"To sleep in? Isn't that why all you pilferers take them in the first place? To feel closer to us in your dreams?" He shrugged, clearly pleased with his playful arrogance. "Which, if I may say, is a complete rip-off for us men. Our clothes get far more action than we do. So I'll let you know now . . . if you have any intention of stealing my T-shirt with the hopes of sleeping in it, think again."

I finished wiping off the counter and turned on the exaggerated pout. "You'd really deny me that? I find that insensitive."

"Nah, it's reality, baby." He put the pan away and slapped the towel over his shoulder. "If you want to feel closer to me while you sleep, you're more than welcome to curl up next to me at night."

"How generous of you." I nearly choked on my words as he leaned against the stove, my mind too busy trying to turn off the switch to the images of him in bed. It was like one of those movie scenes where porn was playing on a computer when the boss walked in, and no matter what they clicked or pressed, the moaning wouldn't stop. Yeah . . . just like that.

"What can I say? I'm a generous guy."

His smile stopped my heart and warmed my insides. It also left me with damp panties. I wondered if he had any idea of the havoc he wreaked. Then again, from what Kelsey had told me about his younger days, there was a good chance he knew *exactly* what he was doing.

He flicked his head to the side and said, "C'mon, let's get you dry."

"What? I *am* dry. You didn't make me wet."

Singing in the middle of a very crowded restaurant was no longer the most embarrassing moment of my entire life.

Although thankfully, Jason didn't taunt me—other than by dropping his gaze to the apex of my thighs before finding my eyes again, adding a single wag of his brows.

"Oh, *this*?" I tugged on the front of my top. "It's just a few water spots."

"Tatum . . ." His deep, throaty voice made me want to follow him to the ends of the earth. "Do you want a dry shirt?"

"Yes, that would be positively lovely. Thank you." Apparently, my humiliation had turned me into an eighty-year-old British woman.

I followed him into his room, but while he moved to his dresser, I lingered near the side of the bed. It took everything in me not to sit on the mattress or sprawl out on top of the comforter. The wine had clearly served its purpose. I wasn't drunk by any means, although I doubted I'd pass a Breathalyzer if I had to take one. I was at the perfect level of intoxication to go with the flow and hope the easiness between us lasted after a few bottles of water.

"This one should fit." He brought over a folded T-shirt and handed it to me. "Feel free to change in here. And when you're done, we can throw your shirt into the dryer. I'm sure it won't take long if it's the only thing in there."

I haphazardly tossed the shirt onto the bed and then counted his steps until he made it to the door. "No need to leave. It's not like you haven't seen me naked already."

As much as I loved the freedom wine offered, I hated how it often became a truth serum. I'd made it this long without bringing it up— which, to begin with, had taken monumental effort on my part. But after a bit, the initial embarrassment had waned, and it was no longer the first thought on my mind. That was, until he suggested I change in his room for privacy.

"What?" He stopped and turned to face me, his genuine shock making me pause—had I taken one second to realize my snarky remark would lead to a conversation rather than just making a point, I likely would've kept my mouth shut.

I'd said this much—no need to hold back now. "Today . . . you came to my apartment while I was sleeping. You *saw* that I was sleeping. I wasn't wearing any clothes, which means you saw me naked. So there's no reason for you to offer me privacy when you didn't give me any earlier."

"I used the restroom." His voice was strained, and his jaw nearly clenched, profound emotion deepening his green eyes. "The door to your room was open. I saw you were in bed and that you weren't dressed, so I closed it enough to keep from waking you."

"You want me to believe that you noticed I was naked but didn't take a peek at the goods?"

"Like I said, I saw enough to know you weren't wearing anything. Beyond that, no. You didn't give me permission, so I didn't look." Honesty stared back at me. "No one has the right to see those parts of you unless you allow them to, Tatum."

His words hit me hard, like a curveball to the gut. They sang a beautiful melody in my ears and tempted me to dance along, my heart thumping to the beat. The desire to give him permission to see me now propelled me into action. I yearned to find the confidence amid the unease, so I grabbed the hem of my shirt and lifted it over my head.

He kept his eyes on mine, never dropping them—not even when I unclasped the back of my bra and let the straps slip down my arms. Other than his Adam's apple bobbing like it was in a bucket of water at a carnival, he showed no sign of being affected by my breasts on full display.

After several long seconds of complete silence, reality smacked me in the face. I stood before him, naked from the waist up, and he hadn't once shown any interest in admiring what I had to offer. Doing the only thing I could think of, I gasped and covered my chest with my hands.

It took less than two seconds for him to stalk toward me, closing the distance between us. At this point, I contemplated picking up my bra and shirt off the floor and running to my car, but the burning hunger in his stare kept me frozen in place.

Jason came to a stop in front of me, threaded his fingers into my topknot, and tilted my head back. His eyes locked on mine, and in them, I desperately searched for answers, for something to explain why he refused to do what any other man would—ogle my body like a starving hyena. Okay, maybe that wasn't a sexy image, but I was lost in the unfamiliar sea of bravery, so I didn't have much brainpower to work with.

"If you want me to look at you, Tatum . . . you have to tell me."

I heard the words, yet their meaning seemed like a philosophical riddle, one I didn't have the mental capacity to understand. Yet I couldn't ask for clarification, because just then, his hand fell from my hair to my shoulder, where he softly traced my clavicle with his fingertip. Then dipped low, following the line of my cleavage before trailing the natural curve beneath my breast. The entire time he explored the sensitive flesh, his eyes remained on mine, held me hostage, and refused to let me go.

Every nerve ending was on fire. My legs were weak, my insides quivering, and untamed desire twisted low in my abdomen. I'd never experienced a need this strong, this powerful. If Jason could do this to me with a few tender strokes of his finger along my chest, I was desperate to find out what else he could do with other parts of his body . . . on other areas of mine.

In an instant, I reminded myself that I deserved this.

I deserved to *feel*, to let go and *live*.

No longer caring to hide myself from him, I fisted the front of his shirt, lifted myself to my tiptoes, and pulled his lips to mine. The last time I'd done this, I was too stunned and mortified to enjoy it. Now, without anything holding me back, I willingly immersed myself in the high his mouth offered.

It took only a handful of seconds before Jason released his restraint. Though I couldn't exactly blame him. I mean, just a few days ago, I'd practically mauled him the same way, only to jump away as if ashamed and disgusted. So, I imagined he waited this time, making sure I wouldn't do the same. And when I didn't, he gave in.

Oh boy, did he give in.

When his tongue met mine, a moan reverberated in my chest. Oddly enough, I wasn't the least bit embarrassed by it. And apparently, the sound of my excitement enticed him. He deepened the kiss, and his grip on my hips grew tighter as he pulled my body flush with his. The evidence of his desire taunted my lower stomach until I was practically feverish with need for him.

With one hand fisting the front of his shirt, I snaked the other over his shoulder to the back of his neck, where I held him close, keeping his lips on mine. And even though he had a firm hold on my body, I had just enough room to roll my hips against him.

As much as I enjoyed this tango we were in, if he didn't do *something* soon, I'd likely lose all self-control—and quite possibly most of my self-respect as well. But I was incapable of translating what I needed from him, which only frustrated me, increasing my impatience.

He broke the kiss, yet he kept his lips close to mine when he whispered, begging, "Please, Tatum . . . ask me to look at you."

My stomach was in my throat, making it hard to speak, but even that wasn't enough to silence my words, the ones he yearned to hear. And nothing in the world had ever felt better than when I muttered, "For the love of fried rice, look at me, Jay."

In an instant, he unleashed his desire, freeing the powerhouse I suspected he'd be. He lifted me up with a firm grip around the backs of my thighs, tossed me onto the bed, and stole a moment to take in every inch of bare skin, as if memorizing my every pore. When neither of us could waste another second, he crawled on top of me and settled his hips between my legs.

We were sideways, the head and footboard to our left and right, though I didn't care. The *where* wasn't important, unless it was in reference to the *what* on my body. In that case, only two places were acceptable, with one—the southern one—currently taking the lead in priority.

He trailed his lips from my jaw to my shoulder, down my chest until his tongue flicked my nipple. Suddenly, my bravery vanished, as if sucked out by an industrial-strength vacuum. I brought my arms up to cover my chest, and then I enticed him to return his attention to my lips.

Something needed to happen, and fast. We either had to take the rest of our clothes off, or I had to put mine back on. I still had a few brain cells that hadn't succumbed to lust, which warned me of everything we risked by taking this further.

But there was a very real chance I'd give my core a complex by depriving it of what it wanted. I mean, it could only constrict around nothing so many times before it'd give up and tell me I was on my own from now on.

In the end, the future of my lady parts far superseded the chance of my best friend finding out I had offered her cousin my promised land. She'd eventually forgive me, whereas *I'd* never forgive *her* if I dried up like a desert.

It was time to take matters into my own hands.

And that's literally what I did.

I ran my hand down Jason's side to his hip, where I spent a few seconds toying with the waistband of his cargo shorts. Then I slid my fingers to the front, between our bodies, just enough to let my intentions be known. He pulled his mouth from mine and dragged his lips along my cheek. With our temples pressed together, he panted in my ear. I couldn't be sure, but I thought I even heard him whisper my name. If he didn't, I pretended he did, because that was hot. And then he tilted his ass into the air, giving me the permission I didn't exactly seek yet appreciated all the same.

The second I had his erection in my grasp, I cried out in both celebration and fright.

Until that moment, I wasn't aware a man's size could evoke both emotions—*at the same time.*

Luckily, he probably couldn't hear me over his own satisfied groan.

11

Jason

Her palm was so soft, so small, so . . . warm. If I didn't stop her soon, it would end before I ever took my shorts off. That hadn't happened since puberty, and I would be damned if I allowed it to happen now.

I slowly pulled away, too selfish to make her stop yet fully aware she needed to. Well, more like *I* needed her to. Then again, she'd given me enough signals to confidently say she'd agree with me. I doubted she'd be okay if I finished in her hand. So I made my way down her front, dragging myself out of her hold until I knelt on the mattress between her legs. I tugged my shirt over my head and tossed it to the floor before dealing with the button on my shorts, and then the fly.

Desperation to be with her almost sent me over the edge of the bed rather than slipping off the side until my feet touched the floor. Yet I didn't let the little fumble get to me. Gravity stripped me of my boxers and shorts while I focused on ridding Tatum of what little clothing she had left. In a perfect world, I'd have trailed my fingertips along the insides of her thighs, tempting her with what was to come. But this wasn't a perfect world, and my throbbing erection wouldn't allow me to drag this out any longer.

I hastily unfastened her denim shorts and then pulled them down her legs, taking her panties with them. Her soft gasp captured me like a warning I would be smart to heed. And as I made my way back onto the bed, between her bare legs, the sexiest purr reverberated in her throat. I was lost by that point. Thank God she was just as impatient as I was. Hell, I was so ready to be inside her I almost forgot to grab a condom from my nightstand before climbing back over her.

Rubbers were a necessary evil. They required forethought, and when the sexiest woman I'd ever seen sprawled out beneath me, *any* thought became a struggle. Not to mention, they took time. In the grand scheme of things, it was mere seconds at the beginning. Any idiot knew those few seconds at the end weren't always reliable. So yes, necessary, yet that didn't mean I rejoiced at the sound of the foil between my fingers or the feel of the latex rolling down my shaft.

Until this time.

For whatever reason, Tatum's eyes widened ever so slightly with desire while she watched me open the packet with my teeth. And as soon as I placed the tip over the crown of my dick, she lost control of her breathing; her chest frantically rose with each desperate inhale, and then fell as each rushed exhale wafted past her lips. If this was my reward for using a condom, I'd never complain about them again.

I lined myself up and rolled my hips enough for the tip of my dick to sit just inside her entrance. She closed her eyes and curled her legs against my sides. After a few gentle thrusts, I felt confident she was prepared for me. But first, I had to take care of something.

I wrapped my fingers around one of her wrists and raised her arm over her head. Then I repeated the action with the other until nothing hid her breasts from me. She watched intently, though she never uttered a word.

"Tatum . . ." I exhaled against her lips as I finished filling her.

Her spine arched off the bed, and she gasped. I knew by how tightly her core gripped me that she needed a moment to adjust, so I lowered my lips to her exposed neck and licked a line to the spot just below her ear. It was enough to spur her into action. She wrapped her legs around my waist, pulled my body closer to hers, and then turned her face in search of my mouth.

"If you want something, baby . . . you'll have to speak up. I can't read your mind." I wasn't a fan of dirty talk; I found most of it distasteful and eye rolling. However, communication was important, so while I didn't need her calling me Daddy or announcing that she was coming as if I wouldn't know, a little guidance would've been helpful.

"Usually, this is the part when you move."

I smiled against her lips and breathed laughter into her. That was definitely a first.

"Yes, ma'am." I pulled out slowly, and in the same unhurried pace, I rolled into her again.

"I'm not a violin, Jason," she protested in a hoarse voice. "Keep this up, and you'll put me to sleep. Maybe no one's told you before, but the term *sleeping together* isn't literal."

I wasn't sure if I should be offended or find the humor in her teasing. But since I'd never had a complaint before, I chalked it up to her being cute and did as she demanded. Meeting her gaze, I smirked and slid back, then captured her sassy mouth and slammed into her. It elicited the sexiest moan from her throat.

It didn't take long until she fought against my grip on her wrists. When I released her, she immediately took hold of my shoulders and rode out her first orgasm with her eyes shut, teeth gritted, and a strangled whimper ripping from her chest. It caused her to tighten around me so much that I wasn't sure I'd last long enough to earn another from her.

"Shit, Tatum. That was so hot I need you to do it again for me."

A lazy smile lingered on her lips while her eyes slowly opened. But the second I ran my hand up her stomach to her chest and circled my finger around her hard nipple, she was back on the defense. She covered my hand with hers and lowered her lids again, but this time, to guard her downcast gaze.

I stilled and took her mouth, hoping to bring her back. Tatum gave in enough to join the kiss, yet it wasn't what I was looking for. Desperate for more, I slid out until I was on my knees in front of her. Her surprised stare lit a fire in my gut, and I had a feeling we were about to turn the tables on her shyness. I needed the sass, the snark, the part of her that was eager to be with me. And I wouldn't quit until I had it back. Until it was just her and me in this room—her head filled with what I was doing to her and nothing else.

In one swift move, I turned to the side and sat against the headboard with a stack of pillows supporting my back, pulling her body with me. It was all so fast I doubted she had a second to contemplate my motivation. And once I had her straddling my lap, I guided her closer with a firm hold on her hips until her heat taunted my dick. She was hesitant at first, though I refused to let her uncertainty win. I trapped her in my gaze, urging her with my eyes to take control, practically begging her to see the truth on my face.

And then she wrapped her hand around my sheathed erection and lined us up a split second before impaling herself on my cock. We both released a tangled chorus of satisfaction. I wasn't sure if being on top was something she didn't typically enjoy, or if she simply didn't have much practice with it, because I had to guide her body, my fingertips digging into her ass cheeks with each push, each pull I directed.

"I hate to be the one to tell you this, Jay . . ." She was breathless as she tried to offer me insight. "But I can't get off this way. So if that's your goal here, you should know you're wasting your time." Then her eyes widened just a hair, and her brow furrowed slightly. "Don't let that stop you from getting yours, though."

My cheeks burned from the strain of my grin. This woman . . . she went from not saying anything to having a conversation while I sat balls deep in her. "Don't worry, baby. I'll get mine. After I make you scream my name."

Her hands stilled on my shoulders, and she narrowed her gaze, while I continued to roll her hips. Never in my life had I been in this situation—fucking a woman, going through the motions, yet both of us acting as if we were discussing our likes and dislikes over a cup of coffee. Ironically, it was sexy as hell, and it didn't once threaten to ruin the mood.

"I'm *not* going to scream your name, Jay," she promised, her tone full of seriousness.

I hadn't meant it in the literal sense, but now that she'd put it on the table, it became a challenge. A challenge I wouldn't lose. After watching her come undone beneath me, I wouldn't give up until I witnessed it again while she rode my dick . . .

She began to move on her own, now only needing a little guidance from me, so I slipped one hand to her lower back and threaded the other into her hair. Her shaky breaths were sucked into a heady gasp as I gently tugged on the loose knot of silky strands that twisted through my fingers, exposing her neck. With her spine now arched, her chin tipped up and throat elongated, she steadied herself with her hands on my shoulders, nails digging into my skin. Her breasts heaved closer to my face due to her curved posture, and I salivated at the sight of her pink, beaded nipples.

I flicked one with the tip of my tongue and waited for her sudden rigidness to subside. Then I closed my mouth around it and lightly sucked. Her strangled moan rumbled through her, practically vibrating my lips. Though nothing compared to the way she frantically rotated her hips against me when I pinched the hardened ball with ease between my front teeth.

"Jay . . . ," she pleaded. "*Jason.*"

I released that nipple and licked my way to the other, repeating the same action. Her core clenched, her movements uncoordinated, and I knew she was close. That realization alone was enough to finish me off, but I needed to get her there first, so I dropped my hand from her hair.

Her forehead fell to mine, her eyes closed and breaths erratically hitting my face. I'd never been more desperate to make a woman come than I was right now. I cupped her breast with one hand and palmed it roughly, unable to control my strength. Every muscle in my body had coiled so tightly I didn't think they'd ever relax again. And as soon as I had her nipple rolling between my thumb and forefinger, a whimper escaped her lips.

"Tatum," I grunted while lifting my hips to meet hers. "Baby, come on."

"*Jason.*" It was breathless, it was almost unheard, but it was *my* name, followed by a gasp and then the most incredible whimper to have ever hit my ears. "*Jay . . .*"

I tightened my arm around her, holding her impossibly close while I buried myself as deep as her body would allow. My skin was on fire as bursts of relief shot through me. My heated exhales billowed along her neck, where I grazed the salty skin with my teeth, tasting her against my tongue.

It took us both a few moments to calm down and slow our racing hearts. And while I fought to control my breathing, I realized it was over. We would enjoy this time, wrapped up in each other, but in a couple of minutes, she'd slide off my lap, and I'd no longer be inside her. I'd no longer be connected to her this way.

Never in my life had I dreaded this moment.

It was easy to think, *Next time . . .* but considering *this* time shouldn't have happened, anything beyond this wasn't guaranteed. She was supposed to be off limits. Her best friend had warned her to stay away from me. And it wasn't until right now that I remembered why.

Breaking things off with Jen had been difficult enough with the relationship she and Marlena had built over the last few years. Except they weren't *best* friends, nor had they ever lived together. Marlena hadn't thought twice before coming to my defense, but this wasn't the same situation. I couldn't even compare the two. Kelsey and Tatum were like sisters—the repercussions of our actions had the potential to be devastating.

"Stay the night, Tatum." It wasn't a question; it also wasn't a command. It was a plea, a desperate request, a wish on a shooting star to keep her for a little while longer. I couldn't take back what we'd done—not that I wanted to—so there was no point in putting an immediate end to it if we didn't have to, especially since this would more than likely never happen again.

She lifted her head until our eyes met. "I can't. Kelsey will wonder where I am."

Just the sound of my cousin's name pained me. "So?"

"She can't find out, Jason." Her tone wasn't filled with anxiety but rather was stern with fact.

"She doesn't have to. Are you not allowed to stay over at someone else's house? Why would she automatically assume you were here?"

"I hate the idea of lying to her. When I don't come home, she'll ask where I've been. If I tell her the truth, she'll be pissed. And it's not like I can just avoid giving her an answer. Anything other than saying I stayed here would mean I'd have to lie to my best friend's face. I can't do that."

I dropped my forehead to her shoulder and tried to accept her answer. But I couldn't. I wasn't done with her yet, and the thought of her leaving left me on the verge of insanity. "Okay. Tell her you had too much to drink so you slept on my couch. She'll be pissed at me. Not you." I brought my head back and found her eyes again. "Stay. Please."

"And why did I come here in the first place?"

"Cooking lesson. It's not a lie. You can tell her everything without betraying her—taking the pasta machine to my aunt's house, running into me, following me back to help me cook. She was here when I first brought it up, so it's not like she'd even question it."

Her eyes glistened, and a smirk tugged at one side of her mouth. "I don't know, Jay."

"Stay the night." I'd say it a hundred times until she agreed.

Her body relaxed against me. "Give me one good reason."

"I've lived with someone for the better part of the last five years. I haven't gotten used to the constant silence yet, and by you staying, you'll spare me one night of loneliness."

The way she stared intently into my eyes, I could tell she questioned my sincerity. Little did she know, but every single bit of that had been painfully true, though I'd never admitted it to anyone, and I had no desire to repeat myself.

She nodded once and whispered, "Okay."

And just like that, the weight threatening to crush me vanished. I pulled her lips to mine and silently thanked her. And with her hands on either side of my face, she accepted my gratitude.

Oddly enough, once we were both dressed and the sex haze had mostly dissipated, we moved to the couch and watched a movie like two friends who hadn't just fucked like it was our last opportunity. Her guard was down, and it didn't return for the rest of the night. Things were just easy between us, and I spent the majority of the film wondering how long this would last.

But for now, I wanted to enjoy whatever this was.

There was no need to complicate it.

12

Tatum

My eyes blinked open, the faint morning sun filling an unfamiliar room. It took a few seconds to realize it was Jason's, then a few more to recall why I was in his bed. When the memories of last night caught me up to speed, I took a deep breath and allowed myself one more minute of satisfaction.

I rolled onto my back and glanced to the side, taking in the sight of Jason. He was asleep on his stomach with his arms tucked beneath his pillow. He had his face turned toward me with his eyes closed, softly breathing through his mouth. A light shadow of scruff lined his jaw, and I couldn't ignore how innocent he looked. Yet I knew differently. The things he'd done to me last night had not been innocent. They hadn't been learned from a textbook nor picked up from locker-room talk.

Even without having known Jason when he was younger, I whole-heartedly believed the rumors. There was no way he could've made my body sing like he had without years of diligent practice, so I was in no position to pass judgment. After all, I was the one who'd reaped the benefits this time.

I slipped out from beneath the covers and tiptoed to the desk in the far corner, where he'd neatly set my folded clothes. The burn in my thighs was enough to remind me of him for a little while longer. It also made it that much more difficult to change out of his T-shirt and into my own clothes to leave. Regardless, I couldn't stay. Hell, I shouldn't have stayed overnight, but I'd found myself powerless to say no to him—especially while he was still inside me.

Ironically, after the movie had ended, we'd climbed into bed and fallen asleep. Sure, there had been a little touching, some kissing, a few strokes here and there, but eventually, we'd succumbed to the exhaustion only sex could provide while wrapped in each other's arms. At some point during the night, I'd moved to one side and curled up, facing the edge of the bed, and it seemed he'd shifted into a more natural position as well.

We had managed to move past the uncomfortable, awkward boundaries of my personality and just existed. Like two people—two *friends*. Not only that, but we'd also managed to get naked and each take advantage of what the other had to offer. That was completely out of character for me, yet with him, it didn't freak me out. If anything, it gave my confidence a boost. It was like a shot of assurance to my ego. Then again, it was difficult to lose myself in my head when I was so busy losing myself in his touch.

I stalled in the doorway of his room and took one last look at him before sneaking out as if I were his mistress. One thing was for sure, though . . . that was *not* the last time I'd let him have his way with me. I wasn't sure how we'd make it work without Kelsey finding out, but if there was a will, there was a way.

And by God, there was definitely a will.

I drove from Jason's house to Samson with my mind lost in blissful thoughts of his skilled hands. And mouth. And the glorious package the schlong gods had bestowed upon him. But as soon as I made the turn down Oasis Boulevard toward my apartment complex, reality set in. I would have to face my best friend with the image of her very naked cousin on my mind. She'd sniff out the betrayal seeping from my pores before I even opened the door.

I'd taken one step inside when she popped out of her room, eyes narrowed and forehead taut with suspicion. She pursed her lips and watched as I closed the door behind me.

"Where have you been?"

I froze. I didn't just clam up or stare blankly at her while quickly forming a lie in my head. Every muscle locked up. I literally stopped moving, quit breathing, and . . . *froze*. My brain even shut down, and all its functions—such as remembering the excuse Jason had told me to use—vacated my head. I was utterly useless.

At least I never had to worry about anyone asking me to falsify an alibi for them.

Her expression relaxed into a goofy, pleased grin and soft eyes, complete with excited, jumping brows. "You're totally doing the walk of shame, aren't you?"

I shook my head, but that was about all I could do.

"Yes . . . yes you are, you little hussy. It's seven on a Friday morning, and you're in jean shorts and a wrinkled shirt."

I glanced down at my attire and pulled on the hem of my top, stretching out the front. "My clothes are always wrinkled." That was true. I basically lived out of a hamper—I would've lived out of the dryer if Kelsey hadn't constantly stuffed the clean laundry into a basket and put it in my room.

"Oh, yeah? Were they wrinkled when you put them on yesterday?"

"As a matter of fact, they were." My tone practically screamed "told ya so," which mirrored her obnoxious, gloating smirk. It confused me for a second until my brain returned and replayed what had just happened. *Holy smoked salmon.* "I grabbed them off the floor this morning and put them back on. I didn't have time to find anything else to wear."

"I don't doubt that one bit. Except we both know you didn't grab them off *your* floor."

"So what?" I shrugged, giving up on denial and hoping that admitting it would make this end. "I had sex. *Great* sex. It was so amazing I just might do it again."

"If you're lying to me, we're going to have issues."

"Nope. I'm telling the truth. You're the one who told me to go out there and have a little fun. So I did."

"I'm so proud of you. I honestly didn't think I'd ever see the day." Her cheeks had to hurt from how hard she fought against her evil, satisfied smile. "Who was it? Is he hot? Oh!" Her eyes grew wide. "Is he a random? I won't lie . . . I'm a little conflicted about that. Sure, there are certain risk factors when introducing yourself to a stranger by shaking his dick with your hoo-ha. But let's be real, if it got you to spread 'em for someone other than Michael, then *hallelujah*."

I propped my hand on my side and cocked my head at her. "Being with only one person isn't a bad thing, Kels."

"You're twenty-five, Tater. One day, you'll be married, which means no more swimming in the pool. Do you really want to wake up one morning and realize you've wasted your life on the sidelines with water wings?"

"Better that than herpes." I gave up and headed for my room.

Apparently, that wasn't a clear enough hint for her, so she followed. "Come on, Tatum. Who was he? I need to know . . . it's *imperative* that you tell me."

"Trust me, Kelsey . . . you don't. Let's just leave it at that."

She was silent for a minute, probably running through the options in her head. A second later, her posture slumped, and she gave me the most pathetic pity eyes I'd ever witnessed. She didn't need to say anything—her reaction made it clear enough that she'd figured it out—yet that didn't stop her from voicing her opinion anyway. "Really? Please tell me you're kidding. Or lying. Better yet, tell me you're delusional and made it all up in your head, that it didn't happen but you *think* it did because you're so hard up."

I dropped to the edge of my bed and stared at her, hoping she could feel the remorse rolling off me in waves rather than the gratification I felt when my sore muscles refused to let me forget last night. This was the worst situation to be in. The last thing I wanted to do was upset her, yet at the same time, I didn't believe I'd done anything wrong . . . other than sleep with her cousin after she'd adamantly begged me not to.

"*Why*, Tatum? You're so much smarter than this. Why would you do it?"

"I don't know. It just happened."

"Sex doesn't *just happen*. Okay . . . sometimes it does, but never for you."

"Well, it did. One minute we were laughing and having a good time, and the next thing I knew, my top was off and my hand was down his pants. Can we please go back to like ten seconds ago when you were excited for me?"

"Absolutely not. Just promise it won't happen again."

"I'd prefer it if you didn't make me."

"Fine, but can you at least promise to be smart about this?"

"It meant nothing—you taught me well. So yes, I can promise that if it happens again, I'll be smart about it. Things might be a little awkward at first, but you'll see . . . you have nothing to worry about."

Kelsey sighed and rolled her eyes. "Doubtful, but whatever. I just hope you know what you're doing. Now get some rest. The last thing you need is to burn the restaurant down because you fell asleep at the stove. Good luck explaining to everyone why you were so tired."

"Yeah, so . . . I forgot to tell you. I was suspended until Monday."

She turned her head and blinked rapidly. "Wait, what? From the restaurant?"

"Yeah. I found out yesterday morning when I showed up for my lunch shift."

"And then you went out and celebrated by having sex?"

"Uh, not exactly. I came home and took a nap first. Then I dropped off the pasta machine at your mom's house."

"You slept with him after you left my mom's house?"

"No. After I left, I made dinner. Then I, uh . . . cleaned the kitchen."

"Oh, for fuck's sake, Tatum. You cleaned his kitchen? And *then* you slept with him?"

"Something like that. Yeah." I didn't understand how the sequence of events was important, but if she needed to know every step I'd made that led me to her cousin's bed, then so be it.

"I just can't with you right now." She shook her head in disappointment, and I silently took it because it was the least I deserved for doing the one thing she'd asked me not to. "Clearly, you're *not* being smart about this, because if you were, you wouldn't have climbed into Michael's bed the same day he suspended you from work."

She stomped out of my room before my shock subsided.

I fell onto the mattress, closed my eyes, and wondered how I'd managed to get myself into this.

I technically hadn't lied to her. And considering she'd run out without giving me a chance to say anything, I couldn't really be held accountable for not clearing it up, either. It didn't mean she wouldn't still be livid if she ever discovered the truth, but for the time being, I chose to find comfort in her confusion.

Sleep never came, probably because my mom decided that seven thirty on a Friday morning was the perfect time to call and fill me in on Dad's colonoscopy. When she got to the part about the actual procedure, I told her I had to go, and by then, there was no way in hell I could close my eyes and think of anything else. So I decided to give up and take a shower.

"Shouldn't you be gone by now?" I asked when Kelsey stepped out of her bedroom to join me in the kitchen.

She nudged me out of the way with her hip so she could pour another cup of coffee, forcing me to butter my toast over the sink. "Where would I be?"

"Gee, let's see . . . work?"

"And what exactly do you think I would be doing before eight in the morning?"

"Uh . . . moving furniture?"

"Good thing you know how to cook. It's pretty much the only reason you're still here, because you're not very funny." The lack of humor in her blank and bored expression was almost convincing, yet the glimmer in her eyes gave her away—that tiny flare betrayed her impeccable poker face every time.

All I had to do was smile or show some indication that I'd acknowledged her teasing commentary as it was intended, and we'd pick up where we had left off.

"I have to get ready for an open house tomorrow." She brought the mug to her lips and blew on the steaming liquid. "They had one last month and got no offers. I told them it wouldn't sell the way it is—the old woman who owns it has knickknacks all over the friggin' place. They finally agreed to let me come in and do an overhaul, but the woman wanted to get her things boxed up first. She must be senile, because if she thinks I want any of that crap, she's sadly mistaken."

"When are you doing that?"

"She won't let us in until eleven, which means I'll be there all day, and more than likely, early tomorrow morning as well. Trust me—that was *not* how I planned to spend my Friday evening." She took a sip of her coffee and then leveled a stare at me. "What are you doing tonight?"

Just then, my phone rang, and I said a silent *thank you* for the interruption. That was, until I noticed the name on the screen. I grabbed it before she could see it, fumbling with the device until I had it up to my ear. Answering the call seemed easier than ignoring it and having to deal with Kelsey's questions . . . though at the time, I hadn't stopped to consider the entire picture.

"H-hello?" I figured if I played it off, then she wouldn't find it odd that my phone rang and I picked it up. I blamed the lack of logic on the early hour.

"Mmm, hello to you, too. You must've snuck out early . . . I woke up alone." His voice was even sexier first thing in the morning. I nearly swooned at the sound of it. Thank God I didn't, because when I glanced up, I caught Kelsey eyeing me with considerable interest.

I only prayed she couldn't hear him—or that it was a *him*.

"Yeah, just getting a head start. You know how traffic is."

His laughter rumbled into my ear and ran through me until the vibrations settled between my legs. This man had turned me into a nympho. "Well, I was just calling to see how things went when you got home. Did Kelsey give you a hard time?"

"Yup, sure did."

Kelsey's curiosity morphed into concern as she continued to watch me.

"Let me get out of bed and shower. I have to drop off some paperwork at the office later," he mumbled. "Maybe we can get together? I don't know if you're much of a coffee drinker, but there's a place on the way into Samson we can meet at. Or if lunch would be better, I can do that, too."

"Oh, absolutely. That sounds awesome. I'd love to come see you." Had I not been so worried about what Kelsey could hear or who she thought I was on the phone with, I might've been more perceptive about what I was saying. Unfortunately, I was incapable of doing *and* thinking at the same time.

"Really?" He didn't sound convinced.

"Of course. Just tell me when to be there, and I'll . . . well, I'll be there."

Jason was quiet for a moment, likely thrown off by my intense excitement. "Oh, okay. Give me a couple of hours to deal with the office, and I'll call when I'm on my way home. We can make plans then. Sound good?"

"Sounds great!"

"See you later, Tatum."

"See you then." I disconnected the call with an exaggerated smile burning my cheeks. It took far more muscle strain to fake a grin than it did to showcase a real one.

Kelsey raised one brow and tucked her chin slightly—the "what are you not telling me" expression. When she realized I wouldn't offer her anything, she asked, "Who was that?" Her singsong tone pissed me off.

"My mom." It was the only person who came to mind, thanks to the call that had kept me from falling back asleep this morning.

"You're going to see your parents?"

"Sure am."

"Didn't you just see them a couple months ago?"

"Yup. But Dad had a colonoscopy. I need to be there again."

She nodded, and by the heavy creases in her brow, I could tell she struggled with whether to believe me or not. "When are you going?"

"Today."

"Really? Don't you go back to work in a couple of days?"

"Monday morning." Then I actually broke it down in my head and realized why she was so confused. "It's just for the weekend. I figured I'm off anyway, and since I rarely get the opportunity to go, I took her up on the offer."

"To fly there and back for . . . what? Two days?"

"Well, I'm certainly not going to drive."

"When's the flight?"

I stuffed half the piece of toast into my mouth, needing a moment to formulate this new lie before I got caught. "In an hour," I said, particles of bread spreading through the air.

"Your flight *leaves* in an hour?"

I shook my head, then nodded, unsure what the right answer was. But as soon as I understood her concern, I shook my head again. "No. Have to *be there* in an hour."

"Oh, thank God. I was gonna say . . ." She shook her head, stepping away from the counter. "Let me drive you to the airport. There's no sense in you wasting money on parking. That shit's expensive."

"No, really. It's okay. I can totally drive myself."

She shooed me off and stepped around the counter. "Nonsense. Let me finish getting ready, and I'll take you on my way into Langston. It'll give me a chance to make sure everything is on the truck before I head over to the hoarder's house."

Before I could stop choking on my toast and argue with her some more, she was in her room with the door shut. I didn't know how the hell I'd get out of this one, but as I packed a small suitcase—by that, I mean I mindlessly shoved stuff inside the rolling carry-on—I frantically ran through my options.

Turns out, I didn't have any.

"You know . . ." Kelsey spent the entire drive from Samson to the international airport in Langston talking, to which I did a lot of humming and nodding. "I think this weekend will be good for you. It'll get you away from Michael and the crap he's trying to pull. Maybe when you come back, your head will be clear, and you'll be in a better place."

"Mm-hmm." I stared out the window, only halfway listening to her. It was damn near impossible to pay attention to her while contemplating what I would do once I got to the airport. Not to mention, if she doubted my weekend plans at all, I wouldn't put it past her to walk me in and wait until I'd made it through the TSA checkpoint. If that happened . . . I was screwed.

"Speaking of . . . when do you get back?"

"Oh, I'm not sure."

"Didn't you buy a ticket?"

Only a moron would get this far into a lie without realizing the issue of a plane ticket. "No. My mom bought it for me."

"Well, when you find out what time your return flight lands, let me know, and I'll pick you up. Maybe it'll get me out of going to my parents' house on Sunday. She's making some kind of pasta, which would be fabulous if you were going to be there to make sure she doesn't mess it up. But since you won't be . . . I'm kinda scared."

We pulled up in front of the departure doors, and she shifted the car into park. This was it. Time to grab my suitcase from the back and head inside as if I belonged. With my luck, the security would think I had a bomb in my bag and arrest me.

"Thanks, Kels. See you Monday." I closed the door and waved, standing on the curb with my carry-on next to me.

She continued to sit there and watch me.

And I continued to wave.

"Ma'am . . ." An older man approached me, and my heart sank. This was it. He was about to ask what I had in my bag. The FBI were already on their way with the SWAT team. I was about to hold up my hands in surrender and tell him I didn't have a bomb when he leaned into the car window and said to Kelsey, "Goodbyes are hard, but we have to keep it moving. There are others who need to be dropped off as well."

I sighed in relief, took the handle to my bag, and stepped away from the curb. I had no idea what to do once I'd made it inside, but I'd have to figure that out later.

I wheeled my suitcase through the airport, following every exit sign I could find. And once I made it down to baggage claim, I did my best to fit in with the other travelers. After all, I didn't want to look suspicious. I couldn't have possibly been the only person in the entire world who came to an airport to get out of telling someone the truth.

Sitting on a bench outside the arrivals gate, I thumbed through the contacts on my phone in search of someone to pick me up. Granted,

I needed someone who wouldn't question why I was here or why I needed to be dropped off at a hotel so close to home, so that narrowed my options . . . considerably.

Down to one. Jason.

Amanda would have too many questions. Anyone in Kelsey's family—*aside from her cousin*—would be too risky. There was a good chance someone would say something about it, and it'd get back to her. Not to mention the whole Sunday lunch thing made calling her mom a bit messy. And as much as I would've liked to believe I could call Carrie or Rebecca or any of the other people I worked with, there was no way I could without either getting caught in my lies or forming new ones.

So, Jason was it.

"Hey, have you by chance left yet to deal with that thing at the office?" I asked after he answered his phone.

"I'm on my way now. Why? What's up?"

"I was just wondering if you could pick me up while you're out."

He hesitated for a moment. "Uh, sure. Is there something wrong with your car?"

"I guess you could say that."

"What's wrong with it?"

"It's at my apartment."

Silence met me, followed by his tentative question, "And . . . where are you?"

"The airport."

He laughed for a second, but when I didn't join in, he grew quiet. "Why?"

"Because Kelsey was standing in front of me when you called, and I somehow gave her the impression I was flying out to see my parents for the weekend."

"How'd you do that?"

"I told her I was flying out to see my parents for the weekend."

His laughter returned, louder than before. Normally, this would be the time I'd feel stupid and pray for a cloak of invisibility. Instead, I let the hilarity of the situation roll through me.

"I'll pick you up, but it might be half an hour before I get there."

"That's fine. Thirty minutes sure beats all weekend."

His chuckle flowed through me. "How exactly are you going to explain being home instead of at your parents'? Don't you think she'll notice it if you're in your room?"

"Not if I'm really quiet."

"Yeah . . . how about we discuss this when I pick you up."

I told him where I was and then disconnected the call. While I waited, I called my brother, since I hadn't returned his text from yesterday. I woke him up, but that didn't stop him from talking to me until Jason pulled up to the curb almost forty minutes later.

Jason stepped out and helped me with my bag while I said goodbye to Tanner.

"Who was that?" His husky tone could've been perceived as jealousy—probably because he'd heard me tell someone I loved them—though the slight hitch at the end conveyed curiosity. And since I was stupid enough to believe he'd be upset at me for talking to another guy, relative or otherwise, the meaning was clear.

"My brother."

His curiosity turned to confusion while he continued to stare at me. "For some reason, I thought you were an only child. Then again, maybe it's because I am, so I just assume everyone else is, too."

"I might as well be, considering Tanner was seventeen when I was born."

"Damn. Talk about starting over," he said, laughing to himself as he pulled away from the curb. "I always thought the six-year age gap between me and Kelsey was hard . . . I can't imagine almost two decades. Are you very close with him?"

"Yeah. We don't get to see each other much, but we talk all the time."

"Where does he live?"

"Alaska." I sighed, and for the first time, I actually *wanted* to talk about Tanner to someone else. "He moved there about eight years ago to get away from the close-minded idiots who came after him with pitchforks."

"*Pitchforks?*"

"Well, more like an investigation." My heart still broke every time I thought about the things he had endured. "Tanner doesn't have a . . . *conventional* marriage. And apparently no one could understand his choices. Rather than try to get to know him, people slung accusations around and chased him out of state."

"Does he have more than one wife or something?"

I laughed, not because I found it funny, but because I was sure Jason wasn't expecting the answer I was about to give. "Four." I waited for his mouth to fall open, and when it didn't, I added, "And two husbands—used to be three."

That got a reaction, though not what I was used to. Rather than shock, he appeared more contemplative. With a slight smirk, he kept his eyes on the road and slowly nodded, as if making sense of it in his head. "Why are there only two now?"

Yeah . . . *not* the question I thought he'd have. Nor was it an answer I wanted to explain, yet I gave it anyway. "The authorities opened an investigation on their family because they thought it was a cult. I think the stress got to Richard."

"He left?"

Tiny needles stabbed the backs of my eyes when I said, "No. He had a heart attack. That was when Tanner decided they needed to get away. And you can't really get much farther than Alaska. But they've been happy there. Lots of privacy, which is what they needed."

Jason was quiet for a moment, making me almost desperate to hear his thoughts—I just knew they wouldn't echo the criticism I'd heard most of my life. And he didn't disappoint when he asked, "Does he have any kids?"

He seriously amazed me.

"Uh, yeah. He has five with Melinda, three with Peggy, one with Loraine, and three with Vikki. But they're all called Mom and Dad. They're just one big happy family; although, they kind of have to be in order to raise a dozen kids. In their eyes, they all share the same DNA."

"I get it. Bill was my stepdad, but I never looked at him like that. To me, he was my father. He called me his son, treated me like his blood ran through my veins, and loved me like he had created me. The heart doesn't know the difference."

God, he really *did* get it.

"Yeah." I nodded, almost speechless over how easy it was to tell him about Tanner. When I'd told Michael, he'd seemed put off by it. And the few times they'd been around each other, Michael had been standoffish. I'd questioned him multiple times, yet he always told me I was "reading too much into it." That might've been true, but after seeing Jason's immediate acceptance of my brother's lifestyle, I doubted it.

He continued to drive toward the airport exit, clearly contemplating something. Coming to a stop at a red light, he finally asked, "Where to?"

"I figured I'd just get a room at a hotel or something."

He narrowed his gaze, which looked very much like the expression Kelsey used when she heard something ridiculous. "That sounds expensive."

"You're right. I should totally make you pay for it."

"*Me?*" Somehow, the feel of our entire interaction changed with his phony, exaggerated reaction.

"Yes. I mean, this *is* all your fault. I wouldn't even be here if it weren't for you."

"You're right. You'd still be on a bench waiting for someone to pick you up."

I shook my head and released any residual hesitation through soft waves of humor drifting past my smiling lips. "Except I wouldn't have been at the airport. You see . . . had you not made me stay over last night, I would've still been asleep this morning when you called—not standing in front of Kelsey. Actually, if you want to get technical here, you probably wouldn't have even called at all. So really, this all comes down to the fact that I slept over . . . which was *your* idea."

"You're absolutely right, Tatum. Had I not asked you to—"

"*Made* me. Don't make it sound like it was a request. You forced me to."

"Oh, that's right. I'm sorry. I forgot about your Stockholm syndrome. My bad." He cleared his throat and fought against the smirk threatening to tip his lips. "Anyway, as much as I'd love to pay for a room so you can hide out for the weekend, that's simply not going to happen."

I turned to face him, gasping in feigned shock. "You'd leave me homeless for three days?"

"I didn't say that." He peered at me from the corner of his eye as he turned at the green light. "But it's ridiculous to pay for a hotel room when I have my own place you can stay at for free."

Butterflies swarmed my stomach, while fear swelled in my chest. "I can't do that."

"Why not?"

"Because, Jason. It'd be weird." I didn't want him to think I was moving in the day after sleeping with him. "I'm not a stage-five clinger, and if I stay with you, that's exactly what I'll look like."

"Do you plan to tell anyone about last night? Or that you're staying with me instead of going to see your parents?"

"No. Why in the world would I do that?"

"I don't know; that's why I asked. If no one knows, then why are you so worried about how it'll look? If you're worried about me, don't. I wouldn't offer if I had an issue with it, or if I thought you were capable of clinging to the fifth stage."

I settled into the seat and stared out the window. Without any other options, I didn't have much of a choice. "Fine. But I'm staying in the guest room."

"Yeah . . . we'll see about that."

"Jason." I glared at him with enough effort to burn a hole into the side of his head. "Don't be stupid. Staying over last night was one thing, but we're not going to make a habit of it. Got it?"

"They say it takes doing something for thirty days to create a habit. I think we'll be fine with three."

"Let me guess," I said with my arms crossed like a defiant child. "You expect sex every night?"

I'd meant it as a joke, yet seeing his wide eyes showed he hadn't taken it as such. "N-no. That's not, uh . . . that's not what I meant."

"So you *don't* want sex every night?" This brazen side of me was new, brought on by a wild night with Jason. I felt powerful. Not to mention, it was entertaining to watch him stumble on his next words.

"I'm kind of scared to answer, if I'm being honest."

I hummed and turned my attention to the window again, knowing I wouldn't get it out while looking at him. "That's too bad, because the only way I'll sleep in your bed is if you make it worth my while."

He hit the brakes a little too hard and swerved, scaring the everloving crap out of me.

"I'm sure there's something I can do," he said with a smile, as if he hadn't almost driven off the road for no reason.

"Just as long as it's not dinner, I'll be fine."

13

Jason

"Your friend decided not to come?" Aaron asked when I joined him in the back seat of the Uber.

He'd gotten us hooked up with a VIP section through the chick he'd met at Taste of the Town. I was surprised, considering it was a Saturday night and he'd apparently set this up recently. Then again, when Aaron wanted something, he usually found a way to make it happen.

I shrugged, trying to act like Tatum's decision to stay at the house didn't bother me. "She's not much of a partier." While that might have been true, her decision had more to do with not wanting to get caught in a lie than it did her lack of desire to go out.

Technically, I hadn't even wanted to come, but Aaron had made a big deal about how he'd set it all up for me, my last hoorah before starting my job on Monday. I'd eventually given in, mostly to shut him up, and figured I'd just leave early if I wasn't having fun. It was ten, so midnight would give me a solid two hours, and if I was enjoying myself, I'd stay later.

"Tell me again who she is? Do I know her?"

"She's just a friend who's crashing at my place for the weekend." I left out the part that they had met once before—not for any particular reason other than my own personal need to keep her to myself.

"*Oh.*" Insinuation flooded his tone. "A postbreakup booty call of sorts?"

"Something like that."

"Does she know that's all it is?"

I groaned to myself, not really wanting to discuss this with him. "We talked about it."

That made me think about the conversation Tatum and I had had over lunch yesterday. We'd just gotten back from dropping off my paperwork at Wiseman, and to my surprise, she'd made us both sandwiches. We'd needed to discuss everything before any assumptions could be made, yet admitting that I wasn't interested in more than sex had basically justified Kelsey's accusations. I'd never felt like more of an ass than I had then.

"We're both basically dealing with the same shit as far as relationships are concerned," I continued.

The driver parked next to the curb and waited silently until we exited his vehicle. If the thumping of the bass and throngs of people crowding the door were any indication, I wouldn't be here long.

However, Aaron's hookup didn't disappoint. We were escorted to the far side of the dim room, just past the first packed bar. A small balcony-like area sat raised about four and a half feet higher than the main floor, with a few steps that led to the platform. A waist-high rail lined the front of the space, making it semiprivate. I'd seen roped-off sections like this one in the past, and I had always wanted to know what it was like to be in one. Now that I was here, I found it rather depressing—I didn't feel like the rock star I'd thought I would.

I followed him, feeling very much like an outsider as he greeted four other guys in the secluded alcove with man hugs. I didn't know any of them, and while I'd never had much of a problem meeting new people, I simply lacked the enthusiasm to do so tonight. Not to mention, loud music, flashing lights, and a packed club didn't exactly make for the best time to gain new friends.

A small hand settled along my lower back, and for a split second, I thought it might've been Tatum. But when I turned around, I noticed the girl with pink hair who'd hooked us up with the space. It shouldn't have left me disappointed, yet it did.

"I have the bar stocked for you guys tonight," she yelled close to my ear while pointing to a buffet-style table against the side wall. "If you want something that's not there, let me know, and I'll see if I can bring it up. If not, I'll have to get it from one of the bars on the floor, but it won't be complimentary."

I leaned over even more and brought my lips to her ear. "These drinks are free?"

When I saw her bright smile, my night started to look up. However, the change in my mood had nothing to do with her and everything to do with free alcohol, but that didn't need to be admitted out loud.

Two love seats sat in the center of the small space, a table between them and a chair on either side. This area wasn't meant for a crowd, although I wouldn't be surprised if it surpassed its maximum number of occupants on a regular basis. Like now, for instance. Aaron had told me we were meeting up with a *few* of his buddies, yet from my spot on the sofa, I counted nine guys—not including me—and four girls. And that number continued to fluctuate as others came and went from either the restroom or the dance floor.

I enjoyed a few drinks while the company around me continued to rotate. At least Aaron did a decent job *pretending* to make this night about me and my job, so I couldn't really complain. And the alcohol was free. The women I could've done without, probably because I wasn't interested in having them hang on me, though the other guys didn't seem to mind. One thing that was hard to ignore, though, was the lack of female attention Aaron seemed to garner. Back in high school, he'd talked a big game, and I couldn't help but wonder if that was something else he hadn't grown out of.

"You look lonely." A feminine voice came from my side, taking the seat Aaron had just vacated. When I turned to her, she smiled and held up a shot glass. "Here, take one with me."

I accepted the green liquor she offered and brought it to my nose. "What is it?"

"It's called a leg spreader." She giggled at my shocked reaction. "Just take it."

"What's in it?"

She playfully batted my arm and held up her glass, waiting for the friendly clink she assumed I'd give. When I didn't so much as lift my hand, she rolled her eyes and gave in. "It's vodka and Midori."

Well, that would explain the color. I sniffed it once more and then tapped the edge of her glass with mine. We both tossed our drinks back and set the empty shooters on the table in front of us at the same time. I had to admit, it wasn't that bad, although it wouldn't be something I'd ever voluntarily ask for—unless Tatum wanted to give it a try.

Damn . . . I needed something stronger. If I didn't get her off my mind, I'd be a miserable couch potato in the middle of a VIP section at a rather popular nightclub. If that didn't prove how much I'd changed over the years, I wasn't sure what would.

"Did you like it?" she asked, and for the first time since she'd sat next to me, I realized she hadn't even told me her name.

"I've had worse." I was about to introduce myself when she held up one finger and pushed off the cushion. Right before I was about to get up and make a new drink, she returned with two more shots. This time, when she handed me mine, I could tell by the first whiff what it was. "Crown?"

"I'm impressed."

I tipped it back, savored the familiar flavor as it went down smooth, and then set the empty glass on the table at the same time she put hers down. But this time, instead of getting up for more, she waved Sherry over. Wait, that wasn't right. Tatum had told me her name as I'd helped her from the tent to her car, yet I couldn't for the life of me remember what it was. It started with an *S*. Maybe. Probably not.

I didn't care.

I still had no idea who this other chick was, let alone why she was hanging out with the pink-haired girl, who had probably pulled a lot of strings to get this section reserved for Aaron. It seemed these two women were familiar with each other, though. Either that, or I had just become *that* guy—the one who paid more attention to a fly on the wall than the barely covered ass in my face.

I figured I needed to come up with something to call her, since she clearly wasn't interested in introductions. So, Megan Fox it was. With her long jet-black hair, it seemed fitting. Granted, absolutely *nothing* else about this woman resembled the famous actress, but it was either that or Cher, and I had a hard time reconciling the thought of drinking *anything* dubbed leg spreader with the songstress.

I blamed my mother and her Sonny Bono obsession.

"She's going to bring up a tray from the bar, but she said they have to be all different kinds so they won't ask too many questions." Her smile stretched so wide it caused her to squint, and I wondered if knowing the shooter girl had given her some sort of pride.

"Awesome. I'm going to grab another drink. Would you like anything?" It was a good thing she said no, because I wasn't sure I could mix whatever girly shit she had in her cup. Rum and Coke was simple; cocktails that came with a list of ingredients and sexually provocative titles were not. If someone had asked me to make a sex on the beach, I'd likely come back with water infused with salt and a handful of sand.

"She's hot, isn't she?" Aaron nudged my shoulder while nodding toward Megan. "It's her birthday, so we invited her up. Too bad you can't take her home with you . . . unless your *friend* is into that shit. If that's the case, I'm totally in."

"There's so much wrong with that I can't even begin to sort through half of it." Although, I had to admit, the goofy grin that hung lazily from his lips made me laugh, even if it was *at* him. "Do you know who she is? She literally sat down and started pouring liquor down my throat without so much as introducing herself."

"Just call her baby or sweetness or honeypot. Just don't call her tomorrow." He jabbed his elbow into my side and wagged his brows.

"If that's what I used to sound like, I need to go to confession and say about a million Hail Marys. And that might only cover freshman year."

"You're not even Catholic." Aaron shook his head, his shoulders jumping with the laughter that rolled through him. "Come on, man, have a little fun. You're single. It's time to mingle, brother."

"Why do I have to fuck some random chick in order to have fun?"

The childish humor fell from his face. He slapped his hand on my shoulder and stared at me with slightly intoxicated yet sincere eyes. "You don't. But you don't have to act like you have a ball and chain at home, either. Because you don't. Whether you want to admit it or not, you *are* single. I'm just trying to loosen you up some."

I tried to ignore his not-so-subtle reminder of Jen and smiled. "I am loose. I promise."

He squeezed my shoulder and walked away, leaving me to pour my drink alone.

Megan was busy with Shirley when I returned. Rather than sit and watch them converse, I dug my phone out of my pocket to give me something to do so I didn't look so pathetic, and while I had it open, I decided to text Tatum.

Me: Hope you're having fun going through my medicine cabinet and sniffing my boxers.

I hadn't expected a response, yet seeing the bubbles pop up as she typed something back put a smile on my face.

Tatum: I finished with that hours ago. I've moved on to Photoshopping us in various stages of our relationship. Working on the wedding pics now. I should have them all framed and hung by time you get home.

Me: You might want to have Kelsey do that for you. I have standards for my decor, you know. Can't have people see my walls covered in frames that don't match.

I couldn't help myself, nor could I hide the smile that left my cheeks aching.

Tatum: You're so right. Crooked pictures are so last season.

Me: Got any of our kids?

I didn't think about that one until after I sent it, but before I could retract it, I got back a smiley face. And to my surprise, a bubble indicating a response.

Tatum: I tried a few of those sites that generate a picture of a baby by mixing two faces together, but they were all hideous. I hate to say it, but I can't have your babies. I can't risk having an ugly kid.

Tatum: Although, Ashton Kutcher and I are totally gonna procreate.

I couldn't stop the laughter that tore through me.

My thumb hovered over the keyboard, but before I could type out my retort, Megan grabbed my attention by tugging on my arm. My cell dropped into my lap, and a new shot glass filled my hand. Her eyes sparkled with excitement when she said, "I have no idea what any of these are, so it'll be a surprise every time."

The idea of puking all night did *not* appeal to me, and I was old enough to understand what would happen if I mixed different liquors. "Yeah . . . I think I'm going to pass on this one. I have to be able to function tomorrow."

"Oh, come on." She pouted, as if that would somehow have an effect on me. Now, if she'd shown real tears, that might've worked in her favor, but poking out her bottom lip didn't faze me one bit. "Please? It's my birthday, and all my friends ditched me."

"They did? Are you sure it wasn't the other way around? From what I hear, my buddy invited you up, and you came alone."

"Yeah, because they already left."

Okay, so that tugged on my heartstrings a little. "Why'd they leave?"

"Take this shot with me, and I'll tell you."

Fucking curiosity. Got me almost every time.

I agreed, but only to this one. After that, she'd have to find someone else to help her finish these tiny concoctions. I tipped my head back, let the liquid run down my throat, and slammed the glass on the tray at the same time she did.

"So . . . why'd your friends leave you on your birthday?" The similarity alone made me think of Tatum and what her ex had done to her on her own birthday. And that filled my mind with thoughts of what she was doing right now, and if she was doing it in my bed.

"That's how I ended up running into your friend."

"Wait . . . *what*?" There was no way I'd taken a shot in exchange for an answer I didn't hear because I was too busy thinking of Tatum. I used to be way smoother than this. "Repeat that, because I didn't understand what you said."

She eyed me suspiciously, and the instant the corner of her mouth tipped in a knowing smirk, I could predict what would come next. "That'll cost ya," she said with a new glass in her hand for me to take.

Why her friends had ditched her wasn't important, yet that hadn't stopped me from accepting the challenge. And before I knew it, I'd had too many. I'd lost count of how many drinks I'd made myself, let alone how many Aaron had poured for me. Add in the straight liquor this chick had made me choke down in some twisted game of twenty questions, and I'd far surpassed my limit.

At least I was enjoying myself.

I was only this intoxicated because . . . well, I didn't really have a reason, other than it was the only way to get answers I could've gone my entire life without knowing. And as it turned out, I'd taken shots for nothing. One in particular had been to get her to tell me her name. Sure, she'd told me what it was, yet I'd forgotten two seconds later, only realizing it when I'd called her Megan Fox to her face. Shortly after that, she'd been dubbed Foxy Lady. Luckily, she'd seemed flattered by that. And at some point, it'd been shortened to just Foxy.

I was in the middle of talking about Tatum when my phone vibrated against my ass. Had I been able to see straight, I would've recognized the number across the top of the screen and ignored it. Instead, I proceeded to tell the bad influence in the short skirt next to me that it was Tatum, and she needed to be quiet so I could hear her.

A few sentences into the conversation, I sobered up enough to understand who was on the other end of the call. "Where are you? It's so loud I can barely hear anything you're saying."

I plugged one ear with my fingertip and pressed the phone against the other to block out some of the music. She didn't deserve an explanation as to where I was. And she certainly hadn't earned a follow-up question. Although, in my inebriated state, I offered both. "I'm at a club. What do you want?"

"I was hoping you could talk. I'm trying to book a flight to come see you, and I wanted to run the dates by you first to make sure you won't be busy."

"You're doing that this late at night?"

There was a brief pause, followed by a faint giggle. "Jason, it's not even nine here. Which means it's . . . what, a little after eleven thirty where you are?"

I twisted my forearm in front of me and stared at my bare wrist. Under normal circumstances, I would've immediately understood that I hadn't put my watch on before leaving the house. But right now, the news of her possible visit had left me too stunned to realize what I was even doing, let alone the fact that my skin couldn't tell me the time.

"I have to go." When it came to Jen, I didn't need to make up an excuse to end the call.

"Can I at least give you the dates I'm looking at?"

"Text them to me in the morning." And with that, I tapped the red circle on the screen and dropped the phone into my lap.

Two minutes ago, I'd been enjoying my night, laughing and having fun with people I'd likely never see again. And now I sat alone yet surrounded by strangers, my head back and eyes closed as I fought to calm down.

"Are you okay?" Foxy must've had her face close to mine, because the heat of her breath blasted the side of my neck. "Hey, Jason . . . can you hear me? If so, open your eyes. If not, then keep them closed."

Resentment did wonders to the mind. Like right now, the bitterness I harbored toward Jen had me so focused, so in the zone, that everything had become much clearer. Yes, I still wasn't in any shape to drive, and I still couldn't remember anything the woman pressed against my side had told me, but my head no longer felt stuck in a bottle of liquor.

If I hadn't been so pissed over answering Jen's call, I might've kept my eyes closed, just to see what Foxy would do. Yet I didn't, because my ex had stolen every ounce of fun from my night.

I opened my eyes, only to jump in my seat at the close proximity of Shania's face. That was another answer I'd taken a shot for—Pink's name. I thought Marlena had told me, but there was no way that was possible, because my cousin wasn't even here. Anyway, I specifically remembered thinking there was no way I'd forget it again. Yet here I was, the tip of my nose inches from hers, and I couldn't think of it to save my life.

"Oh, thank God," she breathed out, leaning back with a hand over her chest. "I thought you might've passed out or something."

"Unfortunately, no." I glanced around, wondering who else had rushed over to make sure I was still alive. The conclusion was depressing. It appeared the only two people who showed any concern over my well-being were the two women who'd forever remain nameless.

Shawna left but then quickly came back with two bottles of water. "Drink these." She pointed a finger at the woman who'd attached herself to my side and added, "Make sure he finishes those. And when he does, let me know so I can bring him more."

Ignoring the fullness in my stomach, I chugged two-thirds of the first bottle. I only stopped because Nurse Clingy felt the need to wipe my chin every time a drop escaped my mouth. There was only so much a thirty-one-year-old man could take.

"Listen, I appreciate your concern and, um . . . helpfulness. But I think it's time I go home."

"Oh, for sure. I should probably head out, too. Here, let me give you a ride."

I froze and blinked at her in bewilderment. "Hell no. Please tell me you're kidding."

She laughed and waved me off. "Don't worry. I'm totally responsible."

"You've had just as many shots as I have—maybe more, since your birthday celebration started before we met. If you think I'm letting you get behind the wheel, you're insane."

"No." She shook her head and rested her hand on my chest. "I have a driver. He's waiting outside. I'm sure he won't have a problem taking you home, too."

"As much as I appreciate the offer, I'll just get an Uber."

"And pay for a ride rather than accept a free one from me?"

She must've mistaken my silence for acceptance, because she practically jumped off the sofa and reached for my hand. Before I knew it, I was on my feet, following her as she led me toward the steps.

Aaron came out of nowhere and slapped the back of my shoulder. He was such an idiot. He must've noticed my hand in hers, realized we were on our way out together, and assumed it meant we'd wind up naked and sweaty. Technically, there was a very real chance *I* was the one who'd misread the entire situation—the whole "free ride" thing had been slightly vague. For all I knew, she was about to take advantage of me in the parking lot.

I really hoped that wasn't the case.

14

Tatum

As awkward as it had been to be at Jason's house last night without him here, it was a walk in the park compared to waiting around for him to wake up. When he'd stumbled through the front door at around midnight, I'd just finished a word search and was about to go to sleep. Needless to say, my plans had changed.

The chime of an incoming text came from the kitchen. My phone was next to me on the couch, which meant it was Jason's. And as much as I respected boundaries and privacy, by the third alert, I decided to check on it—you know, in case it was important.

> **Jen:** There are two weekends this month I can come. If those don't work for you, let me know and I can look at the calendar for September.

The second message contained the dates for her trip. My chest ached, which pissed me off because I shouldn't have had an emotional reaction to his ex coming to see him. After everything that had happened with Michael, I had no right to be upset. Regardless, the sense of unjustified betrayal didn't go away.

There were five other messages below hers on the lock screen. I didn't know his passcode, so I couldn't see his conversations with these people. And while I didn't necessarily need to read their full transcripts prior to these texts coming in, the unknown ate at me.

Three had come in at the same time—the alerts that prompted me to check his phone in the first place. Two were from Jen, and the third was just a number, no name. Could've been a guy or a girl; although, if I had to guess, I'd say it was a female, based on the punctuation alone.

A *young* female.

Unknown: How are you feeling today?? I had so much fun last night! BTW you left a shoe in the car... I put it by your front door LOL!!

The other four had come in last night, probably while I had tried to get him cleaned up and in bed. I recognized the names, yet I read their messages anyway.

Marlena: I didn't even see you leave. Text me when you get home so I know you made it safe.

Aaron: Cheryl says that chick's loaded. Let me know if you wanna make it a threesome. I swear I won't touch you.

Marlena: Hello?? Don't make me come knocking on your door to make sure you're alive!

Kelsey: Wow. You've really changed all right. Not judging or anything, but I don't think you can say you're not the same player from HS when you've got a girl's hands . . .

If I had any way of getting into his phone, I would have, just to read Kelsey's entire message. The preview wasn't enough, especially when it ended with someone's hands doing something to him. I assumed the girl Kelsey had referred to and the one Aaron had mentioned were one and the same. And if that were the case, I had a good idea of who she was. Well, not personally. But it was more than likely the one he'd been with while he sent me texts and voice messages throughout the night.

No matter what, none of it was my business. And I refused to be the kind of girl who staked a claim on someone or something when I had no right to. So, I set the phone down and turned to go back to the couch. Except I didn't get very far, because the figure in the doorway of Jason's room startled me, making me jump.

"Oh my God, Jay." I clutched my chest and took a few deep breaths to calm my racing heart. "How long have you been standing there?"

The slightest hint of an impending grin settled in the corner of his mouth, though there was a chance I'd imagined it, because it didn't seem to fit with his response. "Long enough to see you snooping through my phone."

I picked it up, turned it over to inspect it from all angles, and then put it back down. With a slap on the counter and wide eyes set on him, I said, "Would you look at that . . . it *is* your phone. I thought it was mine. It chirped, so I came to see who had texted me. No wonder I didn't know what these people were talking about."

"Listen, Tatum . . ." Guilt laced his voice and lined his face. "If it has anything to do with last night—"

"Don't do that." I held up my hand to stop him from unnecessarily explaining. Sure, I wanted to know a few things, but I didn't care to risk giving him the wrong impression. I had meant what I'd said the other day when I told him I wasn't interested in a relationship, and questioning him about his night—or the girl—would only contradict that. "It's none of my business. You don't owe me anything."

He stalked toward me in nothing but a pair of boxer shorts. His eyes held mine with a level of intensity I didn't think I'd ever seen in them. It was hard to take him seriously while parts of his hair stuck straight up and an imprint of wrinkled sheets covered half his face, though.

"Then why were you going through my phone?" His deep morning voice had to be the sexiest sound I'd ever heard.

"I-I wasn't." I handed it to him to prove it. "It's locked, so I couldn't if I tried."

He eyed me suspiciously.

"Honestly, Jay . . . it went off a few times back to back, and I only looked to make sure it wasn't something I needed to wake you up for."

He glanced at the device in his hand, almost as if he were scared to see what it contained, and then brought his attention back to my face. "I had a lot to drink last night, so I have no idea who said what. I know I didn't do anything stupid. Well, anything I'd regret, at least."

"Hey, really, it's totally cool. You sounded like you were having a blast with Foxy Lady." I wagged my brows and smirked. "Although, I'm not sure she appreciated you telling her to pull her skirt down all the time."

His eyes widened in surprise, the green and yellow striations brighter than usual.

"You don't remember sending me voice texts?"

I guess that was all he needed to hear to make him unlock his phone and check his messages. It was incredibly awkward to stand there and watch him, so I went back to the couch, leaving him in the kitchen.

It couldn't have been sixty seconds later when he joined me on the sofa.

"Tatum," he started, but then waited until I faced him. "About that girl . . ."

"Seriously, there's no reason to explain. You wanted a piece of ass; I get it." I shrugged, as if my stomach hadn't been in knots all night. "You don't owe me anything, so please, don't make a big deal about it."

"You're a shit liar." He smiled, though it was weak and proved just how hungover he was.

"Am not. I don't have an issue with you getting it where and when you can. You're single, so there's nothing wrong with it."

"But . . . ?"

Damn him. "I guess I just find it a little distasteful to do that while I'm here. In your bed. But I hate saying that because it's not like you even invited me to stay for the weekend. I have no right to complain about it . . . which is why I had no intention of bringing it up."

"I really wish Kelsey had never said anything to you."

There was something in his tone that made me settle in and lay it all out on the table. "Your cousin doesn't have anything to do with it. If this comes across as a lecture, please know that's not how I mean it, but what she's told me—be it the truth or otherwise—has no bearing on what you do. You went out last night, had a lot to drink, and then did whatever you did. None of which can be blamed on Kelsey."

His eyelids fell, nearly closing, and I wondered if he'd done that on purpose to shield me from his emotions, or if it'd been instinctual, an uncontrollable reaction to defeat. And when they lifted, his gaze unfocused on something over my shoulder, my heart shattered at the lack of brilliance in the color. They were no longer limes on a tree, but rather two uncooked artichokes.

"I'm not blaming anything on her, Tatum. I just wish she hadn't filled your head with this image of me, because it's not who I am. And now, your first assumption is that I fucked her, even though I didn't."

I held my breath and replayed his words in my head. "You didn't?"

"No. That's what I've been trying to tell you."

As much as I wanted to soak in the relief I felt over knowing he hadn't disrespected me like I'd thought, I didn't want him to get the wrong impression—especially since I had no clue where these emotions had come from. So rather than wipe my forehead and reward him with an elated smile, I said, "I appreciate that, Jay. I really do. But I meant it when I said you don't owe me anything."

"Maybe it's not you I'm trying to prove myself to. Maybe it's me. Maybe it's everyone in this damn town who refuses to accept that I'm no longer the grade-A asshole who used to live here."

I couldn't stand watching him beat himself up over something he'd already changed. "Oh, come on. You couldn't have been that bad. At least, I haven't heard anyone say that about you. A player, yes. Womanizer, sure. I've even heard man-whore and skirt chaser a time or two. But asshole? No."

A lazy grin tugged at his lips, and with a flippant roll of his eyes, he reclined against the back of the couch. "You must not have heard it all, then. I was a dick back in the day. And the worst part was I knew it, yet I didn't see any reason to change."

"What kinds of things did you do?"

He ran his palm down his face and set his attention across the room, avoiding any eye contact with me. "Samson, as you know, is a small town. Which means high school is just as small. Sleeping with someone once wasn't an option, unless I wanted to run through the entire school before finishing my freshman year. So, I had my favorites and stayed in their good graces, while rotating between new students and incoming fresh meat. Most of the time, that meant I was with several girls at once."

"*At once?*" Why this was the most shocking of it all was beyond me.

"Well, no." His chest rumbled with laughter, and finally, he met my stare. "Not at the same time. I just mean I'd be with one girl on Friday night, and another on Saturday. And I made sure they didn't know about each other. On the bright side, I never cheated on anyone, because I never actually dated them."

I wondered if he purposely tried to make himself sound like the biggest prick in the world. "Okay, so you were a player. Every high school has one."

"Yeah, except I was that way in college, too. It was just worse then, because there were more women on campus than the entire population of Samson."

"So what changed? Aside from time, obviously."

"I moved to a city I didn't know anyone in, got a job that required me to be an adult, and I started dating. Nothing serious at first, but it was enough to see that I hadn't given anyone a chance because I was too wrapped up in getting laid. Then I met Jen—my ex." Just the sound of her name made my blood pressure rise.

"How'd she tame you?"

He hesitated for a moment with his focus on the ceiling fan. Either he really put a lot of thought into my question, or he'd fallen asleep with his eyes open. Eventually, he sighed, letting me know he was awake, and then readied himself to explain. "To tell you the truth, I'm not sure. We started out as friends, hung out when we could, and before I knew it, we were exclusive."

"Your mom said you guys were together for a while?"

He nodded. "Almost five years."

"Holy shit." I wasn't sure why, but his answer surprised me. I mean, I had heard he'd been with her for a long time, yet with everything else I'd learned about Jason, I guess I'd assumed anything past a couple of months would be considered a serious commitment. "How do two people in Vegas date for almost five years and not wind up at a drive-through wedding chapel?"

His hoarse laughter drifted over me before settling into my chest. Considering how little we knew each other, he had this effortless way of bringing me into an easy conversation. Well, once I stopped freaking out and acting like someone who'd never been allowed in public before.

"Tourists are the only people who actually get married at those places."

"You mean to tell me you never thought about it? About how easy that would be?"

"We talked about marriage, sure. But mostly, it was the idea of it. Like . . . we knew we'd eventually get there, but we hadn't made any plans for when. We never put time limits on it. It was always this thing in our future that we were aware of and never doubted, but it wasn't ever something either of us felt the need to rush out and do. Although, I did end up buying a ring a few months before I left; I just never made it to the actual proposal."

The last time his ex had been brought up, he'd made it very clear he wasn't interested in talking about her or their relationship—or subsequent breakup. Which made this conversation slightly uncomfortable, because I wasn't sure how many more questions I was allowed to ask. So, instead of pushing my luck, I simply said, "She should be happy you never gave her the ring. I can tell you from experience that taking it off isn't fun."

"Have you talked to him since the breakup?"

Well, giving him that easy out had certainly backfired.

"Sort of—he finally pulled his head out of his ass and apologized, or as close as he'll get to one. Only took six months."

"I hope you told him to shove it."

I stared blankly at him for a moment, noticing the way his jaw clenched. I refused to believe he felt any emotion at all over whether I'd take Michael back, which pretty much meant he must've developed lockjaw. "You're telling me if your ex moved here right now, you wouldn't take her back? If she begged and pleaded and told you she messed up?"

"Nope. Not for a second." His tone alone told me he meant exactly what he said. "I don't give second chances."

"Why not?"

"What's the point? If it failed the first time, why offer someone the opportunity to ruin it again? It shouldn't take someone very long to realize they made a mistake and try to fix it. If I fuck something up, I know immediately. It doesn't take weeks or months to see that what I did was wrong."

"Why didn't she move with you? What was her reason?" Thank God we were back to talking about him instead of me. I'd learned my lesson, and from now on, I planned to just keep asking questions until he stopped answering them.

"She's a Vegas showgirl. Kind of hard to get a job doing that here."

I crossed my arms over my stomach and bent forward, unable to control the hilarity that kept me from taking a breath. "Back up a minute." I fought to calm down long enough to get out a full sentence. "Your one and only long-term relationship was with a stripper? And you can't fathom why your cousin thinks you haven't changed?"

He blinked for a moment, as if he'd never thought of that before. "That would be a valid argument, except she wasn't a stripper. She danced in shows, not on a pole. Two completely different things. But don't change the subject. Would you take *your* ex back?"

Guess my time was up. The spotlight was back on me.

"I don't know. As long as he's not single, I refuse to waste my time contemplating what I *would* do if and when they ever broke up."

"You shouldn't waste your time at all," he mumbled, practically to himself. "He's playing you, and you're allowing it."

That comment was a surefire way to put me on defense. "How am I allowing anything?"

"It's obvious he's keeping you on a string. The fact that you don't know if you'd take him back is proof of that. It's been over six months—he's moved on, yet here you are, refusing to close the door. If you think he doesn't realize all this, you have a lot to learn."

"People make mistakes, Jay. And sometimes, it takes them a little longer to realize it."

"In my opinion, second chances are worthless. They get passed around like condoms in a high school health class, except they never protect anyone against getting hurt by the same person again."

"He's the only guy I've ever been with." I swallowed hard, unsure if I should've admitted that or not. "I don't know anything but him."

"Wait." He moved closer, caging me between his arms as he searched my eyes. "What do you mean he's the only guy you've been with?"

"I guess that's technically not true anymore. But aside from you, he's the only one. Maybe you don't offer second chances or waste your time with the same person because you've been with so many. But I haven't. It's hard to turn off that switch when I don't have the same kind of experience as you."

Understanding lit his gaze, and regret flowed past his lips with a sigh. "I'm so sorry, Tate. I had no idea." He brought his hand to my face and stroked my cheek with his thumb. The faintest smile played on his lips, though it shone brightly in his eyes. "Although, that doesn't mean I've changed my mind about second chances. I still don't think you should give him one . . . he doesn't deserve you."

Leave it to Kelsey to interrupt our moment with a text.

"Shit. She's asking what time my plane lands. What should I tell her?"

"You haven't looked up what flights are coming in from where?"

"No . . . why would I do that?"

"Umm . . . I don't know, Tatum, maybe so your lie might be a little more believable?"

Crap. I couldn't even lie the right way. All the fibs I'd told over the last week would catch up with me if I didn't start thinking like a con man.

I'd been stuck in the bathroom for almost an hour, waiting for Marlena to leave. As it turned out, even after reading her texts this morning, he'd never replied to let her know he wasn't dead in a ditch somewhere. So, she'd stopped by to check on him.

It was a sweet gesture and all, though I might've appreciated it more had she called first. Instead, she just showed up. I was about to step into the shower when the doorbell had rung, and being the paranoid person that I was, I'd waited for him to answer it before turning on the water. In the unlikely chance it was Kelsey, I hadn't wanted her questioning why his shower was running without him in it. And thank God I had, because it turned out to be his *other* cousin.

Unfortunately, I couldn't just walk into his room and put my clothes back on or wait on his bed for her to leave, because he'd left his bedroom door wide open. Which meant I was stuck in the bathroom with nothing but a towel wrapped around my body and a cabinet full of various hair and skin products without labels to occupy me.

Aside from painting my toenails with an odd shade of brown, I also shaved my legs with one of Jason's razors that I'd found in a drawer—an old razor with dull blades that ended up taking off a few layers of skin. Lotion was a necessity at this point, and even though I hadn't expected to find any in a man's bathroom, I searched anyway. As luck would have it, I discovered a small jar beneath the sink.

It was *not* lotion.

I had no idea what it was, but if I had to guess, I'd say it was creamy battery acid.

It burned, and I couldn't even turn on the water beyond a slow trickle to remove it. Instead, I used part of my towel to scrub it off. If that hadn't helped calm the pain, there was a very high chance I might've resorted to bathing in the toilet.

With more time to kill—and desperately needing to take my focus off my legs—I decided to test out some of his hair products. A small voice in the back of my mind had questioned why a guy with relatively short hair would have all this, but I ignored it. It could've very well belonged to his ex, and he'd accidentally packed it when he left . . . and then stored it in case she ever asked for it back. That theory had sounded far better in my head during a very desperate moment of boredom. To anyone with the ability to think clearly . . . not so much.

I was seconds away from using a bar of soap to write the song lyrics for Alanis Morissette's "Ironic" on the mirror when the bathroom door opened. Thank God, because aside from the chorus, I didn't know the words. Talk about ironic. *That* could've been embarrassing.

"Did you do that on purpose?" I held the towel close to my chest and pulled myself to my feet.

Jason squinted and pursed his lips. "Do what on purpose?"

"Not warn me when your cousin showed up?"

He shrugged, and I imagined seventy-two different ways to dismember him.

"What would've happened if I'd been in the shower?"

"I don't know, Tatum . . . I'm too tired to think of these things. Can't we just be happy that you weren't and she didn't catch you?" His eyes pleaded with me to take it easy on him. And with a face like his, it was hard to be mad.

"Fine. But now I have even less time to get ready to leave for the airport. I'd tell Kelsey my flight was delayed, but then I'd have to look up information for that lie, too. And I think we've already established that I suck at falsifying alibis."

He took a moment to appraise me and then pulled his fist to his mouth, clamping a knuckle between his teeth. "I'd ask what you did to entertain yourself this whole time . . . but I don't need to. What did you put in your hair?"

I glanced to the basket on the counter and took note of all the products. "Dry shampoo, leave-in conditioner, some kind of oil . . ." I moved a few things around to see if I had missed anything. "And a small amount of gel—because, you know, I didn't want my hair to be gross if I used too much."

He stepped into the bathroom and closed the door. "Well, for starters, I think about the only thing you used that's made for hair was the gel. The bad news is, I'm not entirely sure what the other stuff is."

"I'm sorry, do what?"

"Let's start over. Which one did you say was the dry shampoo?" He took the aerosol can with the torn label from my hand and set it on the vanity. "Yeah, that's starch. What about the leave-in conditioner?" Again, he studied the small tube I handed him and then set it down. "That would be the acne wash I used in middle school—don't judge, it still works to dry up the occasional zit. I take it this is the oil?" By the time he picked up the small glass bottle with the dropper inside, I was scared to hear what that was.

"If it'll make me bald, just lie to me and tell me it's vitamin E."

His grin stretched wider as he shook his head. "Nope. But don't worry; it won't do anything bad to your hair. I use it on my skin when I have an allergic reaction. It was something my mom got me years ago from a woman she worked with, and so far, it's the only thing aside from a prescription that works."

I chose to take that as a good sign and ignore the fact that I had sprayed my roots with starch and combed face wash through the strands. Although, we still hadn't addressed whatever chemical it was that I'd slathered my legs with. "There's a small black jar under the sink that at one time contained lotion . . . any idea what's in it now? Because it's most certainly *not* what the label claims to be."

He squatted down and peered into the cabinet. When his eyes met mine again, they were filled with confusion. "Why? What'd you use it for?"

"Well, I shaved my legs with one of your razors, and when I finished ridding myself of about nine layers of skin, I thought it'd be best if I moisturized them."

He winced, which wasn't normally a good sign. "At least you used that one correctly. But I can't imagine that felt great. It's aftershave balm. That shit burns."

"I don't think the word *burn* accurately describes the pain. I'd compare it more to death—of the slow, torturous variety."

Jason closed the cabinet door, but before he stood, he noticed my toes. "Where'd you get nail polish from?"

"In one of the baskets in there. I assume it was Jen's that somehow ended up in your stuff."

"Do you read the directions before you use anything?" He laughed and pulled himself off the floor. "I knew I recognized that color. It's the same as my old kitchen cabinets, which means you more than likely painted your nails with wood corrector. It's meant to cover scratches without using filler."

At least one of us found the humor in this.

By the way . . . it was *not* me.

"In my defense, you keep things for decades and the labels are either ripped, faded, or don't exist. Kind of difficult to read directions that *aren't there*."

"Come on, babe." He took my hand and led me to the shower. "Let's get you cleaned off."

"I think I'll need more than soap and water to fix all this."

He tugged his shirt over his head and winked. "I just might have something that'll help."

In Jason's world, helping me didn't equate to removing the wood stain from my toes or properly washing my hair. I had to give the man credit, though . . . by the time I stepped out of the shower, I felt so good I no longer thought about my burning legs or cared that my roots were still stiff as a board.

15

Jason

"You're wearing half your burrito on your face." Laughter shook my shoulders as I watched Tatum wipe her mouth with the back of her hand. "Maybe if you worried more about where you were aiming that thing and less about who might see you with me, you might not have that problem."

She curled her top lip, silently telling me to shut up.

Between starting my job and Tatum going back to hers, we hadn't had a chance to get together. I'd figured this art festival would be the perfect way to hang out before she started her Saturday dinner shift. Plus, I'd specifically chosen to meet up here knowing Kelsey was busy with work, which meant Tatum wouldn't have to worry about getting caught.

Unfortunately, that hadn't stopped her from scanning the crowd every two seconds.

"Are you seriously that worried about someone seeing us together? You're starting to give me a complex. First it was the club last weekend when you decided to stay home. Now it's—"

"You can't throw that in my face. It was a darn good thing I didn't go, considering Kelsey *did* show up—as well as Marlena—despite your constant reassurances that I wouldn't know anyone."

"I still don't believe they were there."

"Jay . . ." She cocked her head to the side. "You had a full-blown conversation with Marlena."

"I don't remember it, so it didn't happen."

"Well, Kelsey certainly remembers it, as well as the girl you left with." The flash of mirth in her eyes told me she was only teasing, though that didn't stop the foreign feeling of regret from washing over me.

I rolled my eyes and ate the last bite of my burrito—the one she had pretty much forced me to get because all the other food here didn't appeal to her. Somehow, I wasn't sure how a ball of grease contained in a flour shell and decorated with limp lettuce seemed appetizing, but who was I to argue with the food snob?

"We have about"—I checked my watch, noticing the time and doing mental math—"twenty more minutes before you have to leave for work. I don't know about you, but I need to walk this meal off."

Tatum leaned back in her chair and rubbed circles over her stomach. "I think I'm too full to walk. I feel bloated."

Ignoring the fact that it looked like she lovingly caressed a baby bump rather than a full belly, I added, "I'm not entirely sure how you could be stuffed. You spent most of the time on the lookout instead of eating—not to mention, I'm fairly certain you got more on your face than in your mouth."

One brow arched perfectly while she quirked her mouth to the side. As much as I loved her initial awkwardness, seeing the sass she offered once she became comfortable had to be my favorite. Even after last weekend, it took her a bit to shed the uneasiness around me, though I kind of liked it that way. It proved I still affected her.

"Keep that up, Sherlock, and I just might sleep in my own bed tonight." She might've sounded convincing, yet the sparkle in her raven eyes paired with the slight upturn at the corners of her glistening lips told a very different story. There was no way she was sleeping alone tonight.

"Sherlock?" I asked, ignoring the rest of her idle threat. "Where'd that come from?"

"Watson." The lilt added to the end of my last name echoed the nonverbal *duh*.

I shrugged, giving her credit for the creative twist. "Touché."

We rose and meandered toward a booth with silk scarves hanging from posts on either side.

It contained nothing interesting, so rather than browse the items sprawled across the top, I stood back and watched Tatum. She intently studied a necklace made from twisted wire that created a tree with small colored stones meant to resemble leaves. She picked up a blue one, held it close to her face, and then set it down in exchange for a pink one. The soft grin lining her lips as she examined each piece captivated me; I could've stayed right here all day just to see her expression change with each item she picked up.

Yet it didn't last long—much like most moments that involved Tatum. When she set down the pink necklace, she happened to glance up, becoming alarmed at the sight of something on the aisle across from us. A gasp hitched in her throat seconds before she twisted herself in the dangling scarves, leaving her body visible only from the waist down.

It was a rather comedic sight, especially once I realized what—or *who*—had sent her into hiding. I didn't have to look farther than a young redhead, probably in her mid- to late twenties, who grazed the booth behind the one we were at. She seemed to be eying whatever was on display at the stand, so she had her attention down, shielding most of her face from our view, though I could say without question that it was *not* Kelsey.

"You're going to get us kicked out if you keep doing this," I leaned closer to the silk cocoon that protected Tatum. "Stop freaking out. She's not here; I promise."

Slowly, she uncurled herself from the fabric and peeked over the table. When she realized I was right, her shoulders dropped, relief swarming her like a warm blanket on a cold night. Still, I knew she wouldn't fully relax until we left, until she could be certain that Kelsey wouldn't catch her out in public with me.

Dismissing the ridiculously large pendants as if she hadn't spent the last few minutes ogling them, she moved along, stopping at another stand to admire something else. I followed, biting my tongue since she didn't seem eager to discuss her completely unwarranted paranoia, and found something worth taking a look at.

My mom had collected ornaments of angels for as long as I could remember, so when I spotted one dangling from a red ribbon, I picked it up to check the price on the yellow sticker. I was the world's worst gift giver. Regardless of how cheap something was, I had a hard time purchasing it without someone else's opinion—that way, if it sucked, I could blame it on their bad advice rather than my bad taste. I turned toward Tatum with the ornament in my open palm, but before I could ask what she thought of it, I swallowed my question in favor of asking a different one.

"What's wrong?" I couldn't ignore the way she was tugging at her left hand, her face beet red. Nor did I miss the protruding vein on her temple. "Tatum?"

Finally, she released the air that she'd trapped in her lungs in a wave of defeat. Without shifting her stance, she cut her eyes to the side and peered in my direction. "It's nothing. I got this."

It was obvious that Tatum, in no uncertain terms, did *not* have whatever "this" was.

"Oh yeah? So you're good? I'm thinking we should shop around some more before we have to leave. So many things to see, so little time. What do you say?"

She glanced at the figurine in my hand. "Aren't you going to buy that?"

"Nah. If I still want it when we're done checking everything else out, I'll come back." I just stood there and imagined the wheels turning in her head in a desperate attempt at an excuse. This woman could provide hours of entertainment.

"Someone might buy it before then. You should totally get it." Then she snapped her attention to my face, her head now turned my way with her eyes wide and expressive. "Actually, you might want to think about it some more—you know, *really* make sure it's what you want. But you shouldn't walk away from it, because by the time you make up your mind, it'll likely be gone."

She hadn't dropped her hands, and her right still clutched the left. Whatever she was trying to keep from me had something to do with that, and considering she stood in front of a tray of silver rings, I assumed she'd gotten one stuck on her finger.

So, I did the only thing I could think of to get her to drop the act. I held out the trinket and asked, "What do you think of this for my mom?"

Tatum regarded the kneeling angel with detailed wings for a moment and then nodded, not once taking it from me. "I think it's nice. But something as sentimental and precious as that should require a lot of thought on your part. Seriously, Jay . . . take all the time you need. I'm in no rush."

I twisted my wrist to check the time on my watch. "Technically, you should be. You have to leave for work in a few minutes."

Her chin dropped, practically hitting her chest, at the same time her arms fell to her sides. Defeat clung to her posture like dew on grass, and if the whole thing hadn't been so comical, I might've felt bad for her. Finally, she held up her left hand, not once raising her head, and mumbled, "I can't get it off."

Just below the knuckle on her fourth finger sat a braided silver band adorned with a clear heart-shaped stone that I knew without a doubt was not a diamond. Surprisingly, it looked good on her dainty hand, as long as you didn't pay attention to the swelling and redness caused by her frantic tugging.

I grabbed her wrist to get a better view. "How'd you get it on in the first place?"

"It went over the knuckle just fine, but when I tried to take it off, it wouldn't budge."

"That might have something to do with the massive amount of salt in those burritos," I muttered under my breath as I attempted to twist the ring. It barely moved, so I didn't dare do anything else, knowing it would only make it worse. "Do you happen to have any lotion?"

At that, the woman behind the table perked up. She lifted a small bottle of what I assumed to be lotion and squirted a pump just above the band. And while Tatum just stood there, shoulders sagging and a pout lining her lips, I proceeded to rub the creamy lubricant into her skin. It didn't do any good, though. I tried to twist it again, and while it moved a little more than before, it still wasn't enough to get it off.

"Looks like you just became the new owner of a fake diamond ring."

"It's recycled glass," the woman corrected, more than likely offended by my remark. "I made it myself. And the metal is sterling silver."

Or recycled aluminum . . .

"I can't buy it, Jay," Tatum whispered with her head cocked toward me.

"What?"

"I said . . ." She clamped her teeth shut, jaw clenched tight. "*I can't buy it.*"

Leaning forward to prevent the now nosy lady from overhearing, I brought my lips close to Tatum's ear. I had to force myself to ignore the scent of her hair and the memories it brought to mind. "I got that part . . . but why?"

"I only had ten dollars in cash on me, and I spent that on lunch."

A growl reverberated within my chest. "Had you just let me pay like I'd tried to do, this wouldn't be an issue."

"Actually, it would. The ring costs more than ten dollars. So either way, I wouldn't have enough regardless of who bought lunch." The satisfied smirk on her face from being "right" made me laugh, although she didn't appear to appreciate that very much.

I relented and straightened my spine, turning my attention to the saleswoman. "I'd like to buy the ring and this ornament." I set the angel down in front of her and tugged my wallet from my back pocket.

After handing the lady cash and retrieving the small gift bag containing the figurine, I grabbed Tatum's left hand and led her out to the parking lot. She fought me for a moment—either insecure over someone seeing us or distracted by the discomfort of having something cutting off blood flow to her finger, I wasn't sure which—but she eventually gave in and pulled herself closer to my side.

"Just leave it alone, and it'll come off. If you keep messing with it, the swelling won't go down, and you'll just make it worse. And when you do try again, put oil on both sides of the band before twisting it side to side. That'll get the oil beneath it, which will help it slide off easier."

"I'll pay you back. I swear." Her voice was weak and sad.

"Don't worry about it, Tatum. It's not a big deal. Trust me . . . it didn't set me back. After all, I'd planned on covering lunch, but you wouldn't let me. So I'm fine. Let's call it even and be done with it."

She scoffed and slid her hand from mine just as we reached her car. "I'd hardly say this is equal to a burrito. I feel awful that you had to buy me a freaking ring just because I was stupid enough to put it on and get it stuck. I'm sure that makes me look like a . . . like a . . ."

I pinched her chin between my thumb and forefinger and tilted her head back until her eyes met mine. "It doesn't make you look like anything, so stop thinking that. Okay?"

"Jay, don't be delusional. We agreed to keep this casual, have fun, nothing serious. Yet so far, I've stayed at your house for an entire weekend, and you just bought me a ring." She held up her hand and pointed to the jewelry that sat just below a very painful-looking knuckle. "And not just any ring . . . one with a stone that most people might assume is a diamond."

"It's recycled glass, Tatum," I corrected with the same terse tone the woman had used earlier. "Get it right. You wouldn't want to offend anyone." I smiled, even though she didn't. "Come on, babe. It's fine. I swear. Don't worry about what other people will think."

"Easier said than done. I work with a very nosy group of gossipers."

"Okay? And? You've made it impossible for *anyone* to know about me, so what does it matter? Aren't they all aware that you're single?"

"Yeah . . . except there's the fact that you brought flowers, which no one will shut up about."

I shrugged, not caring what anyone said about that. Tatum and I knew what it meant, and that was all that mattered. "Stop worrying about shit you can't control. Just go to work, feed the hungry, and when you're done, I'll take your mind off everything else. Got it?"

A wave of pale pink took over her neck before licking its way to her cheeks.

"Now hurry so we can get to the good stuff." I swatted her hip, unable to reach her backside with the way she leaned against her car door. "If I have to jack off to the memory of you one more time, I think my dick might protest until he gets the real thing."

Tatum's head jerked to the side, her eyes wide as if concerned someone had overheard me. But I didn't care. There was no point in hiding how much I loved being inside her; I wasn't ashamed. Yet it seemed she had a different opinion. She slapped my arm and silenced me with a glare. "Discretion goes a long way, Jason."

Dismissing her lecture, I wrapped my arms around her shoulders and pressed my lips to her forehead. "See you tonight." Then I released her and stepped away to head toward my own car not far from hers.

It only took one backward glance, catching her watch me as I walked away, to halt my exit. The desire burning in her eyes lit an identical inferno low in my stomach. While I knew I couldn't have my way with her here in the parking lot, I could at least leave her with a taste of what to expect later—as well as a way to ensure she didn't change her mind about coming to my place after work.

I eliminated the space between us with a few long strides, coming to a stop in front of her with her face trapped between my palms. My hips met hers, pinning her to the SUV, and the second she held her breath, I covered her mouth with mine.

The most surprising part of it all was that she didn't once attempt to push me away. Instead, she fisted the sides of my shirt, holding me to her, and parted her lips to deepen the kiss. The second her tongue met mine, my dick twitched, and I immediately pulled away. What had started as a way to guarantee she'd end the night in my bed had quickly turned into impatience to have her writhing beneath me.

"I'm going to go home and sleep until your shift is over. There's no way I'll survive watching the clock until then. Plus, spending the day napping will give me plenty of energy to make you come all night."

"You always say the sweetest things, Jay. Maybe you should look into writing greeting cards. I'm sure there's a market out there for 'Thinking of you . . . naked' and 'Sorry for your loss . . . of clothing.' *Oh!*" Excitement danced in her eyes when she added, "What about 'Congrats . . . on getting me off'? I'm sure that would be a big seller."

"Yeah, I'll get on that while you're at work." I leaned in to kiss her again, but at the last second, I decided to nip her bottom lip, tugging on it before letting it go. "Now hurry. I can't wait to congratulate you . . . on getting me off."

Her soft laughter danced in the breeze behind me as I walked away, refusing to look back. I knew if I did, she'd never make it to work . . . and we'd never make it out of the back seat of her car.

16

Tatum

What had started out as a full stomach quickly became uncomfortable bloating. And by the time I got to work, it'd turned into nausea.

As I got busy setting up my station for what I knew would be a chaotic shift, I continued to rub my belly through my opened chef's coat, hoping for some sort of relief before things got going in the kitchen. A few people had stopped to chitchat, but after getting short, dismissive responses, they all left me alone.

Except Rebecca.

"You doing okay, Tatum?" Her focus bounced between my face and where I held my hand to my stomach.

I glanced down, unable to miss just how bloated I was. It was disgusting, really. I'd never had the kind of flat stomach every girl aims for, but this unsightly protrusion was definitely *not* part of my normal figure. I could just picture the burrito growing and expanding in my abdomen until it literally exploded, which made me shudder. "Lunch didn't agree with me."

Rather than respond, she grabbed my hand away from my stomach. I knew the moment she noticed the ring on my left finger. Her wide eyes brightened so much it looked like someone had plugged her into a wall, light shining through the brilliant blue. "When did you get this?"

Pulling my hand away, I mumbled, "Today."

She clapped her hands, which made me want to do the same with a couple frying pans . . . on either side of her head. Her enthusiasm was too much to take on a normal day, let alone one where I felt like vomiting all over the place. "It's so pretty. I bet there's a story behind it."

Vic's harsh tone made Rebecca scurry away when he barked, "Stations. Now."

I couldn't have been more thankful for his militant demand.

As much as I didn't want to, I had to button my coat. At least it hid the disgusting bubble gut I had going on, but it made me so hot I wasn't sure I'd last without running to the toilet, especially once the burners got going.

Lynn, my station assistant, got started on the garlic while I frantically tried to catch up. I'd spent too much time talking and not enough filling the ramekins with spices or getting my utensils the way I liked them. Unfortunately, I still hadn't finished the task before I had to excuse myself to the bathroom.

After the second time leaving the burners to empty my stomach in the toilet, Brooke, the sous chef, slid to my side in front of the stove. "You all right, Tatum?"

"Yeah, I just ate something bad for lunch, and it upset my stomach."

"Do you need to go home?"

"No." Yes, but I wasn't about to admit that. Not less than a week after returning from suspension. "I'll be okay. I just need to sip ginger ale, and I'll be fine."

Brooke smiled and rubbed a few circles on my upper back before returning to her post at the back end of the pass. Which was where she was when I took off for the bathroom for the third time in less than thirty-five minutes. Except this time, it wasn't Brooke who towered over me after I'd freshened up and slipped back into my spot in front of the burners.

It was Victor.

"You need to go home." Not a question or even a suggestion. Just his typical command with zero room to argue.

Yet that didn't stop me from trying. "I promise, Vic . . . I'll be all right. There can't possibly be anything left in my stomach. That should be all of it."

"It's not up for debate, Tatum." He crossed his arms over his broad chest and nailed me in place with a single glare. "If this is more than your lunch, I can't risk you spreading it to the rest of my staff—or, hell, the customers through the food you're cooking. I don't care to turn on the evening news and hear about some outbreak that's hospitalized dozens of people; the only thing they all have in common is eating dinner here tonight. Go home."

"Vic . . ." I pleaded, my posture slumped due to defeat and just overall weakness after losing about thirty pounds of undigested food and bile in the toilet. "I wasn't here last Saturday. I can't afford to miss another weekend dinner shift."

"Tonight's different. You're not walking off the line. You aren't abandoning your post. You're sick, and you need to go home and rest. See how you feel Monday morning, and if you still aren't any better, give Brooke a call and go see a doctor." If he didn't watch it, people could've easily gotten the impression that he had a soft spot. Although, we all knew better.

Conceding, I walked away. The entire time my feet shuffled down the hallway, I prayed I could escape without catching Amanda's attention. For once, it seemed luck was on my side, because when I peered around the corner to the hostess stand, she wasn't there. I spotted her in the middle of the room, seating a table for two, so I quickly darted out the front doors before she noticed me.

When I climbed behind the steering wheel and proceeded to strip out of the coat that felt more like a sauna than a piece of clothing, I remembered I'd agreed to spend the night at Jason's. The small bag that I had packed for the morning taunted me from the front seat. As much as I tried to ignore it, I desperately wanted to sleep next to him tonight. The thought of curling up in my bed alone just made everything worse.

I dialed his number and listened to it ring through the speakers with my head resting on the back of the seat. "Hey. Everything all right?" Somehow, his voice sounded even deeper through Bluetooth.

"I'd be better if people would stop asking me that."

"What happened?" His concern was so palpable that it flooded the interior of my SUV and drowned me in the heaviness of the emotion.

"I've been sick since I got here, and they finally sent me home after I ran to the bathroom for the third time. It's probably best if I stay at my apartment tonight. In the event this isn't just a case of Mexican food gone bad, I wouldn't want to give it to you."

"Don't worry about me, Tatum. Come over. We'll put on movies and relax."

That sounded like a dream. "What if you get sick?"

A whispered chuckle floated across the line right before he admitted, "I can guarantee it's the lunch and nothing else. Trust me—you don't have to worry about me getting it, too. I already have it. I've been chugging the pink shit for hours, and I think it's finally starting to work."

"Oh my God, you have Pepto?" I probably sounded like a druggie, excited by the mention of her favorite party pill. "Do you have any left for me?"

"Only if you come and stay the night."

"You had me at 'pink shit.'"

I woke up with my forehead pressed against the warm, hard wall of Jason's chest. It took me a moment to put all the pieces together, but once I recalled leaving work last night, coming here and curling up with Jay while we watched a couple of movies, and then falling asleep in his arms, I settled into him and breathed in his natural, clean scent.

He stirred a little before tightening his arm around me. It was odd waking up like this, considering the other times I'd stayed over, we'd separated at some point during the night and settled into opposite sides of the bed with plenty of room for another body between us. As much as I hated to cuddle—personal space and all—I enjoyed being trapped in his embrace immensely. It didn't suffocate me like I was used to. In fact, I felt safe in his arms, comforted . . . precious. It was enough to make me burrow into him and never want to leave the cocoon.

"How are you feeling?" he asked, his voice hoarse and scratchy from sleep.

"I think it's finally over. You?"

"So far so good."

When I lifted my leg to hook it over his hip, I was rewarded with his glorious erection. Considering I'd technically stayed the night to get laid, and that hadn't happened, I decided to take advantage of the situation. I pressed my lips to the bare skin just below his clavicle and slipped my hand between us to tease him through his shorts.

"I think I'm still asleep," he mumbled into my hair. "This feels very much like a wet dream."

I trailed the tip of my tongue to his neck while dipping my hand past the waistband to wrap my fingers around his silky shaft. "I'll be quiet, promise."

His laughter flooded my ear as he rolled on top of me, settling between my legs. He propped himself up on his elbows and peered down at me, the undeniable hunger in his vibrant eyes holding me hostage. "What if I don't want you to be quiet?"

That was all it took to spur me into action. I straightened my legs enough to shimmy my pajama bottoms to my thighs, and then curled them back against either side of his body. It wasn't how I would've preferred to do it, but by this point, as long as he had access, I didn't care.

Using my heels, I shoved his gym shorts past the roundness of his ass. Then I stretched my arm between us to take hold of him and line him up where I needed him the most.

Jay dropped his face into the crook of my neck at the same time he rolled his hips inward, sliding into me like he belonged there. But that was all I got from him—one thrust, followed by the sight of his panicked eyes when he lifted his head.

"Wait, babe. I don't have a condom."

"I don't care, Jay. I need you. Right now. I need you to move and take care of this ache because you're the only one who can." I had no idea where that had come from, though it was pointless to question it. He had a way of bringing out a brazen side of me I never knew existed.

"And I will; just let me grab a—"

I dug my heels into the backs of his thighs and grabbed two handfuls of his ass cheeks, more than likely marking the flesh with my nails. It was enough to shut him up and force him to drive into me without making me beg again.

My orgasm came on quick, peaking and tapering off just as fast. And once I came down from the high, blowing out the breath I'd held in my lungs, he tried again to press pause in favor of a rubber. In a move completely unlike anything I would've ever done before, I wrapped my arms and legs around him, preventing him from breaking free.

"Screw the condom, Jay, and just fuck me already," I panted breathlessly, begging him to keep going. Had I taken a second to realize that I probably sounded like one of those girls who tried to get knocked up to trap a man, then I might've relented and allowed him to get the protection he clearly wanted. But I didn't take a second. Nor did I think twice about what I had asked of him. All I could focus on was the building of the next orgasm that taunted my lower abdomen.

It seemed he'd lost interest in it as well. Rather than argue or pull away, he picked up the pace and slammed into me with even, rhythmic thrusts, hitting the spot that I swore had been made for him and him alone.

I pressed my head into the pillow, elongating my neck and chasing him with my hips. Ecstasy was right there, within reach. I squeezed my eyes shut, teetering on the edge yet unable to let go and give in to the explosion of warmth. Jay must've sensed my struggle, because he softly captured my earlobe between his teeth and slipped one hand beneath my shirt until he palmed my breast. I no longer fought him on that—not only because I wouldn't win, but also because he'd taught me just how amazing it was.

He simultaneously pinched my beaded nipple and bit down a little harder on my earlobe. In an instant, I was flooded with endorphins and drowning in warm tingles that spread throughout my body like a wildfire. I knew he loved it when I used his name in the throes of an orgasm, but I couldn't manage anything other than strangled gasps of air seeping past my constricted vocal cords.

In fact, I was so consumed by what he'd given me that I completely missed his erratic thrusts, the way he buried himself in me as deep as he could go, and the shudders that overtook his body during his own dive off the cliff. It wasn't until we were both panting, our chests heaving as we fought for air, that I realized he'd gotten off, too.

Although, had I missed that, I wouldn't have made it past the "*Shit*" he hissed into my neck. Or the "*Fuck*" he growled as he lifted himself onto his elbows. And the way he stared at the sliver of skin beneath the hem of my shirt while gritting out "*Son of a bitch*" certainly wouldn't have gone unnoticed.

I was almost afraid to say anything, except a small voice in the back of my head warned me that this had something to do with the condom I'd refused to let him use. "It's okay, Jay." When his head snapped back, I held his face in my hands and did my best to console him with my eyes. "I'm sorry; I don't know what I was thinking. If it helps any, I'm on birth control—and not the kind I have to remember to take."

"As much as I appreciate that—and yes, it does help—it still leaves us both open to other dangers. I've never *not* worn a condom, so this is . . . well, while it was fucking amazing, it'd be a lie if I said it doesn't freak me out."

I nodded, unable to do anything else. "I know. I'm clean, though. After my failed engagement, Kelsey convinced me to go get tested, just in case he hadn't been faithful during our relationship. I'm hoping the fact that you say you've never done this without one means you're good, too?"

Even if I hadn't heard my own voice, the softness in his eyes would've made me pick up on the fear that laced my words. His lids fell halfway just as he lowered his forehead to mine, the tips of our noses touching. "Yeah, I'm clean, too."

It would be stupid and reckless to assume we were both in the clear, regardless of how slim our chances were of contracting something and passing it to the other, but I had to admit, hearing him tell me that calmed my nerves.

"I promise I won't make you do that again." I tried to smile, though it was likely weak and unconvincing. "I don't know what I was thinking."

He pulled his bottom lip into his mouth and dragged it out. "I don't know, baby . . . I didn't think being with you could get better. Now that I've experienced just how amazing you feel without anything between us, I'm not sure I can bring myself to use them again with you."

"That deserves a serious conversation, one that doesn't take place while you're still inside me." I turned my head to the side to read the clock next to his side of the bed. "And considering we have to be at your aunt's house in a little over an hour, I think it'll have to wait until later."

He winked and pressed a chaste kiss to my temple. "I'm going to need a miracle to get me through lunch without fucking you in a closet."

Oh, if only he knew how easily I'd give in if he tried.

17

Jason

Tatum had left my house twenty minutes before I did, and it had taken everything in me to wait as long as I had. If I cared, I would've worried that I had become obsessed with her. Still, I'd gone an entire week with only a few calls and texts rather than having her in my bed. After this morning, I wasn't sure I'd be able to last that long again.

Something needed to give with our schedules—either that, or she needed to stop worrying so much about Kelsey and what she would do if she found out. Granted, it wasn't like I had any desire to deal with my cousin and her phobia when it came to men, but I wouldn't let her stand in my way when it came to Tatum.

I'd just crossed the bridge into Samson when my phone rang, yet my cell had slipped between the seat and the center console, and I was once again reminded that I hadn't programmed any numbers into Bluetooth. The display on the car's navigation screen simply read "Incoming Call."

I pressed the green button on the steering wheel and answered, only to groan when Jen's voice floated through the speakers. "Hey, stranger!" That had to be the fakest greeting I'd ever heard from her. "Did you decide on a good time for a visit out of those dates I gave you? The first one is less than two weeks away, so I'm assuming that might not work out so well. But I was able to find a couple more in the last part of September."

I regretted very little in life—it was my motto: *Do everything; regret nothing.* However, not shutting this down from the beginning had become the exception to my rule. When I'd ignored the first two texts, she simply sent more. Then I'd tried to say it wasn't a good time with my new job and that asking for time off so early was frowned upon. She still hadn't gotten the hint, because after that, she came back saying the dates were all weekends and none of the flights arrived in Langston before seven on Fridays. That's when I'd gone back to ignoring her, which had spurred the phone calls. Until this one, I'd managed to avoid them all.

"Honestly, Jen . . . I don't understand the point in you coming here."

She giggled, as if what I said was funny, which was impossible, considering the tone I'd used. Nevertheless, she ignored the obvious and carried on with her delusions. "Well, there are a few things you left at the house that I wanted to bring you, and . . ." Pauses were never a good sign. "I was hoping that if we were face to face, we might be able to work things out a bit better."

"Yeah, maybe . . . if I had any interest in working anything out. But I don't. I thought I made that clear when I left. And again when I didn't reach out to you after your call with Marlena. Oh, and every day since you brought up the idea of visiting, by not responding or confirming a weekend for you to come."

She was silent, which had the potential to be worse than a pause. Our years together had taught me that either she was angry and needed a moment to string together the perfect insult that would hurt worse than a knee to the groin, or she was sad and didn't want me to hear her cry. When she sniffled, I knew it was the latter. It was also my Achilles' heel.

"Jen, please don't. I'm sorry for being so abrupt with you, but I'm at the end of my rope here. I'm at a loss for what else to do or say to make you realize I'm done. You made your choice. You stayed behind in Vegas, chose the show over me. That's the end of it. I don't know what more there is to say."

"I get it, Jason." Emotion distorted her voice and tightened my chest. "I guess I just thought we had something bigger than your rule against second chances. I assumed you'd eventually cool off and . . . I don't know, miss me or something."

"I think it's bigger than that," I explained, driving on autopilot while my mind drifted away from the road in front of me. "Face it . . . be honest with yourself for one minute, and you'll see that this isn't about what we had together or how much either of us miss the other. My family is here, and this is where I want to be. This is where I want to raise my kids, surrounded by loved ones. You'll never be happy in Samson *or* Langston. Or any other city around here. And I'll never be content living so far away from what little family I have."

"You've never taken me there, so how do you know I won't fall in love with the area and feel the same way you do? How can you say with such certainty that I won't get along with your aunt and uncle and become just as much part of the family as you are? You've never given me the chance, Jason."

Over the last month, I'd given this a lot of thought. And the one thing I continued to go back to was the fact that she wasn't close to her own family—not because anything had happened; simply because she'd allowed distance and time zones to stand between them. And if she couldn't maintain a relationship with the people she shared DNA with, I couldn't realistically expect her to have one with my family, who were essentially strangers to her. But that wasn't something I could tell her without it coming across as a slap in the face.

"Do you really think you can come for a weekend and know without a shadow of a doubt that you'd be happy spending the rest of your life here?" I already knew the answer, as well as the one she'd try to sell me, yet I asked anyway.

"I mean, it's possible. But even if I do, it's not like I can just rip up my returning plane ticket and stay there. I'd have to come back to pack up the house and give the show enough notice to replace me." She made it sound like that would be difficult—there were dozens of girls who danced in rotation or waited in the wings in case someone couldn't perform. "If it takes a few trips to know beyond the shadow of a doubt, then I'm willing to do that."

I cleared my throat, knowing this would be as hard for me to say as it would be for her to hear. "Jen . . . I think you're so eager to make this work that you'd convince yourself of just about anything. You'd say you love it here, that you want to move and start a family with me here, just to keep from losing what we had for the last five years. But where would that leave us in the future when you wake up one day and realize you miss the lights, the climate, the people and shows and fast-paced lifestyle?"

"You can't assume that'll happen."

"It already did—when you refused to leave it behind and come with me."

"That's not fair," she whispered.

"Maybe not, but you can't blame me for questioning it. And if we have kids when that day comes, how would that work? Would you take off with them and leave me to either follow or only see them during summer breaks? Or would you leave them here with me while you chased after your golden years in Vegas?"

"You're thinking too far ahead, Jason."

"But I'm not. I've lived it. My dad left when I was little because he went stir crazy in this town. I saw him for one summer after that, and most of that time was spent with his girlfriend while he did his thing. Until Bill came into the picture, I basically didn't have a father. That's *not* what I want for my kids—if I ever have any. And you can't blame me for doing everything I can to prevent that from happening."

She sighed, and when she spoke again, her tone had dropped an octave, full of the heartache we both felt. "The bottom line is, neither of us can predict the future. You do what you can to protect yourself and your future children, but at the end of the day, you could very well be turning your back on your soul mate out of fear. Which basically leaves you with two options, Jason: one, stick with your decision and we both move on, never knowing if we could've worked it out; or two, let me visit and trust that I'll be honest with you about whether or not I'd be happy there for the rest of my life. The decision is yours."

I'd pulled into my aunt and uncle's driveway before she even gave me the options, and now, I sat with my car in park, staring at the closed front door, feeling torn in half. Tatum was inside. She was someone I enjoyed spending time with, someone who, over the last couple of weeks, had taught me to breathe again. Yet at the same time, she wasn't my forever. She was exactly what she was—fun, amazing in bed, and a breath of fresh air. And Jen was on the phone, states away, begging me for the forever we had talked about for so long.

"Listen, Jen . . . I just pulled up to my aunt's house. I'm going to have to let you go before someone comes out and wonders why I'm sitting in the driveway on the phone." I was a coward for not giving her an answer, but the truth was, I didn't have one to offer.

"That's fine. Will you at least think about everything and let me know where your head's at? I'll wait for you until the earth stops spinning, just as long as I'm not doing it in vain. And if you decide that working things out isn't what you want, I'll respect that and let you move on. I just need to know what direction I'm going in. I don't want to give you up, but if you don't want me, there's nothing I can do."

I hated the pain in her voice, almost as much as hearing her tell me she'd wait forever if she had to. I didn't want that, yet I also didn't want to look in the mirror years from now and realize I'd made the biggest mistake of my life by turning her down. "I will. I promise."

She said goodbye, and I echoed the sentiment, though it was barely a whisper. She likely didn't hear it before I disconnected the call. And then I took another minute to shed the suffocating emotion she'd left me with. By the time I made my way inside the house, the knot in my stomach had loosened, though the ache in my chest remained.

That is . . . until I reached the end of the front hallway and found Tatum next to my mom, both standing in front of the stove with aprons tied around their waists. Apparently, that was all it took to bring me back to life—not an extra minute in the car, not a few deep breaths, and certainly not an ultimatum that either way could affect the rest of my life.

"Something smells good." I moved between the two women and peeked over their shoulders at what they were doing on the stove. While Tatum remained focused on the pan in front of her, Mom shifted to the side to plant a kiss on my cheek.

"Tatum's teaching me how to make her mother's green bean recipe." Mom wiped off the lipstick she'd left on my face and went back to snapping the ends off the fresh beans.

"I keep telling her she needs to write a cookbook or something." I knew that would get a rise out of Tatum. Except this time, rather than make a comment about how it would be a wasted endeavor because the only people who'd buy it already had most of her recipes, she glared at me through her lashes.

Then I realized what I'd said and who I'd said it around—I had basically admitted that we talked. Often.

"Oh, that would be a wonderful idea." Mom's bright-pink cheeks grew rounder with her smile. Someone seriously needed to give her some makeup tips before Marlena's kids thought she was a clown. "Why don't you do that, Tatum?"

"Because I don't know the first thing about writing one."

"It's a cookbook." I'd explained this to her a dozen times. "How hard can it be?"

"Don't talk to her like that, young man." My mom was an amazing mother, but discipline had never been her forte. I was in my thirties, and she *still* hadn't realized you weren't supposed to coo while correcting someone.

I leaned closer to Tatum's ear and whispered, "Sorry, babe."

She elbowed me. I told myself that meant she forgave me.

Mom took the empty bag the beans had been in to the trash and pointed toward one of the windows that faced the dock. "Fred's at the grill if you wanted to give him a hand."

"What kind of meat are we having?" I stretched my neck to peer out the window, catching my uncle swat at his neck, more than likely annoyed with a fly that wouldn't stop pestering him. It made me laugh. No matter where he was, the time of day, or even the weather, there could be a hundred people around, and he'd be the only one with either a fly buzzing in his ear or a family of mosquitos munching on his legs.

Aunt Diane always said it was because he was so sweet.

Kelsey always said that it was because he'd owned a pest control company and the insects all had banded together to enact their revenge on the man who'd killed their friends.

"Diane said he's doing beer-can chicken. But I'm not entirely sure. You should go see if he needs any help." My mother had a horrible habit of shooing me out of the kitchen.

Honestly, if Tatum hadn't been in here, she wouldn't have had to tell me twice before the patio door shut behind me. But I wasn't ready to walk away from her, so I rounded the counter and perched myself on one of the barstools.

Tatum dumped a pile of sautéed onions into a bowl and took the pan to the sink. It amazed me to watch her wash dishes—both here and at my house—considering she couldn't pick up after herself to save her life.

"Where's everyone else?"

Mom glanced around the room as if my aunt and cousins had just been here and then vanished when I'd asked where they were. "Well, Marlena is in one of the bedrooms putting Lizzie down for a nap, and Nick's in the pool with Connor."

Normally, hearing that my cousin's husband was here would've excited me—given me another guy to hang out with in this house full of women—but this time, I was torn. As much as I wanted to hang out with Nick, I didn't care to walk away from Tatum to do so.

"Oh, and Kelsey ran up to the store earlier with Diane to grab drinks." Mom watched the pot of water, probably waiting for it to boil, completely oblivious to Tatum's silence.

But it didn't matter, because just then, my cousin and aunt waltzed through the front door at the same time Marlena rounded the hallway into the living room. Tatum finished washing the pan and dried her hands to help the women with the drinks.

Marlena came up behind me and squeezed my shoulder. "How's it going?"

"Better now that you're here." I gave her the cheesy grin I saved for my favorite people, which earned me a playful smack across the chest. "I heard Nick came. How'd you manage to drag him with you this time?"

"I told him he could either come with me or I was leaving the kids at home with him." An evil glint flashed in her eyes. "I guess he wasn't excited about babysitting."

"You should be nicer to him," Aunt Diane piped up. "The poor man needs to sleep. You know he would be up all day with those kids if you left them at home."

Marlena grabbed the digital camera off the counter and handed it to her mom. "Here. Go take pictures of that *poor man*. I'm sure he'd love it."

Kelsey snickered to herself while Tatum fought off a grin. Aunt Diane just rolled her eyes and continued to unpack the sixteen different kinds of soft drinks. "I probably should. Connor's getting so big, and since it doesn't look like Kelsey will give me grandbabies while I'm young enough to enjoy them, I should capture as many moments as I can of the ones I have."

"You do realize Lizzie's only two, right?" Kelsey glared at her mom. "Can't you just enjoy her for a few more years until I'm ready to settle down?"

My aunt waved her off with a few bats of her hand. "That would require you to find someone to settle down with, dear. And at the pace you're moving these days, I'll have great-grandchildren to spoil before you make it to a second date."

Tatum giggled but abruptly stopped when Kelsey turned her hateful stare on her. "Who knows, Ma . . . maybe Tatum will give you little tater tots to fuss over."

My mom's eyes grew wide, almost alarmed. "Oh? Are you expecting, dear?"

"Not yet," Kelsey answered for the wide-eyed goddess who clearly couldn't speak. "But she's been hooking up with her boss, so who knows how long it'll be before there's a tiny tater in her Easy-Bake."

Instead of denying my cousin's claims, Tatum focused on the sleeves of Ritz crackers that she crumbled into a bowl, keeping her back to her best friend. I practically held my breath while I stared at the top of her head, waiting for her to look up or offer *something* to tell me this wasn't true. After all, she'd told me she hadn't been with anyone other than her ex and me. I should've dismissed it the second the lie spewed from Kelsey's mouth, but the longer I went without anything from Tatum, the more doubtful I became.

The chatter continued, though I didn't listen to any of it, too busy trying to make the woman in front of me glance up. And before I knew it, the kitchen had emptied out. Mom put the baking dish in the oven and then moved toward the sliding glass door. "You coming, Tatum?"

I was left to watch as my temporary fun just became a little more short lived.

I hadn't stayed too long after the table was cleared off, unable to deal with much more of Tatum's avoidance. I had no idea what I'd done to cause that kind of reaction. The only thing I could think of was that it had more to do with Kelsey's claims of Tatum sleeping with her boss than it did with me. And if that were the case, I hadn't wanted to wait around for confirmation.

"I don't get it . . . is she not allowed to sleep with other people?" Aaron tipped his beer to his lips while keeping his eyes glued to me.

I propped my feet on the coffee table in my living room and downed a quarter of my bottle before responding. "It's not that. I guess I just don't like the idea of her letting some other guy between her legs while she's fucking me."

"Wouldn't you know if someone else was there while you're fucking her?"

I raised my middle finger in his direction. "You know what I mean, asshole."

"Yeah, and I get it, but how is that any different than what you did last weekend? And technically, what you did was worse. Not only did you get it on with that chick from the club, but then you came back here and crawled into bed with this other one."

"Her name's not *the other one*. Not *what's her face*. Just Tatum."

He held up his hand in surrender. "So sorry. Wasn't aware you'd be so offended by that, especially considering you don't remember *any* girls' names," he muttered under his breath.

I ignored his comment, refusing to analyze why Tatum's name was the only one I could remember—and *had* remembered without any problem. "And I didn't do anything with that girl. She had her driver take me home. End of story."

"Then what did you guys do all alone in the back seat?"

I shrugged; that ride was still a little blurry. "Not sure, but I can guarantee there was no touching . . . of *any* kind. And I have proof. She texted me the next day to see how I was feeling and thank me for being a perfect gentleman."

"You gave her your number?"

"I must have. But I don't remember the details."

"Yet you're positive you didn't touch her? Yeah . . . sure."

I needed new friends. "You don't have to believe me. I know I didn't."

"How can you be so sure?"

"Why the hell would I fuck anyone else when I had Tatum in my bed?"

He remained quiet, just sat there and nodded slowly.

"Go ahead and say it, Aaron. I know you want to."

"Say what?"

"Whatever you're over there thinking."

He smirked and then finished his beer, making me wait even longer to hear what would probably end up pissing me off anyway. When he set the empty bottle on the table between the recliner and the couch I sat on, he wiped his mouth and leaned forward. "If you don't want Tatum hooking up with other guys, you should probably tell her."

"I don't want to give her the wrong impression."

"Wrong impression about what?"

Apparently, I had to spell everything out to him. "Kelsey is convinced that I'll hurt her, whether I mean to or not. I'd stay away if I could, but it's clear that I can't—nor do I want to. We've been on the same page so far about keeping this casual, and I worry that'll change if I tell her I don't want her to sleep with anyone else."

"And why don't you want it to be anything more than casual?"

"Aside from what it would do to Kelsey and Tatum's relationship, as well as Tatum's relationship with the rest of my family? How about the fact that I *just* got out of a serious relationship, and jumping into another isn't a good idea. I thought you of *all* people would recognize that reason."

"That's why you should explain your reasons. I'm sure she's a smart girl. She'll understand. What she *won't* understand is you getting your dick in a twist because she didn't follow rules she was never given."

Making friends with an opinionated psychologist had its pitfalls—unless you were interested in hearing about *everything* you did wrong.

"And since we're on the topic of you being a hypocrite, let's discuss the pole dancer." Aaron had never met Jen, yet that didn't stop him from being the self-appointed president of her *anti*–fan club.

"Nothing to talk about. Conversation's over."

"Fine, then I won't point out that you're wasting her time by not telling her to stay in Nevada. Face the facts, my man . . . if you really thought she could be *the one*, you wouldn't have to think twice about getting her on a plane." He clapped his hands together and stood. "I need another beer; you want one?"

"Nah . . . I'm good, but thanks."

Aaron hadn't even opened the fridge when a few soft raps against the front door caught my attention. I hadn't expected any visitors other than Aaron, so I had no idea who would show up at . . . I groaned when I caught the time, unsure when eight fifteen had become too late for someone to stop by unannounced.

But when I turned the knob and swung it open, only to find Tatum standing on my front step, I no longer cared what time it was. It could've been two in the morning, and it wouldn't have changed anything.

"Hey. What are you doing here?" I opened the door wider to invite her in and then glanced over my shoulder toward the kitchen, wondering where Aaron was or what he'd do when he realized I had company.

"I wanted to talk to you about what happened today."

I dug my phone out of my pocket and checked the screen, surprised to see no missed calls or texts. "So you drove all the way out here?"

Tatum followed me inside and took one step toward the living room. Without warning, she stopped and began to twist her fingers in a show of nervousness. "I, um . . . I'm sorry. I had no idea you had company."

Confused by her reaction, I followed her line of sight, hoping to understand what had tipped her off. That's when I noticed not only my beer sitting on the coffee table where I'd left it, but Aaron's empty bottle on the side table as well.

"You're right; I should've called first. It was stupid to just show up." She put one foot behind the other, her hands now clutching the front of her shirt over her chest.

The thought of her leaving was enough to force me into action. I grabbed her elbow to at least stall her exit and explain that Aaron had parked across the street, but I didn't get the chance.

"Hey . . . I know you." Aaron came around the corner, his eyes wide with surprise as he grinned with excitement. For what, I wasn't sure yet, but I certainly wasn't *excited* to find out. He stepped closer and held his arms out. "You're the hugger from the food festival."

I shot him a silent warning, which he understood immediately. It could've been the raised brows, the wide eyes, or the tic in my jaw. Whatever he'd recognized in my expression, he got the hint without me having to tell him twice.

Instead of following through on the embrace, he stuck out a hand. And it seemed the brain doctor was back—Aaron's professional alter ego. "It's really nice to see you again. I had no idea the Tatum he's talked about is you."

She turned with surprise my way, probably her reaction to hearing that I talked about her.

"Uh, yeah. Aaron stopped by to have a few drinks. Did you want one?" I hoped that offering her a beverage would help smooth things over, even though I didn't hold my breath that she'd accept the invitation.

"N-no, but thank you." Finally, she smiled at Aaron and slipped her hand into his. "It's nice to see you again, too."

"Don't listen to anything this bastard says about me. Got it?" It appeared the good doctor had left the building. "They're all lies. Unless he happened to mention how intelligent and good looking I am, or how great I am in b—"

"Enough, Aaron." There was no mistaking the warning in my tone.

"What?" He genuinely appeared offended, yet that didn't mean he was. "I was about to say I'm great in bad situations. Good God, man. What did you *think* I was going to say?" He regarded Tatum again, who now had the corners of her lips turned up in amusement. "It seems he also thinks I'm disrespectful. Honestly, I'm not sure why I'm still friends with him."

"I've been asking myself the same question for weeks." My retort earned me a breathless giggle from the otherwise silent woman at my right and a wink of approval from the asshole on my left.

"I was actually on my way out," Aaron lied, which I appreciated.

Tatum eyed the cold bottle of beer in his hand. "Didn't you just open that?"

He looked at it for a second and then passed it over to me. "It's his."

At this point, I didn't know what the hell was going on, but if it came down to one of them leaving, it better not be Tatum. So, I took the beer from his hand even though it wasn't mine and started to drink it.

Tatum glanced over her shoulder, yet I wasn't sure what she was looking at, considering the front door was closed. "I didn't see a car out there. Do you have a ride home?"

"Oh, no. Jason makes me park my truck across the street because it leaks oil, and this neat freak would have a coronary if there were any stains on the driveway of the house he *rents*." He cupped his hand around his mouth and added, "He takes the whole 'care for it like it was your own' thing to a whole new level," as if I couldn't hear him.

She eyed me, mocking me through her thick, dark lashes. Tatum enjoyed making fun of me for being a clean freak, even though I was sure she secretly wanted me to come clean her room. If she didn't . . . she really should.

"Are you really going? Or are you just saying that so I don't leave?"

Aaron slapped his hand over his chest and dropped his mouth wide open. "Trust me—I would never walk away from drinking someone else's beer, especially so some other guy can spend time with a pretty girl."

Tatum glanced between the two of us, yet she didn't say anything.

Aaron slapped me on the back, slid between me and Tatum like Moses parting the Red Sea, and walked out the front door. As soon as it closed behind him, she made her way around the recliner to the couch.

"That was totally his beer, wasn't it?" she asked, taking a seat on the sofa.

I took the cushion next to her and regarded the bottle in my hand. "Why do you say that?"

"Well, that one's half full." She pointed to the one on the coffee table that I had been drinking and then turned her finger to the one Aaron had left behind next to the chair. "And that one's empty. You'd never leave an empty *anything* sitting out—you would've finished drinking it while standing over the trash can, just so you could throw it out after the last drop was gone. Which means this one's yours." She picked up my old beer, brought it to her lips, and tipped it back. "Also . . . you hate the recliner, so you wouldn't have sat in it."

I couldn't exactly argue with her, so I shrugged. I tipped my new bottle back and gulped, hoping she wouldn't be able to read the reaction

I had over her knowing these things about me. It turned me inside out, flipped me upside down, and hung me out to dry.

But when Tatum cleared her throat, preparing herself to begin, I paid attention.

"That first night I stayed here—when I helped you cook dinner and then we . . ." She nodded in the direction of my room, as if I could've forgotten. "Well, when I got home the next morning, Kelsey was up, and of course, she wanted to know where I was all night. I'd forgotten all about the excuse we came up with and just tried to pass it off. At some point in our conversation, I thought she figured out I had been here with you, so I tried to explain as best as I could without making her mad."

There had to be more to this story, considering my cousin had never mentioned this, and if she didn't get to it soon, I'd end up dragging it out of her.

"I'm still not sure how it all went down," she continued, "but while I was telling her about *you*, she was referring to Michael, both of us under the impression that we were talking about the same person. It wasn't until the very end, right before she stormed out of my room, that she said his name. That's when I realized she thought I had slept with him, not you."

"So Michael's your boss?"

"Yes, whom she hates. Which is why she's making such a big deal about it. I didn't correct her because I thought the truth would be worse—in *her* eyes, I mean. I never expected her to bring it up at her parents' house in front of everyone, and I *really* didn't think she'd ever tell you."

"But you're not sleeping with him, right?"

She laughed and shook her head, humor sparkling in her eyes. "No. Don't you think that would've come up this morning during the whole no-condom conundrum?"

I shrugged, unable to give her a real answer.

"I thought you would've put two and two together—that every time I came here, I had to tell her I was somewhere else. But then you kind of took off after lunch without saying bye, and I started to worry that you might've believed her."

"Honestly, I hadn't at first. The only reason I even questioned it was because you refused to look at me all day, like you were ashamed or had something to hide. It started to feel a little more believable after a while."

Tatum placed her hand on my thigh and scooted closer. "If I looked at you, I would've given us away. And let me be real with you for a second, Jay. Standing next to your mom while replaying every second of our morning in my head was *not* enjoyable. Got it? So, my refusal to make eye contact with you had absolutely *nothing* to do with you and *everything* to do with not wanting your entire family—your mother included—to know that you basted my turkey."

I covered my face with my hand and let my laughter roll through me. Finally, when I was able to breathe again, I released the longest, harshest, most obvious sigh of relief known to man, like a brick house had just been lifted off my back.

"Did what Kelsey say really bother you that much?"

I cleared my throat and dropped my hand to look into her eyes. Here went nothing. "Whether I thought it was true or not, it got me thinking. I know you've said that you don't have an issue if I get it elsewhere—*as well as from you*—but after today, I realized I'm not okay with that. Not just for me, but for you, too."

She didn't speak, but rather listened intently as I poured out my thoughts.

"Maybe it was talking about being clean and having been tested, and how neither of us have been with anyone but each other since our exes. But the thought of you being with someone else the night before sleeping in my bed, or leaving here and going to another man's house . . ." I shook my head, hating the images that came to mind. "I don't know, Tatum. I don't like it."

"For both of us, right?" she asked, seeking clarification.

"Yes. I honestly have no desire to juggle more than one woman. I'm not saying I think we should be in an exclusive relationship or anything. Just that maybe it's safer and wiser if we keep things between the two of us. When the day comes that your ex is single and wants to work things out, or if you happen to wake up and realize you have interest in someone else, then we end what we have. No hard feelings." God, that tasted awful.

"Sounds good to me."

Well, that proved to be way easier than I had anticipated.

I walked her to the door, but before I let her out, I laced my fingers through her hair and said goodbye with my tongue and lips. I couldn't imagine ever walking away from her without doing this.

I barely had the door closed when Aaron came in through the garage. He headed straight for the fridge, grabbed a beer, and strolled into the living room to reclaim his spot in the recliner. I glared at him as I made my way around the chair to the couch.

"I thought you left. Were you eavesdropping?"

"No. Not at all. You had the side door into your garage open, so I waited in there. But I have to say, I'm super proud of you. Talking to her about keeping the sex between just the two of you couldn't have been easy."

I couldn't help but laugh. "You're such a dick."

"For real though, man." He became serious, no sign of jest on his face. "I completely understand why you don't want another guy getting a taste of her before you get your head out of your ass and figure out why you aren't interested in anyone else."

The only thing that saved him from getting pummeled was the taste of Tatum's lips lingering on mine.

18

Tatum

My nerves had been fried all day, which made my shift fly by, although I didn't put on my most graceful performance in the kitchen. Luckily, I was with the slow staff today—no one in the kitchen sucked, but there were the ones who could handle the heat and the others who . . . well, had more difficulty keeping up without sacrificing accuracy.

Rebecca always had Thursdays off, so without Michael's girlfriend around, Victor typically kept him out of the kitchen. Amanda had Thursday-morning classes this semester, so if she was scheduled, it was for the evening shift. The only person I had to deal with today was Carrie, and oddly enough, every time she stepped foot past the swinging door, Victor leveled her with a stare, and she retreated without saying a word.

Their interaction intrigued me. It also offered hours of entertainment as I worked on autopilot, imagining what kind of secrets those two kept. I didn't know much about Fifty Shades, and I had only seen the first movie, but I could totally see Victor dominating Carrie in the red room of pain. I prepared an entire order while envisioning him walking her on a leash.

I had to switch to something else when my libido took over and had Carrie on her knees in front of him. That took it a little too far, and if I hadn't put an end to it, I doubted I'd ever be able to look him in the eye again.

But at least it gave me a little reprieve from the anxiety that coursed through me anytime I thought about the plans I'd made for after work. I'd met up with Jason on Tuesday at his house. He'd gone home for his break and eaten me for lunch. Aside from that, we hadn't seen each other since Sunday . . . a pattern I wasn't interested in continuing. So, last night, he had suggested I head over to his house after work today and wait for him.

It had seemed like a great idea at the time.

Until I'd woken up this morning and thought about the whole situation—not just the amazing sex I'd get to have. That was when I realized he'd given me access to his house. While he was gone. You know, the kind of thing you do when you're *dating* someone.

I honestly didn't think I had anything to worry about, considering Jason and I had been very up front with each other about everything. But as far as feelings and what we both wanted or didn't want, we'd agreed that a broken heart didn't equate to a broken sex drive. Neither of us was interested in anything other than physical companionship, and that sentiment had been echoed as recently as last weekend. So, I shouldn't be freaking out, yet I was.

I was lost in thought as I walked outside beneath the blazing sun to my car. Between the heat, chest pains, and disturbing mental pictures of Carrie and Vic that just wouldn't go away, I almost missed Amanda heading toward me, screaming my name.

"I'm going to tell myself you didn't see me, and you weren't trying to rush out of here to get away from me."

I rolled my eyes and tilted my head to the side in exasperation. "I didn't even know you were coming in today, Amanda."

"Yeah, well, Michael scheduled a meeting for the front of the house before dinner shift today, so I had to come in early." She tossed her keys into her purse with attitude, her way of telling me what she thought about this meeting without saying the words. She didn't have to. We all hated his scheduled lectures—I was just thankful this one didn't involve the kitchen staff.

"So . . . did you only want to say hi? Or was there some other reason you stopped me from leaving?"

"Oh yeah, I hear congratulations are in order." Her dancing brows did nothing to help me understand what she meant by that.

"Like always, Amanda, I'm going to need more here. I have no idea what you're talking about."

Her gaze dropped to my stomach for a brief moment. "I heard you're pregnant."

If this moment were made into a cartoon, my eyes would pop out of my head and roll on the ground while flames shot out of my ears. "You heard I'm *what*?"

"Uh . . . pregnant?" If she dropped her attention to my stomach one more time, there was a good chance I'd stab her in the eyes. "I take it you're not?"

"Yes! I mean no!" I was so turned around I had no idea what I was even answering. "No, I'm not. Who said I was?"

"Well, I, uh . . . several people."

"Like *who*, Amanda? I need names here."

"Michael, for one."

It took me a second to wrap my brain around that one. I mean, he hadn't said anything to me, so I wasn't sure why he would've brought it up with the hostess. "Even if it were true, why in the world would he talk to you about it?"

"He didn't *talk* to me about it as much as I overheard him grumbling about it in his office." Well, that made more sense. "From what I gather, he asked Rebecca why you left early last weekend. That somehow led to you being pregnant."

"Oh my God." It was like someone had lit a match inside me, making my blood boil. "I ate something bad. Can a woman not barf without it being morning sickness?"

"Hey," she said, holding up her hands like a hostage. "I'm just the messenger."

I was fed up with being talked about behind my back and annoyed that I couldn't just set the record straight. Not without admitting I was a liar, that is. As desperate as I was for everyone to stop talking about me like I was a Kardashian, it apparently wasn't bad enough to sacrifice my own reputation to make it stop.

I turned my face to the sky and inhaled deeply, calming myself before carrying on with this conversation. "So, he didn't say anything to you? Or you overheard him complaining about it and asked?"

"Who, Michael? I just heard him talk shit in his office to Rebecca. He never said anything to me about it. But Carrie did. She wasn't happy to hear that you're not only carrying the cheater's baby, but you're marrying him, too. She had a few choice words to say about that. And then there was—"

"Back up." It might've taken me a minute to interrupt, but once I realized I hadn't heard her wrong, I couldn't allow her to keep talking when I had serious questions to ask. "*Marrying* him, too?"

She pointed to the piece of glass that adorned my left ring finger. I hadn't taken it off because I liked it, and aside from Rebecca asking about it on Saturday, no one had even noticed.

"How does a cheap ring on my finger mean I'm engaged?"

"The fact that it's on your left hand should answer that question. Although, if you're more concerned about it being cheap, you should probably think about the guy who put it there. If he's the kind of boyfriend who would bring a date to your restaurant, then you shouldn't be surprised when everyone expects him to give you a fake diamond to pacify you during your time of uncertainty."

I stared at the silver band and clear piece of glass on my finger, twisting it while wondering how something with such a great story, one that used to bring a smile to my face, could cause so many problems in my life.

"Why would everyone automatically assume it was Jay?"

Amanda laughed—*at* me, though not in a hurtful manner. "Really, Tatum? It took you six months to move on from Michael—or so you say. We're not stupid enough to believe you jumped from Jay's bed to someone else's so quickly."

"Fine." I held up my hand, conceding that point. "This conversation is futile anyway, since I'm *not* pregnant. Someone should probably tell Michael that. It might make him happy."

"Yeah . . . I'm sure he'll be thrilled to know you're not turning into your brother."

Those words were like a slap in the face. "What's that supposed to mean?"

"I don't know, Tatum. I was *eavesdropping*, remember? I couldn't exactly jump in and ask why he'd say that." She narrowed her eyes and shook her head as if she couldn't believe I'd suggest such a thing.

"No . . . like what was he saying about my brother?"

"Something about how he has a bunch of kids with a bunch of different women. Although there was something else about other men. Honestly, I had no idea what he was talking about. I assumed he meant your brother is a man-whore who's spread his love around, and his exes are all married so they're like one big family. Who knows. I met him one time at your birthday dinner, and he never struck me as the type."

"That's all he said?" I felt like I couldn't breathe.

"Basically. He was talking to Rebecca, and after she left, I asked about the pregnancy part—not about your brother. The only thing I really remember him saying was about how he made the right decision by leaving you before you guys got married . . . something about him knowing this would happen. Whatever that means. I brushed it off, because I doubt you would've gotten pregnant by another guy while married to him."

I was too stunned to speak. Her words just bounced around in my head while I stood there, motionless, my legs practically going numb beneath me.

"Just so we're clear . . . you're *not* pregnant?" she asked.

I could only nod. The anger over the rumors and assumptions had vanished, and in its place a sadness and immense pain filled me. Somehow, the betrayal of Michael's words trumped everything else I'd learned in the last few minutes.

She'd said something else, but I wasn't listening, and before I knew it, she'd walked away, leaving me alone next to my car.

"Who died?" Kelsey asked when I got home.

"Hope." I dropped my coat on the floor next to the front door, tossed my keys onto the coffee table, and then fell into the empty spot next to her on the couch.

She was quiet for so long that I wondered if she'd even heard me, but then she cleared her throat and turned toward me on the sofa. "Considering the severity of this situation, I'm going to ignore the fact that you just threw your jacket on the floor rather than remind you that I've asked a million times for you to put it away when you get home."

Any other time, I would've laughed at her joke. Not that I didn't find it funny, but I wasn't in the mood to smile. Instead, I came back with, "And rather than tell you to shut the hell up because I'm in a bad mood, that you'll just have to deal with where I leave my shit, I'm going to keep it to myself. Shall we pour champagne and toast to our progress at keeping our thoughts to ourselves?"

It seemed my sarcasm was enough to set the mood.

She turned and set her sad eyes on me. "I know you always accuse me of not listening to you when you speak, and I always argue and say that I do. But at the risk of making myself sound like a bad friend who never listens to you . . . who's Hope?"

I wanted to laugh, but I was too confused by her question to give in to the humor tickling my chest. "Am I supposed to know who it is?"

"Well, yeah. You just told me she died."

Once I realized what she meant, the laughter bubbled out. "No. *My* hope died."

She stared at me, blinking so dramatically I wondered if she expected her lashes to carry her away. "Does this have to do with Michael?"

"Why? Would you not be interested if it is?"

"Not in the slightest." She was such a liar; we both knew she couldn't ignore me no matter what I had to complain about.

"That doesn't seem very fair. You're supposed to be my best friend."

"And as your best friend, I warned you about sleeping with him. You ignored me. And if I listen to you cry over something he's done, I feel I'd only be enabling you."

"Good point. But it's not about that."

"All right, fine. What's going on?"

I knew she'd cave. She always did.

I turned to face her and tucked my leg beneath my bottom on the couch. "Apparently, he dumped me because of Tanner."

"That doesn't make any sense. He told you that's why he broke up with you?"

"No. He was talking to Rebecca in his office, and Amanda overheard part of it." I threw my head back against the cushion and huffed, needing to contemplate how to maneuver around the land mines—all the other parts of what had led to this discussion—because I couldn't tell her that without everything else. The huff was genuine, though. It was seriously exhausting having to edit my own stories to keep Kelsey from finding out what I'd been doing with her cousin behind her back. "Basically, he believed I would wake up one day and want the type of lifestyle Tanner has."

"That's a rather close-minded accusation. Let me guess . . . he assumes you think all relationships are that way just because your brother's in one?" Leave it to Kelsey to go from one to a hundred in the blink of an eye.

"I don't know. Amanda doesn't remember everything he said."

"Listen, Tater . . ." She placed her hand on my knee and offered the soft, gentle voice she used when playing the supportive role of my best friend—as opposed to when she tried to ease the discomfort by making me laugh. "He's an idiot, and you're much better off without him. His reasons for breaking up with you shouldn't matter. All you need to focus on is the fact that you're free of him . . . or you *should* be if you aren't already."

"Oh, I'm *so* done with him."

"Good. Does this mean you aren't having sex with him anymore?"

Well, shit. I hadn't thought that far ahead. Now I'd have to convince her I had found someone else to get it on with when I went to see Jason. "Absolutely."

"Thank God." She sighed dramatically. "I was really worried this would end badly."

I stared at her, wondering how she didn't get just how bad this was. Then again, she hated Michael, so any reason for him to be completely out of the picture was considered good.

"Listen, I know it hurts, and I'm sorry that he's done this to you, but know it's for a good reason. Without hearing that, do you honestly think you would've completely gotten over him?"

When I glanced away, pondering how to respond, I noticed the notebook in her lap and the name of a high-end builder written at the top of the page. I pointed to it and asked, "Is this that big break you were hoping for?"

She had an important showing coming up that could possibly cata-pult her into the big-time realty market. It was what she'd been working toward, and I knew that took priority over hearing me complain. So changing the subject benefited not only me but her as well.

"Yeah. I have to head over to Crenshaw in a little bit to take pic-tures of the house and measure some of the rooms. I'll have to get new furniture for this one, since nothing I have goes in mansions."

"Does this mean you won't be here for dinner?"

"No, I'm sorry. I meant to tell you, but I forgot. I probably won't be home until at least eight." Crenshaw Lake was a solid forty-five minutes away, and that was with good traffic. "It might be late, but I can bring something back for us to eat, if you'd like. That way you don't have to worry about cooking something for yourself."

"No, but thank you. Instead, you should stop on the way home and pick up a carton of our favorite men. We can double-date on the couch with a movie." Kelsey and I hadn't had a "double date" with Ben and Jerry in a while. With everything going on, it was definitely something we needed tonight.

"I think I can make that happen. I'll grab the men; you pick the flick."

"Deal. When are you leaving?"

"I really need to leave here in the next ten or so minutes."

I smiled and patted her leg. "Thanks for listening to me, Kels."

"Always, Tater."

I pushed off the couch to put my things away before she started to twitch. Living together should've helped one of us with our issues—either by keeping me organized or lessening her need to have everything in its place. But no. It seemed her issues had gotten worse while I'd learned to keep my mess centralized in my room.

While she got ready to leave, I occupied my time with a short video call to my brother. After hearing what Michael had said about Tanner, I needed to see my brother's face to ease the irrational guilt that ate at me.

About ten minutes after Kelsey came in to say goodbye, my phone rang next to me on the mattress. The second I saw it was Jay, I realized I'd never let him know that I had changed my mind about going to his house after work.

"Where are you at?" Just the sound of his voice made me regret that decision.

"My apartment."

"I thought you were coming here?"

I could've told the truth, but I didn't see the point in ruining my unbeatable lying streak. "Yeah, I was, but then I thought about how weird it would be to sit at your house while you weren't there, and I decided against it."

He was quiet for a moment, but then he said, "You were here all by yourself when I went to Boots. How was that any different?"

"For starters, it wasn't like I had any other option."

"Good point." He laughed. "Well, I just got home. It's not too late to come by."

I sighed and closed my eyes, thankful that he couldn't see my face. "As much as I would love to, I think I'm just going to stay in."

"What's your excuse now?"

Too bad I didn't have another lie readily available. It looked like my streak had ended—for the time being. "I had a pretty craptastic day."

"Is everything all right?" God, I hated it when he did that.

"Yeah. I mean, it will be. It's fine. Just a bad day. Nothing important."

"I'm coming over."

"W-what? No! I-I mean . . . you don't have to."

"I know I don't have to. I want to, Tatum."

My heart sputtered and then paused, waiting for the kicker it knew would come. "Why?"

"Why do I want to? Babe, I spent all day counting down the hours, then the minutes until I got to leave the office, all because you were supposed to be here. You're not. And I'm not about to let that keep me from getting what I've been looking forward to since last night."

And there it was. "Ahh, I get it now. You want sex."

"Doesn't every man?" His gravelly amusement rolled through the line like a boulder tumbling down the side of a mountain, and all I could think about was how gorgeous his smile was when he did that. "But that's not why I'm coming over."

"If it's not for the sexual pleasure that I offer, what other reason is there?"

"You've had a craptastic day." Somewhere, an angel sang.

"Good line, but you said you wanted to get what you've waited all day for."

"Oh, you want the list? All right . . . to see your smile, look into your eyes, and for the love of God, I need to kiss you before I fucking go crazy. Your lips . . . *damn*. I'm convinced you lace your lipstick with crack or something."

I checked the time, noting that I had approximately two and a half hours before Kelsey came home. Realistically speaking, there was no reason he couldn't stop by. And before I could think of all the reasons he shouldn't, I said, "Hurry. You have to be gone by eight."

"I'm so fucked," Jason groaned against my neck while we frantically tried to slow our racing hearts and erratic breathing.

"Oh yeah? Why's that?"

"Well, for starters, you've ruined lunch breaks for me, and now . . ." He pushed up onto one elbow to see me better. "You've likely tainted vehicles in general. If we keep this up, there won't be anything left. Everything will make me think about being balls deep in you."

I'd met him in the parking lot less than an hour after we hung up. He'd insisted I let him in the apartment, but I was too scared Kelsey would come home and find him in my bed. That was far too risky. So, we lifted the back gate on my SUV and ate the takeout he'd grabbed on his way over. That was also when he had surprised me with information about taking part in a cooking segment for the local news station.

This man just wouldn't give up.

And the more he mentioned it, the more I began to warm up to the idea.

After discussing the opportunity he'd snagged for me—thanks to the husband of someone he worked with—we'd wound up in the back with the hatch closed . . . *naked*. It was good to know that there was enough room for two grown adults to have sex without cramping up or being uncomfortable. It would boost the resale value.

"Yup. You got me, Jay. Lunch, car . . . next it'll be your office. You didn't know my master plan was to ruin everything in your life?" I teased.

Jason trailed the tip of his finger down the center of my chest, then circled it along the bottom of my bare breast. When he covered it with the heat of his palm, I grabbed his wrist and tried to push his hand away. I let him have his fun while we were in the moment, but that didn't mean I was comfortable or confident enough to sit back and let him analyze the part of my body I had the biggest issue with.

"I don't get it, Tatum. Why must you refuse me the joy of playing with your tits?"

A laugh bubbled out at his crassness. "As I recall, you enjoyed them quite a bit a few minutes ago. In fact, I'm fairly certain my right nipple will be bruised after all the fun you had with it between your teeth."

The lights from the parking lot filtered through the tinted windows just enough so I could see his eyes sparkle with his wide, infectious grin. "You know what I mean, brat. You never let me just *see* them."

"How willing would you be if I wanted to sit between your legs and just *see* your dick? It's not show-and-tell, Jay. And considering you've gotten me naked a lot recently, I'm surprised you don't have them memorized by now."

He huffed like a spoiled child, even though he smiled like a kid in a candy shop. "I'm buried in you almost the entire time you're naked. And I'm sorry, but I usually have my mind on other things—like the way your cheeks turn pink just before you come, or how you lightly rake your nails over my shoulder blades when you're focused on getting me off. I'm not paying attention to the exact shade of your nipples or the degree of the curve along the bottom. And almost as soon as we finish, you cover yourself up again."

Flattery would only get him so far—like maybe a blow job or a highway handy—but he wouldn't get his way with this. "They're asymmetrical; one's bigger than the other. There, now you have all the information you need."

"You make it sound like one's a golf ball while the other is a grapefruit," he teased, yet it was obvious this bothered him. "They look the same to me."

I didn't argue, because really, it wasn't a noticeable difference—well, it was to me, thanks to Michael commenting on it once. But that didn't mean I wanted to feel like a mannequin on display while Jason studied the design of my breasts.

"Baby, we're all asymmetrical. You have to own that shit. Nothing is sexier than a woman who's comfortable in her own skin." One corner of his mouth turned up ever so slightly. "And considering you're already sexy as hell, I bet you could have a guy coming in his pants if he walked in and found you just lounging on the couch in nothing but your birthday suit."

"Too bad we'll never know, huh?" I gently pushed him off me so I could sit up.

Before he gave me space to grab my clothes, he brought his face close to mine, so close that I felt his words across my lips when he whispered, "You're fucking perfect, Tatum. Don't ever doubt that." And then he moved away, giving me room to sit up.

Either he didn't care that he left me breathless, or he'd done it on purpose.

He leaned against the side panel with his legs bent between us. His forearms rested on his knees, and he didn't have a care in the world that he was as naked as the day was long. In truth, I envied that about him. And he was right—it was utterly erotic to see.

"You never answered me earlier. Are you going to call Charlie about the show?"

"I don't know, Jay," I mumbled while slipping my tank over my head. "Why is it so important to you? I understand you like this Mary chick—"

"Maryanne. And I'm not asking you to do it for her. I want you to do it for *yourself*."

"Fine, but going behind my back and getting her husband to set this up was a wasted effort on your part."

"Charlie said it wasn't a big deal if you said no."

I huffed, nearly giving up on pulling my leggings back on. That task proved to be a million times more difficult than taking them off in the back of an SUV had been. "Except it's not. He's giving me an opportunity, and I would feel like an ungrateful fool for not doing it. Not to mention, I'd feel bad letting *you* down."

Once I finally got my pants back on, Jason moved to his knees in front of me, holding himself up with his hands on the side panel behind me. "You could never let me down, so don't even think that way. If you truly don't want to do it, then don't. But if it's fear holding you back, just close your eyes and take the plunge. I'll be happy with whatever decision you make."

I cupped his cheeks in my hands, ready to claim his mouth, when the heavy thump of a door closing came from the parking space next to us. I tilted my head to the side just in time to see Kelsey round the back of her car. "Oh shit."

Jason peered over his shoulder and stared at his cousin while she grabbed her messenger bag and a grocery sack from her trunk. "Do you think she can see us?"

"I've never stood outside at night and tried to look in from a few feet away. How am I supposed to know?"

"We should probably come up with something in case she can."

I swallowed hard to keep the panic inside from consuming me. "Jay . . . you're not wearing a stitch of clothing. I'm not sure we have many believable options with your dick dangling between your legs."

As he brought his attention back to me, his hushed chuckle brushed across my face. "It's a good thing you're dressed. We can use that to our advantage. Now we just have to think of a reason we'd be in the back of your car in a parking lot at night without the engine running. It would also need to explain why only one of us is naked. Sex trafficking?"

Out of the corner of my eye, I watched as Kelsey shut the trunk and walked toward the building. I covered his mouth with mine, nearly getting lost in the impatient kiss, and then quickly shoved against his chest.

"I have to go. She saw my car, and I'm not exactly dressed for a stroll—not to mention, I don't stroll. So I need to get back inside . . . like now."

"And make me walk to my car in the buff?"

I twisted my lips to the side, taking a moment to envision it. "As much fun as that would be, I don't have time to watch it. Just get dressed in here, and when you're done, lock it up." I kissed him once more and then climbed over the back seat. In my head, it was a stealth, almost James Bond–type of move, but in reality, it was more of a tuck and roll gone bad.

His laughter echoed behind me as I hopped out, and I replayed it in my mind as I raced back to the apartment before Kelsey could question why I was outside without shoes.

19

Tatum

"You got this, Kels." I'd never been very good at pep talks. Thank God my best friend didn't expect more from me. "Go shine like a diamond. Show those bitches who's boss. Kick ass and take names."

Kelsey might have released a hint of laughter wrapped in an exhale, but it did nothing to mask the nerves that currently made her right eye twitch. I understood . . . kind of. I mean, I'd never been in this position before, where my hopes and dreams were dependent on one night, but I could totally imagine.

The moment grew heavier, and despite my reservations, I pulled her into a hug. "Really, Kels . . . you're going to do great. I bet everyone will put in an offer. Alabaster Builders would be insane if they don't recognize what you bring to the table."

"We shall see." She patted my back and let go.

"Don't worry, Kelsey. If they don't see it, another company will. You've been working with realtors for years. It's only a matter of time before the big builders want in on what you do for a sale."

She smiled and shuffled her feet toward the door. "I have no idea when I'll get home. What are you going to do in the meantime?"

"Word search." That was probably the most believable lie I had ever told. The truth was, I had invited Jason over. I had quite the surprise planned for him, and if she came back early, she'd get an even bigger one.

"After tonight, I'm all yours. Got it? I haven't been a very good friend to you this past week. You've needed me, and I've been too wrapped up in this project to offer you the support you deserve. But starting tonight, I'll be up your ass so much you'll need an enema to get rid of me."

I loved this woman and the constant support she gave, but if she didn't get out of the apartment now, she'd be the one with something shoved up her ass. "Thanks, Kels. I'm looking forward to it."

"Bye, Tater."

"Good luck," I called out before the door closed all the way.

I counted to ten, just to be sure she hadn't forgotten something, and then sprang into action. I wasn't entirely sure when Jay would get here, but I wanted to be ready. He'd told me he would come over after work, yet I hadn't thought to ask if that meant straight from the office or after changing his clothes. Either way, he had about a thirty-minute drive from Langston to Samson, depending on traffic.

Checking the time, I realized I had at least half an hour before he'd show up. But that didn't mean I could relax. There was still so much to do to get ready, and I hadn't been able to do any of it until after Kelsey left. If I'd started cleaning in front of her, she would've known something was up.

I tore through the apartment, picking up anything that didn't belong, and tossed it all into my room—it was faster than putting things away. Jay was a neat freak; I was not. So, I wanted the place to be as spotless as possible for him. After all, we had a couch; he didn't need to go to my room.

Once I had everything looking like a maid had spent hours cleaning, I stripped down to my panties and bra and sat on the sofa. With my feet propped on the edge of the coffee table, I waited impatiently for Jason to arrive. I'd seen poses like this before and thought it would be sexy. Although, those had been in magazines, which had probably been edited. I was quickly reminded that real life didn't come with Photoshop to buff out the crease—*I refuse to call it a roll*—that ran across my waist. Thank God I had time to get this right.

I tried a few more positions, yet nothing felt right. I assumed it was the outfit and decided to shed the rest of what I had on. At first, I stuffed the bra and panties between the cushions, but then I thought better of it. As much as I wanted them close by for comfort reasons, I knew Jay would appreciate it more if I just bared it all. And the only way to prevent myself from changing my mind before he showed up was to lock them in my room. I took two steps before deciding to lock the bathroom door as well. You know, to *ensure* I didn't chicken out and put them back on.

And then it was back to finding the right pose.

I tried stretching out with my arms above my head. That left *nothing* to the imagination, so I tried draping my arms across my body in various ways. Then I repositioned my legs a few times. But no matter what I did, nothing *felt* sexy.

So I rolled onto my stomach.

Same issues, different pose.

But the knock on the door prevented me from switching it up again—good thing, too; otherwise, Jason might've found me in the fetal position.

I'd told him to just walk in, but apparently, he hadn't listened. So, I propped my head on my hand and called out for him to come in. My heart raced as time stood still, my bravado waning by the millisecond. But then the handle turned, and the door cracked open.

Here goes nothing.

I'd planned this out for days, ever since Kelsey had told me that she'd be gone for hours. This was my only opportunity to surprise Jay by owning my imperfections. He'd mentioned finding me naked on the couch . . . and since I wasn't very creative in the face of fear, I couldn't come up with any other ideas. Naked on the couch would have to do.

Jason was turned on by confidence. I had that in spades in a kitchen—in the nude, not so much. So, I closed my eyes, took a deep breath, and imagined I was in front of a stove. I called to mind the aroma of fresh herbs and lemon, the sizzle of homemade ghee in the pan, and the heat of the flame beneath the burner. It was enough to slow my racing heart and bring my breathing to an even rhythm.

That's when I released the air from my lungs and opened my eyes.

I could feel the easy, effortless grin in the corners of my lips as my sight landed on the man in the entryway. I took him in, starting with his polished shoes as he stepped inside. I trailed my gaze up the length of his pressed pants, along the creases of his white shirt, and paused at the perfect knot in his tie. All bets were off when I made it to his face.

At the sight of his slate-colored eyes, I gasped.

The natural silver accents in his thick hair made my throat close up.

And when he said, "Wow, Tate," I rolled off the couch, no longer caring about being sexy.

I landed on my front with a hard thump, and then I pulled myself to my hands and knees to crawl to safety. The carpet burn would hurt later, as well as every other body part that slammed into the floor, but that didn't matter right now.

I scurried around to the back of the couch in search of a blanket or towel to cover myself. Hell, I would've appreciated a damn sock. But no . . . I had to go and throw *everything* into my room before posing like a Playboy Bunnabe. Realizing I had nothing to shield my body with other than the sofa, I pulled myself onto my knees and peered over the back. "What the hell are you doing here, Michael?"

The lust on his face was obvious, though it was nothing compared to the desire in his tone when he said, "I came to talk to you."

"You literally just saw me at work a couple of hours ago."

"Yeah . . . but this is something I didn't want to discuss there."

I shook my head, dumbfounded that I had even allowed this conversation to go on for this long. "Turn around!"

Reluctantly, he pivoted on his heel until he had his back to me. And when I shouted, "*Close the damn door, Michael!*" in the same threatening tone my mom had used when I'd air-conditioned the neighborhood, he swept it closed.

I used the pathetic excuse for privacy he gave me and bolted into the alcove just outside my bedroom and bathroom.

There's an art to swiftly entering a room. You simultaneously grab and twist the handle while also leaning into the door with your body. It's technically three steps, but all are performed at the same time, making it one fluid motion. Works like a charm.

Fun fact: The door has to be unlocked for it to work.

I wrapped my fingers around the knob to my room, but before I realized it wouldn't turn, I'd already slammed my face into the wood. And because I'd pushed instead of leaned, I didn't just stumble back . . . I fell onto my ass.

Not only did my forehead, nose, and cheek ache from being smacked into a door, but my butt also hurt from the lack of padding beneath the cheap carpet. I might've cried out in pain, or maybe he'd heard the literal head-on collision. Either way, Michael came running. He knelt next to me while I held my hands to my face and pressed my thighs against my front.

"Are you okay?" The asshole couldn't even hide the laughter from his voice.

"I'd be a lot better if I could put some clothes on." I thought about that for a second and then added, "Or if you'd leave. Whichever."

He reached up and tried the handle, only to say, "It's locked."

I lowered my hands and glared at him. "Obviously."

Leddy Harper

Then he glanced around, probably looking for another option. Seeing the bathroom, he tried that, too. "Why would you lock yourself out of your room . . . naked?"

"Because Jay's coming over, and he's—" I froze, eyes wide and mouth hanging open. "Shit, Jay's coming over. You have to leave."

"He's on his way now?"

"Hell if I know. What time is it?"

Michael pushed back the cuff on his work shirt to check his watch. "Quarter after five."

I released the breath I held and allowed a small amount of relief to wash over me. "Yeah, he's on his way. But he probably won't be here for another fifteen minutes." I glared at him again. "That *doesn't* mean you can stay."

Rather than say anything, he began to loosen the knot below his chin. Then he released the buttons at his wrists, followed by the ones down his chest. When he had his shirt untucked and open, he hung his tie on my doorknob and slid the crisp white fabric down his arms.

Without a word, he held his shirt out for me to take—a peace offering of sorts. And in that moment, all I could think about was covering up. Since everything I owned was out of reach, I took it from him. At least he gave me some privacy to put it on.

Luckily, Michael was quite a bit taller than me, so it hung low enough to cover all the goods. And with it buttoned up, he couldn't see anything, which was all I cared about. But now that I was somewhat dressed, all I wanted was for him to leave.

He didn't get the hint—evident in the way he made himself comfortable on the couch.

"Seriously, Michael . . . you can't be here."

"Why? Because your boyfriend's coming?"

The jealousy alone was enough to tire me out, but the undercurrent of anger riled me up. I mean, he had no right to be pissed at me for dating anyone—or sleeping with . . . whatever. I'd dealt with it enough over the last several weeks; I would *not* put up with it in my own home.

I stood in front of him and set my fists on my hips. I probably looked like the love child of a scorned woman and Superman, but that was beside the point. "This *has* to stop, Michael. You don't get to decide when we talk. For *months* I tried to get you to have a conversation with me, but you refused. Well, guess what? I don't want to hear whatever it is you want to talk about right now."

He leaned forward and buried his head in his hands with an exaggerated sigh. I hated it when he did that. It didn't matter what the situation was; he had a way of using that one act to make me feel like I'd done something wrong, and then he'd use it to his advantage. Like he did now. When he lifted his head, he gently wrapped his fingers around my wrist and directed me to sit next to him. And like a child, I obeyed.

"I'm sorry, Tate." His voice dropped low and filled with exasperation. "I was too caught up in my own head, trying to sort through my own issues. I wish I could go back in time and change it, but I can't. That's what I'm trying to do now. I'm trying to make it right and praying like hell it's not too late."

I swallowed harshly, needing all the courage I could muster to get this out. "In case you were wondering . . . dating someone else doesn't bode well for your argument."

"I ended things with Rebecca."

I had to take a second to absorb that, because I honestly hadn't expected those words to come out of his mouth. "You did?"

"Yes, I did. I've wanted to for a while, but I needed to figure a few things out first."

"And what exactly did you figure out?"

"That I love you. And I miss you. I fucked up, Tate, and I'm ready to own it. I'm ready to do what it takes to make you mine again. Tell me what it is, and I'll do it."

My head spun, and I felt like I was being pulled in all directions. But that was what he did to me. He'd make me so turned around that I didn't know which way was up anymore. Over the last several weeks, I'd been his personal yo-yo. When he'd first heard about Jay, something had changed. And as much as I'd thought this was what I wanted, I wasn't so sure anymore.

"Why now?"

He shook his head and turned into me, placing his hand on my thigh. "Because I can't wait another day. If it were up to me, you'd put *my* ring back on, and then I'd take you to your room and make love to you."

I began to wonder if he'd sniffed a few bottles of glue before coming over. "Michael, don't you have to be in love with someone—or at the very least, *love* them—in order for it to be called that?"

He brought his hand to my face and cupped my cheek, much like he'd done a thousand times before. "I *do* love you, Tate. I never stopped."

It was like the clouds had parted and the sun shone through, basking everything I'd been blind to in a sea of light. I placed my hand near his shoulder, the heel of my palm over his clavicle with my fingertips along the side of his neck.

It was all so clear.

My heart spoke up.

And I listened.

"When you found out about Jay, I prayed it would make you jealous. I believed with my whole heart that if you saw me happy, you'd realize what you walked away from and try to get it back."

"And I did."

I licked my lips and nodded. "I know. I've waited seven months to hear you admit that. I spent nights dreaming of this moment, days thinking about it. I knew you'd come around. If I just remained in front of you, never let you forget me, forget what we had . . . I knew you'd see it."

"I didn't forget," he breathed out, his airy words blasting my face as his mouth drew nearer.

My heart knocked against my sternum, and the thunderous beats resounded in my ears as my entire body flushed, my next words perched at the tip of my tongue. And when his lips were in reach, I whispered, "Too bad I don't still feel the same."

He stilled, no longer leaning in yet not backing away, either.

"You don't deserve a second chance to break my heart, Michael."

He pulled away, though his palm remained on my face. Confusion darkened his grey eyes while he studied my expression, likely searching for a sign that what I'd said was a lie. He wouldn't find one.

"Is it true? Are you really having his baby?"

I shouldn't have laughed while he sounded so sad, but I couldn't help it. "No. It's not."

Finally, he gave up the act of being hurt. His brows dipped, pinched together, showing me his true feelings over my rejection. "You've been playing me this whole time?"

"Excuse me?" I balked. "You think I played you? How?"

"By trying to make me jealous, then stringing me along. And once I come around, you laugh in my face, like this has all been a sick game to you."

It took monumental effort to keep from rolling my eyes. "I never told you to leave her. I never even asked you to. Whether or not you stayed with her was your decision, based solely on what *you* wanted. Yes . . . I wanted you back. Hell, last week I felt the same."

"Then what changed?" His desperation was as clear as day in his unsettled eyes; it must have burned through him, considering his hand scorched my cheek where he touched me.

"I've wanted us to make it work ever since you broke up with me, but I never actually stopped to think about why. Maybe it's because you're all I ever knew."

Before I could go into the real reason I refused to ever give him another chance, he asked, "Then how can you be so sure that you don't want this?"

"Because there's not one ounce of me that wants to be with you."

"It's him, isn't it?"

"You think I'm turning you down for Jay?" That notion made me giggle under my breath.

The lines between his eyebrows deepened. "Didn't he give you that ring?"

I glanced at my finger, admiring the piece of glass that now sat on my right hand—I hadn't been able to bring myself to take it off completely after hearing of the rumors at work. "Well, yeah. But it's not an engagement ring, if that's what you're thinking."

"Then why'd you let everyone believe it was?"

"I didn't. If you assumed it was, that's on you. I never told anyone I was getting married—hell, I never even said it came from a guy. In fact, had it not been brought to my attention, I never would've known what was being said behind my back."

"Okay, but if you knew what everyone thought, why didn't you speak up and correct it? By not saying anything, you purposely allowed that rumor to stay afloat." He might've had a *small* point there, but I wasn't about to admit that.

"I told Amanda, the house gossip, that it wasn't. No one ever came to me to ask, so I didn't feel it necessary to hold a press conference and clear the air."

"Well, maybe you should have, because everyone's still under the impression that you're pregnant and engaged to that asshole."

"Why would they still think that if Amanda told them all it wasn't true?" I now had both hands on his shoulders, seconds away from shaking him out of pure frustration.

"They think you're too embarrassed to admit it, so you're denying it."

This was all very unsettling.

And rather insulting.

"Basically, what you're telling me is, everyone I work with thinks I'm a liar. What have I ever done to make them think that?" I mean, aside from the fact that almost everything out of my mouth over the last month had fallen anywhere between "half truth" and "utterly ridiculous whopper" on the fact-o-meter. But they didn't know that, so it was a moot point.

His lids lowered while he sucked in a lungful of air. As his exhale passed his lips, he opened his eyes, first setting his sights on my mouth, then meeting my gaze. "Why won't you give me a second chance?"

"Because of the reason you broke up with me in the first place."

"Which was?" Clearly he didn't know what Amanda had overheard.

But before I could answer, the front door opened.

And in walked Jay.

20

Jason

When Tatum had invited me over, letting me know that my cousin would be gone for hours, I won't lie, my dick had gotten hard. And I knew without a doubt that this would be a night I would never forget.

I just hadn't anticipated the memorable part coming at the beginning of the evening.

She had told me to just walk in, so I opened the door and took one step inside. But one step was as far as I got before the wind was knocked out of me. Tatum sat on the couch looking sexy as hell in a man's work shirt. The problem was, it wasn't *my* shirt.

I stood motionless in the doorway, two sets of eyes locked on me. Shock marred Tatum's features, while irritation and abhorrence pinched his. Even though they both had their heads turned my way, their hands never moved from each other.

"Am I interrupting something?" I wasn't sure how my voice remained so steady through the intensity of my heartbeat pounding in my throat.

"No, you're not interrupting anything." Tatum pushed him away— something she *should've* done before I'd shown up. Oddly enough, she didn't act concerned or even guilty for being caught half-naked on the couch with this guy. "Michael was just leaving."

Names weren't my strong suit. But in this case, even though I'd only heard his name once or twice, in *one* conversation a while ago, there was no way I would've forgotten it.

"Michael? As in your boss?" It was a common name . . . *could be a different Michael.*

"Umm . . ." She glanced between him and me a few times. "Yeah."

He huffed out a wave of incredulous humor while shaking his head. "That's what you told him I was to you? Your *boss?*"

A violent shade of red colored her cheeks, her uncertain eyes trained on me. But when she spoke, she directed her answer at him. "Yeah." It seemed she'd lost her vocabulary . . . along with her clothes.

"Congrats, Tatum—you won. You made me jealous." He pushed off the couch to stand and turned to her. If he said anything, I didn't hear, too lost in my thoughts to recognize much else.

Michael was Tatum's ex . . . *as well as* her boss.

He glared at me as he moved toward the door. When he stopped, I thought he'd take a swing at me, so I took a step farther inside. However, instead of turning this physical, he shook his head and peered over his shoulder. "I'll get my shirt from you tomorrow." And as he walked out, he mumbled, "Have fun with the cheating douchebag," under his breath, leaving me frozen in a state of utter confusion.

Tatum seemed slightly flustered, but then again, it was Tatum . . . slightly flustered was normal for her. Yet she managed to shake it off and stand, which did nothing but remind me of the fact that she was wearing her ex's shirt.

"Jay . . ." It was so hard to tell if she was nervous and scared or just uncomfortable.

But I had things on my mind other than how *she* felt. "I thought we agreed we wouldn't fuck other people. The least you could've done was not invite me over to watch."

She held me in place with her wide eyes. "Nothing happened, Jason. I swear."

"I have a hard time believing that while you're standing here in your boss's shirt. Or is he your ex? It's all very confusing to me. Because, you see, when you told me about your boss, you left out the fact that you used to be engaged to him. And when you told me about your ex, you neglected to include the part about him *being your boss*."

Tatum fell back onto the couch in defeat, yet she made eye contact anyway. "Kelsey called him my boss. And when I went to talk to you about it, I didn't think anything of it. It wasn't intentional—I swear."

It wasn't like I could argue with her about that. After all, it was entirely possible she was telling the truth.

However, it didn't do anything to calm me down.

"Did you use me to make him jealous?"

Tatum closed her eyes and shrugged.

"So you told him we were fucking? Did you tell anyone else?"

She started to shake her head but then stopped, opened her eyes, and looked right at me. "It's complicated, Jay."

"By all means, uncomplicate it for me. Kelsey won't be back for hours, so we have time."

Her shoulders rose when she filled her lungs with air and then dropped during her harsh exhale. "The week before I met you, he hired his new girlfriend at Fathom. It wouldn't have been so bad if she didn't talk about him all the time."

I could tell this would be a long story, but I didn't have any desire to sit next to her on the couch, so instead, I crossed my arms and made myself more comfortable where I stood.

"Everyone there knows what happened with me and Michael, so anytime Rebecca would talk about him or what they did on their day off together, they all just watched me with pity. I got tired of it, so I blurted out that I had moved on."

"And telling her that we were sleeping together somehow made you look better?"

"No, it wasn't like that. This all happened *before* we started hanging out."

There had to be an answer in there somewhere; I just wasn't sure what it was.

"Do you remember that picture your aunt took of us on my phone after you first moved back here?" she asked, waiting for me to answer. There was no way in hell I could've forgotten it, so I nodded and let her continue. "Well, when people asked to see what my new boyfriend looked like, I used it to show them."

"I'm confused. You told her we were dating before we started sleeping together?"

"Yes. I didn't think before I did it, which was stupid, because if I had—or if I had planned better—I would've shown her a photo of some other guy. But we were at Taste of the Town, and that was the first picture I could find."

Well, that explained the hug and her odd behavior, though I was still confused. "You used me to make the others stop feeling bad for you every time your ex's new girlfriend talked about their relationship?"

"Yes," she said with a sigh, as if relieved that I understood.

"And then what? Got the idea to tell your ex about me, too? To make him jealous?"

"No. I didn't tell him directly. I'll admit that I kind of hoped he'd hear about it and then realize I wasn't sitting on the sidelines waiting for him. And he did."

"*Think*," I corrected. And when her brows dipped in confusion, I added, "You said he'd realize you weren't waiting around for him, but you were, so really, there was nothing for him to *realize*, only think."

"Okay, fine. *Think*. Whatever."

Honestly, this shouldn't have been a big deal. So she had told people we were dating when we weren't. But technically, we *were* sleeping together and hanging out, as well as talking every day, so it wasn't that big of a stretch to say we were more to a bunch of people who didn't know us.

"Is that why you never wanted us to be seen in public together? In case someone came up and started talking to us, possibly saying things you didn't want me to find out?"

"No. By the time we started hanging out, they all thought we were broken up."

Oh, this just kept getting better and better. "Why didn't you just tell me?"

"I didn't want you to think I was crazy. Admit it, Jason . . . no guy wants to find out that the girl he's sleeping with has gone around telling everyone they're dating—*especially* when they've both agreed to keep things casual. You would've freaked out and disappeared."

"Or I would've found it funny." I couldn't guarantee that, but it was certainly a possibility. "You have done and said the most random, off-the-wall things ever since I first met you. I've laughed them all off, so I don't understand why you automatically assumed I wouldn't have done the same with this."

"You don't understand, Jason. That all happened *before* us. By the time I got comfortable talking to you, where I felt like I knew you well enough to just be me, warts and all, they believed we weren't together anymore."

"Exactly, which *should've* made it easier to tell me." I took a deep breath to rein in some of the frustration I felt. It wasn't fair to attack her on this; it was silly, and there was no point in making it bigger than what it was. "So why did you tell them we broke up? If it kept others from pitying you, why end it?"

"I didn't. You forced my hand." She seemed a little bitter about that, though I wasn't sure why.

"Me? How?"

"You came into the restaurant with another woman. Everyone thought you were on a date with her—including me. I didn't know it was an interview, because we didn't really know each other at the time, so it wasn't like I could justify it to everyone."

An image of Tatum came to mind. A plate of chocolate cake, a couple of very confused customers, singing, a fake candle . . . utter humiliation in her eyes. Then I recalled the way the hostess had regarded me, the snide comments and horrible service from the waitress. It all made sense.

But before I could say anything about that night, Michael's words from earlier came back to me. And suddenly, this became a much bigger deal than it had been. "So they all think I'm some piece-of-shit asshole who cheated on you?"

"What was I supposed to tell them? That I had lied and we'd only met twice?" Fear darkened her eyes, and the longer I stared into them, the less angry I was about it.

I ran my hand through my hair and then dragged it down my face. "I don't know, Tatum. I've been in there a couple of times since—I brought you flowers the next day; I stopped in once to see you on my way home from the office."

"Yes, and the card on the flowers basically reiterated what everyone thought."

I didn't care to waste my time trying to remember what I had written on a card, so I ignored it and moved on. "You don't see it, do you? When everyone looked at you with pity, you fabricated a boyfriend. Yet you don't think there's anything wrong with allowing me to walk in there and have all those same people look at me with disgust? Unfairly, at that?"

"I'm sorry, Jason," she cried, her eyes sad and remorseful. "The whole thing just spun out of control. One lie led to the next until I was buried under them all."

"What do you mean? What other lies have you told?"

"That's just it . . . I *haven't* told any others. They just keep assuming things, starting these rumors I don't know how to get out of, all because I would have to admit that the very first one was a lie. It's gone on for so long now that I can't do that without looking like a freaking psychopath."

I took a few slow breaths, hoping enough oxygen would reach my brain and things would start to make sense. "What rumors?"

"Just stupid things that are being said behind my back. None of it's true. And I only found out because Amanda—the hostess with her nose in everyone's business—mentioned it in the parking lot last week." There was a reason she circled her ass to get to her elbow, and I had a feeling it wasn't to save time.

"What did she tell you?"

"Well, it all started that night I was sick at work and left—the same day I got that ring stuck on my finger. Apparently, throwing up meant I was pregnant, and wearing a ring, no matter what kind, on my left hand couldn't mean anything other than I was engaged. Put the two together, and they all convinced themselves that you knocked me up before I dumped you, and now we're planning a shotgun wedding."

My chest tightened, my throat closed up, and no matter how hard I tried, I couldn't get enough air to make the room stop closing in on me. "You corrected them . . . right?"

"I *thought* I did."

"What do you mean by you *thought* you did, Tatum?"

"I told Amanda that it wasn't true. If anyone could spread the truth, it would be her. And considering no one said anything to *me*, that was my only option to clear the air. Oh, and I moved the ring to my right hand."

"I'm confused . . . are you saying this girl didn't tell everyone?" The longer this went on, the more frustrated I became.

"I don't know."

"Why didn't you just walk in and set the record straight instead of waiting for someone else to do it? You wouldn't have even had to admit to any of the other lies by doing so."

Her posture grew rigid, and she began to fidget with her hands in her lap. "I don't know, Jason. I was so pissed when I found out what was being said that all I wanted to do was storm in there and tell them all off. But by the time I got to work the next day, all I kept thinking about was how I'd have to relive the whole Michael thing all over again."

"What do you mean?"

"We were engaged. If I wasn't asked about when the wedding was, they were asking when we were going to have babies. After he broke it off, everyone felt sorry for me and felt the need to console me by pointing out how I'm still young, there's a guy out there for me, my chances of having a family aren't over. So, walking into work and announcing to everyone that I wasn't engaged, *again*, and that I wasn't pregnant just brought all that back. But that doesn't mean I didn't *attempt* to make the truth known in another way."

"You said no one has said anything to you . . . so how do you know your friend didn't clear it up?"

"I honestly thought she did until Michael came over. I just found out today—like ten minutes ago—they didn't believe her. They think I'm embarrassed and trying to hide it because I don't want to look like the fool who's marrying a cheater simply because I wasn't responsible enough to use protection."

"Oh, that makes me feel all warm and fuzzy inside, Tatum." I couldn't hide my anger or rein in the frustrations that burned within me. "Everyone you work with thinks I'm a complete piece of shit who not only cheated on you but also knocked you up. I'd say at least I look like the kind of guy who'd step up to the plate and do what's right, but they think I gave you a piece of recycled trash stuck in fucking tinfoil. So apparently, I'm not only an asshole who doesn't respect women, but I'm also a cheap son of a bitch. Thanks."

When her lower lids lined with tears, I had to look away, though that didn't save me the agony of hearing it in her voice. "I'm sorry. I never meant for it to go this far. It was just a stupid little lie to keep me from looking like a fool. How was I supposed to know this would happen?"

"A stupid little lie?" My throat was sore, like someone had choked me with their bare hands, yet I didn't let that stop me from forcing out the gritty words. "I find it a little ironic that your motivation for that little lie was to keep you from looking like a fool, yet it sounds like you made that worse. Because now, they don't pity you for some guy breaking your heart; they think you're stupid and likely believe you've ruined your life. And on top of that, they think I'm a deadbeat, washed-up piece of garbage."

"They don't know you, so their opinion is worthless."

I fisted my hands, wondering how she didn't get it. "I'm beginning to think I don't know you at all. Or maybe, *you* don't know *me*. Ever since I moved back, I've done *nothing* but hear about what a player I am, how I'm just a womanizer, that I'll fuck anything that walks and not think twice about who it hurts. And now, not only am I still dealing with that, but it seems I have a whole new reputation I have to battle. What's worse is I can't defend myself to people who don't know me. At least with Kelsey, I can prove her wrong; I can fight and yell and argue until she sees how wrong she is. With these other people . . . I basically have to sit back while my character is torn to shreds. No thanks to you."

"Jay, wait . . ." Tears filled her soft yet desperate plea, and if I didn't get out of here, the sound alone would leave me completely unraveled. I didn't handle a crying woman very well, but that woman being Tatum would be the end of me.

I moved the few feet to the front door and grabbed the knob to open it. "It seems you got what you wanted, Tatum. I served my purpose—your ex came back. Let him save you from the douchey cheater."

She stood just as the first tear rolled down her cheek, but she didn't say anything.

And then I left, refusing to give her the power over my destruction.

When I'd driven out of Langston on my way to see Tatum for a sexy evening alone in her apartment, I never expected I'd be heading back so soon. But there I was, navigating the roads on autopilot while I tried to work through it all in my mind.

And by the time I pulled into my driveway, I realized why I hadn't been able to give Jen my decision—why I hadn't been able to *make* one until now. Regardless of the arrangement Tatum and I had made, her presence in my life over the last month had prevented me from seeing where things would go with Jen. Somewhere in the back of my mind, unbeknownst to me, I hadn't wanted to give her up for someone who had already failed me once.

I no longer had an excuse.

I pulled out my phone and sent Jen my answer.

21

Tatum

In four and a half hours, I ran through every emotion known to man.

Shocked.

Confused.

Offended.

Defensive.

Angry.

By the time Kelsey came home and found me in my room, guilt and grief consumed me. The tears wouldn't cease, and the pain in my chest only grew worse the longer she stood in the doorway, assessing the entire situation.

"What happened, Tater?" she asked, concern dripping from her tone as she attempted to find a safe route to the bed.

"I cleaned."

Her wide eyes met mine before observing the chaos that was my room again. "Okay . . . that explains a few things. I guess at some point, I'll need to clarify the definition of cleaning, because it seems you have that a bit backward." She took a few more cautious steps while mumbling, "I'm sure walking in heels isn't the safest choice, but I doubt being barefoot would be much better."

Less than two feet away, she more or less jumped onto the mattress and situated herself in front of me. She placed her hands on my knees, which acted as my own personal barrier, and regarded me with a level of pity I wasn't comfortable with.

"We'll discuss the mess later. I'm sure you aren't crying over that." She waved her hand around my room. "Unless you're crying because you twisted your ankle getting in here. But that doesn't seem to be the case. I've seen these tears and bloodshot eyes before, which can only mean this is about Michael."

"No," I argued, and then I shook my head. "I mean, kind of, but no."

"Let's go back to the *kind of*. What did the asshole do to you now?"

I let my head fall to the headboard behind me and stared at the ceiling fan for a moment. "He broke up with Rebecca and came here to tell me that he's ready to work things out."

"Oh, really? Does this mean he no longer feels you'll want what Tanner has?"

"I don't know. I didn't get that far into the conversation before we were interrupted." A longer explanation was needed, though I didn't have the words quite yet.

"Interrupted by who?"

I took a deep breath and prayed this wouldn't blow up in my face. "I had invited someone over today while you were gone."

"Okay . . . you're being a little vague here, Tatum."

Huffing, I admitted, "Yeah, because you'll be pissed if I tell you I was going to have sex on our couch."

Her nose scrunched in disgust. "Ew. I don't want Michael's naked ass on my sofa."

"No. Not Michael."

"Then who? How many people are you sleeping with?"

"I wasn't sleeping with Michael."

Silence passed the time, her mouth wide open and eyes full of bewilderment. "Then what were you doing with him when you spent the night? And before you answer that . . . oral *and* anal are both considered sex."

"No, I mean I wasn't with him. At all."

"But he came over today?"

This could take all night. "Yes . . . uninvited."

"When someone else was supposed to be here?"

"Yes."

"To have sex with you?" The way she asked that made it sound like I had put out an ad.

"The same person I've been sleeping with ever since you caught me coming home that one morning. Not some random guy I found online or anything."

"If you weren't having sex with Michael, why did you tell me you were?"

"Because I didn't want to tell you *who* I was with."

I could visibly see the wheels spinning in her head. "Tater, I would've been more accepting of you boning Old Man Wilcox downstairs. You could've literally told me *anyone*, and it would've been better than telling me it was Michael."

"I doubt that."

"Try me."

"Jason." *Let the show begin.*

She blinked a few times, opened and closed her mouth without speaking for several seconds, and then shook it off. "Jason who? Because I only know one, and there's *no* way you would've been dumb enough to climb into his bed."

I could only stare at her, unable to verify anything with words.

"Are you kidding me? I'm gonna kill him." She moved to climb off the bed, but I stopped her.

"He didn't do anything."

"Oh, so you just enjoy sitting in your room alone, crying like a child who lost her puppy? I doubt that. What the fuck did he do, Tatum?"

Her anger was enough to scare even me, which meant I had to put a stop to this before she led Jay to believe I had told yet another lie that painted him in a bad light. "I'm telling the truth. He didn't do anything. I'm the one who messed up. I told one innocent little lie a month ago, and it spiraled out of control. He found out about it and stormed out of here. He won't answer my calls or texts."

At least she calmed down some, though now she just stared at me, utterly perplexed.

This was the time to come clean . . . about *everything*.

I started at the beginning, at Taste of the Town—Rebecca going on and on about Michael, Amanda trying to help me out, and Jason showing up. Then I explained the early rumors at the restaurant and Michael's change of heart, which I used to defend my choice to carry on with the lie. Once I'd filled her in on Jason's job interview and the debacle that ensued with the cake and my subsequent suspension, she stopped me.

"Wait a minute. So that's why he came here that night to see you?"

"Yes," I whispered. "He came to make sure I was all right."

She didn't have to speak for me to understand the battle in her head at the idea of her cousin being concerned about me. "That means it was *his* house you stayed at that first night. When you came home and told me you were with Michael."

It was about time it started to click for her.

"In my defense, I never told you I was with Michael. You assumed it was him, and I didn't correct you. I thought you knew I was talking about Jason until you said otherwise. And by that point, I figured it'd be easier to let the lie stand."

When Kelsey nodded slowly, it meant she had something to say yet chose not to. She didn't often keep her thoughts to herself, unless she knew they would unnecessarily hurt someone she cared about. Although, considering I knew that about her, whenever she did it, it didn't matter if she spoke her mind or not, the implication alone had the same effect.

"Well, that happened weeks ago. What happened today?"

I carried on with the story, telling her about the art festival, the ring, and what had happened at work that night. That led to the next day—minus the amazing sex, of course—but when I got to the part about going to his house that night, she rolled her eyes and released a frustrated "*Ugh!*"

"He's such a pig. I *almost* believed he might not be as big of an asshole as I thought . . . but then you tell me this. We *have* to do something with your self-esteem. If you don't find anything wrong with being told that you can't sleep with anyone else while he continues to get it where he can, then this issue is bigger than I thought. *Especially* since you two aren't even dating!"

I immediately came to his defense. "No. He meant *neither* of us would sleep with anyone else. We agreed it was safer this way. You know . . . diseases and whatnot. So, it's not like it was one sided or anything."

Her brows dipped, casting a shadow over her hazel eyes as she concentrated on a thought. "He told you this after I let it slip at my mom's house that you were sleeping with Michael?" When I nodded, an irritating display of vindication brightened her face. "I'll have you know, the weekend before, while you were visiting your parents, he was out drinking and went home with some skank in a short skirt."

I hadn't planned to mention this, but it seemed I didn't have much of a choice. Jason had made it perfectly clear that he was hurt by my inability to stand up for him when he couldn't do it himself, so regardless of whatever backlash I'd get, I had to speak up. "He didn't go home with her."

"Don't be a fool, Tatum."

"I'm not. He left Boots just before midnight and got home about ten minutes later."

Confusion narrowed her gaze. "How do you know?"

It wasn't until this very moment, on the cusp of proving to Kelsey that she had been wrong about Jason, that I realized what a fool I'd been. She'd doubted him, and honestly, until he'd admitted to me the next day that he hadn't slept with anyone, I'd doubted him, too. But now, as the words sat at the tip of my tongue, pooling in my mouth, I saw him in a way I should have that morning—as the good, thoughtful guy I'd never taken the time to appreciate.

"He texted and sent me voice messages for most of the two hours he was at Boots. And then we spoke about it the next morning. Apparently, you and Marlena were there, but he doesn't remember seeing either of you."

"I stayed with the girls near the bar. I saw him, but I don't know if he ever saw me. I guess he ran into my sister on his way to the bath-room, and then one other time when she wanted to check out the VIP section he was in, but I don't think they actually hung out for more than a few minutes. She said he was wasted. Either way, he can't lie and say he didn't leave with Exotic Barbie, because I watched him exit the building with her, hand in hand."

The image of him holding her hand bothered me. Then again, my feelings about it might've had something to do with the immense guilt that continued to eat at me over tonight's events. I ignored it for the time being and carried on with my attempt to clear his name. "Yes, he technically left with her, but that's only because she took him home."

"And you believe that?" Kelsey groaned and threw herself against the mattress, arms out wide and eyes locked on the ceiling. "Guys will never stop being players as long as women continue to eat up their bullshit."

I held my breath, counted backward from five, and then blurted out, "I believe him because I was there."

She jolted upright and gawked at me. "You were at Boots?"

"No. I was at his house while *he* was at Boots." I let that sink in for a moment before continuing. "His friend had invited him out, and he didn't feel like he could turn him down because it was supposed to be some sort of celebration of his new job. He wanted me to go with him, but I chose to stay behind. He sent me a message when he left the bar, and since I was at his house, I know what time he came home."

"Then we're talking about two different instances, because this was the weekend you were in South Carolina at your parents' house."

I slowly shook my head. "Nope. We're definitely talking about the same weekend." I took her silence as a warning that I needed to elaborate. "I didn't go see my parents. That morning, when you asked me who I was on the phone with, I didn't want you to know it was your cousin. One thing led to another, and before I knew it, I was at the airport waiting for him to pick me up."

"Come again? You mean to tell me that you went as far as packing a bag and letting me drop you off at the airport just to keep from telling me the truth? My God, Tatum . . . I picked you *up* from the airport on Sunday."

"Yup. You sure did. He dropped me off about thirty seconds before you got there."

"What the hell is wrong with you? And he just let you stay the weekend at his house? As well as leaving you there alone while he went out drinking?"

I nodded, and when that didn't feel sufficient enough, I added a one-shoulder shrug.

Kelsey sighed; she seemed to be on the verge of relenting. "You still have those messages he sent you from the club?"

As much as I didn't want her to hear them, I hoped his words might prove to her that he wasn't as bad as she thought. I scrolled through our texts, taking a bit longer due to the number of conversations we'd had since then, and when I made it to the audio messages I'd saved, I handed her my cell.

She pressed play on the first one.

"I'm in a debate with Megan Fox. She said you're s'posed to drink certain wine with certain foods. You're a wine person; is that true?" Loud music filled the sound clip, making his slightly slurred question a little harder to understand.

"Megan Fox?"

"The girl you saw him leave with. He couldn't remember her name."

"Doesn't surprise me. He can't remember anyone's name, especially a girl's—unless he's related to them. I bet he called you Meghan Markle behind your back until he learned your name."

I got caught up in the memory of running into him at Taste of the Town—okay, *running into him* was an exaggeration, but that was neither here nor there. I couldn't be too sure, but I would've put money on the fact that he'd known my name then . . . and used it. Not a moniker, not a celebrity whom he thought I resembled. *My name.* But before I could confirm that to myself, Kelsey interrupted my thoughts by playing the next message.

"I'm gonna have to look into this. I gotta make sure I get you all the wines you need. But since you'll prolly haff'ta help me cook, I should jus' have you tell me what bottles to get."

The next message came a little while later, though I doubted she paid attention to the time stamps to notice.

"This chick needs shopping help. You should be her friend."

I didn't need to see the screen to remember the question marks I'd replied with.

"I like your clothes. I like them better on my floor." His laugh was drawn out and lazy, painting a clear picture of just how drunk he'd been. "Pull your skirt down, Foxy."

"He was talking to the girl," I clarified when Kelsey's judgmental eyes met mine. "He was referring to her skirt being too short. He mentioned it in a text earlier, so I knew what he was talking about. I think the first part was for me, that he wanted me to take her shopping for clothes because he likes what I wear."

"Seems he likes you naked better," she droned before playing the last message.

"I'm leaving the club." Other than the sound of a car door closing, silence filled the background. "Her driver's driving me. If something happens to me, issa black Es'alade. This guy looks like Liam Neeson."

He'd lowered his voice, attempting to whisper when he added, "He's kinda scary lookin'." Then his tone returned to normal. "I'd give you the tag number . . . but I'm already in the car. Shoulda thought about that earlier, huh?"

While his rambling was cute, it was the next part that I hadn't been able to listen to since he'd sent it.

His voice softened but not in a whisper. It was closer to contentment, like he'd been seconds away from falling asleep. "I'm comin' home to you, babe. I'll be there soon."

"Clearly, he was drunk. I think he thought he was talking to Jen," I said, feeling the need to excuse it before she read too much into it. It was the same thing I'd told myself that night when I'd heard it. And the ache in my chest then returned now, like I could physically feel my heart breaking—at the time, I'd assumed it was his heartache, but now I wasn't sure what to believe.

Kelsey finally set the phone down and lifted her eyes to mine. "Did you ever ask him about it? Does he remember sending these to you?"

"I have no clue. I saved them, but if he didn't do the same on his phone, then they probably disappeared. I think they only stay for a couple of minutes once they've been played, unless you keep them. But I've never played them for him or asked about it. He was drunk. I doubt he even knew what he was talking about."

"Okay, so how did you get from there"—she pointed to the device on the mattress—"to sitting in here crying over him without it being his fault?" At least she seemed willing to give him the benefit of the doubt, which was all I could ask for.

I caught her up to present time, which included the ring and rumors, and ended with what had taken place this evening after she left the apartment.

The only thing she had to say was, "I don't understand why he's so mad."

"I don't know that he is. I think he's hurt and betrayed, which I totally understand, but I don't know how to fix it."

"Just give him time to calm down; he'll come around. But I would suggest trying to fix it on your end first. I doubt he'll get over it if everyone you work with still assumes he's a loser."

Advice I already knew. "He doesn't give anyone a second chance, Kels."

"He'll either have to, or his Sundays will be very lonely, because my family would totally choose you over him." She leaned forward and perched her chin on my knees. "Am I allowed to say how relieved I am that you turned Michael down?"

For the first time all night, I laughed. "Yes. You're allowed, but only if you admit that Jason's not as bad as you made him out to be. He might've been an asshole back in the day, but that's not who he is anymore."

"He got in your pants the first time you two hung out. You really want to argue this?"

I shrugged, though I refused to let it die. "And he could've very easily sent me home when we were done. He didn't have to pick me up from the airport the next day or even offer to let me stay at his house rather than dropping me off at a hotel. He could've slept with the girl from the club while I was in his bed, but he didn't. When you told him I was sleeping with Michael, he could've used that as an excuse to add other women to his rotation. Not only did he *not* do that, but he talked to me about his reservations regarding *either of us* sleeping with other people."

She waved me off before I could give her more examples. "Fine. I get it."

"I want to hear you admit he's not an asshole."

A long sigh slipped past her lips. "I never really thought he was. I mean, I obviously had my reservations about him—he had no regard for women ten years ago, and while I understand he was in a serious, committed relationship for a while, he's not anymore. This is the first time he's been single since someone figured out how to tame him. It's not that crazy of a thought that he might spend a little time enjoying his freedom, especially now that he's in a new place with new faces and new ass to chase."

It was hard to argue with that.

"Plus . . . you're my best friend, Tater. You're practically family. I didn't want something to happen between you two that could potentially mess everything up. If any other guy hurts you, he's dead to me. But it's not like I can do that with Jason."

"No, I get it, Kels. And now, I've messed it all up."

"I don't think that's true. You probably won't have any more slumber parties with him, which would make me happy, but I doubt this will be an issue in the long run. I'm willing to bet he'll be over it by lunch on Sunday."

As much as I wished for that to be true, I refused to get my hopes up. "Knowing Jay, I bet he doesn't come."

"Keep calling him Jay, and he won't."

"I always call him that."

"Really?" She sat back, bewilderment narrowing her eyes. "He *hates* that name."

I could only shrug, not having a reason why he'd allow me to use it.

Wiping my face, I shifted on the bed to sit with my legs crossed— more inviting than keeping them bent in front of me like a shield. "Enough about me. Tell me all about tonight. Did you get the deal?"

Her eyes lit up, which ignited undeniable happiness within me. And then we sat there for another hour, talking about her night and what was to come of it. I couldn't have been more excited for my best friend.

Coming clean to my coworkers was not as easy as admitting it all to Kelsey.

I figured it'd be better to get it all out of the way at once rather than tell a couple people and then deal with new rumors. But it wasn't as simple as gathering everyone into the kitchen for a "Tatum has a confession" press conference. I would have to deal with it one person at a time, all within the same day.

As much as I didn't feel Michael deserved the truth, I gave it to him anyway. And as much as the staff liked to talk, I figured he should hear it from me first before someone else filled him in on whatever twisted version they wanted to share. Thankfully, it wasn't a long conversation, nor did he have much to say about it. He nodded and grunted a few times, and then once again accused me of playing him. I didn't argue. There was no point; he'd think what he wanted no matter what I had to say. I was just thankful for the opportunity to speak my mind about his reasons for breaking up with me. And then I rejoiced in the vindication I felt when I'd gotten everything off my chest and left, refusing to give him a moment to refute it.

The next person had to be Rebecca. After all, that's where the whole lie had started, and considering she'd ended up a victim of my carelessness, I felt it was best to go to her before any of the others. Although, after hearing what she had to say, I wished I'd gone to her first and *then* to Michael.

"So . . ." Her eyes sparkled as she rubbed her hands together in excitement—excitement I was not at all expecting. "What's the plan to win him back?"

"Excuse me?" I was confused, unsure if we had both been part of the same conversation. "Rebecca, did you not hear me? We weren't together. I lied about the whole thing."

"Well, clearly you *were* together. Just because it wasn't what we all thought it was doesn't mean you two didn't have something. Now we just have to figure out a way to fix this. What can I do to help?"

Either she was incredibly dense, or she had a heart of pure gold. My money was on the heart of gold. Which honestly made me feel even worse about how this all had affected her.

"Aren't you mad?" I asked, deflating some of her enthusiasm. "I mean, if I hadn't lied, none of the other rumors would've gotten started, and without the last one, Michael wouldn't have left you."

"Sure he would have. Maybe not when he did, but eventually. I *should* be thanking you. Without all that, who knows how long it would've taken me to see his true colors."

"So you aren't upset that he broke up with you?"

She seemed confused by my question, yet she answered anyway. "Not really. I tried to end things with him a couple of weeks ago—after we all thought Jay had cheated on you. But he talked me out of it."

"Hold on." I paused to take a deep breath, and then I asked, "How did he *talk you out* of dumping him? I don't get it."

"I knew that you two used to date and were engaged for a brief period of time. But I thought that was like a long time ago. I didn't know it all happened at the beginning of the year. It wasn't until the night that Jay came in with that girl that I learned the truth. I was mad that he'd ever put me in that kind of position. I must've looked like a heartless idiot talking about him in front of you the way I did. You never said anything—neither did anyone else—so I didn't think it bothered you. When I confronted Michael about it, he swore that you knew about me before I was hired and everyone was making a bigger deal about it than there needed to be. I wanted to ask you about it, but you were gone all weekend, and when you came back, it didn't feel right with everything that happened with Jay."

My heart actually hurt for Rebecca. And even though I didn't need another reminder of how relieved I should be that I wasn't stuck with Michael for the rest of my life, she'd given me one anyway.

I dismissed her desire to plot ways to win Jason back and moved on with my confession tour. Carrie was next—only because she was there and could sniff out a secret from a mile away. I wasn't sure what I'd expected from her, but being told that my lies made me more fascinating than my real life hadn't been it. She lost interest in my boring reality and told me to let her know when something exciting happened.

The rest of the night went about the same—me setting the record straight with anyone who came within ten feet. Most of the time, I got a blank stare or a hearty laugh. The others just brushed it off and went back to work. Honestly, had I known it would be this way, I might've contemplated coming clean a long time ago.

Amanda came to the kitchen at the end of the night. I could tell by the satisfied smirk on her face that she'd already heard, yet I told her again anyhow. I'd repeated it so many times I had it cut down to the main points, the truth, and then my apology. The only thing that heifer could say was, "I knew it." And then she left.

I thought I would feel better once the secret was out, but instead, I felt worse. It was silly to think I could tell the truth about a few things and make everyone see that Jason was an amazing person rather than the jerk they'd assumed him to be, and everything would be fine. Life didn't work that way, and even though I knew that, it didn't make his silence any easier to deal with.

It might've taken a couple of days and a long weekend spent mostly locked in my room, but I eventually called the news station Jason had set me up with. Against my better judgment, I agreed to host a cooking segment for their Saturday morning broadcast. It was scheduled to film in one week and then air that weekend.

I'd more than likely make a fool out of myself on TV.

But it was a risk I was willing to take.

22

Tatum

If I wasn't at work, I was in my kitchen. I'd pull random things out of the fridge and cook whatever came to mind, taking notes as I went and then tweaking what didn't work. Before I knew it, I had page after page of creative meal ideas.

"Where'd you come up with these names?" Kelsey sat on the counter, flipping through my spiral notebook while I prepared my next dish.

"I don't know," I answered, my attention set on the task in front of me. "Just whatever came to me at the time, I guess."

"Sherlock Holmes–Made Pizza? Alexander Graham Bell Peppers? These are pretty catchy, Tater." She continued to flip while I continued to focus on the sauce bubbling in the pan. "You're Not a Jerky sounds good, but I think my favorite is Sorry for Jambalyin'."

Had I actually listened to her instead of just pretending, I would've known where she was going with this, and I might've thought about snatching the notebook from her hands. But I didn't. Because apparently, I had yet to learn my lesson.

"Are all of these about Jason?"

I peered over my shoulder, catching the glint in her eyes that told me denying it would be a waste of my breath. In case it wasn't already obvious, I hadn't learned that lesson, either. "I don't know what you're talking about. They have nothing to do with him."

"Okay . . . then what was the inspiration behind Missing You So Jam Much?"

"What's your point, Kels?"

"My *point* is . . . I'm sure there's something about Jason in every one of these, whether it's in the title or the dish itself. Have you talked to him at all?"

My chest tightened, but I attempted to ignore it and focus on what I was doing. "Not really. I texted him a couple of times to tell him that he didn't have to worry about anyone at work thinking he was an asshole, but all I got were really short responses."

I stirred the sauce, disregarding the hum that came from behind me.

"Do you think he'll be at your parents' house this weekend?" I believed if I could just get him in the same room, I'd be able to make him talk to me. Even if it were only for one minute, it would be better than nothing.

It had been a little over a week since he'd left my apartment, and still, I'd heard almost nothing from him. To make matters worse, he'd skipped lunch last Sunday. Truthfully, it hadn't surprised me; I'd prepared myself for it, pretty much knowing he wouldn't show up, but that hadn't made it easier when I'd stood next to his mom and he wasn't perched at the bar in front of me.

"Oh, uh . . . no, he won't be there." That was enough to lock up every muscle in my entire body. "He's actually out of town this weekend—left yesterday."

I set the wooden spoon down and slowly faced my best friend. "Where'd he go?"

"Aunt Lori said he went to Vegas."

Pretending to be unaffected by something when the person you're trying to hide it from can see your face never works out. Yet I tried anyway. "Any idea why?"

"Honestly, no. But I didn't ask. I knew I wouldn't be able to lie to you if it had to do with Jen, so this way, I can tell you that I don't think you have anything to worry about. He's probably going to see a friend or relative or something."

"Kelsey . . . you're his cousin; you know all his relatives live here." I appreciated the smile I got from that, even if it was small and only lasted two seconds. "And we both know he went there for her. There's no reason to kid ourselves."

"You don't know that."

"Uh, yeah I do. She was making plans to visit him; probably to work things out. I mean, this was bound to happen sooner or later." *Later* would've been an easier pill to swallow than the one I'd gotten, which had left me thinking he'd run out of here and headed straight to her.

"I just hate seeing you upset about it."

"I'm not." Yeah, I totally hadn't learned *anything* over the last week, because it seemed I was still lying. I waved her off and went back to the pan on the stove. "We weren't dating, Kels. It's not like he broke my heart or anything."

"Tatum . . . I just went through this entire recipe book that you've *made up* since your fling with Jason ended. You can't tell me that you aren't in love with him. Pretend all you want that him visiting Jen doesn't bother you, but we both know that's bullshit."

"We were sleeping together for a few weeks. That's it. There's no way anyone can fall in love that fast. You've clearly watched too many Nicholas Sparks movies."

"If that were the case, I'd be convinced one of you would die soon." She laughed at her own joke, and no matter how lame I thought she was, I couldn't bite back the amusement that played on my smiling lips.

"You know you can be honest with me, right? It doesn't matter that he's my cousin; I'll always listen to you, no matter what it's about."

I peered at her over my shoulder. "I know. Thanks, Kels."

She held up one finger and added, "That's a lie. I don't want to hear details of his appendage . . . or sex. I draw the line there."

"Were you able to get Saturday off, Tatum?" Mrs. Peterson asked, pulling me from my daze.

I was on the patio with Kelsey, her sister, her mom, and her aunt, while her dad and Nick manned the grill on the dock below. This was the second Sunday I had to be at this house without Jay, and I wasn't sure how many more I would be able to handle. There was a good chance I'd spent the last hour lost in my thoughts while staring at the sun dancing off the lake. If he didn't show up next weekend, someone would have to spoon-feed me and wipe the drool from my mouth.

I smiled at Diane and nodded. "Oh . . . yes, ma'am. I switched shifts with someone. I'm working Wednesday night now." That meant I wouldn't have to see Michael, and nothing made me happier than an entire shift without his moody ass.

Genuine happiness shone in her bright smile. "That's so good to hear. I hated the thought of rushing through your very first TV appearance or pushing the celebration off until Sunday. I would have, of course, but I want it to be special for you, not feel like every weekend."

"I really appreciate it, Mrs. Peterson, but please don't go out of your way for me."

"Nonsense." She tsked. "Saturday will be *all* about you, and now we won't have to cut the party short for you to go to work." Her eyes glimmered with excitement. "And Jason will be here, too. He's flying back from Nevada late tonight. I'm sure he wouldn't miss it for the world."

While the conversation carried on around me, I tried to tell myself that just because he was in Vegas, that didn't mean he'd gone for Jen. And even if he *did* see her, it didn't mean they were trying to work things out.

Fun fact: It's much harder to lie to yourself than it is to someone else.

But it didn't matter what I tried to tell myself, because my heart was shattered. I'd adamantly denied having feelings for him, citing the impossibility of becoming attached to someone so quickly, and while I still believed that to be true, I couldn't explain the emptiness in my chest or the pain where my heart used to be.

When Lori mentioned getting the salad ready, I couldn't have been more relieved. At least if I had food in front of me, or if I were in a kitchen, I'd be able to concentrate on something other than my pain. Not to mention, I wouldn't have to continue listening to Kelsey argue with her mom over what was better—tile or hardwood. Those two didn't understand the concept of an opinion to save their lives. Kelsey would gripe about this for a week, until they found something else to argue about next Sunday, all the while oblivious to the fact that she was *just like her mom.*

After using the restroom and washing my hands, I joined Lori in the kitchen. She already had the bowl sitting out and the vegetables on the counter, waiting to be shredded and diced into a beautiful garden salad. I didn't need direction, though I accepted it anyway. She pointed to the container of cherry tomatoes and slid a knife my way. The gesture alone was calming, considering our roles were typically reversed.

"Did I ever tell you about Jason's seventh birthday?" Lori's sweet voice caught my attention. She smiled and then returned to chopping the carrots. "He has always been indecisive. Ever since he was a baby."

I didn't know where this story was going, but I began cutting the tomatoes and listened.

"Bill had moved in a few months before, so while it wasn't exactly new, there were still a lot of learning curves we all had to figure out. Anyway, I thought it would be nice to let Jason pick his own birthday dinner. He was seven, so I figured he was old enough to have a say in what we ate on his special day."

"I probably would've asked for mac and cheese," I said through laughter.

"I would've been happy with that, just as long as he picked *something*. But dear Lord, that boy didn't make it easy. At breakfast that morning, I asked him what he wanted. He said he didn't know, so I told him to take a bit and think about it. A few hours later, he came up to me, his little face scrunched and his tiny hands balled into fists."

I stopped what I was doing and looked at her. "What happened?"

She shook her head and laughed beneath her breath. "He didn't know what he wanted to eat for dinner. I offered a few suggestions, things I knew he liked, but he didn't want any of that. So, I told him to think a little more about it. By three that afternoon, I kind of needed to know what I was making in case I had to make a trip to the store. But he still hadn't made up his mind."

"He spent that whole time thinking about it?"

"You know it. He sat up in his room for most of the day, and the more he thought about it, the more frustrated he became. And as I'm sure you can guess, I was just as mad as he was. I must've suggested every dish under the sun, and he turned them all down. I told him if he didn't tell me, I would have to order pizza." She looked at me and added, "He about lost his mind when I issued that threat."

"Did he not like pizza?" I couldn't imagine any kid not liking it.

"Oh, that wasn't it at all. It's just that he didn't *want* pizza. Finally, Bill stepped in. He must've realized I was about to explode and decided to help out. He was great when I needed moral support, but up until that time, he hadn't ever asserted himself in a parental role. Jason was never one to argue or give me problems, so Bill never *needed* to step in before."

She stared ahead and smiled, more than likely lost in the memory.

"He calmly sat next to him at the table with a piece of paper and a pen. And rather than ask Jason what he *wanted*, he asked him what he *didn't* want. Once they had a very extensive list of everything he wasn't interested in, they started thinking of foods that didn't have any of those things in it. It took maybe two minutes before he decided on something I'd never made before." She dropped her chin and swayed her head side to side as silent humor shook her shoulders.

"That's a cute story. You've never told me that one before."

Her eyes sparkled when she turned to me, stepping closer to add the carrots to the bowl. And in her natural, motherly voice, she said, "It takes him a while to know what he wants. Sometimes, he has to figure out what it is that he *doesn't* want first. But give him time . . . he *always* comes around." She winked and then returned to the cutting board.

I was speechless for a moment, but the second I opened my mouth to ask her what she meant by that, Kelsey's dad walked in with a pork loin on a tray. Seconds later, the others followed, effectively silencing my question.

Jason might not have been there, but that didn't stop me from staring at the empty seat at the table, picturing a frustrated little boy who couldn't decide what he wanted to eat on his birthday.

The day had come to film the cooking segment for the news station. Nothing had prepared me for the onslaught of nerves that wrecked my stomach and left me stuttering like a fool.

"You almost ready, Ms. Alexander?" one of the production assistants asked after knocking on the open door to my dressing room.

That had to be the best part of it all. I had my own room with a table and mirror. I might not have had a team to style my hair or apply my makeup, but at least I had a place to do my own.

I gave my reflection one last glance and then hopped off the chair. "About as ready as I'll ever be," I mumbled while making my way out of the room.

The young woman led me down a narrow hallway to the empty studio. I'd pictured a full audience, yet that wasn't what greeted me. In fact, they didn't even have rows of seats lining the back wall like I'd expected. Instead, the only people around were a few cameramen, a couple of guys wearing headsets in a closed-off sound booth, and the host—well, I *assumed* she was the host—in an area set up to look like a kitchen.

She wore her light-brown hair twisted into a bun and pinned to the back of her head, which I typically thought made women appear old, but on her, it worked. Her eyes were heavily lined, the lids perfectly smoky, and I couldn't help but be jealous of it. No matter how many tutorials I watched on the process, I always ended up looking like I'd just rolled out of bed with three-day-old mascara smudged beneath my eyes. And don't get me started on the tight skirt that hugged her hips or the blouse that showed off her cleavage while still being classy. Her simple black pumps gave her calves definition I could only dream about. Without a doubt, this woman could have made a Victoria's Secret model insecure.

Standing in the manufactured kitchen located in the far corner, she instructed someone I couldn't see about the lighting. She'd say something, and one of the overhead bulbs would become dimmer or brighter. This happened several times until she gave the invisible person the thumbs-up. In my opinion, it looked exactly the same as it had before she started to tinker with it, but I wasn't the professional, so my opinion didn't matter.

"Gemma, this is Tatum Alexander." My tour guide smiled while she made the introductions. With her clipboard held against her chest, she turned to me and said, "Everything you requested is stocked in the kitchen and ready to go. We have the dish you already prepared, which is what you'll use to present to the viewers at the end. We'll go through a bit of each step just to show the process, but ultimately, you won't fully cook anything. So don't stress. It's quick and easy. You ready to have a little fun?"

I'd heard this speech before, though it wouldn't have mattered if she'd repeated it a dozen more times; it wouldn't calm my nerves. Don't stress, my ass. Quick and easy? I doubted it. These people had probably never met the likes of me.

They were in for a treat if they thought this would be fun.

Everything was great until the camera came on. That blinking red light did nothing but taunt me until I stood frozen, staring wide eyed into the lens while Gemma used her television voice to seduce the viewers. Granted, the viewers wouldn't come for five more days, but that didn't stop the anxiety from strangling me.

"Tatum, why don't you talk a little about what ingredients we're using today," she prodded in a sickeningly sweet voice.

I focused on the items laid out in front of me and attempted to emulate her tone, hoping it would make me sound inviting and happy like it did for her. So, I picked up the bowl of romaine and said, "Lettuce." Then I moved on to the bottle of oil, doing the same until Gemma leaned closer and whispered, "Speak up—they can't hear you."

"Corn." I made sure to speak louder, more clearly, and continued going down the line. Once I got to the last ingredient, my nerves began to wane, and I finally started to think I could do this.

Apparently, I was living in a fantasy.

"Tatum . . ." One of the crew members stepped up to the counter. This surprised me since they weren't supposed to be in front of the camera, though he didn't give me time to question it before continuing. "You need to look up when you speak, like you're talking to the viewers."

I nodded. Look up . . . I could do that. Talk to the viewers . . . easy.

He went back to his place in the shadows, and we started over.

"Lettuce." I lifted the bowl, same as the last time, yet now, I did so while staring into the lens with a smile on my face. I had to admit, setting it down to pick up the next item wasn't easy without looking at what I was doing. "Butter. Corn."

No one whispered any direction, and the director guy never came back or stopped me. I could just see it now . . . my own show with my own theme song.

I grew lost in the lyrics and beat of what that song would be as we moved from one step to the next. Gemma would ask me a question or turn to the camera, going off on some tangent about food that I didn't pay attention to, while I shined like the star I was born to be.

"What are you doing now?" She must've felt the need to give every detail, and when I didn't, she'd direct me into an explanation.

With the bottle tipped slightly toward the pan on the burner, I said, "Adding oil."

"How much are you supposed to use? I have a tendency to go a little overboard."

"Well . . ." Assuming she had a personal interest in my answer, rather than asking for the sake of the show, I looked at her. "It all depends on what you're making. You should really follow the recipe and use the exact amount it calls for."

Her eyes widened the tiniest bit, but she quickly shook off the surprise in favor of a smile. She grabbed my wrist and pulled the bottle away from the pan, using her hold on me to set it on the counter. "I think that looks like enough; don't you?"

It wasn't until I glanced back to what I had on the stove that I realized I'd continued pouring while staring at her. "Oh, this will be fine." I couldn't guarantee that, but considering we were only doing enough to demonstrate each part rather than running through the entirety of the process, I assumed it wouldn't be an issue. I mean, it wasn't like I'd ever cooked anything without actually *finishing* each step. Gemma hustled me through the next few of those.

"So once we have the breaded corn patties ready to go"—Gemma handed me the plate that had been prepared prior to filming—"it's time to toss them into the pan. Is that right, Tatum?"

I nodded and turned toward the stove.

Two seconds later, any chance I had at being on television blew up in my face.

23

Jason

Mom beamed at me from behind the center island in her kitchen. "There you are. I started to worry that you changed your mind about having dinner with me tonight."

I leaned over the counter to kiss her cheek and then turned to the fridge for a drink. "I told you I'd be here around five thirty. Why would you think I wasn't coming?"

"Because you're late."

Twisting off the top of a water bottle, I glanced at the clock on the stove. "It's five thirty-three, Ma. Which in everyone else's world, falls under the *around* part of 'I'll be there *around* five thirty.' See how that works?"

Before she could say anything, the front door opened and closed. Mom didn't seem surprised by another person walking into her house, which meant it had to be family.

My flight home had been delayed, so I hadn't even landed until after two in the morning, and then I'd had a full day at the office. I was far too tired to deal with anyone I was related to—Mom didn't count; she'd given me life, so she always said that exempted her from situations like this.

As luck would have it, our surprise guest was none other than Kelsey. I would've taken Uncle Fred and his fishing stories over the feisty redhead any day. Hell, Marlena's rambunctious four-year-old seemed like a walk in the park compared to her. What was worse was that my mom had clearly known she was coming over, yet she hadn't warned me; she probably knew I would've bailed—smart play on her part.

"Hey, Aunt Lori." Kelsey's cheerful and bubbly greeting was nothing but a ruse. That theory was proven when she turned to face me. The smile she'd shown my mother vanished, as did the happy tone when she mumbled, "Jason."

Mom stepped around the island to give my cousin a hug, which was more than she'd done for me when I'd arrived. But I couldn't focus on that, because I was instantly sidetracked by my mom's bright-pink zebra-striped pants.

"What are *those*?" I pointed to the ridiculous things painted on her legs.

She glanced down, confusion narrowing her gaze. "They're leggings. Kelsey gave them to me."

"Don't ever do that again." I glared at my cousin. "And who invited you to dinner?"

She raised her brows and cocked her head to the side. "I did. Your mom told me you'd be here tonight, so I figured I'd join you. Since you were in Vegas this weekend, I thought this would be a good way to catch up."

This reeked of a setup.

Ignoring Kelsey's obvious interest in my weekend, I grabbed three plates from the cabinet and set them in front of my mom. I was perfectly capable of making my own plate, but here, Mom determined what everyone got.

"Did you run out of food at your apartment?" I asked Kelsey after we each took a seat at the table. We sat across from each other, leaving the place at the end for my mother. Even though Bill was no longer here to occupy the chair at the other end, I never felt right taking it.

Ironically, Kelsey didn't give me a smug look. She just shrugged and said, "Tater's filming the cooking segment today. I'm sure she doesn't want to come home after that and then make me something to eat."

My stomach knotted at the mention of Tatum. However, hearing that she had accepted the morning-show offer left me feeling like I'd been shocked by a defibrillator—my chest ached, yet it made my heart beat again.

I had to shake it off, refusing to get into a conversation with Kelsey about her roommate. "Are you not capable of making something for yourself?"

"Of course I am. But why would I?"

"Umm . . ." I blinked several times. "I'm just grasping at straws here, but maybe so you have something to eat?"

Just then, my mom set a plate in front of her. She looked at it, then at me. "I can't be sure, Jason, but it seems to me like I *have* something to eat—*without* having to cook it."

I stabbed my fork into the heap of macaroni salad and stuffed it into my mouth. It was the only way to keep from starting an argument about Tatum needing to cook. "This is amazing, Ma."

"Tatum made it yesterday at Diane's." Mom took a sip of her tea. "And swallow before you speak."

"Yeah, too bad you weren't there. Dad did a pork loin." Kelsey was never this nice. Something was definitely up. "So what were you doing in Vegas?" And there it was.

Annoyed, I peered at my cousin while leaning over my plate, hoping she understood the imminent danger she faced if she kept this up. "None of your business."

Meanwhile, Mom sat blissfully unaware with a glass of ice tea in her hand. "Oh, before I forget . . ." She placed her hand on my arm to catch my attention. "Do you have any plans for Saturday?"

This woman lectured me for speaking with food in my mouth, yet it never failed, she always waited until I took a bite before asking me a question. Rather than wait until I swallowed to give her an answer, I just shook my head.

"Oh, good." My mom's eyes brightened with her enthusiastic grin. "Then you can come to your aunt's house."

I took a moment to make sure I understood what she'd said. "She's doing lunch on Saturday instead of Sunday?"

"Yes. We're going to record the morning show and watch it while we're all together." Seeing the pride in her eyes when she talked about Tatum made me wonder if it was visible when she spoke about me.

I quickly shook that thought off; just because my feelings about Tatum had changed didn't mean Mom's had to as well. "Um . . . I don't know if I'll be able to make it."

"Why not? You just said you didn't have plans."

I turned from my mom to Kelsey, only to catch her roll her eyes. At least she didn't make a comment or snide remark; instead, she slid out of her chair and went to the fridge. I wouldn't have been surprised if she'd done that to *keep* herself from saying something in front of my mom.

With the fork close to my lips, I said, "I don't, Ma. But that doesn't mean I want to go." And then I shoveled a scoop of meatloaf into my mouth, preventing myself from having to answer the questions I knew would follow.

Except that wasn't such a smart idea, because she surprised me by asking, "How much longer do you plan to avoid Tatum?" And I started to choke.

My life flashed before my eyes as I leaned over my plate, coughing up meatloaf uncontrollably. And with the strength of a young body-builder, Mom slapped my back—although it felt more like a beating than a lifesaving measure.

Once my airway was clear, I took a chance and played dumb. "Who said I was avoiding Tatum?"

"Kelsey said you two aren't speaking to each other," Mom said when she sat back down.

I swung my glare to my cousin, who annoyingly, still had her head in the fridge. I couldn't see her face, yet I knew she'd heard the whole thing. That point was proven when she called out, "Is this yogurt any good?"

"I don't have any yogurt, sweetheart."

"Oh, then I'm going to assume it's not," she muttered from behind the door.

My fists landed on the table a little harder than intended when I glanced between Kelsey and my mom. "Does anyone in this family know how to keep their mouths shut?"

After grabbing a water, Kelsey decided to stop hiding and moved away from the fridge. "In my defense, all I said was that you were upset with Tatum and haven't spoken to her in a couple of weeks. I didn't tell anyone that it's because she told a few people at work she was dating you, and you found out about it."

I smacked my hand against my face, wishing I had something harder to bang my head into.

"Well, son . . . I don't see what's so bad about a girl telling people that you're going steady. I think that would be a compliment. Why would that upset you?"

"He thinks she made him look like a fool," Kelsey answered on my behalf. "And since he doesn't offer anyone second chances, no matter how sorry they are or what lengths they go to make it right, she's pretty much dead to him."

I groaned inwardly, hoping it would help release some of my irritation.

Apparently, Mom thought that was the perfect time to offer her completely unsolicited advice. "Not everyone is like your father, Jason."

I dropped my hands to the table and stared at her for an obscene amount of time. "What does he have to do with anything?"

"Whenever someone hurts or betrays you, you put up a wall between you and them. Anyone who's watched ten minutes of a *Dr. Phil* show can see you do it to protect yourself. But at some point, you're going to have to realize that while you think you're keeping them from hurting you again, all you're really doing is preventing either of you from healing."

As much as I hated to admit it, she had a point. However, none of that explained her comment about my dad. So, rather than give her insight much thought, I set it aside in favor of getting the answer to my original question. "And that pertains to my father . . . how?"

"What she's trying to say is"—Kelsey leaned forward with her arm stretched across the table to get my attention—"no matter how many times your dad let you down, you continued to give him chance after chance. And he continued to hurt you time after time. But you can't assume everyone will do the same." She sat up straight, slipping her hand back to her side of the table.

My mom didn't wait for me to argue before chiming in. "There will always be people in this world who'll ruin every opportunity you give them, and then continue to crawl back for more. But there are others who'll make mistakes, only to move heaven and earth to keep from ever making them again."

There was nothing quite like a psychological evaluation by relatives—none of whom had ever attended school to *be* a psychologist. Then again, I couldn't expect anything different from my family.

"Listen, guys . . ." I glanced between my mom and my cousin, addressing them both. "I appreciate the insight into my childhood trauma and diagnosis of daddy issues—I really do—but unfortunately, it's unnecessary. Tatum and I were *friends*. That's it. Nothing more. So while you both have some amazing theories about my motivations, it doesn't apply to her. I have no problem being around her, nor do I hold anything against her."

"Does that mean we'll see you Saturday?" Mom had either fallen on her head at Derby practice, or she had mastered the act of sweet old lady and was using it to her advantage.

I picked up my fork and stared at the food in front of me. "I can't make any promises."

My response seemed to pacify Mom—I didn't care how Kelsey felt about it. I just knew I had to hurry up and leave before they could turn back into Oprah and Dr. Phil. If season two started, I wouldn't be able to guarantee it would end as smoothly as the last.

After scooping the last of the meatloaf into my mouth, I pushed my chair away from the table. My mom hated it when I excused myself before I finished chewing the last bite, but I was willing to risk the repercussions.

"I hate to eat and run, Ma, but I have to get home." I kissed her cheek, thankful she hadn't mentioned how fast I'd inhaled my food. "And for the love of God . . . please throw out those tights you're wearing. You should also stop feeding the strays," I added while pointing to my cousin.

"I really need to be going, too." Kelsey stood up, which meant I had about ten seconds to get in my car and back out of the driveway.

I didn't even make it to the front door in ten seconds.

"Jason, wait up. I have something in my car for you." Of course she did.

Reluctantly, I followed her outside and waited while she retrieved something from the driver's seat. When she handed me a notebook, I waited for an explanation, yet she never gave me one. "What's this?"

She rolled her eyes. "My diary from seventh grade."

I grabbed her arm to prevent her from sliding into her seat. "Nope. You don't get to poke and prod at me and then skip out when I need answers."

"You're holding the answers. If you really want them, I suggest you take a look at it."

"Does this have to do with Tatum?"

"I don't know, Jason . . . what'd you go to Vegas for?" She propped her hand on her hip, as if her comeback satisfied her. "See? You won't answer my questions, either."

"What does it matter, Kelsey? You never wanted me with Tatum in the first place, so where did this sudden interest come from?"

She shrugged and dropped the arrogance. "There's a chance—a small, *tiny* chance—that I unfairly judged you when you moved back. But Tatum didn't. Regardless of all the nasty and deplorable things I may or may not have told her about you . . . she never let it stop her from seeing you in a completely unbiased way."

"And that somehow means I owe you something?"

"No. It means you owe *her* something. I'm tired of seeing my best friend beat herself up. The worst part is . . . I'm unable to do anything for her. I just thought that maybe if I talked to you, and you gave me *something* to go on, I might be able to steer her in the right direction."

Thank God the sun had gone down; otherwise, she might've seen the pain register on my face in some way. "Let me guess . . . you want to know if I saw Jen. Because you think if I did, you could use it to make her hate me."

"Not hate you, just maybe stop glorifying you or something."

My ribcage felt bruised from the way my heart beat itself against it, though I wasn't sure what that meant. It was caused either by the idea of Tatum glorifying me or the thought of her hating me. I wasn't sure which. Then again, it could've been both.

"Is she really that upset?" I barely got the words out.

"You're more than welcome to call her and find out for yourself."

"Come on, Kelsey. Why can't you just tell me?"

She sighed and dropped her chin. "Listen . . . I've already given you more than you deserve. I just don't know what the big deal is. Why are you being so secretive about Vegas?"

"Because I don't want to talk about it."

"You saw her, didn't you?"

I nodded, incapable of speaking the truth.

Without another word, Kelsey slipped into her car and closed the door. I stood in the driveway, unable to move, and waited as she started the engine and backed out. Then I waited a little while longer for the chains that had wrapped too tightly around my chest to ease up enough for me to breathe.

And before I got into my car, I pulled out my phone. I had no doubt that my cousin would go straight home and tell Tatum about Jen, and even though I didn't owe it to her, I wanted a chance to explain first.

Me: Can we talk?

I stupidly read through the notebook as soon as I got home, which prevented my mind from shutting off, regardless of how exhausted I was. When Kelsey had given it to me, I'd had no idea what to expect, but it certainly hadn't been what I found.

Tatum's handwriting decorated the papers, and as I flipped through each one, I couldn't help but grow lost in her words. I could almost hear her voice in the loopy letters, teaching me how to cook each recipe the way she had that very first night we'd spent together. By the third page, I began to understand why my cousin had felt the need to give it to me.

Between the ingredients and their names, it was like reading a story about the weeks we'd spent together, the things we'd done, and the conversations we'd shared. In a way, it was a private letter from her to me, a secret only the two of us could understand.

By the time I finished reading the very last word, it was midnight. I still hadn't heard from her, though that didn't stop me from trying again. I opened our text conversation, typed out a message, and hit send.

Me: Please call or text me back.

There was a chance she wasn't awake, so after another half an hour without a word from her, I put my phone down and went to bed.

"How's Tatum?" Maryanne stood in the doorway with a gentle smile playing on her lips. She hadn't been in the office much, and when she had, we'd both been too busy to offer more than a wave to each other.

Confused by her question, I stilled with my hands perched over the keyboard on my desk. I hadn't heard from Tatum at all. And after two texts, I'd given up. Waiting for a response for well over twenty-four hours was enough to prove that I'd made an effort, so Kelsey or anyone else couldn't accuse me of not trying to smooth things over.

The thought of her being with her ex soured my stomach, so I shook that thought loose and returned my attention to Maryanne and the concern that narrowed her gaze. "Uh, I guess she's okay. Why?"

"Oh . . . well, that's good. I was worried about her after the whole incident. But I'm happy to hear that it didn't get her down. She's too sweet to let something like that break her spirit."

I was out of my chair like my ass had caught fire. If the rumors caused by Tatum's lies had made their way to my office, she *would* hear from me again, and it wouldn't be to talk or to explain Vegas. "How did you hear about it?"

"Charlie told me." She seemed confused, as if she didn't understand why I would be upset over my personal business being discussed behind my back. "He was so distraught when he came home Monday. He just feels so bad for her."

"Wait . . . how does your husband know?" Then I recalled Kelsey mentioning that the segment had filmed that day. "Oh, that's right, the cooking show was Monday."

"I take it you didn't watch the footage Charlie made for you?"

It took me a second, but then I remembered Maryanne leaving a CD on my desk yesterday morning. I had taken it home, but by the time I'd made it through the front door, all I could think about was a shower and my bed. It more than likely still sat in the mail basket next to the front door with the stack of letters I'd taken inside.

"No. I'm sorry. My family's planning a big lunch party for her on Saturday. They're going to tape it so we can all watch it together."

"Oh . . ." Her mouth formed a long *O* for a moment before she blinked her surprise away. "It won't air."

"Why not?"

"Maybe you should watch it for yourself when you get home."

"Why can't you just tell me?"

She took a deep breath, and as she let it out, heartache dimmed her eyes. "Because, Jason . . . if I do, you'll panic and think it's worse than it is. Trust me. Watch the clip and see for yourself."

"*Worse than it is?*" I was not excited with how high my voice got, though I couldn't waste the time caring about the fact that I sounded more like my mother than a thirty-one-year-old man should.

"It's nothing, Jason. No one got hurt."

"*Got hurt?*" I was now on the other side of my desk, desperation acting like adrenaline pumping through my veins.

"Yeah . . . *no one* did. Maybe you should call her." She offered a meek smile and walked away.

I didn't care that I still had fifteen minutes left in my workday; I powered down my computer, grabbed my bag, and raced out of the office. Thankfully, no one questioned my hasty exit or attempted to stop me on my way out of the building. I managed to make the trip from my desk to my car in less than sixty seconds—normally, it took a solid two minutes. And before I had the key in the ignition, I had Tatum's number pulled up on my phone.

I pressed the green call button and waited for it to connect.

Once it did, the ache in my chest grew bigger.

The automated recording of her voice mail came on after only half a ring. Anger shredded my heart into pieces, and fear twisted my stomach into knots, but I couldn't separate the two long enough to understand just what emotion I was left with.

The second I walked through my front door, I rifled through the basket that sat on top of the entryway table until I found the disc Maryanne had given me yesterday.

I grabbed my laptop from the top of my closet, set it on the bed, and changed my clothes while I waited for it to come to life. My heart hammered away as I slipped the CD into the drive, and then it threatened to quit beating altogether once the picture finally flickered to life.

It was an unedited copy, so the beginning dragged on with the initial sound check and lighting adjustments. There were other people in the frame, yet I couldn't take my eyes off Tatum. She looked so nervous, completely overwrought with fright.

When the host, whose name I couldn't remember no matter how many times it was said, asked Tatum about the ingredients she planned to use, she kept her head down, making it very difficult to understand her when she spoke. After she had to be corrected a couple of times, they started over.

No one could say Tatum didn't take direction well. She did exactly as she was told—looked right into the camera, smiled, and spoke with clear and concise words. However, her eyes were wide, her smile was faker than the host's tits, and she sounded like a robot that needed new batteries. If I hadn't known better, I would've thought Charlie had given me a clip of a hostage situation.

Tatum's awkwardness aside, I didn't understand why this wouldn't air. With a little—okay, *a lot*—of editing, they could probably salvage enough footage to show something. It saddened me to think they'd decided to scrap the entire thing just because she wasn't born to be in front of a camera.

Unless she had freaked out and walked off the set.

Knowing her, that was probably what happened.

Ironically, I felt bad for the host—and *not* for the obvious reasons. Seeing the two women stand side by side, it was hard not to notice their vast physical differences. Tatum had to be a good five or six inches shorter, though the host had a solid ten to fifteen years on her. Then again, it could've been more; it was difficult to tell with the ninety-seven layers of spackle this woman wore on her face. And don't get me started on her eyes. It appeared she'd used a cotton ball to apply the black lining her lashes and had then gone over it with a pencil eraser.

I couldn't help but think of those Instagram posts Jen used to show me of women trying to re-create sexy poses yet failing miserably. In this case, Tatum was the original, and the host was the poseur with the word *fail* stamped on her forehead.

When I snapped out of my mental comparison of the two women, I realized they'd moved on to the actual cooking part of the segment. Considering I'd just lost track of time picking apart the host's makeup, I had no clue what they were making, but whatever it was, Tatum picked up a plate of it. She turned toward the stove, and a split second later, I stopped breathing.

The pan that sat on a burner burst into flames. Well, it was more like one giant flame. Chaos ensued around the set—the host screamed, Tatum froze, and by the sounds coming from behind the scenes, a pack of wild horses charged the kitchen.

Suddenly, Tatum reacted to the fire in front of her.

Reacted, not put it out.

Still holding on to the plate, she dumped what I could only describe as chicken nuggets into the pan. She must've been under the impression that adding food would help—either that, or she figured the fire would cut down on the cooking time. But when that only increased the flames, *as well as spread them*, she moved on to plan B . . . throwing the plate at the pan.

I had my face inches from my computer screen with my heart in my throat. I had no idea why no one had come in with an extinguisher yet. By law, there should've been one close by, and considering Tatum's unpredictability, the host should've had one strapped to her back, pin pulled, ready at a moment's notice.

Panic consumed Tatum's expression, and I was on the verge of a heart attack. Nothing good *ever* happened when her eyes became that wide. I'd seen it before—at the restaurant with a plate of chocolate cake being the first thought that came to mind. And the second she reached for something off the counter, I literally screamed, "*Don't do it!*"

Unfortunately, my plea didn't travel back in time, because she picked up what appeared to be an oven mitt and tossed it onto the growing fire. The flames now covered the entire cooktop and hid her from view.

Finally, someone rushed forward with their back to the camera. In reality, it couldn't have been more than five seconds, but while I watched, helpless to do anything, it felt like a million times longer. A loud rush of air filled the speakers of my laptop as a white cloud consumed the screen.

After several bursts of the extinguisher, it stopped, and the room became eerily silent. The camera continued to roll, yet I couldn't make anything out beyond the smoke and dust. But then, several moments later, everything began to settle, and the picture cleared up some.

The sight of Tatum had always made me smile, though never like this. Seeing her behind the cooktop, covered in white like someone had thrown a bucket of baby powder at her, I grinned like a fool. The only parts of her that weren't coated in the remnants of the extinguisher were two wide onyx eyes looking right at me in horror. And then the footage ended.

While staring at the black screen, I allowed myself to find humor in yet another one of Tatum's debacles. Too bad her TV career had blown up in her face before it had ever gotten started, because I might've actually tuned in every week just to see her antics.

Watching the video and realizing she was okay should've calmed me down. Yet it didn't. The only way I'd relax was if I heard her voice. However, calling her right now would be pointless. If she hadn't answered less than an hour ago, I doubted she'd pick up if I tried again.

Instead, I grabbed her notebook, exited out of the DVD player on my laptop, and passed the time by trying to make sense of her recipes. At nine o'clock on the dot, I tried calling her again.

Only to be sent to her voice mail once more.

24

Jason

Do everything; regret nothing.

The first thing I noticed when I walked inside my aunt's house was how quiet it was. If it hadn't been for the cars in the driveway when I'd pulled up, I would've thought the party had been canceled and no one had bothered to let me know. But Mom had assured me they would celebrate with or without the segment airing.

Apparently, Tatum had told everyone that the producers had pulled the plug due to an "issue while filming." Granted, burning down the set *was* an issue while filming. I just wasn't sure why she hadn't told them the truth—I would've asked her myself, except she still hadn't returned either my texts or my calls.

The only reason I'd decided to come was because I hadn't been able to stop thinking about her all week. I couldn't get the image of her horrified eyes out of my head, and when I slept, I dreamed of the words she had used to create her very own recipes. I figured if we had a chance to move past everything, it was now or never—and I hated the idea of *never* when it came to Tatum.

When I set her gift on the kitchen counter, faint voices carried through the air around me. Finding the slider to the patio wide open, I moved closer, but just before stepping through the doorway, my feet cemented themselves in place.

Everyone was on the dock. Nick sat on the edge with Connor in his lap, a fishing pole in their hands. Uncle Fred stayed near the grill with Lizzie on his shoulders. Aunt Diane stood in the yard on her phone—taking pictures, not making a call—and the other four were at a table that had been set up along the side, shaded by the neighbor's massive mango tree. Marlena and Kelsey sat with their backs to me, while my mom and Tatum faced them.

All I could do was stand there and stare at her.

I'd seen Tatum in almost every light—first thing in the morning without a stitch of makeup; right after a long shift in front of a stove, hair matted to her forehead from the heat; all put together with her lips painted red. But I had to say, the way she looked right now . . . it wrecked me, and I wasn't sure if that was good or bad.

The saying "She took my breath away" wasn't even close.

She didn't need to take it from me.

The way Tatum looked had me willing to bottle up every last breath I had and hand them over with a bow on top.

That was the thought that wrecked me, because I'd never experienced anything like it before. Over the last sixteen years, I'd been around women who'd turned me on, made me stop at nothing to get them naked. If I didn't succeed, I moved on to the next. If I did, I still moved on to the next—usually after succeeding a few more times. Either way, they'd never brought me to my knees.

There had been other women I'd enjoyed being around. The kind who typically went with the flow. But again, they'd never stopped my world from spinning.

Then there was Jen. She had started off as someone who'd offered the type of friendship I'd left behind at college. For the first time in my life, I was on my own, but Jen kept me from feeling like it. We had progressed into something more, and before I knew it, almost five years had passed. My first and only relationship had made it to the point where we'd talked about weddings and babies and a future. And in the blink of an eye, it had vanished.

But the good times had never made my heart race.

And the bad ones hadn't caused it to cease beating.

Now, watching Tatum as she joked with my mom, I noticed the biggest difference between her and everyone else. I'd always said she was unlike any other woman I'd ever met, though I'd chalked it up to her awkwardness and quirks. But as the sunlight crept between the branches behind her, it lit a halo around her head. And the sound of angels singing the chorus of a song I'd been deaf to blew past my ears, masking itself as the wind.

Her dark-brown hair danced in the breeze, occasionally becoming trapped between her scarlet lips, and despite the canopy of shade above her, she squinted as if she stood directly beneath the sun. While she talked, her upturned eyes gave the impression they were smiling, giving her the appearance of being utterly happy, regardless of what words or tone came out of her mouth. And even though she wore a hint of makeup today, I had no doubt that the pink in her cheeks when she laughed hadn't come from a beauty counter or the mid-September heat.

Unbeknownst to me until this very moment, Tatum had managed to bring me to my knees, stop the earth from spinning, and reenergize my spirit. That completely terrified me, because if she'd done all that in only a couple of months, done what no other woman had ever come close to, that meant she was capable of extinguishing every beat of my heart.

The kind of power she unknowingly had could be crippling.

Lizzie squealed, catching my attention, and when I found her on Uncle Fred's shoulders, I realized he'd caught me watching Tatum. At least it was him and not one of the others; he was probably the only family member I had who could keep his mouth closed. The irony of it all was he was the only one I wasn't related to by blood.

I recited my motto to myself and stepped outside to join the party. Somehow, I almost made it to the edge of the pool deck before anyone else saw me. And once Aunt Diane did, they all did. However, my eyes remained on one, and when she glanced up, I couldn't believe it had taken me this long to see the truth.

Her eyes flashed wide, like two gemstones in the sun. Even though we were more than twenty feet apart, I knew she had stopped breathing, which was evident in the stillness of her chest. Though the way she remained unmoving, regarding me with her mouth slightly open, I couldn't read her reaction. She was either scared, shocked, or overwhelmed, but I could relax a little, knowing she wasn't angry.

Aunt Diane hugged me first—after taking my picture, of course—followed by Marlena. Kelsey seemed to have gone back to her snotty ways, muttering, "I'm surprised you came" beneath her breath as she greeted me.

With one arm over her shoulder, I returned her side hug. "I said I would."

"Technically, you said you couldn't make any promises." That was true; every time I'd been asked, which had been at least once a day since dinner at my mom's on Monday, that had been my response.

"Your point? As far as I'm concerned, that means yes, but don't hold me to it."

"Oh, I took it as you're too much of a coward to show your face." Her smirk let me know she was teasing, yet I didn't doubt for a second that a part of her had meant it.

My mom stepped away from the table and kissed my cheek. To my surprise, she didn't need to wipe anything off. When she pulled away, I noticed her makeup was subtle and classy. "I like the new look, Ma."

She beamed, clearly proud of herself, but then she turned her head to the side and admitted, "Tatum helped me." It was like she knew I needed an excuse to give my attention to the woman I'd come here for.

I tried to smile at Tatum, though I couldn't be sure I succeeded—partly because she kept her beautiful, tense expression set on me. Without any other obstacles in my way, I ambled to her and stopped at the corner of the table. She stood behind the seat my mom had vacated, her hand on the back of the chair as if she needed help steadying herself. Tentative, barely breathing, she moved only to tilt her head back to see my face.

Fucking wrecked me.

"Hey." My voice couldn't have been shredded any more if I had tried.

"Hi," she whispered, apprehension thick in that one word.

"I'm sorry to hear about what happened with the show."

She shrugged and dropped her chin, glancing around the yard. I had no idea how much attention we had on us right now, nor did I care. Nothing else mattered in this moment, and I refused to let my family do anything—inadvertently or otherwise—to end it before I was ready.

"How have you been?"

Her eyes found mine again, though this time, they lacked the undeniable emotion from before, the emotion that told me I wasn't in this alone. Now they were two impenetrable shields blocking me out.

Regret nothing.

I came, I saw her, and even though she'd turned me away, I had no regrets.

This was what she wanted, and I had to respect that, much like she had given me the same courtesy over the last several weeks. So, I nodded and took a step back, offering her the space she wanted. But at the last second, right before I turned to walk away, I caught the slightest dip in her brows. I could've made it all up in my head, or I might have even misunderstood the meaning, but in the single fleeting twitch, I saw disappointment.

I could've stood there all day and questioned it.

Or I could've done something about it.

"*Fuck it*," I growled and cradled the sides of her head in my hands. She barely had enough time to gasp before I covered her mouth with mine, swallowing her surprise. It took her a moment to react, and nothing reassured me more than when she grabbed the sides of my shirt, pulled me closer, and kissed me back. And without a second thought, I lost myself in her.

Despite my avoidance over the last few weeks, it had pained me to think I might never feel her lips on mine again. But now that I had been given a second chance, now that I'd seen her through restored sight, I never wanted to spend one more day of my life unsure if a *next time* existed.

Regardless of the lies we'd tried to tell ourselves, the truth had been there all along.

If we hadn't been too busy looking everywhere else, we might've seen what was right in front of us. The glaring signs, the indisputable proof. And now that I no longer fought it, I refused to go back; I refused to be blind again.

When I pulled away just enough to catch my breath, the sight of her flushed cheeks and dazed, glassy eyes filled me with satisfaction and contentment. But then she became aware of our surroundings, like it had smacked her in the face. She stepped away with her sights on our captivated audience instead of me. She was withdrawing again, and I wasn't about to let that happen.

"Come with me." I grabbed her hand before she could get too far away and led her toward the patio.

Out of my peripheral vision, I could see mouths hanging open, questioning glances between each other. And as I passed the bewildered women of my family, I heard gasps and whispers. One thing was for sure, though; within those subtle actions, I felt assured of their excitement.

"What are you doing?" Tatum asked breathlessly once we stepped into the kitchen.

I glanced over her shoulder to make sure no one had decided to join us and then closed the sliding door. My desire to kiss her again was almost uncontrollable, but my need to understand whatever this was superseded all else.

"Well, you wouldn't return my texts or answer my calls, so I guess if I want you to talk to me, I have to make you." I stood in front of the door, blocking the exit in the event she tried to avoid this conversation.

However, she didn't attempt to go anywhere. Other than blinking at me, she remained still, frozen in place, shock immobilizing her expression.

"I don't know where to begin," I confessed, not caring how desperate I sounded. "Hell, I'm not sure what to even say, other than I'm sorry for the way I left. But I don't want to rehash that. The fact that I was hurt and felt betrayed doesn't change anything, nor does it excuse much. Can we just skip over that and go straight to the part where we figure out what to do now?"

Finally, she snapped out of the spell she'd been under and shook her head. "Hold up, Jason. What do you mean I wouldn't text you back or answer your calls? I've spent over two weeks waiting to hear something from *you*, yet all you've given me is a cold shoulder."

"What? No. I sent you two messages early in the week, and then after I watched the footage of the news show, I called you twice—*both* times I was sent to voice mail. Maybe I waited too long, and if that's the case, I'm sorry. I fucked up. I'll be the first to admit it, but please, don't shut me out without talking to me first." I didn't miss the irony of this—waiting too long, reaching out weeks later, begging for her to have a discussion before closing the door on us.

But luckily, Tatum didn't see that—or if she did, she didn't use it as a weapon against me. Instead, she regarded me with utter confusion and defensiveness. "Jay, I never got them. I don't know what messages you're even talking about. When did you send them?"

"The texts? Monday. One was sometime in the evening, and then another at midnight."

She closed her eyes for a moment while she pulled in a deep breath. When she opened them again, resignation dulled the typical sparkle I'd grown used to seeing. "Well, since you apparently know what happened during filming . . . my cell was among the casualties in the fire. I didn't get it replaced until Tuesday. There are quite a few messages floating around in space that never made it to the new phone . . . as well as contacts that never synced. Not that you'd feel better knowing you weren't alone or anything."

"What about when I called on Wednesday?"

"What time was that?"

I didn't need to think about it; I knew the exact times of both calls. "Just before five, and then again at nine."

"I was at the restaurant. In order to get tonight off so I didn't have to rush through lunch, I swapped with someone. I had the dinner shift on Wednesday. And I didn't send you to voice mail—my phone was off and in the car, just in case another pan decided to explode for absolutely no reason at all."

We couldn't have been more than a few feet apart, but I closed the distance and pressed my palms to her cheeks, needing her close to me. "Seriously? I've gone all week thinking you had said enough is enough. I was a nervous fucking wreck on my way here today."

Tatum wrapped her delicate fingers around my wrists like she never wanted me to let her go. And when her eyes met mine, I realized *I* never wanted to let go. She licked her lips and said, "Imagine how I felt. I've had to go all week knowing you went to see Jen."

A sigh forced its way out as I dropped my forehead to hers. "That's one of the things I wanted to talk to you about. I went to Vegas, yes. And I saw Jen . . . *briefly*. I made the trip because my old boss died, so I went for his funeral, and while I was there, I stopped by the house to get a couple things I had left when I moved."

"You don't owe me an explanation, Jay."

"You're right . . . I don't. But that doesn't mean you don't deserve one." I lost myself in the openness of her eyes, and as if stargazing, I could see the specks of happiness shimmer in the obsidian pools. "When Kelsey asked me about it last week, I was running on no sleep and she'd just finished twisting me up into a hundred knots. I answered the basic question: had I seen Jen. Which I had. But I wasn't in the right headspace to clear up any confusion. I'm so sorry."

She fisted her hands in my shirt, lifting herself onto the balls of her feet while dragging my lips to hers. It was a soft kiss, yet full of feeling and unspoken words. It would be easy to accept this as a truce, but I needed more.

I needed it all.

"Do you think we can move past this?" I whispered across her lips.

"I'm not the one who's opposed to second chances, Jay."

"And I've never wanted to offer one before. So I guess we're both lost."

"I'm more than willing to have a conversation about it once we leave here." She handed me an olive branch, and there was no way I would turn that down.

"Deal. Just as long as you're aware that the second the food is gone, so are we."

She giggled and pulled her head away to see my whole face. "Once the kitchen is cleaned, we can go."

Damn . . . bossy Tatum was hot.

Just then, the slider opened, causing Tatum and me to separate.

Kelsey joined us, though she didn't seem too interested in what we were doing. Instead, she found the wrapped gift on the counter and wouldn't shut up until Tatum opened it. She shot me a death glare while Kelsey peered over her shoulder, deeply confused by what it meant.

"Is this for real?" Kelsey snatched it from her hands and looked closer. "Why would someone name their cookbook *Burnin' Down the Kitchen*? I mean, it's catchy; don't get me wrong. And the flaming pan is a nice touch—very colorful."

Tatum just dropped her chin, shaking her head while my cousin opened the book. I had about three seconds to say my final goodbyes to my mom.

"Oh, this one looks good, Tater—it's called Cheesy Kisses." Kelsey continued to flip, though I didn't dare take my eyes off Tatum, who now stood almost rigid and suspect. It wasn't until Kelsey called out another title that they both became clued in on what it was.

"I'll Scream Your Name Root?" Mom entered, hearing our conversation, and peeked over Kelsey's shoulder. "That sounds like a fun dish."

Tatum yanked the book from my cousin's hands and held it protectively against her chest.

"What's with the title of the book?" It was clear even Kelsey didn't know what had really happened at the studio.

"It's a well-known kitchen phrase." And then Tatum spent the next thirty minutes hiding in the bathroom.

I loved my family, but if they had tried to keep us there for one more second, a war would've been waged in their living room. I couldn't get out of there and drive home fast enough.

Tatum walked into my house like she'd never been there before—timid and a bit cautious. But just like the first time she'd come over, I ignored the awkwardness and eased her into it with a glass of wine.

She took it from my hand and eyed me with a smile playing on her lips. "If you think this will make up for the cookbook incident, you aren't even close, buddy."

"Oh, you're bringing up the cookbook?" I followed her to the kitchen table, slightly upset that she didn't climb onto the counter like she had done so many times before. "Does this mean you're ready to explain why you haven't told anyone about your flaming good time on set?"

Some people had this incredible skill to flick someone off with a simple facial expression—Tatum was one of those people. The way she pulled her pursed lips to one side, arched just one brow, and squinted only one eye, I wouldn't be surprised if a ninety-year-old man two towns over heard that bird get shot.

"I take it that's a no." *Dammit.*

"Correct. I'd much rather talk about us and get it all out on the table."

"It's not too late to forget it all happened, you know."

"I don't want to rehash it or anything." She defended herself with a slight roll of her eyes. "But that doesn't mean I don't have questions."

"Okay." I prepared myself for the worst yet prayed for the best. "I'm ready when you are."

She took a few sips of the wine and got comfortable in her chair. Then she reassured me by meeting my gaze, right before voicing her first question. "What's going on with Jen? Like, where do you guys stand with each other?"

"I told her I didn't think it would do us any good to try and fix something that's broken. I explained my thoughts and feelings to her, she said she understood where I was coming from, and then we didn't speak again until she pulled into the driveway while I was locking the front door."

She nodded in contemplation for a moment. "What were your reasons?"

Oh hell. I cleared my throat and sat forward with my hands clasped between us on the table. "She wanted to come here and try to work things out, but I struggled to give her an answer. I worried I'd be turning my back on my future if I didn't at least see if we were salvageable. But after everything that happened with you that day, I realized my inability to make a decision was because I didn't want to give *you* up. If I tried to figure things out with her, I would've had to put an end to us."

"But you just said that was after you left my apartment. Your mind was already made up about me, so you wouldn't have had to choose. Why tell her no if I wasn't part of the equation anymore?"

"Well, the two biggest and most important reasons weren't contingent on you or us. The first should've been obvious—if we truly were meant to be, I wouldn't have thought twice about ending what you and I had. And the other had to do with walking in and seeing you in another man's shirt."

She balked. "Why?"

"I don't think I've ever felt more territorial than I did in that moment. And during my drive home, I began to wonder if I would've been that pissed if you were Jen. The sad thing is . . . I don't think I would've been."

"Really?" Her tone was barely audible.

"Yeah. And silly me, I carried on for the next two weeks like a blind fool."

"What do you mean?" Oh, she knew where I was going with this, but the glint in her eyes told me she needed to hear me say it.

I fought my grin long enough to answer. "I was hurt over the whole situation, and when I'm hurt, I tend to react angrily. I understood and admitted to myself that I hadn't wanted to give you up for Jen, and that seeing you in that asshole's shirt made me want to tear his limbs from his body . . . but I ignored what it meant. Then last week, I started to come around, but you weren't returning my texts, so again, I wasn't thinking we stood much of a chance."

"But you still came today? Why?"

"I guess I hoped for some sort of resolution. The idea of us avoiding each other and not speaking didn't sit well with me. Honestly, I didn't care *how* we fit into each other's lives. What mattered to me was that we *did*."

She brought her wineglass to her lips, trying to hide the mirth that played on them, but it didn't work because she didn't cover her eyes. "Um, Jay . . ." She swallowed again. "You said about four words to me—two of which were *fuck it*—and then you kissed me. In front of your *entire* family. That's how you resolve things? By attacking people's faces with your mouth?"

I could've played it off or let her think whatever she wanted. But I had no desire to hide anything from her. "You see, my original plan was to say hi and find out how you were doing, start a little small talk, and see where it went. I would've settled for friends, but I had aimed for more. And then I saw you. Right before I walked outside, I watched you laugh with my mom, smile at your best friend, just being *you*. That's when the plan changed."

"See? I always knew that you had it all wrong," she teased with feigned arrogance. "You just can't admit how much I affect you."

"That's where *you're* wrong . . . because I can admit it. I'm fully aware that you have absolute control over every beat of my heart, every breath I take. I can admit that my every smile was created with the sole purpose of giving them to you." I held her unwavering, stunned gaze for a long beat before adding, "And when you're not around, I'm nothing. *That's* how much you affect me, Tatum."

25

Tatum

"The very first time I saw you, I'm fairly certain I ovulated." Had I not paid attention to his facial expressions, I might not have realized how confusing that statement was—which would've been embarrassing. "I mean . . . you were so gorgeous that my body ignored its natural cycle out of desperation to mate with you. I was basically a cat in heat."

His slow nods made me pause, wondering what I had messed up this time.

Highly important fact: The word mate *should never be used in reference to humans. Unless you're Australian. Oh, and never compare yourself to a cat in heat.*

"Let me start over."

Jay reached across the table and covered my hand with his. "No need. I think I understand what you're saying—you thought I was hot. We can come back to the rest of that later. Maybe. Although, let's not."

"Yeah. Okay, that's a good idea. Moving on." My heart raced, which didn't help my state of mind at all. On the positive side, if things got any worse, I could just clutch my chest and get out of the rest of it. "I used to stare at our picture all the time. Well, I stared at *you*, but it was of *us*. Anyway. Before we ever started anything, I would get myself off while looking at your face. Technically, it was more like your profile, considering you were kind of sitting sideways—"

"Tatum . . ." He cleared his throat and shifted slightly in his seat. "The part about you getting yourself off is all that matters. Got it? So let's get back to that."

"Right. Well, once we started sleeping together, I didn't exactly need the picture anymore. But when you left, and I didn't have you to do it for me, I tried again. I missed you, and I wanted to feel good— technically, I wanted to feel closer to you, but that probably makes me sound crazy."

"Nope, just keep going, Tatum."

"Anyway, I missed you, so I went back to what I did before you got in my pants. Except it wasn't enjoyable anymore."

Jason dropped his forehead to the table and groaned.

"Oh, no. It had nothing to do with you." I patted his arm and waited for him to sit up again so I could continue. "I mean, it kind of did, but not in that way."

He stared at me for a while, his eyes growing bigger as the seconds passed. "Tatum! Babe, you can't end a sentence like that. It *kind of* had to do with me but not that way? *What?*"

"Maybe if you stopped interrupting me, I could be done by now."

He rolled his wrist in the "carry on" gesture.

"What I'm trying to say is . . . when I *think* about you, almost all the memories involve one or both of us naked. But when I *don't* think about you, none of that comes to mind."

He stared at me, blinking rapidly. So, I tried again.

"There are times you cross my mind, unexpectedly. I'll be putting a cup in the dishwasher and just stop, overcome with the memory of how you used to always make sure I had a glass of water next to the bed at night. Or I'll get in my car and the stereo is up too loud, and before

I know it, my mind goes back to that story you told me about how you wanted to grow up to be a Hanson brother."

Pausing to see if his reaction changed, I stared into his eyes and prayed he could sift through the words and find what I had meant to say. His expression did soften some, although he still appeared rather lost.

I huffed, on the verge of giving up but choosing to try one last time. "The best of you resides in my chest. It lives in my heart and keeps it beating—*for you.* I told you that I wasn't looking for a relationship, and that was true. I wasn't. I didn't want one. My heart was broken, and the last thing I needed was someone else to come in and destroy what was left of it. And apparently, when I wasn't paying attention, you slipped through those broken pieces, but rather than make it worse, you made it better. You stitched up the cracks and made it whole again . . . from the inside."

He stood, sending his chair flying behind him, and at the same time, he shifted the table out of his way—not far, but enough to give him room to pull me out of my seat. And then his mouth captured mine.

We'd been here a few times before, so I already knew what to expect.

I wrapped my arms around his neck and counted to three. He had me off the floor by one and through his bedroom doorway by three. And the second he had me on his bed, his body hovering over mine, there was no such thing as numbers or counting.

"Are you ever going to tell me why everyone thinks the show was canceled because of filming issues?" He drew invisible lines along my bare breasts with his fingertip.

Rolling my eyes was a wasted effort, though I did it anyway. I lay on my back, facing the ceiling, while Jay stretched out along the side of my body with his head on my shoulder—and his attention on my chest, hence the reason for the wasted effort. At least this way, I didn't have to watch him study my boobs, and while he had his *fun*, I ran my fingers through his soft hair.

"It's seriously not a big deal, Jay."

"Exactly, so you should just tell me."

I sighed, giving up the fight, and I could practically feel his smile against my skin. "Think about it. What would be the only reason I have to keep it from them?"

"You mean aside from embarrassment and inside jokes you aren't a part of? Or gag gifts every Christmas to remind you of it?"

"Yes, Jay. Aside from all that."

His body shook with silent laughter. "Umm . . . you're afraid they'll think you might burn down their kitchen?"

"Yup."

He pushed up on his elbow and stared deep into my eyes. "Seriously? My family would never do that; you know that, right?"

I closed my eyes, unable to handle the heat of his gaze. And when I opened them again, I set my sights on the ceiling over his shoulder. "It doesn't matter, okay? Can we please drop it? You got your answer, so there's no reason to beat this into the ground. I didn't lie."

"No, but at some point, you should start trusting the people around you to give you the benefit of the doubt."

Brushing that comment off, I asked, "Why did you turn the scribbles in my notebook into a printed cookbook?"

"You've said before that you could never write one. Well, now you have one, and *you* wrote it. I just wanted you to see that you shouldn't limit yourself. Sure, the TV idea burned to the ground, but that doesn't mean there aren't half a dozen other options out there."

"I feel like you hate that I work at a restaurant so you're trying to get me out."

He shifted his body over mine, removing any possibility for me to look somewhere else. "No, that's not it at all. I don't care where you work, just as long as you aren't trapping yourself in a box. I'd love nothing more than for you to find your own light to shine in. Even if it's a food cart on the side of the road, just as long as it makes you happy."

I locked him between my legs. "You make me happy."

Fun fact: Distractions were designed as weapons for women.

EPILOGUE

Tatum

"I think you should wear the black shirt. It makes you look more sophisticated." Kelsey reclined on the bed while watching me change outfits for the hundredth time, my official cookbook in her hands.

"It shows too much cleavage. I'm not sure how that makes me look sophisticated."

"Eh, who cares. I'm sure Jason will love it."

"He loves anything I wear. I could literally be in sweats and a two-day-old tee, and he'd rip it off me. I'm starting to think he'll never get tired of having sex with me—not that I'm complaining or anything."

Kelsey jumped off the bed. Usually, she only moved that fast when she saw a spider. She glanced between me and the comforter a few times, lip curled in disgust. "You could've warned me *before* I climbed on your bed. That's gross."

I laughed at her exaggeration. This was one of the things I missed about living with her. "You don't have anything to worry about. Jay washes the sheets once a week, so you're good." I didn't bother telling her it had been days since he'd thrown them in the washer, and we'd had sex several times since then.

Rather than climb back onto the mattress, she settled onto the floor next to the bed and waited for me to pick a shirt and put it on. "It would be nice if you could keep in mind that he's my cousin. Now hurry and get dressed. We don't have all day."

Not long after Jason and I had worked things out, I'd taken the plunge and left Fathom 216. It hadn't been an easy decision on my part, although Jason didn't think it should've been such a difficult choice. He'd hated the idea of me seeing Michael almost every day, and as much as I'd understood his concern, I hadn't been willing to give up the idea of sous chef so easily.

However, having my own cookbook had made it a lot easier.

A cookbook I wouldn't have had if it weren't for Jason.

"Can you and my cousin hurry up and have a baby already so my mom will get off my case about feeding into her infant obsession?" She mindlessly flipped through the pages, even though she'd gone through them a million times already.

"No. We've only been together for four months."

"So?" Her eyes met mine while I slipped on a green sweater, the same color as Jason's eyes. "You're all perfect for each other and shit. I'm honestly surprised you're not already knocked up, as much as you two get it on."

"Stop rushing it, Kels," I droned while moving into the bathroom to apply my makeup.

"I'm not. You *do* live together, so it's not out of the question. You guys have said the *L* word, right?" When her question was met with silence, she rushed into the doorway at the pace of a cheetah. "You've told him you love him, right?"

It probably didn't make sense to her, much like I doubted it made sense to anyone else, but Jay understood. And that was all I cared about. "You know how much I hate that word. It doesn't mean anything to me. I don't need to hear him say it to know he feels it, and vice versa."

She stared at me in the mirror, her expression showing exactly what I'd expected her response to be. At least she didn't voice it. Instead, she rolled her eyes and slipped back into the bedroom. "Hurry up. You can't be late to your own party."

"It's not a party," I argued over my shoulder.

"Tatum, it's your birthday, and my whole family will be there. What would you call it?"

"Uh, a typical Sunday?"

"Well, we're celebrating. So not exactly *typical*."

I rolled my eyes and continued to put on my makeup.

Prior to my decision to hang up my chef's coat for a pen, a spiral notebook, and many nights of trial-and-error recipes, Jason had put out feelers for the cookbook and had run the numbers. I'd told him I wouldn't go into it blind, so he made sure I would have an audience. Surprisingly, there was a big market out there for what I had to offer—make do with what you have in your fridge.

The Petersons had wanted to host a prelaunch party full of dishes I'd created for my first official book—not the same one Jason had lovingly titled *Burnin' Down the Kitchen*. I just hadn't expected them to choose my birthday to do it. My only stipulation was that this would be about the book, *not* my birthday. I even made Jason promise, since his family seemed to have minds of their own.

Less than twenty minutes later, I was dressed and ready to go.

Jason had offered to pick up the box of special-edition cookbooks from the printer and run a few errands for his mom, so Kelsey drove me. To be honest, he'd more than likely wanted to give me time with my best friend, knowing he'd have me all to himself once we left.

By the time we pulled into the driveway, there were cars everywhere. This was supposed to be a small gathering—like a *typical* Sunday lunch, regardless of what Kelsey had said. Panic consumed me, and I couldn't pull in enough air. "Who are all these people?"

"Oh, just a few friends. Amanda, Carrie, Rebecca. No one special." Kelsey's hazel eyes lit up when she turned to me, and I couldn't help but wonder what she had up her sleeve. "Ready?"

"What am I walking into, Kelsey?"

"How would I know? I've been with you all morning."

She had a point there, though I still didn't believe her. "Just tell me now. It's never a good idea to throw me into a situation unprepared. You can attest to that more than anyone. So if you know something, now's the time to come clean."

She flicked her eyes to the front door, and being the best friend that she was, she caved like a twig beneath a pair of boots. "Fine. But you have to act surprised."

My heart sped up, though it didn't stop me from saying, "Deal."

"And you can't let anyone know that I told you."

"If you don't spit it out, you won't be alive long enough to tell anyone anything."

She didn't appreciate my threat. Thankfully, that didn't stop her from giving me what I'd asked for. "They got you a cake with a picture of your cookbook on it."

I glared at her. "That's it?"

"I'm glad I told you. Now you can work on showing a bit of gratitude." She opened her door and stepped out, then waited for me around the front of the car. I was too nervous to question why she walked behind me to the front door, or why she let me enter first.

But as soon as I stepped inside and saw Jason, everything else vanished.

His smile was enough to eradicate every last worry I had over the extra cars and my birthday. It was also enough to remind me just how lucky I was. I stepped closer, ready for him to take my face and kiss me the way he always did, but before I made it to him, movement in the hallway caught my attention.

I turned just as a gaggle of bodies swarmed me. Jason's family smiled with excitement in their eyes. Behind them were three girls I'd never expected to become close with yet couldn't imagine my life without— Carrie, Amanda, and Rebecca. And once they'd finished crowding around me, my heart nearly beat out of my chest.

My parents.

And Tanner.

I was too stunned to do more than stand there while they kissed my cheek and wished me a happy birthday, much like last year. After glancing down the hall to verify there weren't any more surprises, I returned my attention to Jason. His smile told me everything—this was all his doing. My family being here had been his idea, and I couldn't have been filled with more love than I was in this moment.

Rushing to him, I threw my arms around his neck, brought my mouth to his, and melted into his embrace.

"This reminds me of the first time you hugged me," he teased, releasing his hold on me long enough to see my face. "Best day of my life."

"You make me happy," I whispered. "So happy."

He brought his lips closer to mine and breathed out, "I love you, Tatum."

I froze, yet he refused to let me shut down. Cradling my face, he held my gaze. And in his eyes, I saw my future—not the past.

"I'm not him. And while I understand why you don't want to hear those words, I can't hold them in any longer. Yes, you make me happy. And I'll always tell you that. But it's more than happiness I feel for you, Tatum. It's love. I love you more than I ever thought I could."

He'd uttered the one word I hated, the one word that had once brought me unimaginable pain. Pain I never wanted to feel again. But with our families around us, I stood in his arms, in his embrace, and the past vanished. The pain dissipated. The fears drifted away until I was only left with . . .

"I love you, too, Jay." He leaned forward, and I closed my eyes, expecting another kiss. Yet I got nothing but air. What was even more odd was the complete silence that entombed the room. And when I slowly lifted my lids, my hand flew to my mouth, not quite fast enough to catch the gasp that rang out.

In front of me, on his knee, was Jason. And in his hand was the most beautiful ring I'd ever seen. So beautiful, in fact, tears immediately sprang to my eyes. I couldn't see him past the blur of happiness, though I heard him loud and clear when he said, "Tatum Alexander, will you marry me?"

"Yes," I whispered, and then cleared the emotion from my throat before shouting, "Yes!"

As he slipped the shiny ring on my finger, I wiped my eyes so I could admire it. There, on my left hand, as if that was where it'd always belonged, sat a heart-shaped piece of recycled glass set in sterling silver.

"We can pick something out together. I just wanted to put a ring on your finger when I asked you to be my wife."

"No, this is perfect, Jay. I don't want anything else."

"Oh good!" His mom clapped with excitement and added, "This deserves cake!"

"Ma, we haven't eaten yet."

"Exactly. Which is why we should go eat some cake." She disappeared down the hall, and one by one, the entire crowd followed.

Holding on to Jason's arm, I kept him back until we were the last two in the room. "Where are my parents and Tanner staying while they're here?"

"They reserved rooms at a hotel." He stroked my cheek with his thumb. "I tried to get them to stay at our house, but they decided to give us some space. I know you would've rather had them stay with us, and I swear, babe . . . I tried. They refused."

I doubted my smile could get any bigger. "Did Tanner's family not want to come?"

"Oh, they did. But since they'll all be here later this year, he decided to save the money."

"Later this year?"

His gaze bathed me with love when he said, "Yeah, for our wedding."

"I love you, Jay." That had to be the most truthful thing I'd ever uttered.

ACKNOWLEDGMENTS

Kevin: There's no way I would be doing this if I didn't have you on my side. You've been my biggest cheerleader, my biggest supporter, my shoulder to lean on and ear to listen, and without you, I would have never made it this far. I love you more, and will continue to love you more every day.

My girls: Let's get a pool.

My family: I know I haven't seen you much, but I love you. Your support means the world to me!

Stephie: You're my woobie, my person, the other half of my brain. As lame as it sounds, I don't think I could function without you. I would seriously be lost.

Kristie: I'm thankful every day that you agreed to be best friends! Probably the best decision you ever made—HA!

Amanda: Let's do this thing!!

Crystal: We're not going to date ourselves by talking about how long we've been friends. Instead, let's just say I can't remember life without you, and I can't imagine the rest of it spent without your friendship. Love you, Best Friend!!

Angela: You've saved my sanity more than you'll ever know!

Megan: I don't think I'll ever understand what made you email me and give me this opportunity, but I'm beyond thankful for you and the entire Montlake team!! Thank you so much for seeing something in me!

Krista: Thank you so much for making this book better! Your insight has been invaluable!

Kristie: While I enjoy our FaceTime calls, I still think it'd be better if you lived closer! Two hours away is too far!!

Emily: Thank you for putting up with my crap! I'm sure the PR community, as a whole, thanks you, too. LOL! You've saved them from having to deal with me!

Readers: I wouldn't be here without you! At the end of the day, you are the reason I get to live out my dream!

ABOUT THE AUTHOR

Leddy Harper had to use her imagination often as a child: she grew up the only girl in a family full of boys. At fourteen, she decided to use that imagination to write her first book, and she never stopped. She often calls writing her therapy, using it to deal with issues through the eyes of her characters.

Harper is now a mother of three girls, making her husband the only man in a house full of females. She published her first book to encourage her children to go after whatever they want, to inspire them to love what they do and do it well, and to teach them what it means to overcome their fears. You can learn more about Harper at www.leddyharper.com or find her on Facebook at www.facebook.com/Leddy.Harper.